STORMING AREA 51

SURVIVOR STORIES

Compiled & Edited by
Ben Thomas & D Kershaw

There will come soft rains and the smell of the ground,
And swallows calling with their shimmering sound;

And frogs in the pools singing at night,
And wild plum-trees in tremulous white;

Robins will wear their feathery fire
Whistling their whims on a low fence-wire;

And not one will know of the war, not one
Will care at last when it is done.

Not one would mind, neither bird nor tree
If mankind perished utterly;

And Spring herself, when she woke at dawn,
Would scarcely know that we were gone.

Sara Teasdale, There Will Come Soft Rains

TABLE OF CONTENTS

1989 ....**13**

Soldier by David Bowmore 15

SEPTEMBER 20 2019 ....**17**

Janitor Jared Jenkins by Jensen Reed.................... 19

Bradley Lutkins by Stephen Herczeg 21

Sexy_Kikashi_69 by Stephen Coghlan................ 35

Karen Thomas by Brandi Hicks 41

Angela Lazza by Cecelia Hopkins-Drewer.......... 49

Zak "Boomer" Butcher by Gregg Cunningham... 55

Aidan Charles by N.M. Brown.............................. 69

Eric Dyer by Terry Miller 71

Stewie by Gabriella Balcom.................................. 73

Brittany Jenkins by Bob Adder............................. 77

Emmett Trowbridge by Dawn DeBraal 79

Allen Parker by C.L. Williams 91

Belladonna Pryor by Cindar Harrell 95

Alastair Harp by Mason Harold Hilden 109

Evan Dean by N.M. Brown 115

Rachel Montgomery by Cindar Harrell 117

Josh Tillman by Eddie D. Moore 127

Earl Justice by Shelly Jarvis................................. 131

Daniel MacBride by David Bowmore................. 143

Jasmine Smith by Charlotte O'Farrell................. 151

Elayna by Zoe Xolton.. 161

Jordan Matthison by Wondra Vanian 163

Bettina White by Jo Seysener............................. 169

Kyle Koch by Jacob Baugher.............................. 177

Cody Redman by Rich Rurshell 187

Jane by Eddie D. Moore...................................... 195

Al Woods by Eddie D. Moore & Sue Marie St. Lee
.... 197

Ivan Hawks by Vonnie Winslow Crist................. 205

Caroline Walters by Zoey Xolton 207

Cherish Salazar by Marcus Cook....................... 217

Cal Davis by J.W. Garrett.................................... 231

Josh McKennan by J.W. Garrett......................... 233

Emily Sparrow by J.W. Garrett 237

Running by Rhiannon Bird 241

Kelly Lawson by Jacob Baugher 243

Jessie Gilton by D.M. Burdett 245

Claire And Gabe Hammond by Angela
Zimmerman 247

Reaper John Nil by Raven Corinn Carluk...........255

The Knowsiacki Family by J.B. Wocoski 265

Cody and the Agent by Gregg Cunningham.....277

2019 TO 2029 291

Newsfeed by Rhiannon Bird.................................293

Monster Energy by Stephen Coghlan.................295

They Held Their Own by Stephen Coghlan 299

Into the Lungs of Hell by Raven Corinn Carluk...337

Last Night by Jennifer Shelby 369

Two Hundred and Eighty-Four by D.M. Burdett.371

Dark Earth by Jo Seysener....................................373

2219... 395

They Had to Come from Somewhere by Jacob
Baugher...397

2519.. 435

Delaying Action by Peter J. Foote 437

AUTHORS....................................... 461

1989

Soldier

By David Bowmore

Oh my God! Really, Sir? 1989?

Please listen to me, Sir. I come from the future. On September 20th, 2019 more than a million people stormed Homey Airport.

Lethal force was sanctioned, but there were just too many insurgents. They released the aliens. The aliens began killing everyone. It was a total massacre, Sir.

I found myself alone, out of ammo and surrounded by grey-skins. I backed into a metal and glass box in Warehouse One, level 88. Somehow, it must have accidentally activated and now I'm here.

Whatever it takes, Sir, we must stop the storming of Area 51.

SEPTEMBER 20 2019

Janitor Jared Jenkins

Cleaner, Area 51, Q Block

By Jensen Reed

The day they got in I was mopping. Nothing heroic or fancy, just a mop and bucket of water. I wanted to help, to be on the front line, but my boss had placed the mop in my hands and ordered, "Do your job. *This* job."

The mop threads swished back and forth, back and forth, as the clamouring outside grew until it spilled into the base. I took a step towards the commotion but stopped and shook my head. It wasn't my job. If only they knew the hell that was about to be unleashed…maybe they wouldn't have come.

Bradley Lutkins

26, Phoenix, Arizona

By Stephen Herczeg

JULY 19, 2019 – PHOENIX, ARIZONA

"It'll be a gas, man," Jimmy said.

I still wasn't sure. I mean it's a military compound. There'd be soldiers. With guns. Maybe tanks.

"And aliens," he said.

"Don't be an idiot," I said, "That's all just conspiracy theory bull crap. Like the faked moon landing and a flat Earth."

"And the fact Trump is a Russian spy in an orange skin suit?" Jimmy asked.

I thought for a moment then shook my head.

"No. No, that's true," I said.

Jimmy laughed.

"C'mon man, it'll be a blast," smiling wide for a

moment before he said, "Think of the babes."

"What babes?" I asked.

"They're all over Facebook," he said pulling out his phone and bringing up a Storm Area 51 Facebook page. As he scrolled through the posts, I realised that most of the subscribers were women. Young women. They all seemed to say the same thing. They were gonna be there. They were gonna storm Area 51 with everyone else.

"Well, they'd need protecting from the soldiers," I admitted.

Jimmy slapped me on the back.

"Damn straight. And we're just the sort of guys to give them a good level of protection," he said.

I thought for a moment.

Who's gonna protect us?

* * *

SEPTEMBER 19, 2019 – LAS VEGAS, NEVADA

We arrived in Las Vegas after five hours on the road. I figured out quickly that Jimmy was pretty good company in short bursts, but stuck with him in a hot car—my air conditioner was broken—listening to him drone on and on about what he was gonna do to any girls he hooked up with, made me realise I'd be better off with a car full of hornets.

We checked in to a cheap hotel on the outskirts and went straight to our rooms. I had enough forethought to get two rooms.

I flopped on the bed and was about to pass out when I heard Jimmy knocking on the door.

I groaned and let him in. He was ready for a big night. I was ready for a shower and sleep. Jimmy won.

* * *

SEPTEMBER 20, 2019 – Las Vegas – Indian Springs

I hated Jimmy even more.

My head was fit to burst. My gut felt like I was gonna throw up for the tenth time, even though there's nothing left inside. God knows how much I drank last night.

Jimmy looked fine. He was bright and happy and excited about today, and he won't shut up about the girls.

We headed out of Vegas mid-morning. It was about an hour's drive to Indian Springs, where the majority of people were gonna meet before making their way out to Groom Lake, the technical name of Area 51.

I checked the maps. There were some dirt trails out to the lake, but God knew if my old Chevy would make it. I hoped we could catch a lift with someone in a four by four. The last thing I needed was to blow my suspension. And it wasn't as if Jimmy would help out with any repairs. He hadn't even coughed up for fuel.

Just another reason I started to hate him. In fact, I've started keeping a mental log of all the reasons I hate him.

By the time we reached the little one-horse town, my eyeballs were falling out of my head and Jimmy's incessant whining was causing my brain to explode.

Indian Springs existed for one reason, to service the nearby Creech Air Force Base. It's also the closest town to Groom Lake and the mythical Area 51.

We pulled into the parking lot of a gas station that had a whole slew of other cars and pickups in it. A group of guys that look a heck of a lot like the two of us were hanging around the cars.

We stepped out and sized them up. One pretty fat guy with a large red beard held up a fist and shouted, "Storm Area 51."

Jimmy smiled and strode over to introduce himself.

I just looked around for the women. The complete absence was seeding the idea that this whole thing was a joke. I pulled out my phone and check the Facebook page.

A few new posts have been added in the last few minutes. A lot suggested meeting at the Indian Springs Texaco. I Checked-In and saw a couple of the other guys check their phones as my status uploaded.

My phone beeped and several status updates

appeared from the 'women' I'd been keeping a close eye on. I noticed no male updates appeared, but also noticed the other men around me tapping their phones.

The penny dropped and I kicked myself inside.

I'm gonna kill Jimmy.

I put my phone away and walked over to him, ready to drag his ass back to the car and get the hell out of there.

He noticed as I stepped up next to him and threw an arm around my shoulders and introduced me to the bunch of guys he'd met. Their names were just a blur, but I'm sure the big guy with the beard was Chuck, there was a Teddy, a Rufus, and maybe a Jose or Jesus, it was all too confusing.

Jimmy said, "Chuck here's gonna give us a lift in the back of his truck."

Great.

I tried to think of a way of getting out of it, but I've wasted a whole day anyway, I may as well see it through. Most likely we'll get out there, get threatened by guns and run back home with our tails between our legs quicker than a startled rabbit.

* * *

SEPTEMBER 20, 2019 – 3:30PM – GROOM LAKE

Oh, Christ, my head.

There's no road from Indian Springs to Groom Lake. Well not anything that anybody in their right mind would call a road.

We jumped into the back of Chuck's pickup. He was joined inside by Jesus, I think that's who it was, we shared the back with Rufus. Another group, led by Teddy, followed in another pick-up.

For an hour, my teeth and brains were jiggled about by the absolute absence of a paved road. Chuck drove at high speed across a rutted goat track that had more holes in it than an entire backwoods family's mouths put together.

Finally, to my great relief, we came out onto an open plain that led up to a tall barbed wire fence. A large sign said, "Keep Out, US Air Force."

"This is it," said Jimmy.

"Well, it's at least an Air Force base," I said.

We drove along the fence for about two miles before we saw another congregation of pickups and trucks. I surmised this was the rest of the crowd that were planning to storm the base.

By the time we reached the vehicles, we could see that a large crowd was milling around the front gates.

It was a stand-off.

Several soldiers, wielding advanced automatic weapons, not boring everyday M-16's, stood in a line across the main gate. Their eyes were fixed on the crowd, searching for any hint of them attempting to enter the place.

"This doesn't look good," I said.

Jimmy was ecstatic.

"How fucking cool is this?" he said, "It's a Mexican stand-off."

"It's a one-sided bloodbath in the making," I said, glancing at the heavy weaponry on show.

Suddenly, Chuck's pickup slewed around in a half circle and headed back the way we'd come. The other truck followed close behind.

I assumed that Chuck had simply given up and was heading back to Indian Springs, much to my own relief, but after about a mile, he slammed on the brakes and got out.

He strode to the back of the truck and grabbed out a toolbox.

"What the hell are you doing?" I asked.

"Breaking in, what do you think?" he said, grabbing some wire cutters and a pair of long-handled bolt cutters out of his tool box.

He, Jesus, and Rufus headed to the fence and scanned the perimeter. I checked myself and realised that the bulk of the guards were at the front entrance.

Internally, I swore as the first wire succumbed to the cutters. Pretty soon, Chuck had made a big opening in the fence and squeezed through. The others followed, leaving me alone in the back of the truck.

Jimmy turned and shouted, "What are you doing numb-nuts? Come on."

I waved him away and stayed in the back of the truck.

"Idiots," I said out loud to no-one in particular.

I checked my phone. Nothing. No service out this far. I swore and put it back in my pocket.

The sun was moving West, so I laid down in the back of the pickup and found the only shade available. It was hot, I was tired, I slept.

* * *

SEPTEMBER 20, 2019 – 6:30PM – GROOM LAKE

I snapped awake and checked my watch. The sun was low, and the dark was creeping in pretty quickly.

I sat up and looked around. Nobody had returned.

Crap.

I jumped out and ran around to the driver's side of the truck. No keys. I check the other one. Same deal. No keys.

I was in the middle of nowhere, with no way of getting back to town. And I had no idea what had happened to the rest of my group. I'll admit I didn't really care that much, but I was curious.

Too curious it seems.

Going against every sensible bone in my body, I

squeezed through the hole in the fence and made my way across the open ground towards the first set of buildings I could find.

My only reasoning was that I needed to find my friends. I could have trekked back to the main gate, but I was pretty sure they'd just tell me to scram and I'd be in the same boat I was in now.

I found a squat building sitting away from the others and a long way from the runway which dominated the Eastern side of the base.

Wanting just to find some sign of life, I tried the only door I could find. It opened.

I almost chuckled at the lack of security, but then thought what sort of idiot would try to break into this place. I then realised, that idiot was someone like me and my supposed friends.

I entered the dark corridor.

The lights turned on as they realised I was there. I pushed on until I found a small room with a set of laboratory coats hanging from hooks. I pulled one down and put it on. There was a pair of reading glasses in the pocket, I put them on to disguise myself, or at least make myself look more like I belonged. I then found a locker with a clipboard and pen and grabbed both, remembering an old film I'd seen where the lead character had said, "A man with a clipboard and a pen can infiltrate even the most secure location."

I left the room and progressed, with a greater level of confidence, down the long barren corridor before I came to a set of steel stairs that led downwards. Following them into the bowels of the facility, I found a large room filled with strange oblong shaped containers. Each container had a thick set of cables attached which ran up to a series of control boxes mounted well above the floor.

I stepped up to one of the containers and looked over the side.

My clipboard dropped from my hand and clattered on the floor as the shock of what I saw hit my system.

Jimmy.

Jimmy lay inside the box, or coffin as it seemed to be. I was sure he was dead. He was naked. His eyes were closed, and I couldn't see if he was breathing or not.

I reeled back and noticed a nameplate on the side of the coffin. It has Jimmy's full name, date of birth, and address on it.

Several gauges next to the nameplate seemed to indicate his health metrics. They displayed such things as heartbeat, blood pressure and temperature. According to the readings he was alive. The last gauge was a small screen that showed a map with a flashing light on it. Beneath was a label that said, Present Location.

The map showed Groom Lake. I tapped a small plus sign and the map zoomed in. Instead of the building I'd entered, and presumed was the current location of Jimmy, the map showed the front entrance of the facility.

I put it down to an aberration but couldn't work out why they would need to put something like present location on his casket.

I looked in a couple of the other nearby coffins and wasn't surprised to find Chuck, Rufus, and even Jesus. I glanced around the room and noticed a set of viewing screens away from the reposing bodies.

I made my way over and tapped the keyboards before the screens. They came to life and a message simply said, "Avatar Viewing System."

A small popup box displayed saying, "Name of Avatar."

I had no idea what that meant, but something made me turn my head towards the bodies scattered around me.

I typed in Jimmy's full name and pressed enter.

Suddenly, the screens showed a high-quality video. It was of the front gates of Groom Lake Air Base. Sound echoed throughout the room. It was filled with mixed conversations and laughter. I recognised Jimmy's voice and then saw Chuck, Rufus, Jesus, the other guy Teddy.

It must be a recording.

Then I saw the time on the bottom right of the screen. I checked my watch. The times matched.

It's a live feed.

I turned away from the screen, as confused as hell. Then my eyes saw another nameplate. I walked up to the coffin, read the nameplate again. My mouth dropped open with horror.

I edged up to the casket and peered over the side.

I screamed.

A voice behind me grabbed my attention.

"Yes, Mr. Lutkins, there are some things in life that we just shouldn't find out about," it said.

I turned and found myself face to face with a beautiful young woman, dressed in a laboratory coat and wearing glasses identical to the ones I had found. She was flanked by two extremely tall soldiers, their faces fixed in a grimace, their eyes boring holes in my skull.

"But, but..." I tried to speak but my mind was not my own.

I turned and pointed at the nameplate.

It said, "Bradley Lutkins."

"Yes, your friends had the same reaction," she said.

I turned back towards her. She held a small device in her right hand, pointed it and a sharp pain dragged me into oblivion.

The last thing I heard was, "And get my glasses and lab coat back, will you."

* * *

STORMING AREA 51

SEPTEMBER 20, 2019 – 9:00PM – Las Vegas

I woke up on the floor of my hotel room in a pool of vomit. I slowly dragged myself to my feet and searched the room.

Jimmy was unconscious on his own bed, his snores sending out pulsating pain into my head.

I checked my watch and saw the date and time.

I dreamt it all. I must have.

I sat on my bed and dropped my head into hands. My mouth felt like twenty miles of bad desert road. I grabbed for the glass of water on the bedside table and downed it in one gulp. I spent the next few moments trying to keep the water down before my stomach finally calmed down.

Then I noticed my phone. It must have dropped from the table and lay several feet away. The notification light was blinking.

I staggered over, picked it up and crashed back on the bed. I checked the notifications and realised it was the whole Storm Area 51 Facebook group going insane.

We missed the whole thing.

I flicked through the posts. Then almost dropped the phone in shock. There were photos of people at the entrance to Groom Lake base. People I'd never met in my life, could never have met, if I'd never been to Indian Springs and then Groom Lake.

People that I'd seen in coffins below the base.

But I dreamed all that. I was here.

Their photos flashed up. Chuck, Rufus, Teddy, and Jesus/Jose, whatever he was called.

My phone was lying to me, must have been, it said I was friends with them. People I'd never met.

Then I saw my own status update.

It said I'd been to Indian Springs, eight hours ago.

I dropped the phone.

Sexy_Kikashi_69

By Stephen Coghlan

Arms spread wide, Taurine replacing my blood, I lean forward and push off with my feet. I am no longer human as I press my arms behind me. I am a ninja, I am a bird, no, I am a God!

Until, I am passed by someone jogging lightly by, their plastic track suit swishing as they lumber forward. Looking behind, I groan in dismay. I'm only a hundred yards past the starting point. Whose bright idea was it to build the perimeter of the base so far away from the actual compound, anyways?

Gasping, I collapse to my knees. My diet of Cheetos and cheese doodles, liberally washed down with carbonated caffeine drinks has failed me. My rigorous routine of daily sit ups, completing a half of one in the morning when I wake up, and concluding when I lie down at night, excluding naps after meals, has let me down.

Which, is probably for the better, all things considered, because even as I struggle to catch my breath, I hear, over the pounding of my own circulatory system, the artificially boosted voices of "The Man" Demanding that all of us "invaders" turn back now or face dire consequences.

"Fortune," I gasp, "flavours the bold!" Maybe I confused the popular saying with an off-brand chip advertisement, but who the hell would notice over the chaos of all of us charging, limping, or waddling our way towards the quonset huts and whatever else awaited us.

We are a shabby line. The healthiest of us are well ahead, and while I am not the last, I am certainly far from the lead position. I want to stop and return to my parents' air conditioned basement, but, at the same time, I don't want to be left out of finding my alien allure, so I struggle forward, and finally, see, success?

The others have formed a new line, a new barrier, because, I don't know, but it gives me strength and I stumble forwards to see a line of Humvees with their armaments pointed directly at us. The soldiers look at each other nervously while an officer, I recognise the uniform from all my FPS, yells through a microphone.

"Turn back you morons, for your own safety."

Whoopsie, wrong thing to say. The crowd, already agitated from the heat of the desert, surge forward, and I see the leader roll his eyes in frustration.

"We have been authorised to use lethal force."

No one listens, except for me. I know those guns, and I don't have any health packs to patch me up, and, since this is real life, I can't just hide and wait for my body to heal itself. Can I?

Shrugging, as if to say, 'it's not his fault', the officer waves his hands. I expect bullets to come flying out at us, to see us do the machine-gun-jitter, but that's not what finds me. It's instead, a nauseating noise that pierces my skull and makes me bring up all the neon-coloured liquids I had drank for breakfast that morning, while ejecting things from behind with such a force I'm almost propelled forward.

Ew, it really does taste the same coming up as it did going down.

"Have you had enough?" The officer admonishes us. "Don't make me use the Brown-Note-Blaster again."

Strangely though, I feel better for having gotten all that gunk out of my system. It is cleansing. I feel refreshed, if not a little soiled. Renewed, I tear off my pants and wave my formerly white boxers over my head.

"CHARGE!" I scream, and proudly lumber. forth, flinging my multi-coloured underoos over my head. This alone, probably saves my life, as several of the soldiers recoil, afraid of my effluence. Motivated, others struggle forth.

"Goddamn it." The officer shakes his head. "Fine, have

it your way." He looks away from us, to the troops.

"Shoot to kill."

Panic lends me real speed, and I squeeze my way back into the crowd as rifles and Gatling guns begin burping their chunky death into the masses. I'm glad that I'm no longer wearing pants, because what wasn't knocked out of me by the previous attack, is scared from my system. Arms, limbs, faces, pass me buy as I weave parallel to the firing line, while others, more enraged and braver than me, continue to charge towards the ranks.

"They can't kill us allIIIIIIEEEEEE!" screams one of my peers who has climbed aboard the roof of a jeep, only to be shot with a stun-gun.

In the chaos and confusion, we separate and break apart. Some continue the charge, while others retreat, and still others, well, they look for sanctuary. I join a small group of the last, but I am thirsty, hot, dehydrated, confused, and no longer as caffeinated as I would like. Surprisingly, we squeeze past the defenders and find ourselves hurrying towards a series of white-washed buildings covered in desert camo nets.

"In there!" I encourage, but the gang I am with refuse to listen to me as adrenaline pushes them away from the carnage. I can't keep up.

Smashing through the door, I look for something, anything, to save me from the heat generated by my endeavours. Yet, there's no water fountain or vending machine, only a vat that is filled with a glowing green goo.

It looks...

It looks—

Like an energy drink!

I am saved. Sweet salvation!

I search. There must be a way to access the sweet nectar of the nerds. There must be a way to sample the succulent liquid sugar I need for sustenance. There, at the bottom of the tank! Collapsing to my hands and knees, I open the valve, and, fastening my fasting lips, I suck greedily.

Oh, it's delicious, and I try to slake my thirst. It burns beautifully, all the way down my gullet, all the way into my stomach, where it sits like a boiling brew, churning, bubbling, hissing?

I cease my suck, look down at my body, and see the green goo, burning through my flesh.

"Oh, oh God, why?" I gargle, stumbling for the doors. I have to escape, I have to get away. I step into the sun, and feel my body fall away from me.

My head lands onto the earth, and as my world fades to darkness, I watch my body dissolve and sink into the land, vanishing from sight.

Karen Thomas

31, Administrative Assistant, Bloomington, Indiana

By Brandi Hicks

"Of course. Of. Fucking. Course." I kicked the tyre hard and hurt my foot. My flat tyre. "It's only the biggest raid of this lifetime, and now I'm going to be late because of my flat fucking tyre." I was yelling to no one. This stretch of road was completely deserted at this time of night. Thank God I dated a mechanic and he taught me the basics of car repair; too bad he wasn't as good in bed as he was at changing a tyre. But he had made sure I had all the right equipment—in my car at least.

I got the tyre changed, dusted myself off and wiped the sweat from my brow with my arm. When I sat down in the car and looked in the mirror, I saw I had black marks all over my face. I looked down at my arm to see I was covered in grease. "Just fucking great." I mumbled. I wiped my hands on my shirt because I didn't have anything else to use. I wanted to check the Facebook group again before I left, to see if there were any updates. I was still at least an hour away and the first wave was set to go in less than twenty minutes.

I knew I should've brought Chris. He drives so much faster than I do. But for fuck's sake, he doesn't even believe we landed on the moon, why would he believe in aliens like I do? Still, he had the guns and he hates the government. I should've brought him. Too late now. I sped down the highway, keeping a watch for cops. That'd be the last thing I need, a bored cop that's on a power trip. "Oh, Karen is it? Bet you're going to ask for the manager at Area 51, huh?" Har har motherfuckers. I hate those memes. I don't think I've ever asked for a manager in my life. And I have long hair!

I pull into the rally point a good thirty minutes late. Most everyone is already gone, except three twenty-somethings drinking beer who never actually intended to go on the raid.

"Have you all heard any updates yet?" I asked them, hoping they weren't too inebriated.

"Nope. Just saw a bunch of crazy rednecks go in guns a-blazin'. One dude even brought a fucking tank! Where the fuck do you even get that?" The young man was clearly intoxicated and laughing his ass off.

"A tank? For real?" Just then I heard an explosion. "Guess so."

"Yeah, they had grenades and shit too." One of the girls in the group chimed in, also most definitely drunk. The other girl remained quiet. Silently glaring at her friends. This made me think she was a third wheel, and she didn't seem to be drinking, so I guess she was the designated driver. Poor girl.

"Listen, these assholes will be passed out within the hour. You want to go check out the mayhem with me?"

She looked sceptically at me for a minute, then at her two friends who were now making out and grinding on each other. She sighed.

"Yeah, okay, sure." She grabbed her flashlight and backpack and headed toward me. "I thought they were serious about coming here, so I packed a bunch of supplies, then we hit up liquor store and here we are." She shrugged.

"I'm Karen. We should probably get going, since everyone else already left." I picked up my pace a little and the girl matched me stride for stride. Her apathy seemed to be wearing off, she almost seemed excited.

"I'm Lucy." She smiled at me. She was actually kind of beautiful when she smiled. Her blonde hair fell in her face when we started to jog. She kept up with me nicely. Her long legs beating the path we were on.

We slowed down as we neared a clearing. Someone was shouting in the distance—"No landmines! No landmines!"—and then we jolted as another explosion went off. This time we were close enough to feel the ground shake. Gun fire strafed the ground ahead of us from a plane circling the area.

"Are you sure about this?" Lucy asked.

"I came over eighteen hundred miles from Bloomington, Indiana, and I didn't come here to die." I realised then that I still had grease all over me. Lucy hadn't even questioned it. I took my forearm and wiped some grease all over her face.

"Ew! What the hell, Karen?" She started to wipe it off but was only smudging it around.

"Stop it. Use it as camouflage. Pull your hair up." I barked orders at her in a whisper like I knew what I was talking about. I had to take charge or we'd die. "Look, no one is over that way," I pointed to an area on the left, "let's use the cover of trees to get over there."

"But there's nothing over there," she protested.

"I thought you said you prepared yourself for this?" I pulled out my phone and shielded the light coming off it with my hands. "What do you see here?" I pointed to a large white spot on the Google map.

"Nothing." Her smile had faded and she looked agitated. She was kind of cute when she was irritated.

"Look again. See here? There's a road here that just stops. There's nothing marked here, no trees, no rocks, no water, nothing. It's just a large blank space. It's the underground bunker. And I'm willing to bet the entrance is right about here." I pointed again, this time near where the road ended.

"You're sure about this?" I could see hope dawning on her face and I knew I had her with me.

"Positive."

"Then let's get going." She stepped closer to me.

"Well okay then. Let's try not to die." I was suddenly glad Chris hadn't come after all.

We took off through the trees, watching for any signs of defence from the sky or ground. I was being wary of land mines, but I guess the government just thought they would protect whatever it was they were hiding by brute force. We stopped again once we came to the road I had pointed to on the map. It came from an underground tunnel out of the wooded area and went into another underground tunnel not even two hundred feet ahead.

"Why are you doing this?" Lucy asked me.

"I don't know if I can explain. I've always just felt like there was more out there. I mean, you can see the night sky, all the stars, all the planets, so vast we could never really explore it all. You're telling me that out of all that, we're the only living intelligent lifeforms?" I probably sounded crazy, I had a wistful look on my face. I wanted to change the subject and quick. "Look, there. The guards must be out with the main raid."

"I don't know. That's too sloppy for government work."

"You've never worked for the government, huh?" I made her smile. "I'll go first, if anything happens to me, just run back to your friends and get the hell away from here."

"Well, at least take these. Brad, the guy sucking face with my best friend, took them from his dad's gear. Why he had them, I don't want to know." She handed me night vision goggles.

I took a tentative step forward, then another, until I was sprinting to the tunnel opening. I pressed myself against the outside of the tunnel wall and peaked around the corner. Nothing. Okay, this is weird. No mines, no barbed wire, not even a guard? I slipped on the night vision goggles and went into the dark tunnel. With the infrared, I could see just how wrong I was. Lasers scattered the hall. Before I realised it, Lucy was behind me.

"Shit! Lucy?"

"Yeah, sorry, I didn't mean to scare you. I thought you would see me coming, you know, with the goggles and all." She shrugged and started to move forward. I held out my hand to stop her.

"There's lasers everywhere." I grabbed a handful of dirt and threw it at the lasers and they lit up like a Christmas tree. Out of the corner of my eye, I saw something moving at the end of the tunnel. Then, to my complete surprise, Lucy said something in a language I didn't understand and I knew wasn't from this planet. She saw me gawking at her and shrugged.

"Sorry, Karen. I didn't know if I could trust you. We just met and all." The laser field shut down and the figure in the back came forward. He was tall, elderly looking, but fit. He had greying hair and a small goatee.

"Lucy, dear. I'm glad you came. And you've brought someone with you? Is this that friend you spoke of? Susan?"

"No, she decided she wanted to suck the face off her boyfriend instead of coming here. Karen happened to come by and asked me to join her. She had been running late, so we weren't in the initial wave of the raid."

"Suck the face off? Do you mean literally or figuratively? I didn't think humans did that?"

"No, Father, they don't. I meant figuratively. Like this." While I was still standing there gawking, Lucy turned, pulled me to her, and kissed me.

"Ah, okay. I understand. We need to get moving now, the guards won't stay unconscious for long."

In my daze, I turned and looked around. How had I not noticed the guards slumped over surrounding the tunnel? "Lucy? What's going on?"

"This is my father, Abram. He's been in Area 51 for 50 Earth-years now. I was finally able to come down to Earth to try and get to him, but no one I talked to knew how to get here. When I heard Susan talking about the raid, I knew it was our chance. We used our transponders," she tapped behind her ear, "to coordinate everything. But then I didn't have a way in because of Susan abandoning me for Brad. Then I first saw you and saw your determination, I knew you'd be the one to get me in. When you told me your story, I felt a kinship with you. Come with us. I'll fix everything so it'll be compatible with your organs. The way you breathe, eat, everything. You'll be safe with us. Please, come with me." She took my hands in hers and waited for my answer. I hesitated.

"You want me to...to leave Earth? Fuck. I don't know. Maybe. I mean, it's not like I have a lot going for me here. Just a string of bad decisions. Why not make another one? I'm sick of this planet and their Karen meme's anyway."

"Then let's get moving. Lucy, did you bring the locator?"

"Of course, father." She rifled in her bag and pulled out a thin silver tube with a flashing red light. She covered the light with her thumb and when she removed it, it had turned green. "They'll be here in a few minutes. You're sure you want to do this?"

"Not at all," I said. And as I looked up, a giant silver disc hovered above us. A door slid open on its base and a ladder descended. The guards started to come to, but they only stared. One even said bye to Abram. Lucy started up the steps after her father and held her hand out to me. I took it, and with that, I was no longer Earthbound.

Angela Lazza

28, Mommy Blogger

By Cecelia Hopkins-Drewer

My name is Angela. I am a housewife, living in Rachel, Nevada. I have a moderate sense of humour, a good set of pegs and a nice pantry full of cans, but I distinguish myself as an 'influencer' by emphasising the proximity of my home to the fabled "Area 51".

It was the explosion that first caught my attention, because I had never really believed there was anything out of the ordinary behind those 'No Trespassing' signs. After the explosion came the blinding light. I was in the middle of showing my viewers how to make a triple chocolate cake, but I grabbed my phone camera, and jumped into the car to head down to the Air Force base.

When I arrived, there were a lot of people milling around, and the Air Force was shooting in an attempt to herd them to one side. Technically, no photography is allowed anywhere on the Test and Training Range, but my video news provides a community service, so I had my camera rolling.

There was a large pile of rubble on the ground which had uncovered a secret entrance. I dodged the attention of the Air Force and climbed over the debris where I found an entrance to some sort of underground storage bunker.

"Do you see what I see?" I said to my viewers. "I'm going to go inside and check it out!"

The cement steps were intact, so I climbed downwards. The interior was dimly lit, with steel doors to the left and right all along the corridor. Wondering where everyone else had got to, I opened a door and peered inside. It revealed a huge room full of what looked like airplane parts.

"Duh!" I said to my viewers, "What did you expect inside an Air Force research and testing facility?"

The next door opened into a workshop full of all sorts of incomprehensible machines, and shelves full of specialised tools. I shrugged and closed the door, commenting in an aside to my viewers that the technology could be alien for all I understood of it.

"Reverse engineering is a thing...isn't it?" I spoke into the microphone on my camera. "Some of the stuff looks so weird it must be stolen from the Chinese, Russians...or maybe the Martians."

The next room I opened was full of waving tentacles. At

first, I thought this was some sort of hydroponics plant, but then I noticed the tentacles appeared sentient and reached for me. They were growing in huge petri-dishes out of some sort of nutrient culture.

"Creepy," I commented. "I hate spiders, and while I don't see any heads or bodies, there are enough legs in there to frighten me right to death."

Now, on my own, I am pretty cowardly, but with a camera in my hand and a thousand viewers streaming my feed at that moment, I felt emboldened. Marching down the corridor, I opened a number of other doors, avoiding any that opened into complete darkness, or smelled particularly nasty. The final door I opened led into a pristine white laboratory. The lighting in the laboratory was dazzling.

I stepped into the room and passed the benches. A refrigerator lined the far wall, and I thought its contents might interest my viewers. According to the labels, there were a number of viruses, antidotes and experimental cures. A face cream labelled "Eternal Youth" appeared to be in a place of pride near the centre of the shelving.

Like 'Alice' who eats and drinks everything in 'Wonderland', I naively reached for the face cream and unscrewed the top. Dipping my finger into the mixture, I smeared the cream liberally across my visage. Perhaps one of the smells coming out of one of the previous rooms had affected my brain.

"Let's see if this works," I giggled to my audience.

I must admit, it wasn't the smartest thing to do. My face began tingling pleasantly, but the feedback from my viewers became frantic. At first I was pleased, and comments lag behind live streaming, so I had no idea what they were saying. Vapidly, I continued my stream of commentary.

Finally, I noticed that someone had posted: "Look in the mirror!" The post had hundreds of shares, repetitions and likes. I strode across to the sink and looked at the mirror attached to the medicine cabinet on the wall.

I screamed in horror at the sight. My skin was green and growing spikes. Aging would not be a problem for me, because I was rapidly turning into some sort of alien creature. It was impossible to tell what at this stage in the transformation process.

I splashed water on my face and tried to wash the stuff off. To no avail, the change had already set in, and spikes were moving down my throat, onto skin where I had not even put the cream. I ran out of the laboratory and along the long corridor, up the steps, into the sunlight.

The Air Force had rounded up most of the intruders and placed them under some sort of military arrest. I sneaked out around the back of the pile of rubble and got myself lost in the surrounding conservation area.

I found I was photophilic—meaning that my skin suddenly loved light, so surviving the desert was no problem.

I sent the local garage out to retrieve my car from the desert after all the fuss had died down. I'm wearing a veil today, because otherwise my appearance would freak you out. If you want to see what I look like, tune into my morning video blog session...although I'm losing interest in that sort of thing.

I'm spending more and more of my time sunbaking, in strict seclusion because my body is almost totally green.

What comes next? I have no idea. Perhaps I will give birth to multiple larvae? I feel kind of full, like I might be going to lay eggs.

Zak "Boomer" Butcher

Gotta Catch 'Em All

By Gregg Cunningham

Case #A113.

Zak "Boomer" Butcher, 37, from Irvine California. Son to NBAs 2001 player of the year and Wannabe YouTube influencer with 45,000 followers. Famously known for going viral after breaking into one of Hollywood's most elite socialites' coastal properties and throwing the mother of all coke-induced house parties. Constantly gate crashing any media event party he can to be 'seen', and being a general nuisance to his ageing father. Enjoys Pokémon raids and Monster fuelled Fortnite sessions. Ridiculed by Gen-Z online community for being a loser and completely out of touch with kids of today, but regardless he continues to troll at every

opportunity. A legend for all the wrong reasons.

BOOM! So, hey guys, Zak here again with another Zak Boomer Butcher's Roaming Roadshow, livestreaming from Area Five One. I hope ya'll clicked on the subscribe button down the bottom of the screen and liked a few of my other vids on the browser bar up above. Dab on, all you haters out there!

Shout out to LOGJAM, welcome dude!

Oh yeh, before we start, I'd just like to give a holler out to the Code Red Conspiracy crew camped out on the first wave mound lead by my mate Cody...'sup Cody! I met up with him earlier today down by the diner where we filled up our rides. Dude's got some serious Pokémon stashed away in his pocket, hundo P top drawer, and I promised him I'd catch him the area 51 exclusive Legendary if, that is, I can make it over the wire in one piece and get to the gym that the Niantic production team are promising us. And checking out my phone, I see that pixelated egg is still hovering above Runway Four and counting down nicely. Folks are speculating as to what Niantic are actually hatching in there. My bet is we are going to be looking at some sort of spawn of Mewtwo. So, Cody, keep watching my live feed, brother. If Mewtwo is battling tonight, I will gift you one, buddy.

Reading my DMs here, and FIREJACK reckons it will just be another fucked up Tyranataur to T bag. Cheers, bro'...haters finna hate.

As you can see here on my arm, I have one...two...three iPhones, all fully charged and mounted on this handy arm holder, ready to Battle Raid with all you other Pokémon catchers.

WENDYFNAFGIRL...sure thing, babe. Just Slide me a DM.

I'm hearing that all Second Wave cosplay runners should be arriving on the dunes by tonight, and I'm told the Slavs are bringing a fresh supply of Vodka coolers to all you Kyles dirt biking your way up to the wire.

SPADOOFWARRIOR says he's bringing munchies...good girl!

As for all the furries taking up position next to their salty Naruto runner friends warming up on the third wave sand dune...shit, guys...did none of you think to bring shade with you? I mean, fucks sake, its forty degrees out there and ya'll are sat there in your Sonic Hedgehog onesies like you're on a Sunday picnic! Feds ain't finna be in a hurry to help you out once that sun hits the top of the clock! Sun stroke time! Do yourself a favour and take some cover, guys, especially you die-hard furries in those sweaty mascot costumes. It's finna be a long wait till zero hour 9am comes around and you guys break out your rocket men. So, go take a walk over to our spectators over on Randy Quaid flats. I've never seen so many RVs in one place since Will Smith right hooked E.T.

Maybe go do a couple of interviews, mention my

livestream so we get those viewing figures up. I'll give away prizes to those that slide me a DM... BOOM!

Shout out to MAISYDEE, LIMPLOBSTER AND DEEDOG—thanks for tuning in, guys. And yeh, I'm wig snatched for the party too!

Man, this place is definitely next on Disney's shopping list to buy up, for sure. I mean, if Don King hasn't pay per viewed this spectacle already, he'd have the place lit up like the fourth of July, for sure.

Now I'm hearing from DROID1011 that the plan is to kick things off with a little light show of our own tonight, so I hope I'm finna see some serious dog fighting moves up in the skyline. Just mind and keep your distance up there, the sentries will be taking pop shots at any eager beavers straying their drones inside the no-fly zone before we're ready. Don't want to be the first casualty of this momentous alien liberation movement by an itchy trigger finger now do we!

CAPTINHOLTZ wants a tour of the site...dude, I can't give away too much—hills have eyes an all that shit—but, as you can see, Roadshow here is packing his trusty GoPro here, mounted on his helmet. Nothing much to show you to the left; just the jokers, sand dunes and trees an' shit. The same goes for my right; clowns and cactus. I got my quad bike ready to go, and my tent is rolled away, as you can see. I've even tidied my campsite away, don't want the Feds finding any excuses to book me just yet.

Shout out to my spoof brigade watching this circus from Australia! Always first to the action. Hopefully you guys won't be the only team waiting to Raid in the online gym. And if I get locked out because of you dodgy fuckers, I'm coming after YOU, JACKson5!

But seriously, yeh, don't be jerks, dudes! This is the raid of a lifetime, let those who are actually on the fence line have a go. They'll have dodged bullets and Men In Black death rays to get to the gym, for reals.

I'm finna be live streaming my ride down to the fence line while I watch the Pokémon game unfolding on my three screens up my arm, maybe catch a few Hypnos on the way down. Anyone wanting to reach out and friendship me can find my trainer code on any one of my links on this stream. Just look for ZaksRoadshow and pick out the prettiest face.

Cody mate, if you are watching, brother, check back in a couple of hours once you've had your uneventful alien hunt. Hopefully I've got you a little mystery box gift-wrapped for your digital Pikachu menagerie...like maybe a Shiny Mewtwo. But I gotta say, you guys are batshit crazy if you think there is real aliens down there, but hey...whatever floats your boat. I bet you think the moon landing was faked too, dude.

*** *chuckling* ***

Or maybe that the Government is watching you

through your camera phone! Hey, don't forget your tin foil hat when you storm the fence, bro! It will save your brain from all those Bruce Banner Gamma rays they'll be firing at you.

chuckling

Too late for you SOLROCK49... BOOM!

So, subscribe to my page, then sit back and enjoy the view, all you Kyles and Karens. I'm finna take the backlot tour way in as far as I can go, then stash my bike and go on by foot.

Okay, give me an hour and watch the skies, my Naruto ninjas. Glad to see you've all united under one great big banner. I'm so stoked to see the Furries hanging out with the Weebs and rubbing shoulders with the gamers. Shit, it's 1970 Coney Island all over again; gangs congregating on Van Cortlandt Park, waiting for the down-low, and I'm just waiting for Cyrus to pull up in a Cadillac and greet this crowd of Gen-Z deadheads.

WARRIORS COME OUT TO PLAYYYYY!

BOOM! So, we got the Cringe Weebs, we got the Tik Tokkers, we even got the anti-vaxxers. Ya'll be sat back and passing the cones. It's finna be a cold night tonight, waiting for the nod. So, go grab yourself a furry to hug and take it easy guys.

Peace out.

* * *

Okay so I'm whispering now because, just over these bushes, is the trespassing boundary sign...check it out. It's a bit dark now...the sun has almost gone over the hills...but see the lights down there to the left?...that's the first wave. Over there on those dunes...yeh...that's the second wave. And check out the choppers in the sky, guys. I'm counting at least eight of them.

chuckling

Looks like our gangs have split formation and are now formed up into a fine mash up of Naruto runners, furries and gaming ninjas, warming up their drones and taking flight in one big harmonious Age of Aquarius wolf pack.

We got the quad bikes taking formation over there—Oh...oh...guys...look down there. Shit! See the line of humvees leaving the gates? Looks like it's game on. Do you hear the mega phones going off? I'm finna turn this thing up a bit and see if you can hear anything...

"...I repeat you are now trespassing on federal property and liable for prosecution. Stand down or we may use extreme force to subdue any further failure to comply..."

BOOM! Okay, it looks like we are getting ready to dance, so I'm finna just keep moving down to the fence line and see if I can get any closer. Judging by the countdown clock over my egg— Oh look...shit! They've done it! Niantic have opened up a gym bang in the middle of the Area 51 hangers... Fuck me! YEET!

Okay guys, the countdown clock on the egg says 37 minutes to hatching, so I'm finna leg it down to the fence line now and see if I can make it within my reach to join the fight. I'll keep the live feed on and talk when I get closer. Christ, I feel like Richard Dreyfus climbing up the Devils Tower trying to avoid the UFO searchlights. I hope the helicopters don't start spraying the air with any weird alien gas or shit.

Ah well...I'm 404 ...BRB... BOOM!

* * *

* * **panting* * * *

Holy shit! I can see on my screen that the egg has hatched, guys! The egg has hatched! And it's...no way! Are you guys serious... It's Arceus... Holy fuck...look at his Cp level! Holy shit, this is epic, guys...an Arceus! I've never seen this Pokémon, ever! This is epic...but Jesus, he's finna take some beating, for sure. I just hope I've got enough to take him.

Okay, so I reckon there is no other way. I've gotta get inside the fence now, there is no way I can join in the fight from here, I'm just too far away. I've...man...

* * **panting* * * *

...this...wow...blowing my mind, guys...Arceus!

* * **panting* * * *

...Cody Dog...you're finna owe me big time, dude!

Rule one when cutting a big fuck off electric perimeter gate...

*** *panting* * * *

...use rubber gloves. I can feel the vibrations in my knuckles, guys. My teeth are buzzing.

Okay, so over there is the action. I can see lights by wave two and Quaid's flats... Shit! I hope that isn't gun fire! Wave one has its drone in the sky now, man, what a sight.

Sorry, guys, I can't reply to your onscreen messages...busy time...I'll see if I can zoom in... Nah it's no good, the drones are too fast. I'm just finna make my way over to those buildings on the far side and see if I can join one of the fights from there.

I'm getting a lot of noise, guys. NIDOQUEEN11 are you okay?

Guys, can anyone see NIDOQUEEN11? She sounded panicked...

CHRIST SAKE!!! Was that a mortar bomb? Are those humourless dicks bombing you guys?

Cody, dude, I hope you're not involved in that FUBAR, mate. These guys are flexing big style.

Shits got real way too fast guys... But by the looks of things, I'm not the only one trying to get his hand on a Pokémon limited region Area 51 Arceus. The place is lighting up on all sides, I'm finna have to 404, guys...

*** *panting* * * *

...guards...spilling out everyw—
gunfire

* * *

It's a fucking circus out there, guys, but I made it to what looks like a comms hut. I'm just gonna squat behind here for a moment while I catch my breath because we got sirens and bull horns going off all around. I counted a dozen or so of our furry runner brothers dropping to the runway tarmac as three Humvees cut them off, and then some big fucking marines got stuck into them. I hope you guys took holiday insurance.

Someone looks like they got a quad bike inside and is currently doing donuts on the tarmac, and waving a...a Wolverine Red Dawn flag...? They really don't seem to see the funny side to all this at all, guys. We gone all Patrick Swayze on them.

YO' WOLVERINES!!
****chuckles****

Looks like wave three's patch has taken the challenge; I can just make out a group of Naruto runners charging the runway and following the chorus call... WOLVERINES!!"
****laughs****

Boy this is mental... WE HAVE NARUTO RUNNERS IN AREA 51, guys! Hashtag awesome!

Okay, raid on! I'm inside the Pokémon Go gym but can only see one other actual body on the other side of the hanger wall, for real. He's in the shadows, so I'm not sure if he's a Naruto runner or one of the guards. Everybody else inside is a fucking out of town spoofer. Typical. Biggest raid in history and the game is full of Spoofers from Australia.

Yip.

JACKson5, I see you lurking. And what a shock, FELIX_THE_CAT...bet your accounts get frozen tomorrow, you cheating scumbags.

laughing

Okay, so I'm pretty stocked up on potions and my attackers are top notch. Let's raid!

Raid pass accepted... SHIT CONNECTION LOST!

I've got to get closer to the hanger, guys...maybe see who that other dude is that made it over the fence to the raid...

Gunfire! We got GUNFIRE and...no wait...is that fireworks?

Looks like someone is taking his drone flying to a new level and firing bang snaps and roman candles at the Humvees!

CHRIST! The whole area is lit up like Vegas.

panting

whispering

Holy shit, guys, it's like I'm watching the storming of

Anoraks Castle, or Dr Strange rallying the Avengers against Thanos!

Okay, I'm up again and I've gotta' say...Arceus's CP is off the chart!

phone tapping

phone tapping

COME ON YOU BASTARD DIE!

phone tapping

phone tapping

Almost got him...I gotta get somewhere safe...BATTLE HARD GUYS!

* * *

SHIT! It's one of the guards! The other player is one of the fucking guards! He's smoking a vape and leaning up against the hanger wall like he's seen a compound raid like this a million times! The hanger door is wide open, what the actual—

OK LET'S GET TO THE CHASE and get out of here, guys.

DAMN IT! ARCEUS BROKE FREE AGAIN!

THIRD TIME LUCKY!

BOOM... GOTCHA!

ARCEUS IS CAUGHT!

HOLY SHIT, GUYS, I JUST CAUGHT ME A SHINY

ARCEUS!

AND AGAIN... TWO SHINY LEGENDARIES!

Looks like the guard is having the same problem as me, but he ain't got the same moves I have. Looks like we might just get a sneak peek inside that open hanger while we are here, eh? Get some good footage for Cody at Code Red Conspirator while that guard is stood cursing at his phone?

Cody mate, will we open Pandora's box and take a peek inside your hanger?

*** *panting* ***

Man, it's getting wild out there...and my connection is cutting in and out inside here. Not sure if you'll get any of this, but sorry to disappoint you, there's nothing— Wait! I see something! Its shimmering behind...

Shit, it's too dark in here to make anything out clear enough, but I'm finna see if I can make my way over to the far side. God, it smells like ammonia in here.

Smells like burnt hair too.

*** *coughing* ***

Is that a...DO YOU SEE THAT?

HOLY FUCK...

...CODY!...

*** *screaming* ***

*** *thuds* ***

*** *inaudible scratching* ***

*** *silence* ***

Aidan Charles

Licensed Therapist

By N.M. Brown

My wife Louisa babbled about Area 51 for months before she was medicated. We all thought she was crazy, but she was telling the truth.

I awoke that fateful September morning to an empty bed. Louisa's tyre tracks led me exactly to where I thought she'd be.

Chaos consumed the entire valley. Alarms blared, tear gas hung heavy in the air, civilians overran the military. Blackness invaded my senses.

When I came to, Louisa and I were restrained on steel tables. Figures spoke; causing agony to my hypersensitive ears but in a language I could understand.

Human/alien cellular fusion: COMPLETE.

Eric Dyer

By Terry Miller

Storm Area 51. It was simple enough. What started as thousands became over a million. Mission: Impossible became Mission: We Might Just Pull This Shit Off. The military presence was formidable, but we were determined.

We stormed the fences at Gate Four but they never opened fire, I guess they thought they'd just scare us off. What happened when we breached the perimeter could have never been foreseen. A hundred or so feet into the siege, our frontlines disappeared. They were just gone. The curious continued on but many stayed behind. Thousands disappeared behind the 'magic curtain'.

We stumbled into some large facility, humming and buzzing with whatever fluorescent liquid pumped through the pipes above us, illuminating the vast room. I stood bewildered, a sceptic that just wanted in on the fun. Now, if not before, I wanted to know what was really going on.

The gravity inside the room fluctuated with every step

as if it was, somehow, artificial. The further we ventured, the weirder our surroundings became. Before us stood something akin to a window, but as we approached, we noticed many distant, bright objects quickly passing by us. Upon reaching the glass, we gazed out into the vastness that passed us.

We turned and a figure stood before us. It was not green, not grey, but almost wraith-like.

"You shouldn't have come here," it said menacingly.

I then began to understand. We weren't on Earth. We were in a spaceship. Somehow, the portal transported us here.

Sensing my thoughts, the alien quickly corrected me. "You have not travelled from your home. You've been with us all along, or perhaps I should say we've been with you. I believe your kind call us 'Souls'. The planet you call home is but a projection in your minds. Like I said, you should not be here. The problem will soon be rectified."

* * *

We stood outside the fence. The abundance of military personnel quickly dissuaded our intentions as the jets passed overhead.

Stewie

By Gabriella Balcom

Inserting myself into the 'paramilitary' group in the first wave was easy for me. I just spoke like the other men and women and talked weaponry. However, my chest tightened up as we neared the front gate of Area 51, and the worst possible scenarios ran through my mind. Being shot. Rotting in jail. But we easily made it through behind a huge tank with E.T. on the side of it.

The people I'd accompanied walked toward a large building and I went with them. They entered, heading to the left, but I followed a hunch and went right instead. Even though my days as a successful investigative reporter lay far behind me, I just knew being here would change that. At fifty-one years of age, I'd been reduced to writing obituaries for the newspaper in my hometown of Midland, Texas, but this was my chance to redeem myself.

Anyone could write an article speculating about this site, but I'd do better. Way better. Although I knew little green men didn't exist, I planned to do a kick-ass, adrenalin-soaked piece about infiltrating Area 51 and finding hidden secrets.

However, I ground my teeth together later and wondered why I'd bothered to come. Why I'd let myself feel hope. I'd come up empty despite checking room after room.

Then something caught my eye. A floor-to-ceiling shelf stood nearby, but I noticed a very faint line on the wall beside it. I pushed the shelf aside and discovered an unmarked door.

This is it. My sight seemed keener, my hearing sharper. In fact, I felt like all my senses were on high alert, and plans flooded my mind.

I opened the door, stepped inside, and froze, my mouth falling open. I'd expected to see filing cabinets, computers, or accumulated data of some type, not a prison cell. But a cell was exactly what lay in front of me and, as I peered through the tiny window, I could see it wasn't empty either. The creature inside was tall, skinny, and had dark-grey skin and a head larger than a human's. As I gaped, the creature stared back at me.

Comprehension hit like a tidal wave and I felt like cheering. This would bring me a Pulitzer! I'd be the first reporter to ever interview an honest-to-goodness *alien.*

But voices rose in the hallway outside and I heard running feet. I waited till everything died down, cracked the door, and looked out. No one was nearby, but I was terrified that success was about to snatched away from me. I'd come too far for that to happen, and I racked my brain, trying to figure out what to do. Then I remembered something I'd seen earlier. Heading down the hall. I found the door labelled DECONTAMINATION. Bulky, protective suits were hanging on a wall, and I grabbed two.

I've done all kinds of research in the past, and picking locks was a skill I'd honed along the way. So I had no trouble getting the cell door open.

You help? The words sounded in my head and I flinched. At first, I wondered if I was losing my mind, but the dark-grey creature raised a hand, touched his head, and once more I heard, *You help?* I realised he was communicating with me telepathically.

"Yes," I replied. "I'm going to get you out of here."

I helped him get into a suit and it concealed his identity nicely. Then I donned the second one and led him from the room.

Yells sounded from behind us and soldiers soon ran by. From their shouts, it sounded as if they'd discovered the paramilitary people I'd accompanied. That didn't bother me, because it meant facility staff would be preoccupied. Hopefully, they'd pay less attention to me and my new companion.

I led him back through the deserted gate to the truck in

which I'd arrived, and searched for the keys. Thankfully, they were under the driver's seat.

Within minutes, I'd driven away, leaving Area 51 behind me. I felt like cheering.

Brittany Jenkins

The Nest

By Bob Adder

I was so excited...the carny noises, the smell of hot dogs, the music, the laughter, the booze. We were like one huge family coming together. I wanted to take it all in, experience every little bit of it, make new friends, stay up all night and be right at the front for the big push in the morning.

I know, I know...in hindsight, it was stupid; buying the little blue pills off the smelly guy with the weird eye. But he said they were 'Keep Awake' pills, and I wanted to be there for everything.

How was I to know it was a sugar bullet?

When the first symptoms hit—the stomach pain, the racing heart—I tried puking them back up, but nothing came so I staggered back to my tent for an insulin shot.

Kneeling in the hot, sticky air under the canvas, my hands were shaking so much I couldn't even get the little box out of my pack. I had to lie down for a while, get my breath, and I slumped over, the little box just out of reach.

Sometime later, I came to for a moment. My mind was foggy and confused, and the tent was in complete darkness. I had a vague notion that someone had joined me in my sleeping bag—I thought I could feel hands all over me, touching me in the no-go zone—but then I zonked out again.

It was bright when I finally awoke, sunlight was seeping through the tent's opening, but I noticed straight away how deathly quiet it was. The music and partying noises were gone. Bleary-eyed, I crawled over and pulled back the flap.

There was nothing but devastation. All around. Just devastation.

Upturned stalls, cremated cars, blood and gore with clouds of buzzin' flies.

My vision started to go black, dark curtains pulling across the stage of horror, and my head pounded, but then I felt the softest hand on my leg.

I looked back, finally remembering my night-time visitor, just as his tentacle circled my waist and pulled me back into our lover's nest.

Emmett Trowbridge

President, Save the Aliens

By Dawn DeBraal

The S.T.A., (Save The Aliens) meetings are held on the third Tuesday of each month at the Dew Drop Inn restaurant in Rachel, Nevada, population fifty-four. My name is Emmett Trowbridge; I am the president.

Typically, we experience low membership numbers, but recent events have meant many new people are interested in our meetings; especially after a website urged the storming of Area 51.

Thinking back to the meeting before the storming, there was standing room only. Those who attended the meeting passionately believe aliens are being held against their will. We wanted to know what the government was hiding. I called the meeting to order.

A stranger shouted out, "Are you going to storm the base next month?"

I slammed down my gavel responding, "You sir aren't a member of this group. You are not allowed to speak, only listen, because we are a democracy and we can't lock you out of the building. Before anyone talks, you will need to identify yourself, and we will check on the roster to make sure you are a dues-paying, card-carrying member. Do I make myself clear?" A murmur went through the crowd.

Clara White stood; Clara was a dues-paying, card-carrying member from way back. "Are we going to storm Area 51 in September with one and a half million others who have committed to the raid?"

If looks could kill, Clara would be dead. Why would she pick now to be obstinate? The club had planned to be discreet about joining in the storming. Clara brought it up in an official meeting, so now I had to address her question.

"Yes, Clara. In answer to your question, S.T.A. will be joining in the storming. We will be learning the art of Naruto running. Hank Adams learned this form of running when he was stationed in Japan years ago. The training starts tomorrow, and there is a sign-up sheet. Anyone wanting to become a member of Save The Aliens or get on our mailing list should sign up with Maggie over there." I pointed at Maggie sitting at a table with a stenographer's notebook, and a metal cash box. "Dues are twenty-five dollars a year."

People who weren't registered clamoured around Maggie's table while she took down names and addresses.

I continued the meeting despite the background noise, finding most people concerned about raiding the place in the daylight.

I divided the members into sub-groups of Naruto runners, Rock Throwers, and Punchers, the group known to drink energy drinks and punch through brick walls. By the end of the meeting, I assigned over one hundred new members their duties.

The new members took an oath of allegiance to, "Help the aliens escape captivity, seek their favour, and gain advanced knowledge from them." I knew aliens had the cure for cancer and diabetes, and I was going to befriend an alien and get the answers. Big pharma would not hold this country by the short hairs any longer. I informed the new members we would be organising buses to take us from the Dew Drop Inn to the base on the twentieth of September. The buses would leave at 12:30 p.m. If they were late, they missed the bus. I had a group of motorcyclists riding at the rear. I reminded them that they could bet the Air Force would be protecting Area 51 with all their might but, with one and a half million of us, how could they stop us?

I shouted out to all the members, "Do you want to see an alien?"

"Yes!" the crowd responded.

"Are you tired of being lied to by your government?"

"Yes!" they answered.

"Meeting closed!" I smacked the gavel down.

Clara White eagerly approached me as everyone filed out of the restaurant. "There are a lot of new faces. I worry you won't be able to control these new folks."

I had to agree with Clara but was distracted when Maggie brought over twenty-five hundred in cash. I realised we had enough for the buses and some snacks.

* * *

On the day of the storming, hundreds of people showed up parking in the desert around the Dew Drop Inn. I rented three school buses with a capacity of seventy riders each. The motorcycles coming up at the rear sounded like rolling thunder, parking the bikes behind the buses. The excitement was building up to a frenzy. At twelve-thirty we turned down the Extraterrestrial Highway, also known as State Road 375.

I thought that Rachel's branch of Save The Aliens would be first on the scene because our town was closer than any other to the base. We were joined by many others as far as the eye could see. It was amazing how this group had grown. I was responsible for two hundred and fifty-nine people, but the mission had already taken on a life of its own.

A tank stolen off the front lawn of the V.F.W. Hall had been brought back to working order by the very veterans who used to repair and drive the Desert Storm Tanks. The tan-coloured tank led the way. On the sides of the tank, some jokester painted "E.T. Phone Home" with a picture of the glowing finger and an eight hundred number to call for a ride. It made me chuckle. It was as if aliens would be familiar with the movie E.T. and that they would be standing on the side of the road reading the message and conveniently holding a cell phone. You had to respect the resourcefulness of those veterans. The tank managed to get to the front of the line — the full tracks pulling it through the sand at a faster rate than I would have figured. Everyone stepped aside for the M1 Abrams MBT (Main Battle Tank), they gave it a wide berth. It became our symbol of power, and it led the way with an empty gun—at least I hoped it was empty. The fuel tank of only a four-hundred and sixty gallons gave it a capacity to travel two hundred and sixty-five miles, I knew the tank would get to the base, but without a refuel, wouldn't make it back.

Some folks took their four-wheelers and rode in the desert along the side of the road. We were a moving wall, a human force. I knew I was no longer in control; the crowds surrounded my group and absorbed us. S.T.A. was no longer leading. We'd been overrun. The sun caused heatwaves to rise from the ground distorting the vision of the distant Emigrant Valley Mountains. Motorcyclists stopping and starting in the ninety-five, degree weather had to be miserable, but our spirits were high. Naruto runners were loaded in the back of pick-up trucks, and vegetable-hauling trucks waited for their big moment.

We passed the W.T.E.C crew—those Welcome to Earth weirdos. Carol gave them the finger. "Carol, control yourself!" I reprimanded, but I felt undeniable admiration. I was thinking of giving her a promotion in the club.

The first of us arrived at the Gate Three entrance, one hundred and fifty miles from Rachel. A large stop sign, on a massive gate protected by armed guards, stopped us from moving further. Those in the rear pushed toward the entrance. Those in front could not stop the momentum. There were hundreds of guards all along the chain-link fence pointing their weapons at us. A soldier came out with a bull horn telling the masses to move back or they would be forced to shoot if the crowd didn't turn away.

Vern Crawler driving the tank didn't care. He opened the top and screamed a battle cry as he smashed through the gate, drawing fire from the soldiers. We stood in stunned silence. We had not figured on actual gunfire. The trucks carrying the Naruto runners passed through the gates as well and headed toward the buildings on the base. A wild cheer went up from the masses as we clamoured through the gate. Nothing could stop us.

A few F-16's flew over as we travelled further inside the perimeter. Laser beams tracked our movements. How could the government use deadly force against her unarmed citizens? Drones flew around, warning us to turn back. The Air Force had been very respectful of the citizens, but now were beginning to fend them off as if they were a threat.

Due to our large numbers, we were a threat. The Gate Three entrance was overwhelmed. There was too many to kill. How protective would the base be of their military secrets? Everyone wanted to see the aliens.

We soon learnt...as the first shots were fired.

My group didn't get through the gate because the bus succumbing to roadblocks. We exited the vehicles, accidentally stumbling onto the hidden entrance to an underground tunnel. The guards were busy holding off a million other raiders. Somehow, we were fortunate enough to hurry our people down the shaft finding a door to an emergency stairway. Down the spiral of steps we went. The stair-well was well-lit and air-conditioned, or perhaps it was cool because we were so far underground. The steps ended at a locked door. The Punchers loaded up on energy drinks and bashed at the door until it opened. Total silence greeted us. No doubt the Air Force never considered a raid like this would happen. Most of the base was fighting the civilians above.

We entered the main room. Spaceships in various

stages of repair were out in the open. Strange looking aliens watched in stunned silence as the people from Rachel walked through. Robots carried parts from one ship to another. The aliens were tall, slender with large black eyes. Their elongated fingers formed a peace sign. We, the invaders, did the same back.

Along the length of the room were many doors. I knocked on one and was surprised when a slender being in a bathrobe responded, motioning for me to come inside. I instructed the rest of my people to keep looking while I entered the alien being's apartment.

"I come in peace. I am here to rescue you!" I made hand signs as I spoke. The being looked at me with its dark eyes. A small thin black tube, a probe, came out of its neck. It wavered in the air for a moment as if to hypnotise. While I was staring at the tentacle, it split in two and then whipped forwards, sticking into my neck, just behind my ears. It was so painful I fell to my knees.

Everything I ever felt or knew of life was being pulled out of me like a straw at the end of a malted milk drink. I had no will to fight the probes, finding myself in total submission to this being. The tubes penetrated deeper into my brain. The alien sucked out memories of my childhood; growing up, my grandparents, my sister. The creature knew everything about me; where I lived, about my wife and children. I felt so vulnerable, I found himself crying like a baby.

Then the opposite happened. I was being filled again with all my memories. The feeling was coming back in waves. Intense memories, happy and sad, washed over me. Once my own memories were restored, new knowledge implanted at an astonishing speed. I saw where the aliens were from, why they were here, the crash, the way they were living. Our sun was too hot for them to be outside, so they had been kept here underground since 1947; since the crash in Roswell, New Mexico. He was not alone. Several of their crew survived the wreckage, and he was their commander. I saw the planet Giron, outside the Milky Way Galaxy. I saw the alien's childhood, all his feelings right back to his birth. I understood everything with such clarity.

Finally, to my amazement and heart's desire; the cure for cancer and diabetes, the cure for every disease known to man. The government had all these things at their fingertips and never offered them to help people.

The creature found cancer in me. I wasn't surprised, I'd suspected as much; a doctor's appointment the following week would have confirmed my suspicions, I was sure. Prostate cancer was suddenly taken from me. I could feel it being tugged by the very roots, from my body. When the alien finished, he withdrew the antenna probes. I had no words. I lay on the floor, no strength to stand. The alien lay his hands on me, sending warmth, and gave me some stability along with durability.

I found I could communicate with him without talking. I mentally sent a message to him, asking the creature if it wanted to leave the base. The alien explained the sun was too overpowering, and that the Air Force was trying to find a way to repair the ships, but the technology wasn't there yet. Klaigh and his crew were certain their kind would come to rescue them. They were on their way. It was only a matter of time. What felt like years to us on Earth, was only a matter of months for him. Satisfied with his answer, I shook the slender grey hand and went back out to my group.

Calling them back together, we started up the stairs. Floor after floor, climbing out of the bowels of the Earth, we reached the surface. Coming out of the tunnel, we started back to the buses. I suspected many of my crew had experienced the same encounter that I had endured. They all looked a little dazed.

"Halt!" shouted the guard. We stopped just outside the secret entrance.

"We are leaving. We are done with this whole thing," I told the soldier. The guard moved my people forward, marching behind us back through the gate to where the buses were still waiting.

All the club members filed back on the school buses. They appeared shaken to the core. We had found the aliens, communicated with them, and some of us were even cured by them. The Save The Aliens Club finally had the proof we'd longed for. I had no idea where the motorcyclists were, or where the E.T. tank ended up. They went off on their own. But I had safely delivered my club members to the bus, and we were on our way back to Rachel.

The bus weaved around the parked cars like a desert snake heading back home. It was still light out. I looked at my watch; it was only seven p.m. Had we been here a matter of hours, not days? All of us had experienced a profound interaction with beings from another planet.

No one spoke as the buses lumbered along. The S.T.A. members sat in total silence, thinking about the new knowledge given to us and the seeds that had been planted within us.

Allen Parker

23, Cameraman for REAA51 NEWS

By C.L. Williams

I follow Alicia to the outskirts of Area 51 where our boss, REAA51 News is expecting us to cover the infamous "Storming of Area 51". I hold the camera up, point the lens at Alicia, and count her down as she begins her news broadcast.

"BREAKING NEWS! This is Alicia Banner of REAA51 News at the secret Area 51 base where it is being reported that droves of people that stormed the secret military base are now running away from Area 51 in a frenzy! I'm going to see if I can stop someone and get a quick word."

She looks around as she notices some are too fast to catch. She notices someone running slower than the others, "Allan, let's go get a word from him," she tells me. I follow her as she runs towards the guy running slower than others.

"Excuse me, quick word for REAA51?"

"They were locked away for a REASON!" he shouts then looks directly into the camera, "WE'RE ALL GONNA DIE! IT'S TOO LATE! NONE OF US CAN BE SAVED!"

The guy runs off and I point the camera on Alicia once more, I make sure she can see my face as I mouth to her, "We're still live."

"Those are the words of one of our many citizens that stormed Area 51 earlier today! Let's take a look at what is going on," Alicia then signals for me to get a glimpse of what is happening at the secret military base.

I point the lens towards the base, and we see hundreds of people running out of the base in panic. I manage to zoom in on a few faces and you can see the fear. Members of the military are also running out into the desert with fear covering their faces as well. I am about to put the lens back on Alicia when a crashing sound is heard in the distance. I quickly point the camera back to the secret base and I see what looks like lasers making their way out of the roof of the base. A metallic entity is then floating in the air and begins shooting lasers towards anyone and anything in its way.

"NO WAY!" Alicia screams off camera as the two of us see something that looks alien causing terror on everything in its way. Alicia nudges me to point the camera back on her.

"It looks like the conspiracies were true! The military does indeed use this base for extraterrestrial studies. We are going to try to find one of the workers of Area 51 and get a word."

I look at Alicia in protest. I'm unwilling to go anywhere near the metallic being with lasers in its eyes. She asks me if I can turn off the camera for a moment. I oblige and she begins lecturing and motivating me.

"ALLAN PARKER!" she yells at me, "I know you're new to this job, but it is our job. You need to get your panties out of a bunch and follow me into that military base!"

"There's an alien floating in the air, shooting lasers out of his eyes," I say in fear. "I can't speak for you, but I like living!"

"How does that girlfriend put up with you?" she asks as she goes from motivating to berating.

"FINE!" She pushed the right buttons and now I'm following her into the secret military base as we see a metallic-looking alien shooting lasers out of its eyes.

Alicia starts looking for someone in the military to get a word from. She manages to find someone, and Alicia gets near him, mic in hand, and tells me to turn the camera back on.

"The is Alicia Banner here with," she then puts the mic in the man's face. He slaps it out of the way and makes a run for a barricade. Alicia picks up the mic and once again tries to get a word from someone working inside Area 51. She finds another person and tries to get a word from him as well, "What can you tell us about Area 51?" she then places the mic in his face.

"No comment, what I can tell you is you need to get the hell out of here right now! These things do NOT come in peace. I repeat, they do NOT come in peace," he then pulls out a gun unfamiliar to Alicia or myself and he begins shooting the metallic entity. Seeing he doesn't want to talk, I put the camera back on Alicia.

"We did not get much from the man working inside of Area 51, but he did tell us these extraterrestrial beings are not the peaceful type. If you see them, do not approach. We will try to give you more updates later but for now, we are being advised to leave the premises immediately." The two of us leave the premises as we watch people turn to ash by one of the Area 51 escapees.

The second we leave the facility I make a beeline for the van. Alicia may be pissed at me, but I just watched someone turn to ash and I'll be damned if I let that *thing* turn me to ash as well.

Belladonna Pryor

26, Salem, MA

By Cindar Harrell

"It was just supposed to be fun, you know? A joke."

"I know, Belladonna. Just tell us what happened," the woman said softly, a warm, compassionate smile on her face. She was from the... police? The press? CIA? I couldn't remember. I had talked to so many people already, it was all just a blur. All I knew was that my arm hurt, hell *everything* hurt, but inside I had gone numb.

"We do this every year, the four of us."

"Storm Area 51?" she asked sceptically. I waved my good hand at her and shook my head.

"No, no. We plan a trip. We met in college and we promised we'd all stay in touch even though we live in different states. This is how we do that, we go on a trip every year. Different places, just whatever interests us at the time."

"And this year that was Area 51?"

I nodded and unconsciously reached for my arm and closed my eyes. I tried to tune out everything: her, the beeping of the hospital machines, the memories. I just wanted to forget, but all of these people kept asking me to relive it. Why? Haven't I been through enough?

"It was Tom's idea, initially. He always had the best ideas. He saw the thing on Facebook, you know, the event post?" She nodded. "He showed it to us and we all agreed. We thought it would be fun, go and have some laughs then maybe head to Vegas afterwards."

"What happened when you got there?"

"When we got there...?"

And there it was, the thing everyone wanted to know. What happened? What happened the day of the Storming of Area 51?

It was what everyone wanted to know, and I wanted to forget.

* * *

There were so many people there, miles of people all lining up, marching. It was intense. I figured, we would all just get to the gates and, I don't know. Party? But I guess the extremists, the ones who took it seriously, were all up front.

We were pretty far in the back, so I don't know a lot of what happened in the beginning. Everyone was laughing and fooling around at first, but then people started getting hot and tired. Even then though, we still acted like we were at a festival or something.

The first signs of something wrong was the ground shaking and a bright light.

"What the hell was that? You saw that right?" Tom asked us.

We all nodded.

"What do you think it was?" David asked.

"Probably just fireworks or something," Pam said.

"Damn! Why didn't we think of that?" Tom hollered out in disappointment.

They were still smiling, laughing, but something felt wrong. "I don't think it was fireworks."

"What do you mean? What else could it have been?" Pam asked.

"I don't know. A warning?" I answered. I'm not sure why I thought that, something just told me it was.

"Like a warning for what? Don't go getting all weird on us with that Salem witchy sense of yours!" Tom said, rubbing the top of my head, mussing my hair good-naturedly.

I tried to laugh at the usual joke. It's true I am from a family of Salem witches. My parents own a shop in town and sell herbs and charms. They all thought it was cool.

"Are you going to talk to the aliens with your magic, Bella?" David gave me a playful shove.

"I think you are mixing up two very different genres there, Dave." He feigned confusion at my response and shook his head.

Nothing else happened for a few minutes, but then we heard the alarms. We were getting closer to the base and we could hear them going off in the distance. Sounds of planes or choppers overhead made me duck. There were so many people, I couldn't really see anything. Most of the guys around us thought that it was all part of the show, something someone staged, we did too at first, I guess. We never really thought the military would fire on civilians.

We were already past the main perimeter by the time things started really getting to us. It was all a confusing blur of lights and sounds. I don't remember a lot of what happened right after getting in. It's almost like... they don't want me to. Like they had something set up at the gate to confuse us, make us forget. I'm not sure.

David was the first to be separated from us. When the first explosion hit close by, everyone began to wake up, I guess. People started screaming, panicking. It became a stampede to find a way out, but we were all packed in like sardines. The military had deployed and were trying to contain people, there was nowhere to go, no room to move. David tripped and was trampled underneath thousands, hundreds of thousands, of pairs of panicked feet.

That's when it became real for me.

The sense of 'wrongness' that I had felt earlier was screaming in my head in full force and I was running like everyone else. We reached the side of a building, a small alcove where we stopped to catch our breath. Pam got sick and I very nearly joined her.

"What is happening?" she sobbed. "Don't they know that it's just a joke? Why are they attacking us?"

"I don't think everyone got the memo, look," Tom said and pointed out into the crowd further ahead. There were people, civilians, with guns firing on the military. It was an all out assault.

Everything happened so fast, I didn't even have time to think or process what was going on. I just had to move. We started to look for cover. Dust and sand, and I don't even want to know what else, filled the air. It was hard to make out anything in the chaos. I started to see things, things that rationally I knew made no sense. Creatures. I don't know. I felt like I was going crazy. I shook my head to try and get myself to focus, we needed out of the open.

From what I could see, there were three main buildings. We chose one and followed the outside wall until we found a door. It was already broken. I don't think anyone else had made it inside yet, it looked like it had gotten caught in the crossfire more than someone purposefully trying to break in.

The three of us went in. It was weird. Quiet. Dark. Our breathing and Pam's sobs were deafening without all the noise and screaming from outside. I mean, obviously all of that was still there, but it seemed so far away.

Pam collapsed as soon as we entered. "What the hell was all of that? How did this happen? Oh God... David... Did you see what they did to him?" She rocked herself back and forth in an effort to calm down, mumbling in increasingly incoherent sentences.

I didn't want to think of David. We weren't safe yet and I knew we couldn't afford for two of us to fall apart.

"We just need to rest for a minute and then leave," Tom said, rubbing his hand along his dirt-crusted forehead.

"Leave how? It's a massacre out there. We'd never make it back to the gate, even if we knew where it was," I said.

"But we don't have any guns. We aren't attacking them! They should just let us leave!" Pam looked up at us, naive hope filling her tear-stained eyes.

"I don't think they care. To them, we are all the enemy now. We were part of the mob that broke in, I don't think they are making distinctions between those who are armed and those who aren't," I said.

"Then we need to get guns. If they are going to try to kill us either way, then we need to be able to defend ourselves, fight back," Tom said, determined. "I didn't come here to die."

"Neither did I, but even if we could find weapons, we

are talking about the military! They have years of training! I don't know about either of you, but I've never held a gun in my life," I replied. To me, it just seemed like we would make ourselves more of a target. "Maybe we can sneak out. Find a back way out of this hell hole or something. That can't be the only entrance."

"Any exits will be well guarded, whatever they are trying to hide here, it's not like they are going to let anyone just walk out with their secrets."

He was right, of course. He usually was. I hated that.

"OK, well. You stay with Pam, I'm going to look around in here and see if I see anything that may help us." I looked at my surroundings for the first time. Boxes, crates. "I guess this is some kind of storage facility. Maybe there are some extra weapons in here somewhere or, I don't know... hell, maybe a teleportation device." I gave a mirthless laugh. Why did we ever think this was a good idea?

"Are you sure you're going to be all right by yourself?" he asked.

"No, but Pam is hysterical, she can't be left alone and I'm not strong enough to protect both of us."

He nodded.

I sighed, closed my eyes, took a deep breath, and tried to calm myself down. I have a habit of always acting more in control than I am. This situation was no exception. On the outside, I may have appeared calm, but inside I was shaking and screaming.

I walked along the narrow paths between the rows of boxes, looking at labels where I could find them. Most of the labels didn't make any sense, but I was leery to just start prying off lids. Even if there weren't aliens or UFOs hiding somewhere on the site, it was still a military installation. There's no telling what kinds of dangerous weapons or chemicals they kept around. I kept walking. I'm pretty sure at some point, my mind decided to check out, leaving my body to aimlessly wander on auto-pilot. It was all just too unreal.

The next thing I can remember thinking was that I didn't realise it had gotten so bright inside. There was a crate, kind of separate from everything else along one wall. It was on some sort of pedestal and was glowing. Approaching slowly, I held my hands out in front of me. The air got warmer the closer I went to it. It was like it was emitting some kind of pulse of energy in small waves. It was nailed shut and there were no labels on the outside. Despite my better judgement, I began looking around for something to pry the lid off. I don't know why. I should have known better. I should have just left it alone.

I found a crowbar and went back to it. Once the lid was off, the light seemed to dim, almost as if it knew it had done its job, I was already caught in its trap.

A golden box sat inside. Dusty and battered, it had the

look of something that you would see in the movies dug out of the ruins of an ancient civilization, It certainly didn't look "sci-fi-ey" or high tech. Nothing like I expected. Well, truth be told I didn't expect to find anything at Area 51, but if I did, it wouldn't have been this. The surface of the box shimmered and for a moment, I thought I saw strange runes on it. I watched closer. Again, just for a second. On the third time, I was able to identify some of them as old Norse, but I knew others were something else. A fourth time. Egyptian hieroglyphics. Was that Greek? With every new shimmer I thought I saw something else. Mostly dead languages, but some I recognised as modern. Others didn't look like anything I had ever seen before. Maybe the alien theory wasn't completely out the window after all.

"What the hell is this thing?" Needless to say, my curiosity got the best of me. I opened it. Smoke filled my lungs and I began to cough. I stepped back, stumbling on my own feet and fell.

"Belladonna...." a voice whispered. It sounded like it was right next to my ear. I opened my eyes and a grotesque, inhuman face appeared inches from me, then was gone. I screamed.

"You are all the same. Your need to discover what you don't know, don't understand always destroys you. You see a shiny box and you open it, despite all the warnings of the disasters you will unleash."

"Warnings? What warnings?" I asked, voice ragged.

"You must have seen them," it responded.

"The symbols? I didn't understand enough of them. I can't read those, I just recognised a few."

"But surely you have heard the stories? Legends and myths exist for a reason, to warn us, to prepare us. They are lessons." A form, shimmering and ethereal flickered in the smoke, never fully taking shape.

"Myths?"

"Has your species never told a story of a box of disasters?"

"A box of disasters? You mean like Pandora's box?"

"Ah yes, that was it. Pandora." I sensed more than saw the thing smile.

"But that's not true. Just something people made up to explain things they didn't understand at the time. It isn't real," I said desperately.

"Just like a military base in the desert hiding secrets from the world isn't real? I am sure you have heard plenty of rumours of this place. That is why you are all here, is it not? To get the truth? Well, welcome to the truth, Belladonna Pryor. I know you, I know all of you who came here. I called you. I called everyone."

"What do you mean you called us?"

"I am the beacon. This box holds the disasters and plagues of the universe. All calamities and wars. But what good does that do if there is no one to open it? I lure creatures of all kinds, tempt them in to opening the box and unleashing chaos. That is why you have all come. That is why they have all come."

"Who are they? Who are you talking about?"

"The ones all of you humans came here to see. Those you call aliens. They came because they were drawn to the beacon, then your government caught them and contained them here. But now, I have called all of humanity here. And now thanks to you, Belladonna Pryor of Salem, Massachusetts, you have unleashed the pure source of chaos."

"No... I didn't mean to. I didn't know," I whispered, all the air leaving my body, a weight of a thousand worlds descending over my shoulders.

"They never do."

"What will happen?"

"That part isn't up to me. I just bring in those to unleash the evil, the chaos, what form it takes is determined by everyone else."

As suddenly as it appeared, the figment vanished and the smoke faded away. My heart was racing in my chest, heavy like thundering elephants. I couldn't believe it. None of it.

I didn't have time to dwell on what happened, however. A crash interrupted my shattered thoughts. The wall beside me exploded in a waterfall of debris and creatures like giant mutated spiders lurched out from the hole.

Screaming, I scrambled to my feet and ran. I couldn't remember which way the door was, so I just had to trust my instincts to lead me back to Tom and Pam. When I saw them, their eyes were wide, staring at the monsters chasing me.

"Run!" I yelled. Tom tried to get Pamela to her feet, but she was too panicked. She couldn't stand. When I reached them I grabbed her arm and we both pulled her, urging her to move. The thing behind me grabbed onto her leg. She screamed as we struggled to wrestle her free, her eyes wide in terror. It was no use, we were no match for it. Her hand slipped from mine. In an instant, she was gone. There was so much blood, all I saw was red.

"Come on! We've got to go!" Tom grabbed my shoulder and whirled me around. I snapped back to my senses and moved.

We ran as more and more of them appeared from nowhere and everywhere all at once.

"There!" Tom cried, pointing to a crack in the wall that was large enough for us to squeeze through. He went first then held his hand out for me. I took it and was almost through when something grabbed my arm. It burned as it pulled. I thought it was going to pull my arm completely off. Tom held onto me, bracing on the wall. He grabbed something sharp from the ground and stabbed the thing, making it let me go.

There was a cabinet in the room we were in, so we shoved it in front of the crack to try and keep the things out. Both of us were panting and covered in blood and dirt. My head was still filled with Pam's screams, my eyes still seeing the red of her blood.

"What the hell were those things?" Tom asked after he had a chance to catch his breath.

"Aliens? Monsters? I don't know. Call them whatever you want, but I think we just found the secret of Area 51."

* * *

"And I guess you know the rest. We holed up there until rescue teams arrived. We...we thought they were going to kill us, but they helped us." I blinked away the tears in my eyes. I was tired of crying. It seemed to be the only thing I could do anymore.

"It's all right, Belladonna. You're safe now," the woman said running her hand over my hair.

"Why didn't they kill us? The people that found us?" I asked.

"Well," she hesitated, "once the containment on the...assets...had been breached, the military had to focus on containing the outbreak. I suppose everyone realised they were fighting the same enemy at that point. It became us versus them. Once things had gotten under control, rescue units were sent out to look for survivors."

I looked away. "I wish they had just killed me too. It's my fault."

"Don't say that. It's not your fault. You are only one of over a million people to storm Area 51 that day. You've been through a horrible tragedy, but you survived. You both did."

I looked over to the bed next to me. Tom was asleep. I envied him. I had been too afraid to close my eyes for that long.

"You made it. The worst is over."

I just nodded as she stood and left the room. I wish I could believe that, but something in me knew better. Call it my "witch sense," but I knew that whatever had been unleashed that day was far from done and the horrors we had witnessed were just a preview of the devastation to come.

Alastair Harp

The Last Snake Oil Salesman

By Mason Harold Hilden

What the fuck am I looking at, and what the fuck did those spacetards do? I guess my day can get worse, but it started so goddamn good.

Rachel, Nevada, is a one horse town about 20 miles from the military installation cryptically known as Area 51. It was basically in bum-fuck nowhere surrounded by ghost towns, dust, sand, and more sand. And there I was, Alastair Harp, entrepreneur and salesman. My mantra is, there's a sucker born every minute, and that is the only commandment I followed. I'm not young, and not old, medium build, and I am blessed with the look of someone who's appearance one could never accurately recall. I know I'm not handsome by any means, but I do dress well, and thoroughly enjoy my many indulgences and vices—and they are many. I'm not ashamed to admit that I've made a career out of conning people and I am very good at my job. And there I was, in Rachel-fucking-Nevada, about to win the biggest jackpot of my career. When I heard about this Raid Area 51 fiasco, I knew my golden goose had finally arrived.

I had to pull a few strings and grease many palms, deciding I could make maximum bank by selling 'Keep Awake' pills. I purchased the entire stock from a North American pharmaceutical company in Philadelphia. I then immediately brokered a deal with the US military, and sold them the entire stock (ironically, a large percentage of the pills were allocated to the US Air Force and their base at Groom Lake). I easily tripled my initial investment. One caveat was that I was to be able to keep the pill bottles, so I could refill them with sugar pills to sell to the spacetards, as I affectionately called them. I was unconcerned with my duplicity, as was the military liaison who I dealt with while brokering the deal. Man, she had a great rack. Conspiracy theories and wild fantasies would be all that was needed to keep these spacetards awake as they searched for their little green men.

Vendors and hawkers arrived in Rachel a few days before the raid, selling items like gas, MREs, bottled water, sun tan lotion, cheap-ass hiking boots, as well as conspiracy related items like maps to and of Area 51, know-your-alien binders, and tinfoil caps to protect one's mind from being read. The initial count was to be as high as 2.5 million seekers of the alien truth, but much less than that arrived to raid the top-secret base.

We arrived the day before, and I sat inside the air conditioned cube van, watching as Dodo Eyeball sold the pills.

I hated Dodo Eyeball. "Hey Dodo? I fucking hate you."

"Yes, boss!" Always the same response from him.

I'll admit, he was my whipping boy, especially when things went wrong. He stank, was as dumb as a post, and never showed initiative. He would never amount to anything, and that was fine with me. It made it all the easier for me to manipulate and control him. Today however, things were going great!

At $25 per pill, and thirty pills per bottle, I was making a fortune. By the time all the pills were sold, I had made in excess of seven million dollars. Many people popped the pills right in front of us after purchase, and I wasn't concerned. If and when anyone realised that the pills were fake, it would be too late. I would be safely hidden away in Sin City, and the mark would likely be in jail, or partying, or making baby spacetards. I didn't really give two shits what they did or what would happen. Life was good, and air-conditioned cool.

The pills sold out after only a few hours and, because you can never have too much money, I sold all of our bottled water, too. Except two, which I kept for myself. Another two hundred bucks was another two hundred bucks. The trip back to Las Vegas would only take about four hours and two waters was enough for me. Fuck Dodo.

The road was eerily devoid of vehicles as we drove back down the ET Highway. We travelled for almost an hour when it happened—I had to take a piss. Having a hate on for public washrooms, I had trained myself from an early age to only go at home, or a friend's place, or hotel bathrooms, places like that. But never, ever in public washrooms. "Aw, for shit's sake, pull the damn van over!" I yelled at Dodo. His dumb-ass response was to ask if I had to pee?

"No. I want to take some damn pictures of cactuses, cacti, whatever the fuck they are in plural!" He's such a dumbshit.

Then he offered me my phone, which I forgot all about. "I'll get the damn phone when I get back! And keep the windows up 'cause I don't want the A/C going out," I told him as I slammed the door shut. I forgot that Dodo needed the phone for the credit transactions. Cash was the preferred method of payment, and most of them were indeed done this way. Internet access was surprisingly good in Rachel, but the masses of spacetards made it a slow process with regards to transactions. The adage *money talks and bullshit walks* was front and centre at the Raid Area 51 market.

Oh shit, I almost forgot to yell at Dodo but remembered as I turned, "Hey Dodo? I fucking hate you."

"Yes, boss," he replied with a strange shit-eatin' grin.

I was angry that I had to urinate, but did it ever feel great when I finally did. It was one of those shiver-down-your-back leaks, and I'm not afraid to admit that I was momentarily in bliss. In fact, I was so preoccupied with my euphoric urination that I failed to notice the sound of crunching gravel as the van tires began moving on the roadside.

"What the—" was all I could mutter as I watched my van move back onto the highway heading for Las Vegas without me. And Dodo even had the audacity to yell at me, "I fucking hate you too!" while giving me the bird as he drove away. Yeah, away with all my fuckin' money!

Piss dribbled onto my hand and underwear as I finally remembered to put my dick away. I was so mad that I could shit, and that would be all I needed to totally FUBAR my current situation. I was dumbstruck. I just got robbed by Dodo-fucking-Eyeball, the dumbest shit I ever met! I was going to yell back, knowing full well that he would not hear me, but what was the damn point? I was royally fucked! I stood in silence and watched my van continue on its journey when I realised that it was extremely hot, noon sun hot. The spacetards had started their raid, and I was starting to sweat, and get very, very thirsty. I knew my time was numbered. All I had was the clothes on my back, my pissy underwear, and a wallet, complete with numerous bank cards and zero cash. There were no ATMs out here, and definitely no places to get a drink. I thought I'd just sit down and— *Wait! Did Dodo just drop something out the window of the van?* It looked like a bottle of water, and it bounced! Holy shit! Dodo, that bastard! He just left me a bottle of water! Bless that thievin' backstabbing piece of shit!

I ran for the water, already feeling the effects of being out in the sun for what felt like forever (five minutes). I scooped up the bottled water, which was uncharacteristically warm to the touch. As I scrambled to open the bottle of salvation, I noticed it's yellowish discolouration...and then the smell.

I threw the bottle into the bush, feeling some small satisfaction when it exploded, and wondered if his day could get any worse.

* * *

But that was yesterday. A holy hell of shit has happened since then, and I'm still staggering down this highway. Not a car passes, but I hear plenty of screams.

And I'd pay a million bucks for that bottle of piss right now.

Evan Dean

42, Security Detail, Area 51

By N.M. Brown

Being a night guard at Area 51's museum in Roswell has put a lot of food on my family's table.

I'm an avid collector. They even let me keep old exhibits taken down to make way for new ones.

The trip to Nevada will be well worth new additions for my collection; from inside actual Area 51!

* * *

The freshly raided section I arrive in mirrors a sensory deprivation chamber.

I barely get out alive. There's a jagged scar above my heart. Its beats are out of rhythm; looks like I wasn't the only one to add something to my...collection.

Rachel Montgomery

By Cindar Harrell

I made it into Area 51. I mean, after everything that's happened, there was no way I was *not* going to get in. One way or another. It was all I could think about since the time I was 12. I would have found my own way in eventually, but this event was the perfect opportunity, so I seized it.

"Ameri, hold the camera steady! Great, perfect!" my recording of the event went. "This is Rachel Montgomery, and thank you for joining me in this very special video! As many of my loyal followers know, I have spent the past eight years in search of my mother. I got a lead about three years ago in the form of the Akashic Records. If I can find that, then I can find her. According to all of my research, and several reliable sources, the US government got hold of the records and are now storing them in...you guessed it...none other than the infamous Area 51! Today is the Storming, and while everyone else is hunting aliens, I will be going after the real prize! Stay tuned!" My camera went dead after that so everything that followed is recorded in memory only.

I'm sure you've heard all about the actual "storming" at the gates, so I won't bore you with those details. My story is much like everyone else's on that front, however it is what happened once inside that makes my experience exceptionally unique.

I had a contact in the military who helped give me some basic blueprints and maps of the facility. He couldn't guarantee them to be up to date, but it was better than nothing. He claimed that the government has a whole secret sector devoted to finding dangerous artefacts of mystic value. They locate them before anyone else can and use their resources to study them. Or contain them. My mother was an investigative journalist who loved all things supernatural. When one of her sources caught wind of a rumour, well, that was all it took to send her on an obsessive hunt that spiralled out of control and ended with her disappearance. I made it my mission to find her. And this was my chance.

We followed the map to the building my contact had circled; Warehouse Three. He said it was a warehouse of some sort on the surface, but it held all the secrets I was after.

Thankfully, the map was pretty detailed and gave alternate routes; we had to take the long way as the shortcut alley was already occupied by a boozy, gunned-up couple. We didn't fancy our chances against a pair of crazy gun-toters, that's not why we were there.

"Now what?" Ameri asked once we were inside the warehouse. There were crates everywhere, but I didn't pay attention to any of them. I knew it wouldn't be on the surface level.

I waved for her to follow me as I went into a room with several monitors.

"He said that there was a secret entrance in the back that leads to an underground facility. It should be right around here." I ran my hand along the large computer, careful to avoid touching the controls. The last thing we needed was for me to hit a wrong button and set something loose. "Ah, here!" I found a switch and the wall opened up revealing a dark tunnel descending into the unknown underbelly of Area 51.

I entered the darkness without hesitation. Without fear.

I don't know how long we walked. It seemed to take forever. I knew that there was utter chaos above me, but all I could hear was the sound of my own rapid heartbeat. Eventually, I sensed more than saw the passage open up. I cursed my dead and smashed camera as I pulled out my phone. The minute I unlocked the home screen, a charge of electricity shot through it forcing me to drop it.

"What the hell?" I cried out, more from the surprise than the actual pain, shaking my fingers.

"Rachel, look." Ameri tapped my shoulder.

I looked at her, then to where she was pointing further into the room. I couldn't help the audible gasp that passed my lips. Bits of light danced around in the shadows illuminating the room in small pieces. There seemed to be no rhyme or reason to it, but when the light got close to the wall, the flash intensified as if it were bouncing off of something.

I walked further into the dark chamber and approached the wall. Reaching out my hand, I touched the cool, smooth surface.

"Glass?" A loud bang made me recoil and a burst of light cut through the darkness where I was standing. "A mirror."

A chain reaction of light stemming from that initial source where I stood went off, illuminating the room piece by piece. Mirror by mirror.

"They're all mirrors," Ameri said. She was right, both walls were lined with them. They were as tall as us and evenly spaced. I walked to another, following my reflection's progress. The image changed. The glass rippled and a box appeared as if a portal had opened beyond the glass, or a strange version of a two-way mirror, one that could change which way you saw it. Eagerly I went to another, then another.

All were the same, but different. Each one changed as I approached but they revealed something different inside.

"Secrets..." I whispered. "We did it, Ameri! We've found it!"

"You think the Akashic Records are inside one of these mirror-doors?" she asked.

"It has to be!"

"Great, but which one?"

I paused. "I'm not sure." I looked around at the seemingly infinite number of possibilities. "The Akashic Records would be one of the greatest finds in history. A comprehensive knowledge; everything that has been, is, or will be. Even if we are to assume that each of these mirrors holds something of great value, items from myths and legends, something with infinite knowledge and foresight has to be at the top of the priority list, right?" I mused.

"I mean, yeah, you would think so. They say knowledge is power right? And if that's the case then something with all the knowledge in the world..."

"Would have all the power in the world." I looked to the back of the room, still shrouded in darkness. "Following that logic, they would want to make sure it was well protected. Even if someone were to make it as far as we have, they might put it in the back in hopes that other things would distract any would-be thieves." I started walking again, faster. Spurred on by the certainty that what I had been seeking for so long was close, I began to run and didn't stop until I was at the end. The back wall was completely black, but the light reflected in some places giving it the illusion of glass. I touched it like I did the first mirror and once again it rippled, changing the smooth surface to that of a more malleable gel.

"Now what?" Ameri asked, eyeing the strange wall before us.

"We go in." Without waiting for a reply, I pushed through the substance and walked into the unknown. I heard Ameri curse behind me but didn't bother to turn around. I was too close.

The room was engulfed in a darkness so thick that it was like a miasma permeated the air. I stepped forward and a single light formed, a perfect circle showcasing the only thing in the room: a pedestal.

Slowly I approached, only just then worrying about the possibilities of any potential traps or security measures the government may have put in place. In all of my excitement I had almost forgotten where I was. After what seemed like an eternity, I finally reached it and breathed a sigh of relief. I closed my eyes to steady myself.

This has to be it!

I looked at the object displayed on the plush velvet.

I nearly cried for joy upon seeing the ancient tome. "This is it!" Of course, I didn't know exactly what the Akashic Records would look like, but the book before me practically screamed "all-powerful knowledge!" The cover was cracked leather with metal fittings around the edges and a large clasp to keep it closed. Jewels adorned the clasp and centre of the front cover. The pages were yellowed and it was so large and thick, I worried if I would even be able to carry it.

Unable to control myself, I unclasped it and opened the book to the first page. I held my breath, and it seemed that even my heart stopped beating.

Sounds of an explosion suddenly thundered overhead, shaking the room. I was dizzy, my eyes burned and my thoughts grew fuzzy.

"Rachel, we need to get out of here, now!" Ameri called out from behind me. She couldn't have been more than a few feet away and yet she sounded like she was speaking through an ocean of water. I raised my hand to my head and nearly fell. It took a moment for me to realise that I didn't actually hit the floor. I looked up into Ameri's concerned, frantic face. "Come on." She pulled me back into a standing position and dragged me to the wall where we entered. I glanced back to the pedestal, but I already knew that the Akashic Records wouldn't be there.

We passed through the strange veil separating the relic room from the mirror-hall, and the fog over my mind finally began to lift. Another tremor, another explosion. We looked at each other and shared a silent thought: run!

We raced back to the passage that lead up to the

surface level and emerged back into the warehouse area only to find that the chaos from outside had stormed in. Crates were smashed on the floor, their precious relics spilling out like a hoarder's lost paradise.

Wait, is that the holy grail? A scream snapped my attention back to our dire situation. *Focus! Survive now, think of everything else later!*

I looked in the direction of the scream in time to see the girl from the alleyway being dragged by a monster that I'm not even sure how to describe. She struggled in its grip, blood raining down around her. I had to look away from the horror and fight the bile that rose in my throat when her screams were suddenly cut off.

"Move!" Ameri grabbed my hand and pulled me in the opposite direction. Out of the corner of my eye, the monster lunged and I thought I saw someone else trying to escape.

"I think someone's in there still, shouldn't we try to help them?" I asked.

"How? We can't even help ourselves!"

Reluctantly, I had to agree and followed.

We both made it out of the compound alive which is more than many can say. More than that poor girl that was ripped apart right in front of us. I've since learned that her name was Sally. I never met her and yet I know that I will never forget her as long as I live.

"I'm sorry you didn't get what you came for, Rachel. I

know how much the Akashic Records meant to you," Ameri said once we were at the hospital with many of the remaining survivors.

I shook my head to clear it of the invading thoughts and images that I just wasn't ready to deal with yet.

"Yeah, um... It's disappointing, for sure." I nodded, staring blankly at the wall behind my best friend. I was having a hard time focusing, my thoughts too jumbled and scattered. Too full.

"Are you going to be OK?" Ameri asked, sensing my distraction. "We'll find your mom. There has to be another lead out there somewhere."

I forced myself to look at her. "Yes, I'll be fine. And you're right, I'll find her."

"We just need to go through all of her notes for another clue. You know I am always here for you. Who knows, maybe there is a copy of the Akashic Records locked away somewhere." She smiled.

"No, I don't need them."

I can find her now.

I closed my eyes and finally let myself process all the information of the past several hours. Everything that happened, everything that I'd seen. Flashes of images and words seemed to flow through my mind, as if seeing them displayed right in front of me on the largest computer screen in the world, the universe. I didn't need another copy of the

Akashic Records. One was plenty.

I opened my eyes and knew where to find her.

Now, I knew *everything*.

Josh Tillman

By Eddie D. Moore

Everyone knew that the whole Storm Area 51 plan was a gigantic joke. Well, almost everyone anyway. The government knew it, the guards on the base knew it, and the vast majority of people who showed up at Gate 12 with tents and coolers full of beer the night of September the 19th knew it. I only heard of a hand full of people that got too close and triggered a perimeter alert. The MPs took them all into custody without resistance. Looking back, I think they were the lucky ones.

Most of us spent the afternoon drinking and grilling. You would've thought it was Halloween by the way so many people were dressed. All your favourite aliens from science fiction were there. It was one big SF nerd convention and campout.

I crawled into my tent around midnight after about three beers too many. Even the fireworks weren't enough to keep my eyes open, but a few hours later, the panicked screams of the people around me did the trick.

We knew that it was a possibility that the National Guard might show up to break up our little gathering, and as far as I know, there might have been a group crazy enough to rush the gates and force a response. There were after all dozens of campsites surrounding the Air Force base. I was not, however, prepared for what I saw when I stepped out of my tent.

I heard gunfire in the distance, and I saw spaceships of a dozen different designs flying every direction imaginable. It was pure chaos. Tracer fire chased ships that got too high. Explosions on the ground and in the air lit up the early morning sky.

A saucer-shaped spaceship suddenly stopped twenty feet above my head before I could decide which direction to run. An instant later, a blue-tinged light enveloped me, and I began to fall up. The light grew in intensity as I got closer to the ship, and I could barely see the long slender arms that dragged me inside.

I remember screaming and struggling against arms that looked too frail to hold me when something was sprayed in my face. It felt like my body melted and an irresistible relaxation swept over me. Deep in my mind, I was still in a panic. The aliens' oversized heads and dark, bulbous eyes still frightened me, but I couldn't even lift a finger to resist as they dragged me into a holding cell.

Dozens of people were stuffed into each of the cells. Apprehension replaced the euphoria as whatever drug they used wore off. I think we all found comfort in the fact we weren't alone, but there was barely enough room for us all to sit down. An eight-inch diameter hole in the corner became the restroom. At least, we assumed that was its function.

They gave us plastic tubes filled with a green mush to eat. It tasted terrible, but after missing a few meals, everyone decided it was better than starving.

The days crept by at an intolerably slow pace with nothing to do but stare at the men, women, and children around me. Most of us considered it a welcome change when the ship landed and they marched us out of the ship. Those who tried to resist discovered that the long poles carried by our hosts held an electrical charge that was strong enough to make you urinate yourself.

The sun was brighter than we were used to on Earth, and it took several minutes for our eyes to adjust. Besides a few dilapidated buildings near the landing site, there was nothing to see in any direction but row after row of green crops and human slaves carrying buckets of water into the fields. When they returned, their buckets were full of leaves, and they dumped them into a machine that processed the leaves into a familiar packaged green paste.

It wasn't hard to figure out what our new masters wanted. A couple of jabs with the stun stick and a little shouting while pointing at a row of empty buckets, and we all knew what to do.

I don't have a clue what happened on Earth after we were abducted. As far as I know, the invasion could've been planet-wide, but I like to tell myself that it was a local event.

Daydreaming about the life I had before the Storm Area 51 event is probably the only thing that keeps me toting that bucket back and forth under the hot sun every day. Not a single day passes that I don't regret not staying home and sleeping in my own bed in Seattle the night of September the 19th.

Earl Justice

64, Retired Pawnshop Owner, Yawkey, WV

By Shelly Jarvis

I've been waitin' nineteen years for a chance to get them sons a'bitches, ever since they took my wife and impregnated her. Now I don't know what them aliens look like, or how many arms they got or nothin'. My wife don't remember much about that weekend. But she had a boy, looks human, and acts human, but I know he's theirs just as sure as I know the workday is long. I got snipped at forty, she had him after, and it's surely because of them little green men.

I saw the Area 51 raid on Facebook while I was checking out a local yard sale group. Some of 'em were jokin' about rescuing aliens and havin' new space-pets, but I knew better. Those things aren't fit to be around us normal folks. I see it every day with my wife's spawn,

Brandon. Oh, he tries to fit in and he pretends to be normal, but I know he ain't. And he knows I know. But I digress.

Soon as I saw the ad, I knew what I needed to do. I called Steve, Dale, and Rick—my boys from the Legion, sans Darren (that fool would get us all killed). We made plans to head to Charleston for a gun show a couple weeks later. Until then, we'd meet in my garage, throw back a few cold ones, and make a plan.

The plan didn't come together like I thought it would, but it didn't dampen our spirits. We knew we were in the right, and the good Lord would back us against those alien motherfuckers. I talked to Pastor Mac about it and he agreed there was no better cause than to take up arms against them that would enter our country illegally.

Now that I think about it, seems he might've been talkin' about Mexicans. As my President says, they ain't sending their best, but if they can point a gun at the real aliens, I say we let 'em stay.

Anyways, after stocking up at the gun show and borrowing my cousin's winnebago, we were ready to meet our brethren in Nevada. Now I'd seen some mock-ups on the internet, but most of the plans seemed amateur at best. Still, I didn't know what their Nar-you-tow runners were and thought maybe they had some secret weapons, so I had hope.

I kissed Shirley full on the lips while she flipped my eggs—somethin' I hadn't done for years. The excitement of what was about to happen had my stomach doin' cartwheels and I almost couldn't eat the three eggs, sausage, bacon, fried potatoes, and toast that she made me. But I did. Who knows when we may get a chance to eat again?

As I passed through the livin' room, I saw Brandon passed out on the couch with a bag of funyuns on his chest and an empty pickle jar on the floor beside tipped over empty cans of Budweiser.

"Damn aliens," I muttered. "Won't get a job like the rest of us red-blooded Americans, can't pass a damn drug test, and expect my tax dollars to support their sorry asses. Well, I tell you what, Trump won't have it and neither will I."

I slung my duffel bag over my shoulder, grabbed my Earnhardt hat, and marched my happy ass out to the garage with renewed vigor. Steve was there at a quarter to eight and we compared weapons, trying to determine which would be best for sniping, hauling over the terrain from gate to facility, and those for close combat. In the end, we decided to take 'em all. Can't be too careful.

While we were loadin' the camper, Dale and Rick showed up and added their gear to the mix. We climbed in and were just about to pull out when a white '78 Trans Am jerked to a stop in front of us. The bird painted across the front seemed to scream at me as I stared, stunned, at the figure who approached. Shoulder-length hair the colour of mud was tied back with a red, white, and blue bandana. He wore camo cargo shorts and a black shirt with the sleeves cut off, guns over each pale shoulder.

In short, he looked badass.

"What's he doin' here?" Rick asked. "Thought we weren't tellin' him about the raid."

Dale winced. "It might've slipped out."

Now Darren is what I call "batshit." So it didn't bode well when he climbed up in the Winnie and gave a snuff-stained grin. He said, "You weren't leavin' without me, were ya?"

"Course not," I lied. "Figured you was just runnin' late and we wanted to be ready to go."

Darren tossed his bag and weapons on the floor and slumped back against a seat. "Good. I'd've been mighty red if you'd gone on without me."

Without another word, I put 'er in drive and we headed out for our mission.

* * *

We made it to Mount Sterling, Kentucky before we had to stop. Darren's morning constitutional left us gasping for air and rolling down the windows wasn't enough. Fifteen minutes parked with the windows down and doors open, plus Steve's splurge on an aerosol freshener, let us get back on the road.

"You can't be doin' that the whole trip," Rick said. He don't like Darren all that much, never has, and his patience was already wearin' thin.

Darren just stared back with a shit-eatin' grin as he squirted canned cheese into his mouth. I smelled disaster for those two idgets unless I could keep 'em apart, so I called on Steve, my best friend and the only decent man among us, to take the wheel. I moved Rick up front beside him and spent my time watching Dale whittle and listening to Darren fart.

We stopped for dinner in St. Louis. The cornbread muffins were good, the barbecue was fine, but it was the busty gal behind the counter that made the little joint worth rememberin'. Rick took a likin' to her too, and when she went on break he gave her a tour of the Winnebago. We stayed inside and finished our drinks, even having a round of apple pie while we gave him time to finish his business. He's been mighty lonely since Armelia died, and there ain't one of us who would blame him for wantin' a little comfort.

The girl returned twenty minutes later, smoothing her hair and uniform like we didn't all know what happened. When we got back to the Winnie, Rick wasn't there. The bed was mussed and air smelled sweaty, so we rolled down the windows for the second time while we waited.

"Prolly in the pisser," Dale said as he kicked off his boots. He pointed across the parking lot to the gas station.

"Makes sense," I agreed. Steve turned the ole girl towards the station.

A thwap-thwap under the wheels made us all jump. There weren't no speed bumps in this lot. Steve pulled up a bit farther and we checked the mirrors. A flanneled lump lay on the ground behind us.

The cops came and took statements from the lot of us. We didn't know why he'd been under there. The last one to see him alive was the waitress. I went in with the cop to point her out, but she wasn't there. They talked to the manager, who acted like he had no idea who I was talkin' about.

"The one with the red curls and the big tits," I said. It was the only thing I remembered.

"We don't have any redheads on staff," the manager said.

I floundered for words until Steve stepped up beside me and put his hand on my shoulder. He said, "I don't know who you're coverin' for, but we know what we saw."

The cops seemed to take his words as gospel, turning their attention from us to the manager. One of the officers waved us away and said he'd call us when they figured out what happened. Back in the Winnie it was a sombre affair. Rick had been one of our disenfranchised brothers for years. The thought of leaving him behind was heavy.

"Let's turn back," Dale said, his voice seeming to rip as it came from his lips.

Steve shook his head. "That's not what Rick would want."

I looked at him, surprised by his words. Steve is mild-mannered on his most rebellious days. He sings in the choir with his wife every Sunday, he volunteers to take meals to shut-ins, he plays Santa for the Christmas toy drive. He also happens to be a former Special Ops and did two tours in Kuwait in the early nineties. But he doesn't talk about what happened over there. Instead, he talks about his daughter, the teacher, or his son studying up at WVU. So even knowing what I knew about Steve, I never expected him to want to press on.

That's probably why we did. Steve's words were steel, resolve in our backbones, and we kept going.

We were somewhere in Colorado, about twelve hours from the alien daycare, when we lost Dale. The park ranger said he was in the wrong place at the wrong time, a mountain lion dragged him under the bus, and we were lucky he was the only victim.

Course I knew he was fulla malarkey. Losing Rick was bad, real bad, but losing Dale the same way was downright scary. I knew it had to be Darren—he's never been quite right anyway. And in some sick way, I understood why he killed Rick. It had been a constant war between 'em. But

Dale was his friend; his only friend if I'm bein' honest.

I tried to talk to Steve about it the next time we stopped for gas, but Darren was always close. Steve shook his head to keep me from sayin' more, but I knew he understood what I was gettin' at.

"We gotta keep movin'," he said. "We'll be there soon enough and can sort this whole mess out."

He was right, but I didn't like it. There was too much space between us and there, too much time for another strike. But there was nothin' else to do but keep drivin'.

* * *

We reached A51 in the evenin' when all the other campers and trucks and motorcycles were parkin'. As we pulled in by a lifted F150, I breathed a sigh of relief. These were my people, and their presence made me feel safe. Then a Tesla pulled in beside us and that safety dwindled a bit.

There were plenty of people who looked serious standin' around with guns and knives strapped to 'em, but there were also a bunch of teeny-boppers in convertibles drinkin' craft beer and smokin' doobies. I shook my head. My wife's alien freeloader would be right at home here.

When the time came, we were all in it together. The rednecks with the hipsters, the tech-nerds and the UFC wannabes, the bikers and the business men. Turns out everyone wanted to see what the Government was keepin' secret. It's the most united I've seen our great country in a long time.

Nobody really knew what they were doin'. Lotta people got shot. Those runners I'd read about had been a joke about some cartoon. Damn millennials. Still, me, Steve, and Darren got in. Luck, I guess, 'cause it sure wasn't because of our good planning.

Inside was a maze of chaos. I opened a door only to immediately close it when I saw—well, I don't rightly know what it was, but I knew I didn't want to see it again. A line of spidery—things the size of my hound—crawled past and no one bothered stoppin' them. I saw people in lab coats leading chains attached to slendermen, black oozes that left a trail of glitter in their wake, and a short grey thing with a bulbous head that carried a miniature version of itself as it searched through the crowd for an exit.

As I stood there staring at everything and everyone, I didn't even bother to pull out one of my guns. It was too much and I didn't know where to start shootin'. I stepped back into an empty corridor and watched while a warm, wet spot formed on the front of my pants.

Then I saw the weirdest thing of all: the top of Steve's head flipped back and revealed a huge mouth with the biggest teeth I've ever seen. He pulled Darren to him and took a massive bite. Blood and meat fell all around him, but he didn't seem to notice. He flipped his head back over and wiped his mouth. He looked up and our eyes met.

I fell down then. Guess my body was shakin' too hard for my legs to hold me up. Steve pushed his way towards me through the press of bodies. I was callin' down fire from Heaven with every step he took, but he kept gettin' closer. When he reached me, he slid down the wall beside me until he was sittin' on the floor.

"Sorry you had to see that," he mumbled, somehow managing to look sheepish.

"You ate Darren."

He nodded. "Dale and Rick, too. I didn't mean to. I've been keepin' myself in check all these years and didn't think it would bother me. But the closer we got to this place, the stronger my hunger became."

"You gonna eat me, too?"

"I'll try not to. Already did you a disservice once."

"What are you talkin' about?" I ask.

He looked at me with a pained expression. "Knockin' up your wife."

"Shit," I mutter. "So, Brandon really is an alien? I just thought Shirley cheated on me."

"I guess it's both. She cheated, and he's an alien."

We sat there in silence for a few minutes and for that time, it felt like we were in my man cave watchin' NASCAR with nary a care in the world.

Finally, I said, "Well, I guess I should be gettin' back. You gonna stick around for a while?"

Steve nodded. "Yeah. Prolly eat those assholes with the Prius."

I chuckled, "They kinda deserve it."

"It was good knowin' you, Earl," he said, shakin' my hand. "You've been the best friend I've had in the last three hundred years."

"Will I ever see you again?" I ask, hopin' and fearin' his answer.

"Don't reckon you will. Your world won't last long after this mess and I've got places to be."

"Should I give your wife a message?"

"Nah, she'll be along shortly with the kids. But thanks." We stare at each other again before I see Steve's head start to tip back. He said, "Get goin' before I eat ya."

And I did. Ran straight out the building, past the fights ragin' on and the bullets zippin' by. I got in the Winnebago and locked the doors, leaned back in my seat, and spent the rest of the night watching the spaceships dartin' overhead as they made their way home.

At first light, I did the same.

Daniel MacBride

By David Bowmore

"Good evening, viewers. The government may have thrown a blanket over traditional reporting, but this is the twenty-first century. People are the newsmakers now. They can't stop us talking.

"We're here with one of the survivors of the extraordinary scenes you have no doubt seen today online and in other uncontrolled news sources.

"Hello, Daniel would you like to tell the viewing public about yourself?"

"Err, yeah. My name's Daniel, Daniel MacBride. I'm a student, sort of seeing the world on my gap year. You know, just me and a backpack. But I never expected to see what I saw earlier today."

"Before we get to that, how did you get to the site? Tell us about the atmosphere."

"Well, the whole thing reminded me of a line from that old Woodstock song my Gram was always playing. You know, 'By the time we got to somewhere we were half a million strong'. There was an air of rebellion and freedom and camaraderie.

"But we were heading for Area 51, not a hippy music festival.

"Roadblocks didn't stop us. People were travelling cross country by trail-bike and four-wheel drive, some walked, others rode horses. I even saw someone on a camel, and a tank. Armed with nothing more than curiosity and a need to know the truth, we travelled over dessert rocks and dunes to converge and surround the installation."

"Tell us more."

"Er, well the internet was rife with speculation and instruction. But I rode my thumb and got picked up in a flat-bed Ford, driven by bloke called Leroy, but his grandma was the force to be reckoned with in their party.

"As if by silent agreement every man, beast and machine halted about twenty-five miles from the fences to set up camp. The glow of fires could be seen in the clear dessert night. The old lady told me all about watching the moon landing from her father's knee as we shared our food and drink. When the sun rose, all you could see to the left and right was a never ending mass of humanity waiting to move. Behind us was a thick carpet of people. It was beautiful.

"The authorities had made threats online, but how do you stop a million people?

"We started moving. A slow trundling pace at first so that no one was left behind.

"Sirens sounded. Jet planes flew in formation, some quite low, to intimidate us. But we kept moving. The old lady was my constant companion. She held my arm as we rode in the back of the pickup and I asked if she was scared or would prefer to be inside the cab, but she said something about fighting for the right thing all her life, 'When soldiers opened fire at our college, I knew I would always fight'. She was a brave woman.

"Military trucks met us halfway. A voice from a loudspeaker told us to halt, to cease our advance, that we were on Military ground and action may result if our insurgence continued.

"Someone nearby was playing the Star Spangled Banner on an accordion. The old lady had her fist in the air along with the rest of us. We smiled at each other.

"And then a hole appeared in the middle of her forehead and she dropped like a stone."

"Wait a minute, Daniel. Are you saying the military

opened fire first?"

"As far as I'm concerned. Yes. And then there was total mayhem. People were screaming and crying. A million people were panicking. No one expected the soldiers to open fire. I mean this is the twenty-first century.

"I was lying on the bed of the truck, cradling the old lady. But she was gone. I peered over the edge to see other vehicles charging along with us, hundreds of them. When I think about it, there must have thousands, perhaps tens of thousands of ordinary cars and trucks and vans all intent on ramming the fences. Explosions started to rain down on us. For crying out loud they were firing rockets. I saw a camper-van flip over and explode. A riderless horse overtook us.

"I lay on my back praying that Leroy would see sense and turn the truck around. I just wanted to get away. At any second a rocket might have taken us out.

"Drones were whizzing about too. Micro-rockets targeted random vehicles. But someone had thought to bring their own armed drones. Soon there was a mini dogfight going on in the skies above us

"As I watched, the truck rattling my teeth, I saw my first alien. A sort of flying creature, and then another and then more until the sky was full with them.

"Then these things started diving down on us. They plucked people from the backs of bikes, or ripped open the roofs of cars with their claws. People were lifted into the sky in a bizarre lover's embrace. Only to be dropped from hundreds of feet up. One of the swarm descended for me, I scrambled back from it and lifted the nearest thing to defend myself with, which happened to be a pitchfork. It pierced its skin easily, killing it instantly. I'll never forget the black-grey skin and almost featureless face, with a row of needle-like teeth jutting forward. It was very small and lightweight. I threw it out of the truck easily."

"It sounds absolutely terrifying, Daniel. How did you get here? How did you escape?"

"The pickup came to a sudden halt against the wall of a building, well inside the complex. I can't describe everything. Leroy was dead. Bullets were flying everywhere. The explosions. The dust. It was crazy. And those alien things diving on people, soldiers too. I just ran, trying to find somewhere to hide.

"I followed some random guy inside a giant hanger. The door had been partially blown open. He fell down and I tripped over him. Most of his head was missing. The same soldier turned his gun on me, but his superior pushed it away and the bullet went wide."

"Just to confirm, Daniel. You witnessed a US

serviceman murder a citizen."

"Well, yes. Didn't I just say that? And he'd have shot me if his superior hadn't intervened. She bundled me to the back of the hanger. The murdering soldier was saying it was all our fault, we were the ones breaking the law, we were the people who had released those flying things. And she reminded him that we were all American citizens. The true enemy were the aliens. She actually said the word: Aliens.

"Me and her and half a dozen soldiers scrambled into a weird vehicle. I didn't really see it properly, but it floated, you know hovered above the ground. Once inside, I could hear the radio chat. Area 51 lost, immediate evacuation and all that sort of stuff. We were flying low and fast.

"I don't know anything more. I don't know if I can tell you anything else."

"Did the soldiers say anything to you? Did they make any apologies?"

"No. I was left on the highway and I had to walk into town. She gave me a look that said sorry, but nothing more. Then they were gone."

"What will you do now, Daniel?

"I don't know. Prepare for war, I guess. If the things I saw escaping are only some of what was in Area 51, then we're in trouble."

Jasmine Smith

By Charlotte O'Farrell

I first heard about the "storming Area 51" Facebook event when my cousin, Jim, sent me the link. "Looks like we've got something fun to do on your visit!" he'd written, adding that it was just an hour's drive from his house.

I'd been saving money to visit Jim for his 30th birthday for over two years. I work as a waitress, so a transatlantic flight from London wasn't cheap. But we'd been close as kids, before his part of the family moved to the States for his dad's career, and we'd kept in touch online. Our 30th birthdays were only two months apart, so it was a cool family celebration.

Neither of us were really into aliens and stuff. But we didn't take the idea of storming the compound seriously, either. We assumed people would just turn up in nearby towns, take selfies, and have a huge "Area 51" party before heading home. As my trip got closer, I heard a lot of my colleagues talking about the event, and it felt kind of cool to be the one that was actually going.

I touched down in America two days before the storming. Jim and his family played host, taking me for a tour of the area and treating me to dinner each night. I approved of the big American portions—nothing we could ever dream of in the UK! The night before Area 51, we'd celebrated his 30th with his old college buddies and drank too much.

The road trip there's a bit of a blur. It was the early hours of the morning. I kept drinking water and hid behind my sunglasses. If only that was the worst point of that day.

We drove out into the Nevada desert.

"You know we're gonna be the only ones who turn up, right Cuz?" Jim grinned, wiping his sweating face with his forearm (the car's air conditioning didn't work, and it was a warm day for September).

"Then we'll storm it on our own! Their bullets are no match for us!"

But as we got closer, we saw more and more cars parked up, and people walking to the right spot. Some had beer and were shouting to each other, setting up for a party—some were in costumes and we laughed at the bobbled-headed aliens and Pokémon. But far more scary were those turning up in faux-military clothing, bought online or from an army surplus place, looking like they were taking this stuff altogether too seriously.

"Keep away from those guys," Jim whispered to me, as

we parked our car on a dirt road and continued on foot. "They look like the types that'll set the trigger-happy guards of this place off. Know what I mean?"

I felt uneasy, but we'd come this far. Going home without so much as a "look at us, hunting those aliens!" selfie would have felt like a defeat.

At some point the crowds became uncomfortably heavy. I saw the Area 51 facility in the distance; it looked less imposing than its reputation would imply. The security around it, however, did not. But we were surrounded by that point. Hundreds of rowdy people were crushed up against us in all directions. We couldn't fight our way out if we wanted to.

I don't know who shouted "CHARGE!". Whoever it was, it set off an immediate chain reaction. All around us, people shoved towards the facility like a tidal wave. If we'd stood still or moved against it, we would've been trampled.

The gunfire didn't start until we were nearly touching the place. I think we caught them off-guard; they really weren't expecting us to *actually* storm the place. There was maybe quite a bit of hesitation to turn fire on a group full of mostly young civilians following a Facebook prank. But people did start to fall. A guy's head exploded two feet from me. I got splattered with his blood.

The mass of people kept moving. Anyone who stopped would've been caught in the stampede and killed anyway.

And the event's organisers were right, in a way: they couldn't stop all of us.

Jim grabbed my hand as we stormed the fence, so we didn't get separated. It looked menacing but it fell quite easily, with the strength of us all pushing together. I could hear bullets whizzing past me in all directions at this point. It reminded me of those black and white grainy films of the trenches of World War One.

The nearest entrance was a huge grey door. It must have been about four feet wide, reinforced. I noticed it was closing slowly.

Jim and I both dashed for it without thinking. I closed my eyes as we got close, expecting a bullet through the brain at any moment. We slid through, narrowly avoiding being crushed.

We found ourselves in what looked like a cloakroom. White coats were hung up on pegs down one wall, along with face masks that looked like old style plague masks, only with odd breathing apparatus at the end. Still gasping to get our breaths back, we each grabbed a white coat and put it on. I was still on edge, expecting to be caught—but it seems security were still busy with the waves of people storming the compound, and we'd slipped through their fingers.

On the far wall, there was a sign pointing down the next corridor that said "Infirmary". We followed it, down a perfectly ordinary-looking route.

I completely expected to see aliens in the infirmary. But what we saw was people. Patients, to be exact. Rows upon rows of them, lying in hospital beds, machines beeping next to them. The only unusual thing about them was that they were all in glass containers, like see-through cages—the sort of thing you'd see premature babies in, except they were all adults. Some were old, eaten away by cancer and on their last legs. One or two were young, but showing signs of being in an accident recently. All looked about to die. None were conscious, mercifully.

At the foot of each bed was a set of notes. I picked one pad up.

The first page looked like any normal set of medical records. It had the patient's age (around 80), her details and a log of her vital signs. A line at the bottom read "HEART DISEASE – TWO WEEKS TO LIVE". It was on the second page things got weird.

It was headed "Nutritional Information". It had a breakdown of the materials in her body, her exact weight and height, and how much energy she could produce. There was a box at the bottom marked "Special Instructions", where someone had written in typical scribbly doctor's handwriting: "Should provide sustenance for 12 hours."

I passed the document to Jim in silence and checked the next one. I had time to look at four, in all. Each one was the same: diagrams and formulae calculating how much nutrition each person would provide.

"Hey! What the hell are you doing here?!"

The voice made us jump. A middle aged, bespectacled man in a white coat had appeared in the doorway, holding a clipboard.

"You're not supposed to be here!"

He ran towards a red panic alarm mounted on the wall. Luckily, Jim was faster, and rugby tackled him to the ground before he made it.

He kept the groaning scientist pinned to the floor.

"You'd better tell us what's going on here," Jim shouted. "What the hell is this place?"

"I can't tell you anything!"

Jim grabbed his arm and twisted it slightly, making the man wince and cry out.

"What is it, some kind of food farm?"

"It's a...necessary evil," the guy replied, his voice high with the pain of Jim's grip on him. "Just stop hurting me!"

Jim let go of his arm but didn't let the scientist get up from the floor.

"You people have no idea how much trouble you're in, you know that?" the scientist said resentfully, rubbing his hurting arm with the other one. "I doubt you'll make it past the guards on your way out, so I'll tell you. When we first made contact with alien life, we wanted to observe them, but always, they died; we didn't know how to sustain their lives, what they ate, what they *needed*. It took one of them crashing here on Earth for us to work it out. We found a green, oozy substance that seemed to suck things in. It's food, but it consumes living organisms by absorbing them, and then it multiplies like nothing you can imagine."

Jim relaxed his grip on the man who pulled himself into a sitting position but didn't try to run.

"We tried feeding it animals and plants at first, of course. But nothing seemed to keep it well-fed for long. If it died or shrunk away, so would our aliens, and the whole project would be over; all our scientific studies, everything, gone forever. Then one of the researchers got a bit too close to the goo when conducting his experiments. It ate him. And that's when we knew that human flesh was what we needed. Living human flesh. We needed this."

He nodded towards the lines of patients.

"We try to choose people who are already dying. Sometimes we get sent violent criminals. We make sure they're comatose when we feed them in. They don't feel anything, I assure you."

I felt tears welling up in my eyes. So, humanity's grand role on the greatest stage imaginable was just this: three rungs down on the food chain. It fit, somehow.

"Each government sends their fair share over to us. It's been agreed at international level. You idiots probably stormed the best protected holding centre out of the whole world!"

Just as I prepared to say something, my brain swimming with a million questions, we heard the sound of boots running down a corridor.

"Quick, in there!" I shouted, gesturing to a small office room just off the main infirmary. There was a glass pane in the door. Jim and I huddled under a table covered with paperwork and monitoring equipment for the patients. It was a squeeze, but we managed it. The scientist stood awkwardly by the now closed door.

We heard the guards run into the infirmary.

"Gentlemen, what's going on?" the scientist asked through the door. He wasn't a good actor.

"Intruders," one of the soldiers replied gruffly. "You see them?"

He gave an uncomfortably long pause. My heart dropped. All he had to do was say yes, and we were as good as dead.

"No. Quiet as the grave down here. As always!"

The guards seemed satisfied with this answer. I'll never quite understand why he didn't give us up—maybe he would get into more trouble for telling us state secrets with such little coaxing, and it would be better for him if we just left.

In any case, as soon as the soldiers were gone, he ushered us down the labyrinthine corridors and let us out of a quiet side entrance.

"I never want to see you guys again. And tell no-one what I told you," he barked, practically pushing us out the door and slamming it behind us.

Luckily for us, the shooting had stopped. Guards were escorting groups of terrified survivors off the premises. Jim and I blended in with a group of sobbing teenagers quite easily and let them lead us away.

I never told anyone my survival story...until now, at least. I tell people we waited at the back and didn't charge with the others. I don't make a big deal about it when it comes up in conversation.

I used to look up at the night sky and feel at peace. Now all I can imagine is a green, shiny goo, devouring all in its path. I hope I never get unlucky enough to be fed to it when my time comes.

Elayna

18, Gift Shop Cashier at the Little A'Le'Inn, Rachel, Nevada

By Zoey Xolton

I remember all the excitement of the Storm, like it was yesterday. Thousands of believers flooded my dad's establishment, the Little A'Le'Inn, the only hotel, diner and gift shop in Rachel. I remember being so mad at him for making me work! I wanted to join the Storm. I wanted to see some Goddamn aliens!

In a matter of hours, my righteous teen rage was replaced by fear. Chaos fell on Rachel once the gates of Area 51 were breached. I remember hiding under the counter and covering my ears. There were screams and gunshots...

My dad saved my life.

Jordan Matthison

19, Former Airman, US Air Force, Fort Leavenworth, KS

By Wondra Vanian

Groom Lake—that's Area 51 to you civilians—was supposed to be an easy posting. Everyone knew the facility hadn't had anything more interesting in it than a stockpile of old uniforms since its popularity turned it into a tourist trap. Guarding an empty base wasn't a job most airman wanted to do. They wanted to be in the thick of it. They wanted to be up there being heroes.

Not me.

Going into the Air Force wasn't my idea. I didn't want to get my ass shot down in some sweaty foreign land. If there had been any way to avoid it without upsetting my "lifer" father, I would have taken it. But "we're Matthisons, and Matthisons are part of a proud military history...." Blah, blah, blah.

My sisters, they were the lucky ones. They both got married and pregnant within six months of graduation. Lucky bitches. Believe me, if I could have done the same to avoid ten weeks of getting dirt kicked in my face, followed by four years of praying the Moron-in-Chief didn't get my ass deployed, I would have taken it, swollen ankles and all.

But no. I was a healthy—if not particularly athletic—boy so my fate was sealed. Which was why, when my time in Basic was coming to an end, I asked Daddy to pull a few strings for me. Get me a job where the chances of my seeing action would be fewer. Since he'd seen me on the simulators, I knew he'd do his best to make it happen.

And he did.

Spending the next four years protecting an empty building from drunks and weirdos? Sounded like exactly my kind of duty.

How was I supposed to know there were actually three more facilities under the one I patrolled? How could I have known that there really were aliens in Groom Lake Air Force Base? I mean... why would you keep the aliens in the place they think you keep the aliens, amiright?

Okay, so...aliens. It wasn't ideal but, hey, the security systems were top-notch and most soldiers did their time and left without ever having to see one of the creepy little bastards. I should have too...

Stupid Facebook. Stupid Millennials.

When news reached the base of a plan to storm Area 51 to reveal its secrets, we were all pretty amused. But then tight-assed Old Kincaid got it in his head that it was a problem and serious defensive actions were put in place. Me? I was not part of the decision. I got stuck in the basement, guarding Vault 1. I wasn't too worried at the time. Hell, at least it wasn't Vault 3, right? But, then, they stormed.

Honestly, I never expected them to pull it off. I don't think anyone did. Well, maybe General Kincaid... but that could have been wishful thinking on his part. Miserable old bastard sure did love a reason to blow shit up. They tell me he got bitten in half by one of those things. Can't say I'm sorry.

Anyway, I missed most of the action. When it started, I could hear the shouting and the gunshots. I still wasn't worried. Anyone trying to get in would have to get through an entire unit—all of them better with a gun than me. But then someone broke through the barrier.

This guy practically fell into the basement. He wore this ridiculous makeshift armour—I think his chest piece was made from hubcaps—and had a heavy rock in one hand. Poor bastard looked almost as surprised at having succeeded as I was to see him. We kind of stared at each other for a minute, then he spoke.

"Uh," he said, "let me in." His eyes went up and down the hallway, like he was trying to see something he wasn't supposed to see. Did these people really think we'd just leave top-secret shit laying around?

I remember thinking, Wow, this guy looks less of a threat than me. That's saying something...

"Nah," I said. "You should go." I puffed up a bit, tried to look a little more intimidating than I was. He actually took a step back, which made me feel pretty good.

"Let me in," he demanded, "or else!" He was sweating pretty hard and his voice was pretty nervous, so I felt brave enough to laugh in his face.

"Or else what?" I asked. I hiked my gun up a bit, just to remind the guy that I had it. His fingers tightened around his rock.

Don't get me wrong. I wasn't going to shoot him. God, I hate guns. Probably would've shot myself in the foot before I hit him.

"Or... or..." He looked around, like he was considering his options. Then, he did the dumbest thing he'd ever done in his life. He threw the rock at me.

Oh, I was able to move out of the was easily enough— but the rock hit the control panel on the wall behind me. There was a metallic *pffzt* and the massive steel door started to slide open. I could hear the *clickity-clack* of their legs and the *snikt* of their pinchers and I thought, no way. I didn't care how much shame it would bring on my family. I didn't care if I spent the rest of my life behind bars. Hell, I didn't care if

I got shot for desertion. That had to be better than being torn apart by fucking aliens.

Screw the consequences, there was no way on God's green earth I was going up against those things. I had about three seconds to think and to come up with a decision. Am I proud of myself? No—but then I never was so what's new, right?

I said, "Sorry!" to the other guy. He was too busy craning to see into the vault to pay any attention to me so I shoved him as hard as could toward the swarm of angry aliens and ran for my life.

Bettina White

43, Extraterrestrial Activist for WTEC (Welcome to Earth Committee)

By Jo Seysener

I had been following #stormingarea51 and I leave this post so you can understand what—who—is coming. The little flickers in my mind are growing louder.

It's nearly time.

* * *

I started the day protesting as usual. My signs got heavy in the heat and I was sweating, so I took a break from walking the cul-de-sac—if that snotty woman from number eleven comes out and glares at me one more time, I promise she'll be the first to go—I was scrolling through alerts about the Event when I saw that Betty White was going.

That woman is my idol. We share a name, not related,

you know, but just love her style. And if she was heading out, I was all in.

I packed everything into my crusty jalopy—not a lot of dosh in the ET WTEC—and sent two forks to Mrs Shove-it-up-your-nostril with a happy smile.

Out of my bland driveway through the grey living quarters of suburbia into glorious life.

Gas was dear. Every roadhouse had hiked their prices high enough to tickle Jesus' kneecaps, but I'd packed jerries from my zombie-apocalypse cache—a girl can have more than one hobby, can't she? Damn thing leaked on my pillow, but I stuffed it all under some plastic. Maybe we could use it as a flame thrower later to bust the bad boys out.

I trundled across the desert behind trailers, buses and combi vans, right down Extraterrestrial Highway. Dust and flies filled the car and I resorted to putting the windows up and closing the vents. It was worth turning the car into a sauna, just to be part of this. At one stage everyone started beeping, sending a wave up and down the line of vehicles. Super cool.

I knew we were close when a huge wind cleared the dust. It blew right at us, as though to push us away. Some sort of defensive mechanism the government had cooked up to hide their facility from us. Well, it had worked for nigh on seventy years.

I kept an eye out for my girl Betty but knew she wouldn't

be on the road with the rest of us. She'd arrive with pizzazz, a classy broad like her. By helicopter, maybe.

The wind stopped and everything became still, even the line of traffic. The air crackled like it does right before a lightning storm in summer, or before a tornado. Vehicles moved in close, lines of us spreading wide across the salt pans, preparing for battle.

I chatted with the people in cars and vans, winding my windows down now the dust was gone. Some real kindred spirits there. I was definitely in the right place.

Then came a great rumble. Military vehicles surrounded us. I fished about in my bag, hauling out the necessaries. I snapped off some quick photos for the scrap book back home, even though I knew I shouldn't. But I wasn't the only one doing it.

We were breaking all the rules today.

They began inspecting car to car, weapons on display. Did they think we would be stopped by a show of force?

I put on my blandest expression and waved my old ID when they stopped at my car. The young grunt frowned at me in my old car, clearly not accepting the rank and my appearance. I forced a smile.

"Retired."

Forcibly. With dishonour.

He nodded slowly, passing the thin plastic back. I was glad he hadn't smelled the spilled fuel in the back.

More rumbling came from up front. Vehicles skewed about. Suddenly there was a lane clear in front of me, right to the gate.

I charged down the lane, having left the jalopy running. Vans slotted in around me and we all jammed together through the gate, stuck like cattle panicked in their rush to board the truck that takes them to the abattoir.

I rammed the van in front of me and some fool shunted me from behind, turning the whole thing into a derby. We busted through the fences and raced for the facility, the combined speed of the herd propelling us over the lines of spikes that shredded tyres.

Then the doors were ahead and we just kept charging. Smoke wafted around me. The saturated pillow had finally combusted. I tried to push my door open but it was jammed against the combi beside me. The passenger saw the smoke and helped me clamber out the window. I was stretched face down in a stranger's lap when we peeled off, my feet dangling out the window.

The combi rocked with the resulting explosion. Cars were heaped together before a hole in the wall of the facility. I slid off the man's lap with a wave and shot inside, heading as deep into the building as I could, turning and weaving. Bullets pinged around me but I ran hunched over through a whooshing glass door.

Silence permeated the space, a bleak white. Someone

once told me that imagining yourself in a white room was how you felt about dying.

Then death was sterile and cold.

I approached the only desk in the room, pressed against one wall. A single touch screen occupied it and I groaned. I had chosen the most useless spare room in the world's most fascinating place.

I pressed the screen set into the desk, just to be sure. Three cylindrical icons came up, the far one bleeping red. My finger hovered over it, then I touched it anyway. What the hell if I blew the place up with a dodgy reactor? We'd already busted a hole in it.

A section of wall hissed, turning its innards to face the room and I realised I had been mistaken. The occupant inside the glass clearly wasn't a reactor. Elongated legs bunched together in a tight enclosure sent a current of pity through my chest, reminding me of nothing more than a big spider trapped under a glass by some bully kid. I stepped over to the beast which regarded me through a band of eyes. I pressed my hand to the cool glass and it leaned into the touch.

I knew I had to free it. I shot back to the desk, touching the remaining icons. More sections of wall broke open. I was faced with three unique, new species. None of our world; too big and cumbersome, ending in just the wrong places, they would tip over walking on our land. Expect for the final cylinder, which held the cutest little button mushroom with a plethora of coral like roots—legs?—I had ever seen.

How to free them? The room was bare. Movement caught my attention. The centre alien tapped on the glass, tilting its head. I approached, cautious. This one held higher degree of awareness than the others; eyes bright and intelligent. My mind tickled and itched, as though a mosquito was buzzing about inside. I shook my head, but it wouldn't stop. The tapping turned to banging, and I thought it was the alien trying to get my attention.

Wrong again.

Just me, banging my head on the glass. Bloody smears impeded my view of the alien and I wiped them away with the hem of my shirt. Those eyes stared into mine. I tried to understand the message it was sending.

Down the bottom...something near the floor...ah! There were the controls, just underneath the container. I ran my fingers over them in a sequence that seemed so familiar, repeating it for each captive alien. The tiny mushroom smooshed about, shooting toward the door and knocking itself out when it failed to open.

Far too cute. I set him right, opening the door. The prior battle must have moved on as the corridor was empty. Black marks decorated the wall but there were no bodies or blood to be seen. Either there had been no casualties or their clean up crew was amazingly efficient.

I found the first difficult to believe.

The mushroom skittered out the door and down the corridor, bumping drunkenly off the walls. I turned back to the remaining aliens and came face to face with the largest one. He must have been right behind me. I wanted to take a step back, but couldn't. For the first time, I was afraid. Perhaps I shouldn't have let the big guy out? Then I saw the scars and stitches on his torso. The bastards had experimented on him, which was really akin to torture in my books.

I placed a hand near the marks, trying to communicate my sadness with my eyes. Dark, wizened skin covered bony protrusions. Nothing moved in the creature, so unlike us, sending out micro expressions even when we think we have our poker faces on. Nothing is hidden with humanity. No wonder they were scared of this one.

His gaze locked on mine, and I knew he had seen worlds. How old was he? A vision of stars and faces filled my mind, too many to count. This being was older than our god.

My knees wavered and I wanted to bow. More information than I had ever known overflowed in me. I saw planets dark and dead. One black—no, on fire. Smoke covered the atmosphere. It cleared and I saw familiar shapes. This was Earth. The images flowed in an odd sequence. Was this the future I was seeing, but the flow was reversed. I was on the ground, seeing my home. Something had exploded. Number eleven was gone.

But I was standing in front of my house, not on fire. Eleven was still there. My happiness broke. I stared into the vision, trying to understand, like Peter seeing the Revelations. Beyond the capacity of any mortal mind.

Buzzing smashed into me and I saw what caused the devastation the alien had shown me. I couldn't find the words, addled by the information dump.

Swarm.

Go.

I smiled at the alien, patting his insect-like arm. Happy to follow the instructions, I left. My visit had gone well, and now I had a new purpose.

* * *

This is my final blog. I have seen the future and we will not survive.

These feet are sore and swollen. They made me walk all the way back. Through the flames, through the field of bullets. Kept walking, walking. I will do it for them. Deliver the justice they craved with their righteous anger.

The twitches are getting harder to ignore. Snooty Mrs. Eleven will get hers soon. The Swarm will be released soon, but first, the fire.

BOOM TIME.

Kyle Koch

48, Walmart Employee

By Jacob Baugher

Somehow, we made it through the breach at Gate One. I straightened my MAGA hat, raised the AR-15 that I'd stolen from the Birmingham Walmart, and charged through the hole in the chain link. The internet trolls and frat boys and the nerds and the liberal #NeverTrumpers screamed and ran with me, foolishly sprinting right for the first hangar.

Not me though, not Kyle Koch. President Donald Trump had given me a very important mission. So, while the droves of millennial snowflakes and entitled GenZ-ers eagerly ran to their fates as cannon fodder, me and my girl, Sally, held back, ducked behind the first warehouse and headed for warehouse number two—where the real prize was.

That's where The Donald had told me that it would be: the portal. The portal that would send all the liberals to that commie-country that they seemed to love so much—Norway or whatever. Shouts and screams and gunfire pounded, muffled by the warehouse walls. Me and Sally leaned against the back of it, in a small alleyway. The sun was setting, but it was still hot as balls in the desert. I reached into my pack and cracked open a Bud light, tossed it to Sally, and opened my own. We stood there for a moment, just catching our breath.

Two chicks ducked into the alleyway. One was a Megan Rapinoe wannabe. The other had purple hair that fell into her eyes like one of those anime characters. Definitely libtards. I pointed the AR-15 in their direction. No one was gonna keep me from The Donald's mission.

They stared at the rifle like they'd never seen one before. Typical. Megan's double's eyes bugged out like a shih-tzu's. The two slowly backed away to the end of the alleyway, turned, and sprinted away.

"Hurry Kyle, you have to hurry, believe me," The Donald's voice whispered in my head.

The Donald had first appeared to me a few weeks ago, after I finished third-shift at Walmart. I'd gotten home, cracked open a beer and sat back in my EZ-Chair. Sally was asleep on the couch, when all of a sudden, there he was, standing in my living room, golden hair flowing in the non-existent breeze. He leaned close to me, like a real-life Jesus.

"I'm gonna make you a deal, Kyle," he said. His breath

smelled like cheeseburgers. "The best deal. A winning deal. You'll be a winner, Kyle. Someone who wouldn't take this deal would be a loser. You're not a loser, are you Kyle? Believe me, this is the best deal in the history of deals, maybe ever."

He told me about how the dem-o-crats were ruining our country (as if I hadn't already heard from Fox). He told me that they were keeping secrets from the American people and that he, Donald, couldn't reveal them because of some law or whatever. So he needed me.

"There's gonna be a portal, Kyle, a portal in the second hangar. Don't worry, I'll clear the way for you. The Donald will take care of you."

"How will I know how to open the portal, Mr. President?"

"It'll be easy!" he yelled and spread his arms wide. "So easy, Crazy Bernie could figure it out. You're smarter than Crazy Bernie, aren't you, Kyle?"

And so, here they were. Sally shotgunned the beer, crumpled the can, tossed it on the ground. I followed suit, reloaded the stolen AR and tossed Sally a clip of her own.

"Ready?" I asked her.

She nodded. She was shaking. I grasped both her shoulders and shook her. "Hey!" I shouted, "Get it together! The Donald needs us!"

Sand and gravel crunched under my feet as I took the

lead, ran out from the cover of the alleyway and toward the second warehouse. The Donald was true to his word, there were no soldiers in between us and the door. Pride flooded my chest. The Donald had organised this entire charade for me to help save America. A vision of me and the president up on a podium, accepting awards as his birthday was proclaimed a national holiday. "Kyle Koch, Saviour of America. Patriot. Mover of History."

We sprinted across the open ground to the second warehouse. Screams and shouts and gunfire still erupted from warehouse number 1. The big, airplane hangar doors were locked up tight, so we crept, under the floodlights, around to the back. A small, tan metal door stood ajar. I nudged it open further with my gun. Nothing shot at us so I peered inside. Darkness. No movement.

"Sally, grab that lighter out of my pack."

She did. Her hands shook when she handed it to me. I ignored her, flipped the zippo open, flicked it to life, and tossed it through the doorway. It clanked and clattered in the darkness. Nothing.

"Come on," I said, and stepped inside. The moment I crossed the threshold, high-powered fluorescent lights snapped on all at once. My vision went white and I shielded my eyes, blinking at the sudden change. Sally screamed and her gun went off twice. I threw myself to the floor, rolled, and came up in a crouch. My eyes adjusted. Sally sat on the floor, AR discarded next to her, face buried in her hands.

"I can't do it, Kyle," she said.

"Quiet," I snapped at her. "Watch the door."

I dismissed her and took in the room. Unblemished, polished chrome gleamed, shining under the fluorescent lights that hung high above. The warehouse was a single large room. White storage boxes were stacked up to the ceiling. Large, black, snake-like cables wound their way to the centre of the room where a dais of some type of metal that I couldn't recognise extended up to about chest height. The room smelled like bleach and steriliser, the scent that I imagined a set of freshly-cleaned scalpels had. And it was cold. My breath condensed and I stood there like a smoker just taking it all in. But the room was more than just a warehouse. There was something different. Something wrong—I had a creeping shivers-down-your-ass feeling like I was being stalked by a predator.

My family had a dirt cellar when I was a kid. The warehouse had the same feeling you get when someone flips the light switch off on you and you're sure, absolutely sure, as you sprint up the creaking wooden stairs that some dark, dark monster would leap from the shadows, grab you with writhing tarantula hands and drag you off to its lair.

And there were whispers. Whispers; almost inaudible murmurs under a strange humming sound like a speaker's feedback. And it was coming from the dais.

"Do you hear that?" I called back to Sally. My voice echoed strangely, like I was speaking into a box fan.

"Hear what? Kyle, I don't like this. Let's go back to the others."

"No. We ain't come all this way for nothing."

With that, I approached the dais, heaved myself up onto the metal and looked down. Blue translucent light stretched over a pit filled with darkness like a screen. I leaned down, trying to peer into the dark, but it was almost opaque. Smooth. Tranquil as still ink. That was fine, I didn't actually need to go through the portal, just open it, and that seemed simple enough.

A control panel rose up on the other side of the portal, covered in a multitude of buttons and dials and indicator lights that all flashed green. Next to them, was a big red lever with the word DANGER printed on it in white capital letters. I crossed to it and pulled. It slid into place with a satisfying *clank*.

The almost sub-audible humming cut off. In the silence, the whispers swelled and grew louder. Louder. Louder. I turned back to the pit of inky darkness. The void swelled forth in a dome, bubbling, frothing, stretching out like a pregnant belly.

The bubble popped with a sickly squelch and the voices roared out like the crowd at a rock concert. A pair of red, insect eyes glared up at me in the rippling blackness. A face, a terrible, insectoid face opened its mandibles and lunged at me. Klaxon alarms blared. I fell off the dais, skidded across the polished floor. Sally was screaming, She raised her gun and emptied the clip, shooting over my head.

I scrambled out of the way, raised my own gun. A long, insectoid leg burst out of the portal, followed by another. The thing pushed itself up over the dais. Praying mantis face. Eight legs. Somewhere between a spider and a mantis. I emptied my own clip into it, but it kept coming. Behind me, there was a crash and Sally screamed again. Military personnel swarmed into the building from all sides. Sally was tackled to the ground.

"It's loose! It's loose!" Someone was shouting. "Incendiary grenades!"

The thing leapt out, hovered in the air, the size of a Dodge Ram pickup. It lifted its abdomen and spewed white goo all over everything. I sprinted for the door.

A uniformed officer raised his gun. I didn't hear the shot, but my leg crumpled beneath me. He followed me to the floor, pressed something hard and metal against my forehead. I turned back to the portal. More things swarmed out of it, at least a dozen were in the air now. They crushed the control panel. Soldiers hurled grenades. Fire leapt up. The monsters ripped soldiers from their feet, covered them in goo. Sally screamed again. I tried to turn toward her.

"Hold still!" shouted the man pinning me down. His

spittle was hot against my ear. Then I saw her being dragged away by one of the monsters. I tried again, broke the soldier's grip, but that metal rod was still pressed against my head. There was a buzz, a click. My vision went white and wiped the world away.

* * *

An old scientist stared at me from across a sparse metal table. A single, bare light hung, swinging from the ceiling. The room hummed. That hum was going to drive me insane. I had woken up in a padded cell with the hum in my ears and it hadn't stopped. Ever. I figured it was a torture technique.

"Is that all, Kyle?" the scientist tapped a finger against the metal table. A recording device lay between us.

"That's all," I said.

The man nodded, pressed a button on his watch. "I'm through, Shawna. Tell Agent Jackson I'll type a full report up for him in the morning." He clicked the recorder off. His chair scraped when he pushed it back. I stayed seated, not that I had much choice. They'd handcuffed me to the table.

"Where am I?" I asked the scientist. "Where's Sally?"

The man looked at me, removed his glasses. The door buzzed and he pulled it open.

"Sally's dead," he said. "You're in jail."

He walked out and three uniformed guards walked in. I didn't recognise the patches on their uniforms: space shuttles with an eagle emblem. They walked me down a white, sterile hallway. As we passed the only window, I tried to look out, but one of the men blocked my view. Before he did, though, I thought I saw the Earth hanging in a black background, like in those pictures the media liked to air from the space station. But no, that couldn't be right. Perhaps I'd imagined it.

The guards brought me to the cell, opened it, and tossed me inside. I crawled to the cot, held Sally's MAGA hat to my face, and cried for her.

"Good job, Kyle." The Donald's voice whispered in my ear.

I shuddered. "You're not real," I spoke into the silence. "They said you're not real."

"Oh, we're real, Kyle." The voice changed from the president's to a deep, demonic, insectoid shriek. "We are Swarm, and we are coming."

186

Cody Redman

27, Modesto, California
Conspiracy Theorist Youtuber

By Rich Rurshell

"Hey guys, thanks for tuning in to Code Red Conspiracy with me, Cody Redman, streaming live from a little way outside of Area 51 for today's storming. I'm sure many of you have already seen my videos What Lies Within Area 51? parts one and two, but those of you who haven't should go check them out, and if you're new to the channel, then give this video a like, and don't forget to hit the big red button to subscribe to all of our conspiracy theory videos.

As you can see, there are a lot of people here already. We're the first wave of the raid. We got Luke, Andy, and Ed from the Code Red team... Hi, guys! Wave to the camera! We already met a few of our channel subscribers who turned up today to get in on the action. We also got a lot of Pokémon Go players here for the rare egg Niantic are

allegedly putting into Area 51 today, just for the occasion...
an exclusive shiny. Some are even in fancy dress. That
should prove interesting once the advance starts.

Shout out to my boy, Zak, at Zak's Roaming
Roadshow, he's over in the second wave base camp.
What's up, Zak? While you're chasing pocket monsters, I'm
going to be looking for evidence of real extraterrestrial life,
advanced technology and anything else they may have
hidden away on the base.

People have showed up equipped too. We have a
drone team, some on tactical surveillance, ex-paras letting
our front runners know about any resistance from the base
military, and some on infiltration. Even if we can't get any
people onto the base, somebody might get some drone
footage from inside those hangars. We must have close to
two hundred drones in wave one alone! Nice work, guys!

There are people on quad bikes, dirt bikes, jeeps and
four guys even showed up with bulldozers. And—I kid you
not—an E.T. tank! People mean business. We're getting into
Area 51, one way or another.

The word is we set off in less than an hour. I'm going to
go speak with the tacticians and see what the latest is on
how we're going about this. So, check back in to this
channel in about thirty minutes or so to witness the coolest
moment in Area 51 history unfolding live on Code Red
Conspiracy, and don't forget to like this live stream and

subscribe to the channel for more conspiracy theory videos.

We come in peace out!"

* * *

"Hey guys, thanks for tuning back in to Code Red Conspiracy with me, Cody Redman, streaming live from the storming of Area 51. And we are go! Drones are airborne, and the heavy vehicles are leading the advance. The quad bikes have gone on ahead to scout and act as decoys, and those of us on foot are moving fast towards the perimeter fence. No sign of any resistance yet.

If you've just tuned in or you're new to the channel, then give this video a like, and don't forget to hit the big red button to subscribe to all of our conspiracy theory videos, though this could be the most exciting video we've ever had on Code Red Conspiracy, maybe one of the most exciting videos ever!

The mood is pretty good right now, I was feeling pretty anxious when we first set off, not really sure what we would be faced with in the way of resistance, but I'm feeling pretty good about things right now, and as you can see, Andy is grinning like an idiot...give us a wave, smiler.

Second wave should now have left base and be heading towards the perimeter...good luck, guys! My main man, Zak at Zak's Roaming Roadshow is in wave two, if you're not familiar with the channel, go check it out for all your pocket monster needs. Zak, if you find anything more than that egg today, I hope you get some quality footage, buddy.

I was only saying to my—Holy crap!

I'm not sure if you can see this, but there are drones dropping out of the sky like rain! I guess they are onto us now—"

"...Attention, you are approaching federal property and are liable for prosecution. Turn back or we may use deterrents...any further failure to comply, or breach of the perimeter fence will result in the use of deadly force..."

"No shit they're onto us! This is it, everybody!

The front runners are charging, and the heavy vehicles are on course to breach the fence... I'm going to run on ahead to see what's happening...

For some reason the guys on the quad bikes are stopping and tearing off their helmets, and a group of Pokémon hunters dressed in furry costumes are doubled over...are they vomiting? In fact, all the front runners look incapacitated, either laying on the ground, or crouching holding their stomachs... What the hell? It looks like the base guards are pointing some sort of devices at them...and oh, Jesus! It stinks. Hey guys, are you ok? Are you....aarrrgh...ohhh!

Oh, god... I've just been sick... I think I shit in my pants too...they must be using some sort of sound frequency weaponry...vomit pulse rifles or something. Damn it!

Wait! The tank has wiped out the gate and the dozers have flattened the fence, the jeeps and dozers are in! Some of the front runners are up on their feet again, racing into Area 51! We made it! We're in!"

"...I repeat you are now trespassing on federal property and liable for prosecution. Stand down or we may use extreme force to subdue any further failure to comply."

"There are more military vehicles turning up inside the base, just as the rest of wave one are charging at the gap in the perimeter...that's it! I'm stepping over the fallen fence! I'm officially in Area 51, people! Now to go find— Oh, Christ! They're shooting at us!

Shit! The furries are down, front runners are scattered and being picked off...all drivers of our vehicles dead or wounded... a few of the quad bikers are on the retreat... I'm getting the hell out of here too!

Oh shit! People are dropping around me like flies... Run! Turn back! It's a massacre! Oh, Christ! Ed! They shot Ed in the face... Run!"

***

"Hey guys, thanks for tuning back in to Code Red Conspiracy with me, Cody Redman. If you're just tuning in, the storming of Area 51 turned into a massacre. For the first wave anyway. A few of us managed to make it back alive, though Luke and Andy are nowhere to be seen, and Ed didn't make it.

I made it back to my car, I've cleaned myself up, have a clean set of clothes on, and I'm back in the diner where I met up with my buddy, Zak earlier today.

I checked in on Zak's footage and it seems the second wave are having more luck than the first wave, so I'm going to split screen his live footage with this live stream right now."

"Cody mate, will we open Pandora's box and take a peek inside this hangar?"

"No way! It looks like Zak made it into a building! Way to go, man!"

"Man, it's getting wild out there...and my connection is cutting in and out inside here, not sure if you'll get any of this but sorry to disappoint you...there's nothing...wait, I see something. It's shimmering behind..."

"Jesus! What was that?"

"Shit. It's too dark in here to make anything out clear enough, but I'm going to see if I can make my way over to the far side. God, it smells like ammonia in here.

Smells like burnt hair too.

Is that a... DO YOU SEE THAT!"

"Oh my god! It looks like a ball of liquid... no wait... it's changing shape...morphing into..."

"HOLY FUCK...

...CODY!..."

"What the hell is that thing? And what's that noise? That rattling sound? Creepy as hell! I hope you're ok, Zak!

Shit! The connection is dead... damn it!

I'm not sure what we just witnessed, just that was unlike anything I've ever seen before. A liquid creature or something. Capable of morphing into other shapes.

Looks like Zak found his exclusive shiny pocket monster... I just hope he made it out of there alive. What did he call it earlier? Arceus? Seems like as good a name as any.

You saw and heard it here first, people! Proof of secrets being held within Area 51. Arceus, the shapeshifter, caught on camera by my buddy, Zak, and broadcast live here on Code Red Conspiracy. Don't forget to like this video, share your thoughts in the comments, and if you haven't already, hit the big red button to subscribe to the channel.

Wait, there is some commotion over by the window... Jesus! Is that gunfire... I think I can hear helicopters too...

I'm just going to go see what's going on out there...

Holy crap! The military is advancing on the diner! They're coming in force! But what the hell are they firing at... is that...is that Arceus?

Whoa! Those guys are being tossed around like rag dolls! I'm not sure if you can see this, I'm not really sure of what I'm looking at, but there is what looks like a dust devil tearing through those soldiers... Oh God, some of those guys are being torn to pieces. There is something within that sand, but I can't...quite make it out...

Wait a minute...that's my phone ringing...

Andy? Jesus! You made it out alive... I'm at the diner... get to where?...I can't, the military are fighting with something just outside... are you watching my livestream? What do you mean JACKson5? Who the hell is JACKson5?

Holy shit! Arceus just brought down one of the choppers...oh crap...they're all being torn out of the sky at will...

Andy? You're breaking up... I can't hear you...

For those of you watching this at home, share this live stream all over social media... Arceus is in control here...

Shit! It's coming towards the diner...Can you see it? Everybody, what you see here is what the Government has been hiding in Area 51... Can you hear that? It's that rattling noise again...

Oh Christ! The diner is caving in...Arceus is attacking the diner...if I don't make it out alive, at least share this video everywhere you can. Just get the word out. This is Cody Red—"

Jane

By Eddie D. Moore

I wasn't stupid; I let the group storming Area 51 run ahead. They tried using rubber bullets and water hoses on us before things turned deadly. We were a few hundred feet from an aircraft hangar when the bastards started using real bullets.

Bodies littered the ground right up to where Truth Seekers had made entry into Warehouse One. A swarm of multi-legged creatures poured out of the building. Soldiers with flame throwers followed, torching the creatures and humans.

I grabbed a creature and ran. I'm not sure how it slipped under my skin, but at least, we're both safe.

Al Woods

By Eddie D. Moore and Sue Marie St. Lee

"This is Michelle Corker reporting to you live from the northern perimeter of Groom Lake where the recent Storm Area 51 movement occurred. As you can see in the distance," Michelle motions for the cameraman to zoom in on the background, "this looks like a battleground, which indeed, it was. Most of the fighting has moved south, and I'm told that we should be relatively safe here.

"As yet, we have no definitive fatality count, but locals informed us more than humans and wildlife died. Witnesses affirm that strange beings were among the dead. One of those witnesses is here with us now, Al Woods, of Homewood, Illinois."

Michelle took three steps to her right and stood beside Al. His dishevelled countenance appeared tired, as though he hadn't slept in days.

"Al, thank you for taking the time to be with us, and..." Michelle looked at the accordion he was toting and smiled.

"for bringing your accordion along. Are you planning to play for us?"

"Huh? Oh, no. I take her everywhere I go. If it wasn't for her, I might not be having this interview with you."

Michelle looked bewildered by Al's answer, but continued, "Okay. I understand that you've experienced some rather traumatic events. I wouldn't feel right about continuing without asking, how are you doing? You look a little worse for the wear."

"Ah, yes, I suppose so." Al ran his fingers through his dusty hair in an attempt to look more presentable than he imagined he was. "Yep, I'm tired. It's been a rough couple of days, but, I'm doing pretty well, especially considering how many didn't survive."

"Yes, so, Al, tell us a little bit about yourself and what brought you to this movement. Were you here in protest to the government holding secrets?"

Michelle moved closer and held the microphone for Al. "Well, my brothers and I are professional musicians. We were invited to play at the campgrounds in the beer tents for some pretty good money. We thought it would be a fun gig, a lot of opportunities to drum up new business, pardon the pun." Al smiled at his own joke. "Nah, the real truth is, the money was good and we knew this would be a historic event. We wanted to be a part of it." Al took a sip of ice water and forced himself to swallow.

"So, you were here to provide entertainment for the people. When did you and your brothers arrive?" Michelle asked. "What was the atmosphere like preceding the disastrous event? And did people fear an attack from the government?"

"Well, we arrived three days before the actual storming was to happen. People were friendly, some of them acted goofy, you know, wearing alien masks and aluminium foil pyramid-type hats." Al laughed slightly while remembering. "But man, I'll tell you, there were some real die-hards too, you know, people that were so angry that the government was keeping huge secrets from us. Those guys were angry, ready for a fight."

"Were they armed?"

"Oh, hell yes. I think some of them were ex-military, some with severe health issues too."

"Health issues?"

"Well, I got to talk to a lot of new people between sets. I think maybe some had PTSD, but a lot of them felt like they were ignored by the government after serving their country and being wounded in some way, whether it was physical or mental. The government doesn't treat our veterans very well, and that is a fact."

"Okay. So, tell us what happened? You were there, right? You and your brothers? Are you able to tell us what you saw and heard?"

Al wiped the sweat off his forehead, and after a long sigh, he answered, "It's a long story, but I'll do my best."

"Wait, Al, my producer is signalling to me." Michelle pushed her earpiece closer to her ear canal, listening to the producer's instructions.

"Al, we're going to take a little break and move to a cooler location nearby where a tent has been set up with folding chairs and lots of cold drinks." Looking into the camera, Michelle spoke, "Viewers, we'll be right back after this brief message from our sponsors."

In the tent with large fans circulating the hot air, Al sat in a folding lawn chair with a bottle of ice water in his hand. He tapped the lapel mic the cameraman pinned to his shirt, and the cameraman gave him a thumbs up.

"Al, we're on in three, two, one." Michelle faced the camera, "Welcome back viewers. Before I begin, I need to thank our producers for providing this tent to shade us from the harsh sun."

Michelle sat down next to Al. "Before we left for the break, I asked if you could recount the events for us, beginning with the night before."

"Thanks, Michelle." Al cleared his throat with another sip of ice water. "We were playing in one of the beer tents the night before the march was to happen. Everything was going great. People were laughing, dancing, drinking, joking. There was a lot of discussion about what kind of aliens might be discovered. One guy planned to take one home and make it a pet." Al laughed, cleared his throat, and glanced at his accordion before continuing.

"We finished playing around one o'clock in the morning. Only a few of the really drunk people complained. You know, the ones who could hardly walk much less dance. Jock, Rand, and I went to our travel trailer to get a good night's sleep.

In the morning, someone was on a megaphone, telling people to form four groups. Each group would have one designated leader, who was in contact with the other three at all times. It was supposed to be a strategic invasion, I'm pretty sure those four guys were ex-military. They were organised, armed and knew what they were doing. I think their only mistake was that they weren't leading trained militia, most of their followers were jobless snowflakes and terribly hung-over.

"Jock and Rand had coffee in the trailer then left for home. They didn't want to hang around for the main event."

Michelle's voice was full of concern when she asked, "Have you heard from Jock and Rand since you last saw them?"

Al shook his head. "No. I haven't heard from them, but they should've been well out of Nevada before the shit hit the fan. Oops. Sorry about that."

Michelle nodded her head, indicating it was fine for Al

to continue telling his story.

"After coffee and a doughnut, I washed up, grabbed Jenny and headed for one of the groups."

Michelle blinked and leaned in closer. "Wait. Who's Jenny?"

Al pointed to his accordion on the ground beside him. "That's Jenny."

"Oh, okay."

"Yeah, so Jenny and I started at the back of group number four. Four was always my favourite number, that's why I chose it. Anyway, I strapped Jenny on my back, set the cooler onto my wagon and was ready to go."

"You were prepared then. I mean, you had water, right?"

"Yeah, of course. I'm also ex-military."

"With all due respect, Al, why cumber yourself with an accordion?"

"There have been times in my life where I was dead broke, alone, and she was all I had to my name. I don't go anywhere without her. Call it a personality quirk. May I continue?"

"Yes, please."

"I worked my way up to the middle of Unit Four. The closer we came to the gate, the more drones we saw. Loudspeakers blared intermittent warnings in-between ear-splitting wavelengths, the kind used in special operative missions. I put on my ear protection and special eyewear for what I expected next."

"And, what were you expecting next?"

"The blinding light. It's another experimental military tool used to disorient and blind the enemy."

"So, you, the group, the people storming Area 51 were now the government's enemies? They were using secret military weapons on you civilians?" Michelle's face wore a look of outrage and disbelief.

Al stared blankly at Michelle as if she were speaking a foreign language. He found it hard to believe she was so naive. Didn't everyone know that storming a secret military installation would be considered treasonous and punishable by death?

Rather than entertaining Michelle's ignorance, Al continued recounting his story. "That's when the drones began dropping things. I couldn't make out what they were at first, but, when these things hit the ground and started scurrying around, I knew this wasn't a military invention. These were some sort of aliens. They grouped up and swarmed over people. One of them brushed my leg and it went completely numb. I couldn't feel anything. I fell to the ground and..."

Al coughed and took a sip of water. He coughed again and spat blood onto the ground. Terror filled his eyes as creatures with multiple legs crawled out from under his shirt.

Michelle tossed her lawn chair behind her and jumped up, but it was too late. Half a dozen of the creatures jumped on her. The cameraman knocked over the tripod as he struggled to fight off the ones that jumped on him.

Al rested his head on his accordion and stared into the red light on the camera that indicated that it was still functioning. His breathing slowed and stopped. Screams could be heard in the background as the life drained from Al's eyes. A moment later, the red light blinked twice and then went dark as its connection was terminated.

Ivan Hawks

Souvenirs

By Vonnie Winslow Crist

"Let's leave, Sal," I said. "We shouldn't ignore military warnings."

"The Keep Out sign was probably posted by another souvenir hunter. I'm not missing an opportunity because you're spooked."

Before I could protest, Sal opened an access door, climbed aboard. Reluctantly, I followed, closing the hatch behind us.

Once inside, we discovered the ship's automated lights still functioned.

"Something's off."

"Whatever." Sal rifled through cabinets, stuffing his knapsack with equipment.

"I heard noises above us," I warned. "I'm leaving."

"I'm staying."

Suddenly, a dozen praying mantis aliens dropped through ceiling panels onto a screaming Sal.

Alone but alive, I fled.

Caroline Walters

31, State Librarian, Carson City, Nevada

By Zoey Xolton

I arrived in the small town of Rachel, Lincoln County, before sunrise, and already the place was packed; it was a veritable hive of human activity. Aside from Election Day, I'd never seen so many people. There were folks from all walks of life, as if every creed, colour and minority that existed within the U.S.A. was represented right here, in this bizarre melting pot of conspiracy.

It wasn't long until the Push. I don't know whose bright idea it was, but the viral posts across all social media platforms said that our best chance of storming Area 51 was to do so under the relative cover of darkness. And, if it all went arse up, the dawn would either bring relief, hope and comfort—or reveal to us the folly of our curiosity and our sense of entitlement. Either way, that was the plan.

The streets were lit, the actual roads, and the revellers. Eclectic lighting sundered the heavy Nevada gloom; headlights, hand-held torches, rainbow coloured glow-sticks, and the still air hung thick with the tell-tale scent of pot. It was strong, *probably hydro*, I thought. The place was ripe with illicit drugs.

Some were evidently there to party. There were throngs of college aged kids in skimpy outfits made of silver, holographic material. They had signs and balloons, over-sized novelty glasses and fluffy gators. Then there was the religious nut jobs; hollering over megaphones about God and sins, the Devil and Revelations. From the look and sound of it, they were going to run out of steam well before the action even started.

Pushing through to the front of the immense crowd were the truth seekers and news crews. Covered in microphones, with binoculars hanging from their necks, phones and cameras at the ready. Some of the stranger individuals had home-made contraptions mounted on their heads and chests, antennas and coiled wiring poking out of their backpacks.

And last, but not least, were the so-called American Defenders; armed compatriots who'd taken it upon themselves to shoot 'them aliens' on sight; you know, to "Protect 'Murica!", as it were. These guys were wearing their weight in gold, in privately purchased tactical armour, and hunting gear. I couldn't believe it—actually, that's a lie. It's the U.S.A, of course there was going to be guns; but what I couldn't wrap my head around was the fact that they'd kill on sight.

I fitted into none of the aforementioned groups. I was there purely out of curiosity, just a slightly alternative, everyday American citizen who spends her days with her nose buried in books. I wanted to see an alien, a living, breathing, real extraterrestrial...unless it wanted to kill me first. I felt, as clichéd as it sounds, that it was best to come in peace. Why would you shoot an alien on sight? It could be innocent. I mean, we'd all heard the stories growing up. If there really were aliens in Area 51, they were probably there under duress, captured, far from their own kind— merely lab rats to be poked, prodded and tested upon.

Maybe our storm would liberate the creatures? We couldn't know. But the overwhelming consensus was: the U.S government had kept us in the dark for far too long. If there were killer aliens in Area 51, we wanted to know, had the right to know. And similarly, if there were friendlies, like the Greys of vintage comic books, and notoriously mocked U.F.O sightings, we wanted to know about them too! If they had knowledge and superior technology, everyone had the right to know, and benefit.

Before I'd even finished drinking in the spectacle that was The Storm, the Push began. Whistles and car horns blared, righteous voices blazed over megaphones and then, like a tsunami, we moved. The noise was deafening. Millions of hearts raced, legs marched, and all eyes were trained forward. On pure adrenalin we forged our path.

* * *

When we arrived at the ominous, triple razor-wire fortified gate of Area 51, we were blinded. Industrial sized floodlights burned our retinas as they flashed on in the darkness. Curses broke out. There had been no warning to cover our eyes. A formal, military trained voice barked over a loudspeaker.

"You are trespassing on government property. I repeat. You are trespassing on government property. This is your first, and final warning. Leave now, or we will open fire. You have two minutes to disperse."

I blinked my eyes to adjust my vision as the message was repeated. The Storm booed and yelled, crying out for truth, while others shouted of government conspiracies. I had expected this, to be honest, though I couldn't speak for the others. The government was never going to stand down and just let us stroll on in—and we lacked the fire power to break 51's defences. Machine gun towers lined the fence in both directions; men in black stood behind the guns, ready and willing to do their duty, even if it meant opening fire on civilian protestors.

Country of the free? I had my doubts, but that was 'democracy' for you.

The countdown began. "Ten, nine, eight..."

We never made it through the gate.

A great rumble shook the earth, cutting the general at the gate off, cold. The Storm fell silent as shock rippled through the crowd. Moments later, a deafening roar tore through the air, along with great fragments of reinforced concrete and blue metal. Screams erupted, and amongst the confusion of it all, I heard the unmistakable sound of guns loading, cocked for action.

The crush of bodies was instant, as debris rained down upon us. Not three feet from me, a chunk of rubble the size of a station wagon crushed a dozen scrambling revellers. My stomach crawled up my throat involuntarily. The world around me succumbed to chaos. Gone were the truth seekers and the pot-heads, the news crews and most of the scientists. It was everyone for themselves.

Americans trampled their fellow compatriots in terror, crushing skulls and bones into the bitumen as they fled in fear. Suddenly, gun fire rang out, not individual shots, but the blaze of the tower mounted machine guns. Only, we weren't being met with fire. I looked back and my blood ran cold.

If The Storm thought it had any claim as a force, it was

grossly mistaken. Given form in the darkness by the constant blaze of the guns, came the *Swarm.* Creatures straight from the realms of nightmares poured out of Area 51. The gunners tried to thin their numbers, to save themselves and the fleeing crowd—but it was futile. More screams were heard as the gun towers were overwhelmed by the lightning fast, scurrying insect-like aliens.

And that's when I realised that we had no right to storm Area 51. We never did. The government might be shady as Hell, but they'd been keeping these things from spreading; and look what we had done. *Or someone had done,* I thought as I ran, my lungs burning. The explosion had come from within Area 51. Someone, or something had let these horrors out...

Behind me, the gates of Area 51 fell. The guns seemed ineffective, almost as if the bullets merely ricocheted off of the aliens' hard, reflective carapaces. I could hear the aliens gaining on us. It was a skin-crawling sound, something like what I imagined the surge of an army of oversized, lethal cockroaches might sound like. I figured it was the terrifying cadence of their many segmented legs rubbing back and forth against one another, as they swarmed, a skittering tide of black in the dark.

Two heart beats later, and the breath was stolen from my lungs. The world moved in slow motion as I felt myself falling. I'd tripped, or someone had shoved me, I couldn't be sure. It happened too fast. All I knew was terror. I was going to be eaten alive, consumed by a million twitching, pincered mouths, never to be seen or heard from again. And then there was nothing.

***

When I came to, I was in total darkness. There was no sound at all, save for the frantic thumping of my own heart. I remember venturing a 'Hello', but there was no answer. My head ached, and my knees were skinned, the fresh stinging sensation enough to make me grimace. I got to my feet and reached out, trying to ascertain where I was.

The door is open, came a voice, though I heard it inside my head, not with my ears. I froze as a luminescent being came into focus before me. Every fibre in my body screamed with immediate realisation, with recognition. A Grey stood before me, as material and tangible as anything I've ever known. The alien was unmistakable; it looked just like every traditional depiction of the pale-skinned, slanting orb-eyed being I'd seen growing up.

My mouth hung open. I tried to speak, but found I had no voice.

Do not be alarmed. Your voice will return. For now, it is not safe to make sound.

I swallowed hard, and nodded dumbly.

I must leave you, now. I advise that you remain in this bunker until the sun has risen. They are still feeding, but will disperse soon. Humanity needs you, Caroline. Be well.

Before I could do anything more than stare in wide-eyed wonder, the Grey shimmered from my sight. In its place, a small orb of glowing light manifested, hovering on the spot. I don't know how long I stood there, eyes transfixed. At some point, out of shock, exhaustion, terror, or a mix of all three, I curled up on the cold floor of the secret bunker and fell into a deep, black sleep.

When next I awoke, the glowing orb was gone. Carefully I felt my way around until I came upon a lever. With some heavy shoulder work, I got the door open. Warm, brilliant sunshine sliced through the darkness. As my eyes adjusted, I peered outside. There was blood everywhere, but no bodies—but more importantly, no aliens. Breathing a hesitant sigh of relief, I slipped outside and into the light.

I was alone, or so it seemed. I crossed the salt flats known as Groom Lake, and headed back towards Rachel. It was the only place to go, there was nowhere else for miles. With all my heart, I hoped that the swarming aliens were nocturnal, or at least, already far from the area. My goal was to locate my car, if it was still there, and get the Hell out of Nevada. *Canada sounds good,* I thought. *Free healthcare.*

On my journey, I came upon a handful of others who had survived. People who'd had the sense to lock themselves in their cars and lay low in the footwells until the sun rose. For as far as the eye could see, the landscape was soaked red. Over one million souls gone, just like that. My mind reeled as I staggered along.

I found my car, and thanked God when it started. I made it out of Nevada that day, my foot firmly on the accelerator for the full two-hundred-and-fifty mile drive. I wasn't game to hang around to see another night. Taking nothing more than I could pack into my car, I left my old life behind and state-hopped my way to safety before the U.S border officially went into lock-down.

So much has happened since that day...yet my only true regret, even after all this time? That I never had the presence of mind to thank the Grey that saved my life.

Cherish Salazar

19, College Freshman

By Marcus Cook

51 Hours after the Raid

I just wanted Jonathon to like me. I thought he was taking me to a rave. It then seemed to be a prank. Before I knew it, I was running toward a steel gate.

Many people were being gunned down. Me and Jonathon got past and into the facility. What we saw was ungodly. They looked like spiders, but different. They got released and...the carnage...all the *blood*.

Jonathon pushed me away as I watched his body get devoured alive by hundreds of them. I got stung by one. I smashed it.

My skin is boiling and I itch.

1 Hour before the Raid

"Is the Camera on, Matt?"

"Yeah."

"I'm Jonathon!"

"And I'm Cherish!"

"We're going to release some aliens!"

"It's about time the world knew that they exist."

"Wait! Jonathon? Matt? You're not serious, right?"

"Of course, we are. Why else would we be here?"

"To party?"

"Cherish, you thought we drove 200 miles to party?"

"Yeah. Somebody said it was the next Burning Man."

"We are storming Area 51 and finding out what's inside." Jonathon high-fived Matt.

"If they are like E.T., we release them. If they are like ID4 or Aliens, we let the world know!"

Cherish shook her head.

3 Hours after the Raid

Alarms, people screaming, explosions rang out through the night sky.

Matt Underland sat behind the wheel of his mother's SUV sweating and panicked.

He had been parked in the lot of the local café near

Area 51 for hours awaiting his friends.

They had joined hundreds of people in the Raid on Area 51. Matt chickened out at the last moment and started to believe he made the right choice. He felt his friends were either arrested or...even worse...dead! He hadn't even seen any of the raiding party, since the ones dressed as Naruto Anime characters came back complaining about shin splints and cramps.

But that was hours ago.

A thud against the back of the truck startled Matt. He looked through his side mirror to see a female hand covered in blood holding onto the side of the truck. Matt immediately leapt out of the driver's seat and sprinted to the back. There lay Cherish, covered in blood, mud, and sand.

"Holy shit, Cherish!" Matt exclaimed as he attempted to stand her up, "Where's Jonathon?"

Cherish's eyelids popped open and she replied, "DEAD! Everyone's dead!"

Matt started to rub her shoulders in an attempt to calm her down, "Calm down, I'm going to get you to a hospital."

"You can't. I'm on my parents' insurance. They'll find out. You need to take me back to school. I just need some rest," Cherish replied as she began to shake.

"No, we're going to a hospital," Matt argued as he helped Cherish into the passenger side.

"I'll tell them you killed Jonathon," Cherish threatened.

"You are insane," Jonathon stated. "Fine. Let's get you back."

They drove for almost an hour before saying another word. Jonathon watched his friend drift in and out of consciousness. Finally, he needed to know.

"So, what happened?"

Cherish had trouble focusing, but when she heard, the question she seemed ready to answer it.

"It started out exciting. It looked to be a million people lined up like in Braveheart. You could hear over the PA's, the base warning us not to approach the base..." Yadda, yadda, yadda."

"Right. I was there for that," Matt reminded her.

Cherish looked at him annoyed by his interruption, "Fine. Once we had charged, the base opened fire with non-lethal weapons. Beanbags and soft pellets."

"But you guys kept going."

"Who's telling this story?" Cherish grimaced in pain, "Yes we did, until they started to use full pressure hoses. We stopped and watched the lead people get pinned to the ground and soaked to the point of drowning."

"So, you didn't make it in?" Matt questioned.

"No, we made it in," Cherish replied, "We saw a small group of people head off the path. We followed and met up with them. They run a paranormal blog and podcast called ParaTruth. I guess they paid a lot of money to get the codes to the back door entrance."

"Are you for real? This is sounding made up," Matt interrupted.

"Fuck you. Your friend is dead and you're telling me I'm making this up. Fuck you and take me home," Cherish replied, angered and afraid.

Matt focused on the road as Cherish relayed the rest of the story.

* * *

She and the others entered through a secured manhole, walked through who knows what in the sewer, and entered the military base through drain. It was a tight squeeze, but they all fit. Alarms were blaring and strobe lights were spinning. It made everything more terrifying than it already was.

"Where are we?" Jonathon asked.

"Looks like a lab," the one with glasses replied as he looked over a computer generated map.

"There should be holding cages out that door and to the left," his partner added.

Cherish followed closely behind Jonathon as the four snuck up to the door. The guy with glasses peered through the window and gave the all-clear. They exited into a dark, metal hallway. The sounds of gunfire and stomping of feet could be heard above them. Cherish gathered they were underground.

Within a hundred feet, Cherish heard one of them say, "Holy Shit! This is it."

They quickly opened a door and dashed in leaving Jonathon and Cherish in the hall.

"What now?" Cherish asked, frightened and ready to give herself up or try to sneak back out.

"We go in. We came this far. We have to see for ourselves. Right?" Jonathon asked.

"No, we don't. We got in. That's as far as we should of gotten. We haven't thought of the repercussions. If we see something, they may kill us," Cherish pointed out.

The door reopened and Glasses waved them over, "You have to see this."

Cherish and Jonathon took deep breaths and rushed in to join them.

Cherish could not believe her eyes. It was like a zoo. Different size glass cases with indescribable creatures inside. Two legs, four arms, three heads, eight eyes were features Cherish could remember. She was also positive there was a unicorn and Big Foot.

"Guys look at these bugs?" the other one called over.

Cherish was reluctant to look as Jonathon left her next to the unicorn. She watched the three boys ogle over what was inside. Curiosity got the better of her and she walked over to see for herself.

The case was dimly lit, yet she could make out the giant webs build throughout.

"Radioactive spiders...like in Spider-man," Glasses joked.

"There seems to be a lightswitch, let me turn it on so we can get a better look" Jonathon said pointing at a switch to the left of the case,

"Thanks," Glasses' partner responded.

"Jonathon, don't touch anything." Cherish warned.

"It's only a lightswitch." Jonathon's words echoed over and over in Cherish's head.

Then the alarm went off and the glass slid open.

"Holy shit. Close it!" Cherish screamed as a foot long spider-like creature flew out of it holding pin.

Cherish watched as it latched across Glasses' face and its scorpion tail jammed through the top of his head. Glasses collapsed to the ground as other spiders leapt out onto his body. His partner screamed as he and Jonathon headed for the door.

Cherish froze up in fear as she watched the creatures rip into Glasses' flesh. He made no sound or movement.

"Jesus Christ, Cherish move!" Jonathon screamed as he grabbed her around the arm and pulled her away.

* * *

The rest of it was a blur. She remembered Glasses' friend being taken down by the aliens as Jonathon opened the door. She remembered Jonathon pulling open the manhole cover and screaming for Cherish to get in.

Her last memory was watching Jonathon's chest being torn open as he held the manhole cover for her. As she pulled her hand in she'd got stung. The cover was dropped on top of the creature, splitting it in half.

"We're here," Matt called out causing Cherish to open her eyes. It was dawn and she saw they were parked in front of Chi-Pi-Chi sorority house.

Cherish thought she'd never see it again. She started to tear up as she hugged Matt goodbye.

She got out without saying another word, and Matt drove away.

The house was alive with girls. Cherish was shocked by how many girls were awake and active at 6 am on a Saturday, until she saw the banner. Chi-Pi-Chi Panty Party.

"Oh my God, Cherish! Where have you been? Mud wrestling?" a voice exclaimed as she turned to see a Platinum blonde sister standing in shock behind her.

"Oh Riley!" Cherish collapsed to the ground in tears, "The car broke down. It was terrible."

Riley stood over her, fighting the urge to touch her filthy sorority sister, "There, there, Cher. Why don't you go shower and tell us about it at breakfast?"

Cherish saw the disgust as she stood and headed upstairs. Every girl she passed gave her a disgusted look, followed by whispering.

She entered the shower room and stripped off her clothes. She didn't realise how soiled they were; blood, mud and sand. She wanted to burn them, but instead tossed them in the garbage. She stepped under the hot water and started to wash away the filth. The water was warm and relaxing, but she didn't feel right. Her skin felt like it bubbling, blistering. She looked down at her arm; it was red and puss-filled. She scrubbed that spot hard. She thought she felt something move under it.

She screamed.

"Who's in here? Are you alright?" a girl's voice echoed in.

Cherish gathered herself and answered, "It's me, Rachel. It's Cherish."

A tall girl—athletic build with long brown hair—entered the shower area and walked over to the shower stall. "Cherish? Are you alright? You were screaming."

Cherish placed her arm behind her back, smiled and answered, "Yes. I just saw a spider."

Rachel's smile faltered as she looked around and stepped back. "Well, as long as you're okay."

Rachel quickly left the room.

Cherish rinsed off, grabbed a towel and headed to her bedroom. As she entered, she found her roommate with a fellow sorority sister's head between her legs.

"Oh shit!" Alexa screamed as she pulled the covers over them both.

"What the hell!" Lena yelled as she popped her head out from under the covers. "Oh! Cherish you're back." Lena crawled from under the blanket and joined Alexa on the pillow.

"Yep. I'm just going to go to bed. Do whatever." Cherish walked over to her bed not looking at the girls. She felt like all the energy was being sucked out of her body. She collapsed on her bed and faded off to sleep.

She lost track of time as she lay in slumber. Her body ached and she felt she was losing control. She was becoming something else's puppet. She heard voices off in the distance.

"Cherish, you going to sleep all day?"

"Cherish, are you feeling okay?"

"Cherish, the parties in a couple of hours! You better start moving."

"Jesus Christ, Cherish. The guys are showing up!"

That was the last thing Cherish understood. Her world went silent after that.

* * *

"Is somebody sleeping in that bed?" Carl asked as he stepped into the bedroom.

"Yea, that's Cherish. She's been there all day." Alexa started to unbutton his pants.

"And she's okay with us being in here?"

"She went on a bender. If she doesn't like what we're doing she can leave," Lena added as she pulled off her shirt.

The three began to fondle, stroke and kiss each other.

Cherish started to stir in her bed. Suddenly she sat up, startling Lena.

"Holy shit!" Lena yelled as she rolled off the bed pulling the covers with her.

Alexa remained mounted on top of Carl as they watched Cherish turn and stare at them.

"What the fuck is wrong with her eyes!" Lena exclaimed as Cherish stared, her eyes grey around large, white pupils.

Cherish gave an evil grin as she leaned over and bit into Alexa. Alexa started to scream as her flesh ripped from her neck, her blood squirting all over Cherish and the bed.

"Holy shit!" Carl screamed and pushed Cherish away and wrapped his shirt around Alexa's neck.

Cherish began to convulse and Lena watched her chest split and large spiders poured out onto Carl's back. Lena screamed and sprinted out of the room. Carl attempted to fight off the spiders, but they tore into his body. One crawled into his mouth and jammed its sharp needle tail through the roof of his mouth and into his brain.

Lena sprinted out of the room as several spiders bounced off the closed door.

Downstairs, the music was loud, and girls were everywhere, dressed in not much more than bras and panties. Guys were mingled between them dancing, drinking, and touching whatever the girls allowed as Matt and his friend Bobby arrived.

"I'm going to try to find Cherish," Matt told Bobby.

As he made his way through the crowd, he heard a familiar voice. "Hey, Matt!"

He turned to see Riley. "Hey! Have you seen Cherish?"

Riley shook her head. "She hasn't been feeling good. Last I heard she was still in bed."

"I'd better check on her," Matt said as he headed toward the staircase.

Screams suddenly rang out as Lena tumbled down the stairs covered in blood and Matt ran to help her up.

"What happened?" he asked, kneeling beside her.

Lena was trembling as she pointed to the top of the stairs. There Carl, Alexa, and Cherish stood, their skin was tattered and torn, their eyes grey and dead.

Rachel walked to the bottom of the stairwell and shouted, "Nice costumes, wrong theme."

The gathering crowd laughed which seemed to agitate Carl, Alexa, and Cherish and they sprinted down the stairs.

Alexa grabbed Rachel and bit hard into her shoulder, before tossing her to the ground. Rachel tried to fight her off, but spiders poured out of Alexa's mouth and covered Rachel's skin before skittering over to attack the retreating crowd.

Matt fought his way out, clambering over people falling to the ground, screaming in agony. Bobby and Riley were standing on top of the dining table and, as Matt stumbled into it, he put out his hand and Riley stomped on it.

"OW!" Matt screamed.

Riley looked down. "Matt! I'm sorry!"

"We need to get out of here!" Matt said as Bobby helped Riley down.

The three friends headed for the front door but, as Riley flung it open, Bobby was yanked back by Cherish.

"Cherish. No. God No!" Matt screamed as she bit into the side of Bobby's face. Matt reached out to grab him, but a spider leapt out of her hair and onto his arm. He slapped it hard, knocking it to the floor, then turned and fled, dragging Riley with him.

In the car, Matt turned on the ignition and floored the accelerator, driving away without looking back.

An hour later, they were on the open road.

"What the hell were those?" Riley cried.

"I think they came back with us from Area 51. Some sort of alien creatures," Matt responded, "Were you bitten, or stung?"

"No." Riley shook her head and he could see the panic in her eyes. "You?" she asked.

"One jumped on me, but I it didn't get me."

Matt looked back at the road, trying to ignore the movements under the skin on his arm.

Cal Davis

48, Cook, Area 51, Q Block

By J.W. Garrett

Area 51 had been closed to the public, but I feared this day would come. I do as I'm told, cooking food for the facility, not questioning the bits of flesh and bone concoctions ordered.

A groaning gives way to the massive doors crashing outside. Poking my head out, I see what I've suspected all along. Strange beings occupy the space here, and two turn in my direction.

Ahead, my escape looms. One of them grabs me, puncturing my leg. I don't even get a better look before teeth sink into my flesh.

My eyes close. Lunch will be late.

Josh McKennan

24, Kansas City, MO

By J.W. Garrett

I always knew this would be a one-way ticket. I had to be here for the ride though, for this one piece of unfolding history that could cancel all that's come before. I don't want to be around for the famine, the war—the utter annihilation of the planet. In the middle of the action, in a blaze of glory, is the way to go for me. And, in the process, if I can free some imprisoned humans, held here at Area 51 for maybe decades or longer, all the better. Everyone comes here for their own reasons. In the end, we're all bound to our individual journeys.

When Emily and I arrive, the doors are already open, thanks to the hordes of people who've come before us. After we slip inside, chaos ensues. Our day of travel and thought toward a plan don't prepare us for the pandemonium inside. Emily dives to the right, and I follow. Soon I realise the hopelessness of trying to stay together.

Emily and I discuss ahead of time staying away from the masses of people who make for easy targets, and from the executions taking place I know we had formulated the right plan. With the information we had. Yet the alien beings are prepared for us, are organised, and are methodically picking off groups of humans with practiced efficiency, devoid of the emotions their human counterparts display. We scatter. It's harder to get us that way.

I look to my left and my right, but Emily is gone now, almost like she's evaporated. I choose a path away from the aliens doing the most killing. Some puncture humans with claws; others appear to use mind control. The humans in that particular group fall to their knees, moaning, grabbing their heads in pain, before splatting lifeless to the ground.

For now, the monsters don't focus on me. Since gathering in groups attracts the aliens—from what I have witnessed so far—I steer clear of the crowds and act like I know where I'm going. I pass an almost empty hallway and duck in.

What we've been told isn't true—the aliens are smaller than we've been led to believe, outfitted with varying appendages to accomplish specific tasks, like chopping, slicing, piercing, or sucking. The pictures given to the public for years don't give justice to these true-to-life insect-like slithering alien life-forms. The up-close-and-personal versions are so much worse 'cause they're creepy and alive and intent on destroying us.

I hear a rumble and glance up just as a small group of humans beats a path in my direction, a crowd of alien beings hot on their heels. Convinced my chances are better alone, I push against various doors until one of them gives, and I shove my way inside. Just as it clicks shut, I hear a locking mechanism slide home behind me.

A sickening reek envelops the space. The source takes little time to identify. Piled high to the side are dead bodies. Nearby is a noisy mammoth alien apparatus. I turn in an attempt to leave, and something pokes me—a needle.

Bad news.

Later, as my eyelids lift, I see my gruesome future when humans are...fed into the machine's inner workings, making a green mush-like fuel. My eyelids drift closed again, and I hope for the darkness to take me completely before I'm consumed.

I wish I had more...time.

Emily Sparrow

28, Saint Louis, MO

By J.W. Garrett

Whatever is inside me, driving me toward Area 51, I can't stop it, and I've found others on the same mission are compelled, just like me. Mostly I avoid those people. It's a frightening time, and I sense this event could spur the end of humanity. Even with all the craziness happening around me, I still can't stop the obsession within that propels me forward, like some eerie bond has zapped me, yanked tight, and won't let go.

At least I'm smart enough to hook up with my navigation expert, Josh. Who knows what resources we'll need to get there and once we're inside, so he says.

The reality is, we might not make it out alive. If we're able—Josh and me—we'll record our findings. Already I'm wondering if anyone will be left to read them.

Getting in wasn't difficult. Looks like we missed the

initial drive. The masses before us have busted the massive doors wide open. We only need to slip in with the steady stream of others like ourselves. But Josh and I staying together is another story.

Tunnelling through the crowds of people, I dart down a long empty hall. Shots ring out, and minibattles rage on, but—with me and Josh hopefully somewhere behind me— we don't seem to be the aliens' focus just yet. Do these aliens only home in on larger groups, like Josh and I discussed on the way here, or will they eventually crush the life force of all the invaders?

Regardless, the beings swarm everywhere. They're smaller than I'd imagined but lethal and move like giant insects. People are falling, crying out, and in the process of dying around me. I don't stop to get a better look. But the insect-like creatures pick at the dead humans, rearranging them, then stacking and sorting their carcasses. Another set of aliens dumps the bodies into some kind of machine or chute maybe. I glimpse all this in the seconds it takes before I move on.

A door down the hall beckons me, and, just like my urge to come here, I am powerless and give in to the driving force. Once I reach the door, nothing prevents me from pushing my way through, and I suck in a breath at the scene before me.

Various machinery whirs and spins. Four alcoves flash

in a blinding alternation as the alien beings go in and then, in a burst of light, fade away and disappear. Portals maybe? A shrill pitch echoes in my ears, bouncing off my eardrums. I can't focus as I wince in pain.

The haze clears, and a taller alien, different from the ones in the main room, takes notice of me. Its features are exaggerated, even for its elongated body, with huge bulbous eyes, extended forehead, and some type of antennae sprouting in several spots from its head.

The tall monster communicates with another of his kind. When its thoughts are forced inside my head, I realise I'm not safe away from the crowds after all. My feet are frozen in place, but I can still turn my head. What energises these contraptions now hits me. Pieces of human flesh and bone are fed into a vat. Then a pasty green sludge pumps from there through the clear piping connected to the largest machine in this room, spluttering and spitting, while churning and revving the motor harder.

The vision implanted in my brain tells me that I'm going into one of the portals to some unknown destination. At least, for now, I won't become a liquefied power source. A tall, lean alien points me to the second portal alcove. Maybe it will take me away from this place. Maybe it's my chance at life.

As I enter, the door slides shut with an audible click in front of me. My hands and feet tingle. Then the feeling spreads all over, and my body goes translucent before fading completely. When I'm aware again, I exit a door and spill out into the middle of a commotion or battle. But at least other humans are present. I'm no longer in Area 51.

Chaos spins around me. I'm on board a ship of some description. If it's better or worse than Area 51 inundated with aliens, I'm not sure at this point. This human crew is involved in life-threatening issues of their own. I'm sure of this fact from the desperation evident on their faces, the frantic tone of their voices, and the wild look in their eyes—which I'm sure mirrors my own.

I don't see Josh.

I'm not sure if I'm happy or sad about that.

An explosion rocks the ship, sending people and debris flying. We have nowhere to run or hide. I turn toward the remaining grim faces surrounding me, awaiting my fate with those who survived the first blast.

The alien swarm is now here...

Running

By Rhiannon Bird

Everyone was running. The aggressive shouting had turned to screams. Somewhere behind me there was the distinct sound of bones cracking and flesh ripping.

The person beside me was knocked to the ground by something. I choked down a scream and kept moving, I couldn't afford to stop. I made it back to my friend's house who I'd been staying with. I glanced out the window at those things one last time before I raced down into the bunker. Thank god my friend was paranoid. I pulled the door shut behind me, praying the world would survive what we unleashed.

Kelly Lawson

Abduction Coffeeshop, Rachel, NV

By Jacob Baugher

The day the raiders came, dressed in camo and Master Chief cosplays, I was late for my shift at Abduction Coffeeshop, just off Interstellar Highway.

"Who are the freaks?"

"The Raid, Kelly," my coworker whispered.

"Ugh. Kill me."

I clocked in, already sick of freaks. The espresso machine whirred. Freaks got their space-themed lattes.

All at once, they left.

Later, some midget dressed as a praying mantis walked in.

"What do you want?" I snapped.

The freak buzzed in a mushy insect voice, "The Swarm are legion. It has begun."

Buggy jaws distended, closed on my neck. Hot gushing. Darkness.

Jessie Gilton

Three Hundred and Fifty-One

By D.M. Burdett

I want to close my eyes. I want to find a dark space, crawl in, cover my ears, shut out all the sights. Shut out the sounds.

But I have to run; it's that or death.

The klaxons and screams disorientate. The pulsing emergency lights show the world in stilted fragments.

Flash! A bloodied face, a wide-eyed girl.

Flash! A hideous creature with bulging eyes, its pincers *cla-clacking.*

Flash! A white wall, a single crimson handprint.

Flash!

We scramble as one, run across the carpark, find a door ajar. It's metal, thick and heavy, and takes a few of us to push it open. We pile inside, tumbling over each other in the dark.

"Close it!" someone yells from the back.

"There're people out there, we have to help them, we have to let them in," another pleads.

Cla-cla-clack. More screams—outside and in the room behind me.

"They're coming!"

More frantic effort before the door closes with a deep thud we feel in our hearts. Then noises vibrate in the walls, moving parts slam into place, metal sliding over metal.

Then silence.

The lights come on suddenly. We blink, taking in the huge shelter; the stocked shelves, the never-ending lines of bunks.

The illuminated countdown above the door tells us our fate:

3652 DAYS 23 HOURS 59 MINUTES UNTIL UNLOCK

Three hundred and fifty-one survivors sit down to wait.

Claire And Gabe Hammond

26, Twins from Utah

By Angela Zimmerman

"This is the dumbest thing you've ever talked me into," Claire said looking out the window at the vast nothingness that passed by. The lights of Las Vegas were miles behind them. There was nothing here. Just mile after mile of brown, flat, nothing.

"Oh, shut up. You've done far dumber things than this. What happened to Fun Claire?" I glanced over at her. The excitement I felt obviously did not extend to my twin sister.

Since the early part of Summer, I had been following along as the movement to storm Area 51 had picked up steam on Facebook. Since I was out of class for the summer and not doing much other than my boring job, the idea of storming the infamous government conspiracy hotbed took over my life. And I knew when my sister came out west for her annual visit, I would talk her into taking part.

"Fun Claire wishes we had stayed in Vegas. Fun Claire wanted to throw dollars at dancers and get phone numbers. Fun Claire was geared up for all you can eat buffets and day drinking by the pool. Not fiddling around in the desert with a bunch of dorks." She shot a look at me, unclicked her seatbelt, then leaned her seat all the way back and closed her eyes.

I couldn't believe she'd act this way. "But you have a tattoo that says The Truth Is Out There! We marathoned the X-Files like three times when we were kids. We talked about aliens all the freaking time! This is perfect for you!"

"Yeah, well, I also have a tattoo of a rubber duckie. You don't see me trying to find Bert and Ernie, do you?" She sat up and looked at me again. "I'm doing this to be with you, Gabe-o. Believe it or not, I missed your dumb ass." She gestured wildly with her hands, an expression that reminded me of our mother, "But this, this is stupid. It's a live-action role-play version of a stupid meme. Remember when you would dress up as video game characters and go to conventions? This is that times a thousand. This is a bunch of nerds who have nothing better to do than waste time and money travelling to nowhere to potentially get themselves shot by trigger happy military grunts. Have you seen America lately? They could stay home and get shot for free."

I didn't even try to hide the tears that welled up in my

eyes. Of all the things I missed about my sister, her ability to use words as weapons was not one of them. While she gestured like our mom, she spoke like our father. But even he had been unable to hurt me as much as Claire could when she wanted to be spiteful. Out of all the people on Earth, she was the one that knew how to cut me the deepest.

I blinked a few times to clear my eyes. The pain rolled off in waves and seemed to lull Claire back into her seat. She quietly readjusted her seat and without looking at me, refastened her seatbelt.

We didn't talk for the next thirty miles.

It had been dark for a while when we started encountering traffic. At first, it was nothing major. Just a few cars that all looked to be going the same way. Most of them were decorated with witty phrases or drawings on their windows. This brightened my mood considerably. Claire, not so much. Not long after encountering the first few bits of traffic, the signs warning them started showing up. Government warning signs about restricted land ahead, all trespassers will be shot and whatnot. Most of these were new and probably installed just for this event. Some had been defaced.

As the signs began to appear more frequently, the traffic began to thicken. It was when we were at a standstill that Claire broke her silence.

"Gabe-o, I'm sorry about before. I was being an

asshole. Quick question, what's the plan here? If this is an entry, there is no way this is going to work. Are we supposed to just drive up to the gate?"

"That part I don't know. I think we just rush it? Like you know, just run and AHHHHHH!" I karate chopped the air in front of me.

"Ok, no, that's a horrible plan. That won't work at all. They will just open fire on the line of you internet warriors running at them. You got to think smarter. Actually, you know what, let me drive." She was already opening her door. I knew better than to argue.

Once Claire was behind the wheel, she pulled out of the traffic, whipped the car around and headed against the flow. I began to fuss but was met with an outstretched hand. A few turns and ten minutes later, we were alone in the dark.

Claire pulled the car over and killed the motor.

"Alright kiddo, you said you wanted to raid it. Let's freaking raid it. Get the flashlights. Let's go."

"What the hell are you talking about?" I was clueless.

"You wanted Fun Claire, right? This is Fun Claire. Get the flashlights. We'll go in a back way."

And with that, we did.

The fence wasn't the highest we had ever climbed, and once I had laid my jacket down on top of the barbwire, it wasn't the sharpest either. Once we were inside, we picked a direction and ran. I led the way since I had done all the research.

We laughed as we ran, no longer caring that we might be apprehended at any moment.

We turned left, then right, I took us past nondescript building after nondescript building. Every building was empty and dark. There were no guards, there were no cameras, there was no surveillance. Just small, dark, empty buildings and two siblings running through them joyfully.

After fifteen minutes of fooling around, Claire stopped to catch her breath. She turned to smile at me with outstretched arms.

"See, Fun Claire."

I smiled back at her. Out of all the people on Earth, she was the one I loved the most.

That was the moment the door of the building behind Claire opened.

A blistering white light radiated from the door as an unnaturally tall being walked out.

I gasped. Claire, seeing the colour drain from my face, dropped her arms and turned around. She screamed.

Standing before us was something that looked human but in an artificial way. The basic human features were there, but not quite right. The hairless skin glistened with a reptilian sheen. The eyes were too large and too angled. The hands, palms resting just above the knees, seemed too stretched out and long. The thing standing before us was a living embodiment of The Uncanny Valley.

We fell into each other's arms. The being advanced towards us, opened its mouth and released a piercing blast of sound that drove us both to our knees.

We screamed in unison as the creature reached down and lifted us to our feet and stepped back slightly.

The sound stopped. Our ears rang. My nose bled. The being looked at us with a cocked head.

You are the same, but different. Its voice came from somewhere other than its throat and rattled in my brain like a moth in a lamp. *You didn't follow the others, but still you came.*

It held out its hands, cupped together in a welcoming gesture. *What is going to happen to the others like you is going to be ghastly. It will be bloody on both sides. There are bigger plans in place than you know. We have watched as the men in suits unfolded them. I would like to offer you safety. The facility here has been primed to survive these plans.*

In our minds, we were somehow able to see exactly what the creature meant. The social media push for the storming of Area 51 had not been a funny organic thing that just happened. It had been a deep-set ploy by the powers that be to get enough of the young impressionable population to take part in something they could brand as a domestic terror event. They were going to turn the event into a massacre and use it for political talking points. It was an inside job to gain traction in riling up the country for a potential Civil War.

Claire began sobbing into my chest. The creature stood and watched us, unblinking. I took a deep breath and pulled Claire off my chest. I looked from Claire to the creature and then to the light from the open door.

"I guess your tattoo was right after all." I wiped the wetness from her face with a shaking hand and smiled my goofiest smile at her.

The fear retreated for a moment as a familiar smile broke on her face.

"What does rubber duckie have to do with any of this, you dork?"

* * *

The twins were safely relocated by the time the things the creature's warning had become reality. Their new place in the facility was one of comfort and tranquillity. As the battles raged above them, Claire and Gabe were kept safe and sound by creatures that lived underground at what used to be Area 51.

Reaper John Nil

Age: Redacted, Location: Classified Government Black Site

By Raven Corinn Carluk

I and my five team members stepped through the translocation Tunnel at Area 13, and entered Area 51. This whole event had become a minor clusterfuck. Too many bureaucratic fingers in too many bureaucratic pies, and not enough of those fingers believed the civilians would actually follow through on an internet gag. Minimal resources had been deployed for defence, allowing far too many of the stormers to breach the perimeter and assault Facility One.

Only now that it was FUBAR did the Powers That Be realise that hybrids were part of the physical assault.

The other guys immediately broke off toward their designated tasks, tuning out the klaxons and alert lights. All black sites mirrored the same layout, making drop-in ops like this easier. Reaper teams rarely had to lockdown against Earthly threats, normally sent on individual assassination missions, and the occasional sweep and clear of a hybrid nest. I assumed heads would roll for letting the stormers get this far.

I checked my gear while stalking to the security room. I knew what should be where on my body, could tell things were in order just by the feel of how they weighed and hung. Sig Sauer 9MM and extra mags in the shoulder rig. Brace of throwing knives across my chest. Plasma pistol hanging low on my right hip, spare battery packs above on the belt. Kevlar and carbon fibre body armour, the reinforced cowl a matte black skull in honour of our Reaper designation.

Air Force guards nodded as I passed, acknowledging me but not saluting. Far too many people in this hall, and not enough repelling the stormer incursion. White-coated techs scurried about, heads down, and stayed out of my path. Many curious or frightened glances came my way, but I was used to it.

I've never considered myself a big man, but I was enormous compared to the people staffed in Area 51. Well-muscled, over six feet tall, square-jawed and stocky, there was no mistaking my soldier history. Reapers weren't supposed to be stealthy, though any of us could be, but we weren't like our counterparts. Agents suppressed knowledge of aliens, spread misinformation, and controlled the study of technology. Reapers destroyed the evidence and removed threats to Earthly security.

Or, as my mentor more directly said it, "Agents need to blend in, Reapers need to get shit done."

"Shut down those klaxons," I barked upon entering the security centre. "Give me a sit rep and current feeds of the stormers." I loomed behind the privates at the monitoring stations, scanning the video feeds already available, looking for hybrids. Most of the stormers likely didn't realise they ran side-by-side with aliens.

"Reaper, sir." A corporal stepped into place beside me, wringing his hands. I nodded once to acknowledge the younger man, eyes locked on the screens. "It's chaos out there. Civilians broke the fence down, despite the sonic assault, and they made it to Facility One. They've overwhelmed the battalion, claimed weapons, and turned on the guards. It's like something is protecting them."

I grunted, surprised at how nervous the corporal sounded. Area 51 clearly had lower standards for the mental fortitude of its workers. Couldn't imagine the man lasting one day at Area 42, let alone one of the dangerous sites. "Not a thing," I finally said. "Someone. Multiple someones."

"Sir?"

"Hybrids." I frowned at the security feeds. Humans everywhere. Fires, overturned vehicles, broken doors. Labs vandalised, genetic experiments on the loose, alien crossbreeds out of their cages. "These are probably Pleiadeans. Meddling fuckers never keep to themselves."

The corporal moved closer to also stare at the screens. "How can you tell them apart? I thought they looked like normal people."

"Reapers have our eyes enhanced so we can see their auras," I mumbled, following a trail of evidence on-screen. Had they gotten so far?

My hand shot out, pointing at a screen. "Get me every camera in this area." My other fist clenched as I tensed with the need to take action. Needed to confirm what I saw first. Couldn't hare off after false leads.

The privates worked fast; each screen changed to one of the many angles around the containment floor. Two hybrids and a dozen humans with stolen weapons had breached subbasement two, and were currently opening cells.

"Fuck, that's Stevens." The corporal shook his head in disbelief.

I shot him a glare, brows drawn tightly together. "Say again."

The corporal pointed with a shaking finger. "That's Lieutenant Stevens. I don't know why he's dressed like those civilians, but he's on second shift security."

Not much phased me. I was well-trained, had thirty-four confirmed human kills, fifty-six alien, and enough genetic modifications for a dozen men. I'd seen wholesale slaughter, depraved acts committed by all species, and things that would drive a civvie insane.

But the realisation that someone inside the site had helped the hybrids rocked me to my core.

Time to act, to stop them before they caused further harm. I ran from the security room at top speed, opening comms with the rest of my team. "Two hybrids in subbasement two. Humans attempting to break containment. Have a turned lieutenant with them."

Everyone else checked in with similar reports. They'd attempted to follow lockdown procedures, but were met with heavy resistance. Civilians were everywhere, sowing chaos, stealing and fighting back and destroying equipment. There were far more hybrids than initially reported; one for every hundred normal humans, and from many different races. Evidence of internal sabotage and stormer support was everywhere, hampering efforts to regain control.

Better to focus on running rather than the surge of anger. Never understood how people could side with any alien species. None of them were to be trusted, not even the ones that looked similar. Sharing technology and knowledge didn't earn them a home on Earth.

I pounded through halls, past techs and guards, and down two flights of stairs, reaching the containment floor in under two minutes. I passed shell casings, dead airmen, and other evidence the stormers had come this way. This group was willing to kill, all for beings that would as likely eat them as offer enlightenment.

The crowd of civilians seemed surprised by my arrival, but not the lieutenant nor the hybrids.

I halted, stood at the ready, assessing the situation and my choices. Definitely Pleiadean blends; their gemstone auras were brilliant despite the human blood, and they were just a little more beautiful than their companions. Not known for their fighting skills, they were highly resilient. I would absolutely need the plasma pistol to finish them off.

One of the civilians pointed a stolen M16 at me. "Back the fuck off, man. You don't get to keep them prisoner anymore." I approached, drawing my Sig. "I fucking mean it."

I shook my head, glaring at the civilians. Most of them couldn't meet my masked gaze, but they had enough mob bravery to remain where they were. Keeping the gun out but held low, I barked commands. "You will cease and desist, then return back where you came from."

Stevens opened another cell door, narrowing his eyes at me. "Remember, they can't stop us all. We just need to free the innocent."

Civilians grumbled, egged themselves on, took a step forward with guns trained on me. I raised my pistol, sighting at the closest armed man, calculating the best firing order. The extended magazine gave me twenty rounds, but I'd only need a dozen. They'd fire back, but I counted on no more than six bullets hitting me. Drawing a breath, I stilled myself, and squeezed the trigger.

A dozen shots in quick succession. The 9MM had been configured for my enhanced Reaper skills, barely kicked as it belched death at the gathered people. I guided the recoil, using it to drift across the group, knocking them down like pins.

They fired back, as expected, but most of them were incapable of handling the automatic weapons they'd stolen. Bullets pinged against the walls, most of them missing. Those few that hit were extremity shots. I ignored the pain, turning my focus to Stevens and the hybrids.

Stevens fired his sidearm three times.

All three slugs hit me; two in the chest, one in the head. Kevlar absorbed the force of the bullets, but I was still rocked back, unable to return fire. Adrenaline pulsed through my veins, speeding reflexes and recovery. I took a half step back, shot twice blind, then shook my head to clear it.

The two hybrids raced toward me, unarmed, seeking to tackle me. I braced against the attack, managed to stay on my feet, but could not reach my weapons. The three of us struggled; me for my plasma gun, them to subdue me. They were tall and slender, but surprisingly strong. I grunted, gathered all my strength, and forced them off.

A lance of pain stunned me. I couldn't stop the hybrids when they grabbed me and bore me to the ground, stripping me of weapons. I heard crystal bells, as if from a great distance, and tasted honeysuckle on every breath, though they weren't real. The pain lessened, became a weight inside my skull, inside my very mind.

I knew what the pressure was, what the non-existent sound and smell were. "Get out of my fucking head!" The sensation grew stronger, though never became as painful as initial contact.

The chimes grew louder, tinkled like laughter. I attempted to resist, falling back on my training. Visualised a brick wall forming itself around my thoughts, growing thicker and taller, forcing her back out. A simulation was nothing compared to a real Pleiadean, however, and I couldn't keep her from invading my thoughts.

Be at peace. Her mental voice was melodious, gentle. I knew it was a trap, but still couldn't stop myself from relaxing and listening.

We are leaving. You will tell your people to allow us to do so.

I opened my eyes to find her standing over me. Eight feet of willowy grace and shimmering sapphire beauty, she looked like the paintings of Vedic gods. Blinking once, she smiled.

You and your warriors are soon to have much larger things than myself to deal with.

The hybrids rose, releasing me, and moved to stand beside the blue woman. I couldn't move yet, though the tinkling chimes retreated from my head. She'd somehow paralyzed me, rendering me helpless. I growled, straining to move as the trio of aliens retreated.

Stevens stepped into my line of sight, handgun held loosely at his side. "She knows what she's talking about. We both know what's locked up here."

"Bastard. Why?" I managed to twitch a finger, lift my head.

The lieutenant tipped his head. "When you meet The Swarm, you'll wonder why you didn't help." Stevens saluted, then followed the Pleiadean.

I shouted in rage, slowly regaining use of my limbs. I knew what would happen, what his mysterious statement would lead to. The Agents find out more about The Swarm while we Reapers cleaned up the mess created by this entire shitstorm. There were plenty enough escaped aliens and genetic hybrids for us to handle without worrying about an unknown new race.

The hall shook, accompanied by distant booms. I stumbled to my feet just as the klaxons started again. A triple blast, meaning subbasement three had been breached. The level with the most dangerous creatures, the ones too deadly to be experimented upon, that needed to be kept in absolute isolation.

I swallowed hard. Containment breach on that level triggered a self-destruction countdown that could only be stopped when three senior officers gave the all clear. If only one of the monster aliens had been released, it was possible my Reaper team could handle it and halt the self-destruct.

But the fools who thought they were freeing innocents weren't likely to stop at just one, and there were too many dead personnel already. I realised there was nothing I could do to stop the threats from wreaking havoc. "Regroup," I said over comms, swallowing past an icy lump in my chest. "Regroup in Area 13, await further instructions."

The whole event was officially a major clusterfuck.

The Knowsiacki Family

Post-Incident Investigation by Agent Jackson

By J.B. Wocoski

Case Number: SPRS42-Zed

Agent Jackson, ID number CA39427LA, assigned to follow-up on Surveillance Project Rainbow Storm. These are my transcribed notes for the interviews I conducted with a family of witnesses about the Storming incident at Area 51 on September twentieth in the year Twenty Nineteen.

Note: the sole purpose of this investigation is to determine, to the best of our project capabilities, if the interviewee's memories have remained intact or if they have become corrupted about this incident. The interviewee's names and home location have been changed to protect the family from possible corporate, government and/or military repercussions.

Today, I am interviewing the Knowsiacki family of Pasadena, California.

I interviewed each family member separately in their kitchen. I was able to get more from their ten-year-old son, Michael, than from his two parents, Peter and Patricia, or their sixteen-year-old teenage daughter, Micka. When I questioned them, the father, became confrontational and outright belligerent, while the mother was initially nervous and then became hysterical in pain from a migraine.

Like all the rest of those interviewed previously, these interviews contain highly diverse and confusing statements and opinions by each family member about what really happened when they arrived in their SUV at Area 51. What did they witness and/or participate in? It draws into question if they really made it there or not. What did they do there? Who might have stopped or prevented them from entering the base? However, more importantly, is there any evidence they can give me about what happened there?

The most disturbing thing was their partial memory loss of the incident. We know the family members were there, but we are unsure about what really happened. More importantly, they forgot almost everything about their oldest son, David. The family is very distressed over this memory loss and are looking for answers. I have only one chance to help them put their minds to rest, so, they can get on with their lives.

I first interviewed the father. "Please have a seat, Peter. As our website states, we are a non-profit organisation seeking the truth. I am here to help you discover the truth. Any questions before we start?"

Peter shook his head; no. I smiled. "Good, let's get started. How many members of your family went with you to Area 51?

"Ah, five family members, including myself, Patricia, my wife, my daughter, Micka, and my youngest son, Michael."

It was evident that Peter did not remember his oldest son David by name, but oddly, he miscounted his children and thought of Michael as being his youngest son. I decided not to press the issue. "Alright, according to our records, you responded to our article on our website asking for witnesses and participants to contact us about Storming Area 51, is that correct?"

"Yeah, ah, that, that's right. We drove out there to be part of that Storming Fifty One event on September twentieth."

He hesitated as he sat there as if trying to remember what happened next. So, I gently prodded him. "Ok, go on. Did you leave from your home, here in Pasadena?"

"Yes, the five of us left around three AM. It was a long drive. I remember us stopping for fuel and breakfast at, ah, ah, some fast food place. I really don't remember where. Ah, I remember the three kids were cranky. They all used the restrooms. I think their mom had bacon and eggs, no, ah, she couldn't have had that, she's a vegan. Maybe she had gluten-free waffles. I don't know what I had, I remember the taste of sausage. I like my eggs over easy...maybe I had eggs and a muffin...an English muffin, that's it, that's what I had. The three kids ordered their own meals. I'm sorry, I'm a bit confused as to who ordered what. Can we move on?"

I noticed he had more slips of the tongue about his three kids, so I simply smiled reassuringly. "Sure, please go on. Was the sun up by this time?"

"Yes, the sunrise was a brilliant red sky in the east; I remember seeing it as we got into our SUV." He became quiet and momentarily confused, sitting there as if searching for a memory, or what to say next.

So, I helped him. "And you were saying how you drove toward the sunrise, right? How far did you get on the highway?"

"Yeah, that's right, the sunrise, it blinded me, and I reached up, ah, I put the visor down and my sunglasses on. It was starting to get hot, I turned the air conditioning on. It seemed as if we drove forever, the three kids and my wife mostly slept. I remember a traffic jam, and we came to a stop about ten or twenty miles short of, ah, Area Fifty-one." Peter's words trailed off, "I'm not sure about where we stopped."

Peter messed up again about how many kids he had, I pretended not to notice, "Please go on what happened next?"

"Why are you asking me these questions? I didn't do anything wrong. We were stuck in traffic, we never made it to Area 51. Ah, I'm sorry, I don't know what's wrong with me, I'm having trouble remembering what happened next."

I could sense his level of frustration rising as he tried to remember his son, David. "Ok, Peter. Let's take a short break, relax, have some water. Take it easy."

He looked me in the eye and stuttered, "That's easy for you to say! You're not the one being interrogated!"

I sat there quietly as he drank his water. Finally, he calmed down a bit, so I said, "Our agreement is purely voluntary, if it is too much for you and would like to end our interview, I can leave."

"No! Stay!" His abrupt answer startled me.

"Alright, your family is stuck in traffic, please go on."

Breathing heavily, Peter closed his eyes and said, "My gas gauge was getting low it started to bing and distracted me. I looked back up and saw some short state troopers with thick goggle-like sunglasses approaching my SUV from up ahead. I elbowed my wife awake. One of the short troopers tapped on my window, as another trooper tapped on the passenger side window. My wife and I rolled down the windows, and..." Again, Peter's words trailed off as he sat there with a blank look on his face.

"Peter, that's good. What did the trooper want? " I asked.

Peter stared blankly at the kitchen ceiling above my head, trying to remember. Slowly as if reciting by rote someone else's words, he rambled on, "It is so bright, the red sunlight is so bright, take off your sunglasses and look into the bright red light. I remember pulling into my driveway. Yes, have a nice drive home." Peter sat there as if in a trance for three minutes and twelve seconds. He looked me in the face and started getting upset and accusatory, "It's time to go. I have to go now. I hope you got what you came for. That's all I can tell you. Who are you? What do you want from the, ah, five of us?" He stood up dazed and abruptly left the kitchen as if the interview was over. In a pleasant voice, I heard him yell upstairs, "Honey, you're next! "

I documented his constant slip up about the five of them; there were supposed to be only four in his immediate family.

Patricia took a seat across from me at the kitchen table. I politely asked her, "Do you have any questions about this?"

"Can we make this short? Ever since we got back from that dumb road trip, I've had a migraine. I keep worrying that I've forgotten something important, but I cannot put my finger on it."

I paused for a moment. "What do you remember?"

She sat there, massaging her temples with her fingertips "Not really that much. We all got in the SUV, the kids were sleeping in the backseat. I was exhausted from last-minute packing all night long. Peter didn't help me at all. Instead, he slept until it was time to leave, which left me with the burden of work to do. If it hadn't been for David, I don't know what I would have done." She stopped speaking and scrunched up her forehead from the pain across her eyes.

I noticed her slip about David, I made a note about it. Concerned about her health, I asked, "Patricia, are you well enough to continue?"

She slowly nodded her head. I gently asked her, "How much do you remember about the road trip there?"

"I fell asleep as soon as we left, and woke when Pete stopped for breakfast at some diner in the middle of nowhere. I had these dreadful soggy waffles, and the restroom was disgusting. When we got back into the SUV, I dozed off again. It gets weird after that."

"I don't understand...weird? In what way?"

She looked up at me. "Yeah, weird. It was like we arrived at some crowded place in the desert in the middle of nowhere except for a black mailbox. There were thousands of armed people around the five of us, but they didn't have names or faces. My son ran somewhere, but..." She stopped talking and scrunched up her face again as if another shooting pain pierced through her eyes and temples.

I paused my questioning; she was obviously suffering from some sort of repressed memory trying to get out, it was common in alien abduction scenarios and botched memory wipes. I waited for it to pass. "Can you continue, I have just one more question?"

Patricia weakly nodded I asked her, "Do you know anyone named David?" She grabbed her forehead, screaming in pain and passed out. I dialled 911.

Peter came running into the room, looking at me, he demanded, "What have you done to her?"

The 911 operator answered at the same time. I quickly relayed their address and what happened to Patricia then handed the phone over to Peter. "It's her migraine. She screamed and passed out from the pain. You have to get her medical help."

With the arrival of the emergency medical team and the ensuing commotion that followed, Peter forgot about my interviewing his family. As Patricia was taken away by the paramedics with Peter in tow, I quickly figured out how to proceed. If I stopped the interviews, I might never get a chance to help them again. But if I continued, they might consider me shallow and crass. I decided to persevere on, so I left the kitchen looking for the Knowsiacki's teenage daughter. I found her in the living room texting on her smartphone, seemingly oblivious and unconcerned about her mother's condition.

"Excuse me, may I have a word with you about your recent family trip to Area 51?"

She ignored me, as her phone rang at that moment and she started talking trash about one of her friends to another friend. I quickly realised she was too self-centred to be helpful.

Turning around, I spotted Michael ducking into a room down the long hallway. I followed him. Poking my head inside the doorway, I saw he was listening to music on his brother's bed. "Hi!" I said, "You must be Michael."

At first, he sort of froze, like he wasn't supposed to be in there, then he responded, "Yep, and I know who you are. You're that guy, Jackson, who's interviewing my family. How's my Mom?"

"She's pretty sick, I think they'll take her to the hospital for observations."

"Good, I hope they can help her." Michael thought for a moment then said, "She has gotten worse since that nightmare trip to Area 51 when David got killed during the first assault. Of course, you know all about that!"

It took me a moment to digest the fact that Michael remembered everything that happened that day. "Ah, why don't you tell me what happened to David? How did he die? I wasn't there."

As most ten-year-olds do, he looked me over as if trying to decide my fate. "Ok, I'll tell you what happened to David. He was a high school bully and a dumb jock!

"He and my dad headed over to the assault line of losers. They were the most ragtag army of stupid looking geeks, jocks and mental cases, both male and female. It's no wonder most of them got killed or captured in their charge up that ridge behind the black mailbox.

My Dad and David got into an argument with some guy who thought he was leading the charge up the hill. The next thing I knew, David screamed, 'There ain't no land mines!' He runs past the black mailbox and up the road. He stops halfway up and starts jumping up and down, yelling, 'See! No landmines! No landmines!' After a few minutes of doing this, he gets tired and sits down on a good size stone."

I exclaimed, "There were no landmines! Are you kidding me?"

Michael smirked, "No. David was wrong. That stone he sat down on blew him to kingdom come! When the smoke cleared, the hole was twenty feet in diameter. I figure it must have been an anti-tank mine of some sort. At that point, the mob of nitwits went berserk and charged the compound."

I thought for a moment, "Ok, so why doesn't anyone in your family remember this but you?"

"My mom went hysterical, my father collapsed,

blaming himself, and my sister doesn't care about anyone but herself. We were all together when the short state trooper came over to us. Seems I am the only one who remembered the brain-zappy thing from the movies and the comic books. When I saw him get out the metal bar, I scrunched up my eyes really good, and my face too—it worked."

I grinned. "Well, I must declare that was pretty smart of you. Out of curiosity, did you take any pictures?"

"Absolutely!" He jumped off the bed and brought his smartphone over to me., "Get a load of these awesome movies I made! Tonight, I'm gonna upload them to my website and make some real money."

As Michael thumbed through the movies on his smartphone, he was distracted long enough for me to take out my memory stabiliser and delete his memories, along with every file on his phone and laptop.

His sister was easier to do; I caught her between keystrokes.

I felt terrible about the poor job someone did flashing Patricia's memory away so, on my way out of Pasadena, I stopped by the hospital and finished the job for both Patricia and Peter.

All of them are living a happy life, oblivious to what actually happened to them and the others at Area 51.

Another successful cover-up.

276

Cody and the Agent

By Gregg Cunningham

"Shit, I've already told you, this old guy...this boomer punk is like 'hey, Cody, dude, yo bro', you found any aliens yet?' And was really starting to piss me off while I'm chowing down with my crew, and I'm like 'dude, really how old are you?'"

I watch as the prisoner, Cody, hangs his head and slowly inhales on his cigarette, his handcuffs rattle on the wooden table and I can see the angry scar that slices through his hairline from his forehead to his neckline.

"You weren't a fan of his then?" I ask as he sits recounting the earlier hours of the attack.

"Shit no. The guy was a boomer, bouncing around the diner like some wannabee gangster, back slapping and hollering his stupid catchphrase while we set up our cameras and checked our gear. He was just there trying to hook up with Weebs half his age."

He exhales and takes another drag.

"We weren't there to fuck around Agent Smith. We were doing some serious investigation on the manipulation of our society by the Government and what your fuckwits are guarding here!"

"Agent smith, I like that. But I kind of see myself more as an Agent Coulson."

Cody points through the barriers to the guard whose back is turned away from the cell door.

"Yeh, well someone forgot to tell hulk here that he was a good guy. We all knew you fuckers had something down here and were gonna expose you for the liars you are...we're not some school class out to be manipulated by your fake news Facebook adverts for a bit of Cambridge anal...itica probing. We know what the hell is going on in here."

His eyes squint as the smoke drifts into them, and I watch on quietly as his foot bounces on the floor, agitated.

We sit in silence for a minute.

"How bad is it up there anyway?" he asks, but I suspect he already knows. I'm thinking he's worried about his friends as I pull out my report, a file thicker than a phonebook, filled with surveillance photographs and a list of the names of the dead and missing.

"Oh, it's bad," I reply, sliding the file across to Cody.

He takes it and begins thumbing through the images of the dead cosplay kids on the runway. Their lanky young anti vax bodies riddled with bullets. The pathetic look on his face makes me realise he's not ready to see any of that yet. But he needs to know what his madness has cost his country. All those dead college kids who followed his lead into the compound.

"One hundred and fifty-nine," I say as he stares at the dead bloody mascots, Naruto runners and bat shit crazy fame hungry Instagrammers, all lying in puddles of microwaved goo. All of them thinking that their voices mattered for the sake of a selfie. None of them worthy of being scraped up and shovelled into dog shit bags if you ask me.

Humanity's dumbest.

"We didn't know you guys would actually attack us." Was all he could mutter as he hangs his head staring at a kid wearing a Sonic Hedgehog onesie hung up lifeless and bloodied on our perimeter fence. That would be the front page money shot, for sure.

"Yeh, well that doesn't really matter now, does it Cody. You broke into a secret military facility, a treasonable offence, punishable by death. Didn't you get the hint last month? Didn't you watch the fake news?"

I pull out his battered laptop from my bag on the floor and the guard turns around slowly, peering through the metal bars at the two of us. I give him a nod and he walks away.

"We know your guys took him from the hanger, it's all here, on your hard drive." I tap the laptop and open the screen up.

"We watched them take him. What we want to know is where did you take him?"

He stares at me defiantly.

I stare back.

"Look kid, this is serious territory you're stumbling into now. I don't have the time nor the patience to calmly sit here and wait for you to cough it up. People are going to die. Lots of them. And I'm talking six figure numbers here. And that's in the first few days."

He looks at me with a smug grin, sucking on the cigarette like he is Marilyn Brando posing for his close up.

"Do you know who opened the door for that kid? Have you any Idea what the hell he was exposed to inside that lab?"

He shrugs, probably thinking he's holding all the aces and is ready to ask me the same question.

"Nope!"

"Have another look at his footage, Cody. You take a long hard look at what that kid actually found, and then once your dick has gone limp and your balls have shrivelled back into your stomach, maybe try answering that question again."

I stare through my standard issue sunglasses and stand up, spinning the laptop towards him and pressing play.

The guy on the screen, Zak Butcher, is dressed in black, wearing a GoPro mounted on his helmet and strapping some serious hardware to his arms. I see power packs and cables disappearing into Velcro pockets like he is a one-man roving news reporter. He's waving a large can of Monster drink at the shaky cam footage and smiling away as the desert landscape speeds past his face. Just another Kyle.

"BOOM! Yo dudes, Zak here live from Area five one, off to find me some aliens!" He laughs at the camera, slurping his energy drink. "CODE RED TEAM RULE!"

Cody sits there quietly staring at the screen while I walk to the door.

"I'm going to give you a bit of time to think things over, Cody, while I go for a coffee. When I come back, you better start talking."

I leave him in the cell and take a walk for a while.

When I come back, I see the horror on his face.

"Ready to talk now?" I grin.

He nods, wiping his face as the colour drains from his cheeks.

* * *

"He was just some red-neck punk who looked old enough to be my dad. I'd never met him before, but we followed each other on YouTube and played a couple of Fortnite games. Got all Stan on me when he met us in the diner, shaking Andy's hand and drooling, trying to buy us beer all night. He was just another groupie wanting to bask. I gave him my trainer name just to get rid of him so I could prep my gear."

"Trainer name?" I asked.

"Yeh, you know...Pokémon," he replies sheepishly.

"Like the kid's game?" I added with a quizzical look. "Aren't you a little old to be playing that stuff?"

He ignored that.

"He told us he was going 404—disappearing down the back roads down into 51—and wanted to give my blog a shout out. I said whatever. Ed wanted to leave because he was being such a dick, but we had a beer with the boomer and he told us his plan to catch a shiny. And hell, if I got a Legendary from him it would be worth it."

"A Legendary?"

"Yeh, a prize, a boss token, like when Leia hands out medals at the end of New hope, something to pin on your chest. It's a big deal."

"So, you wanted a Shiny so you thought you'd raid Area 51 for the honour?"

I shook my head internally this society today had no idea.

"Fuck that, man. I wanted to see the aliens, but if I could get my hands on an Arceus, I'd buy that for a dollar too. I didn't actually think anything was going to happen, just a bit of shirt fronting, perhaps a scuffle or two, just not...not this!"

I nodded as he threw the images of the dead onto the table.

"Go on."

"Yeh, well Ed and Luke packed up our quad bikes and the old dude left on his after we all went our separate ways. He sent me a few video links during the storming, but I wasn't too bothered about them until he broke through the fence. Then all hell broke loose."

Cody sighed and drew on the cigarette butt again.

"The old guy had balls, I'll give him that. Sorta like that old guy who flew his plane into the alien mothership in that Independence Day movie. He was the first to get the footage onto the net, and it went viral in minutes. We couldn't see much, but the fact that the news channels reported on the blackout—and the fact you were trying to block it—was news enough."

He smiled scratching at his bloody head wound.

"Once we saw he had gotten inside, we thought we'd help him out and create a diversion; sent our drones into the air, set off the fireworks and rode our quads through the fences. Andy led the way; his quad was on the tarmac first, he celebrated with a couple of tarmac donuts…"

He drifted off, staring at the ceiling while stifling the tears in his eyes.

"You fuckers didn't even give Ed and Luke a warning shot before you opened up…"

I said nothing as he wiped away his anger.

"Anyhow, when Andy went through and I swung past Luke's body, you lot opened up on the anti vaxxer kids being used as human shield for the Runners behind the fence line." He shrugged.

"Somehow your stormtroopers missed me. I just took off, weaved through the furries and made for the hangers down the back where the Pokémon gym was; that was our marker. That was where our guy, JACKson5, had said he would be."

"Was he the insider?"

He stared at me again, realising the game was well and truly over.

"Word was that Andy had spoken on the dark web with someone on the inside of Area 51. They said they wanted to talk, show us something that was going down. If we could get inside the camp, he'd be waiting for us at the old Pokémon gym. He knew it was going to be activated the day the raid was on. It was an easy reference point to find with our phones. Just an old game location you couldn't get into when you played."

"You didn't know this guy, then? Had never met him?"

"No, he just went by the name of JACKson5."

"What did he want to show you?"

"Shit, I don't know. He said he wanted to show the world what was really going on, and had some info from the inside. I didn't believe him, but y'know, why the hell not? When we saw Zak's live feed and heard the guy was inside the gym, we checked for ourselves and realised he wasn't spoofing and was actually inside the camp."

"So, you believed him then?"

"Hell, we were just winging it. If we got inside the fence line, the news was going to show the footage on the hour, every hour. We didn't expect to actually break through. It was you guys who forced our hand. A lot of kids thought why the fuck not and just went for it, like they were Avengers or some other super heroes out for revenge. I don't think they comprehended the fact that it meant they would probably fucking die. I mean most of them had rich-ass daddies who they thought would bust them out of jail in a day or two. The others reckoned they would be free after the 'GoFundMe' pages would be set up to pay their court fees and bail money. Anti-vaxxer kids are dumb as shit these days. They don't have a clue what goes on outside Facebook or Instagram, too busy Tik Tokking. They just thought they would get famous, grab an interview, and get on TV."

"So, the plan was finding this JACKson5 conspiracy sympathiser and what...he would just let you inside and show you the Martians. It that it?"

"That was it. We'd get inside, take a few pictures inside the alien hangers, and split. It would get us a few million hits and we'd expose you fuckers for what you really are."

"Patriotic protectors of our country?" I smirked.

"No, Gestapo fascist bully boys!" He sneered. "And you can't keep me here without a lawyer!"

I laughed at that.

"We already know what you fucks have inside those hangers, you can't hide the footage any longer. The game is up!"

My sigh was long, he still didn't get it.

"So, what? You think because you actually saw inside that old hanger and saw that it was filled with nothing more than the relics of old cold war propaganda—Project Aquatone, Project Rainbow—that you somehow exposed some grand old conspiracy for your channel, Cody?"

"I WANT TO BELIEVE!" He leaned forward and sneered. He was smirking at me like he had finally found the truth.

"Listen up, Mulder, even Project Oxcart is over sixty years old now. What you found inside there is nothing but old news, son."

"WE SAW THE FUCKING ALIENS DUDE." He thrust

forward. "ZAK POSTED THE FUCKING VIDEO BEFORE YOU SHUT HIM DOWN, AND ANDY GOT HIM OUT BEFORE YOU COULD DO ANYTHING TO STOP US!" Spittle flew from his mouth.

"THE WHOLE WORLD HAS SEEN WHAT YOU'RE HIDING BEHIND THESE WALLS. YOU FUCKS ARE FINISHED...AND IF YOU THINK YOU'LL BE ABLE TO FIND ANDY AND ZAK...WELL LET ME TELL YOU SOMETHING...THEY'VE GONE OFF THE GRID. YOU'LL NEVER FIND THEM...THE TRUTH IS OUT THERE!"

This was all I wanted to hear. They had got the subject outside the compound. It was only a matter of time now.

I stood up and walked to the door, nodding to the guard who unlocked the cell, then did my best Columbo turn around, saying nothing as I reached into my suit pocket.

"Is this the part where you neutralise my brain Agent Smith?" He shrugged, destined to his fate.

"Cody, I told you already, I'm not the bad guy here. It wasn't me who got attacked and bitten inside that hanger. It wasn't me who became an infected carrier. It wasn't me who released an infected enemy of the state into the American public to spread a virus capable of wiping out nearly the whole of the human race."

I pulled out his cell phone from my pocket and placed it by his hand as I leant over and whispered in his ear.

"Call your mother before it's too late, son. You and

your alien liberators have just released the deadliest pathogen into society since your planet's Black Plague engulfed Europe...and it had nothing to do with the Governments of Earth."

I removed my sunglasses for Cody to look into my exposed slanted green eyes in horror. I blinked for effect as he recoiled in shock.

He had no cell coverage of course; we couldn't let that kind of knowledge get out now. I just wanted to let him see the screenshot of the Legendary shiny Arceus—Zak had left him spinning on his Pokémon Raid screen—just before he realised the whole unbelievable truth.

"Yeh, I guess you do believe now... It's all about the Lizards, Cody. We are amongst you! Always have been."

* * *

"Agent Jackson!" The voice met me in the corridor.

"Sir?" I replied, turning to wait.

"I want a briefing by 0600 hours on Project Arceus. I presume it was a total success?"

"Yes, Sir. Total chaos, as predicted. We have released the subjects into the wild."

"Good, and Swarm forecast predictions?"

"Worldwide domination within days, Sir."

"Good man. I'm sure they will get a few of us, but we

surely can watch them destroy themselves this time?"

I couldn't help myself, replying with a grin, "Sir, they can't stop all of us!"

2019 to 2029

292

Newsfeed

By Rhiannon Bird

They were calling it the *Swarm* now. The thriving mass of aliens that I could see on live footage. I watched as they poured out and destroyed the crowd, practically devouring them. I was practically glued to the screen. A voice broke over the footage.

"It seems some of the Swarm has managed to get near our news crew. But don't worry, they have military personnel there to protect them." The camera shook violently, followed by a scream, and the screen went dark.

Suddenly no one could see what was happening with the Swarm and the world broke into chaos.

294

Monster Energy

By Stephen Coghlan

"We've already lost containment." Brix sighed as she looked up from the screen. The monitor's glow cast an eerie shadow across her stress-beaten features. "It's only a matter of time."

Cursing, Colonel Caruthers shakes his head.

"We warned them." He hisses through his teeth. "We warned them."

"Reno is rendered inert already," Brix continues, pointing to the map of Nevada on the tactical wall. "And once it hits the main waterlines..."

"I know." Caruthers sighs. "Absolute destruction will follow. You almost have to admire it." He chuckles bitterly. "Who knew Mountain Dew would be the death of us all."

Mountain Dew, the nickname the scientists had given the green goop that they had found years ago. It took the lives of several researchers before it had been properly contained from the crash site and it had been nurtured, probed, until it was determined to be a self-replicating food source for the inhabitants of the crashed shuttle.

It was the monster's energy.

Grabbing the radio, Colonel Caruthers yelled into it, making a request of his guardsmen. "How's the evacuation going?"

"Not well, sir," replied the voice on the other end. "It's reproducing faster than expected, and fire does nothing. We can barely stay ahead of it."

Looking back at Brix, the officer asked, "When will it stop growing?"

"From previous tests at Owen's Lake, sir," Brix replied, chewing on her pencil, "when it's satisfied that it's reached its required mass. Only then will it go dormant and be prepared for harvest."

It was one more nightmare scenario, hampering the forces already strained from rampant diseases, released aliens, and in one case, a new and nasty viral, inhuman, STD. It was a war for Earth, which humanity was losing.

"How long, until it reaches us?" the colonel asked, peering nervously at the clock.

"Five minutes, sir, more or less."

"I see. Thank you, Brix. You're free to go, if you want."

She smiled sadly at the colonel, and that was her only reply. She wasn't going anywhere, because there was nowhere to go. Mountain Dew would be on them soon, unless the drivers of the mobile command centre managed to fix the vehicle's engine in time.

What a lousy time for the radiator to pop.

Cursing, Colonel Caruthers pulled out a Camel from his carton. Regulations banned smoking inside operations, *but regulations be damned*, he thought as he pulled out his lighter.

"Sir, could you smoke outside?" Brix asked, smiling at her own disbelief of the situation. "I can't work with you cloying my senses."

"Working to the end?" the colonel asked, and Brix straightened in her seat.

"I'm a scientist first, sir." She smiled sadly. "And, as the surviving knowledgebase on the green goo, I want to make sure my observations are recorded."

It was admirable, and who was he to not understand a duty. Opening the door, he stepped into the dawn's light and saw the drivers of the operation's centre, struggling over the open hood.

"Any news, soldiers?" the colonel asked, and both young men looked up from their work.

"We..." The corporal paused, wiped a stained sleeve across his sweating face. "We couldn't stop the leak. Sorry, sir."

"It's alright soldier, you tried." Holding out the carton, the commanding officer offered a final smoke to his men, feeling very much like he was granting them their last rights. They both refused.

"You've both performed well. You can run, if you want." He offered a final hope, but both of his troopers declined, staring at the glowing green on the horizon.

"Will it hurt, sir?" the other operator asked.

"I don't know." There was no point in lying. "But I can tell you, reporting a failure to stop it would hurt my pride, and that's a pain I can't live with."

It was visible now, flowing towards them.

"Screw it, sir." The first driver grabbed a smoke, and the colonel lit it for him.

"It's been a hell of an honour, soldiers." The colonel smiled as they watched it reach the truck, before he chuckled and shook their hands.

"I'll see you on the other side," were the last words he said as the goop reached their boots.

It was time to become energy for the beasts.

They Held Their Own

By Stephen Coghlan

The 437th Armoured Hussars are no strangers to combat. Despite most of their experience being classified beyond Ultra-Secret, they have earned a reputation as one of the toughest companies in existence, and yet, despite their rich and glorified history, they have never encountered anything before the social media rebellion of two cycles past.

On the morning of May 26th, 2021, Second platoon travelled far from the confines of the local firebase. Led by second lieutenant Yera Ra'id, the platoon was in high spirits. After such a long time into their tour, the platoons had only received a handful of light casualties despite their multiple engagements with alien forces.

The team had been sent into the heavy forests southwest of Bảo Lộc in order to hunt down the last of a group of escapees, who had fled after a limited firefight at the city's walls only the day before. Accompanying the mobile platoon was a fireteam of walkers, hulking bipedal tanks eight meters tall and armed with an array of close and long-range support weaponry.

The lead walker pilot, Cpl Kenward was a veteran warrior who had served one tour already in Southeast Asia and was the recognised local database of knowledge. She was jokingly referred to as "Mom" by the troops. Her partner, Lance Cpl Caspar, was a by-the-books soldier who had landed with the 437th when they had first arrived

Cpl Kenward's best friend, Sgt Theomund Witters, was the die-hard leader of Second platoon. He was a recognised veteran that all senior officers consulted for advice. Although the troopers joked that Witters was older than the United States military, he was considered as the father figure that kept their unit functioning in prime condition.

The 66th would normally have provided air cover, but half of the unit was being shipped out to a higher risk-area of central China away, where another uprising had occurred with the greys, whose space fleet was being a problem for the local 125th mechanised division. Lack of air support did not bother the second platoon, as they had faced the same enemy many times before and had always come out victorious.

Despite being covered in vegetation, the air in the forest was too thin for humans, even those used to high altitude, to breathe, thanks to the terraforming efforts that had been used to suppress the local human population. Therefore, anyone venturing into the local atmosphere had to bring either oxygen, or compressor packs with them. That was why all foot soldiers had to wear the Ormarr combat armour. It was heavy gear, especially with the added weight of a compressor pack added to it, but against the arrows and few stolen weapons of the insurgent greys and whatever humans they had captured and forced to fight on their side, it was more than sufficient for most combat situations.

The only respite a soldier got from their suit was when they were inside one of Second Platoons' four Armoured Personnel Carriers (APC). Two of the APCs were the Las gun carrying Satomi class carriers that carried first and second section respectively, while third section was issued the mortar support Tira class, and the command APC was an older Bast model that had been upgraded with new Railtillary. It was filled with supplies, but even so, it still had more legroom than the other three units, but the excess space could quickly disappear, if needed, to become an impromptu medical station.

First Section, the grenadiers, was led by Cpl Bevin and Lance Cpl Norward. Norward was an experienced grenadier who had joined the second platoon just before deployment after his unit, the 212th, had been decimated only months before. Troopers Tosh and Finlay had become part of Norward's fireteam, as they wielded the Hellbound grenade launcher, which was capable of exploding its ordnance mid-flight.

After her first tour had left her without the use of her left arm, Cpl Bevin had served as an instructor while the limb regrew under the watchful eyes of skilled physicians who had adapted the xeno tech. When the medics had finally given her a clean bill of health, she had rejoined the 437th. Her fireteam was a little heftier in numbers than Norward's, and consisted of Marksman Armand, Nan-Launcher Vojin, and Riflemen Asim and Williams.

Second Section was led by Cpl Knight, aka "Puff-Boy". He was a gruff old dog who had never risen above the rank of Corporal because he did not enjoy the logistics of his job, and more often than not passed all the responsibilities to Lance Cpl Malloy, a recent graduate who had earned her stripe because of her natural leadership abilities.

Second's other gunner, Trooper Lafayette was several years Knight's junior. The two had formed an odd love-hate relationship that many of the other sections considered off-centre, but the rest of Knight's unit just accepted. Dubbed "Pig-Boy", he wielded a LMG, which was easier to maintain than Knight's minigun mark LXVI.

Malloy's boys, as she called them, were composed of Riflemen Gilmore, Lance, and Molan who knew to listen to Malloy when trouble started, but always kept one ear out for Knight's command because, at his order, one of the three riflemen would run for more ammo for either of the heavy gunners. Nan-Launcher Nabhan was excluded from that duty, as well as the platoon's only engineer, Eadwards.

Specialist Eadwards was quiet and withdrawn. She was the only trooper to have a university education, and her brains and mousy attitude made her seem small and tender until one upset her. She was very prone to violent outbursts, and was well trained in close-quarters-combat, which had led to more than one disciplinary action.

Third Section was the mortar support. Its leader, Cpl Quan, was pragmatic, but also able to laugh in the face of danger. His second-in-command, Macen, was often put in defence of the two mortar troopers Gann and Fremont, who had joined together during a recruiting drive at their high school. Marksman Macen, who was Lance Cpl Macen's little brother, Riflemen Viljo, Zander, and Slivergunner Kim rounded out the remaining members of the team.

Outside of the three Sections, Radio-Man Alvar, a slender almost-boy whose father was a field commander for another battalion, and Medic Sgt Leigh, a recognised field surgeon who was on loan as the Second Platoon's normal medic was away on maternity leave, rounded out the trooper headcount.

The first two days of pursuit were uneventful. The fireteams took turns rotating point, with one walker following along behind, ripping up trees where necessary to make room for the APC's. The rest of the troopers marched beside or behind the vehicles and remaining walker, while selected troopers moved as scouts through the woods. Every night, the platoon would stop for a rest, where Medic Leigh would deliver hot-packs to the soldiers, drivers, and technicians. At night, one section would end up on watch, but the section that started on watch would be allowed to sleep the day before in the bunks of their respective APC's.

Although the troopers grumbled about their long marches, they did not envy those who were crammed into the APCs. Each vehicle had two staff who continually switched roles throughout the day in order to stave off boredom. When not driving, the free operator would check the navigation system and supplies, handle communications, and inspect and clean the weapons protecting them. At night, before resting, the APC teams did a formal inspection of their vehicles, before sleeping in their cockpits. It was a cramped and uncomfortable job, but at least they didn't have to walk all day, and they had unlimited access to the sit-toilets, which meant they were the only troopers who did not have to wear catheters.

It was the third evening that would go down in infamy.

The first indication that something was wrong was the appearance of a strange weather pattern that developed directly in Second Platoon's line-of-march. High above, in an orbiting AWAC, Specialist Gliffs, the 66th's meteorologist, stared in awe.

"I'd been watching over Vietnam when I saw this new weather pattern start." He recalls. "At first I thought it wouldn't be that odd; The south had not been colonised for that long, so there was still a chance for unknown systems to evolve thanks to the terraforming."

Gliffs tried to radio down to the troops on the ground, but communication was already becoming garbled. A directly aimed laser signal pierced the forming storm and got him through to Alvar, and although the radioman passed the message on to Lt Ra'id, the platoon commander shrugged and simply continued marching towards the cloud.

Inside Second Section's APC, Eadwards launched one of the platoon's remote recon drones. Called "Frisbees" by those who slogged on the ground, due to their shape, Drones were often found hovering ahead of troops when subtlety was not an issue. Their sensor laden bodies were great for providing forward reconnaissance. If a drone fell, and was not recovered by someone who did not have the right transponder code, they self-detonated.

As the drone was catapulted from the APC, Trooper Gilmore watched it fly into the growing clouds. "The drone took off and accelerated to just under mach speed. I followed its flight and watched it get close to the clouds ahead of us. To my amazement, the craft became unstable before flipping over and falling to the ground."

"It went straight ahead, then straight down." Lance Cpl Norward, who had been unable to sleep, watched from the turret of 1st section's APC. "One moment it was all right, and then it was all wrong."

Because of the drone's failure to fly, Sgt Witters immediately stormed into Eadwards' moving APC.

Their conversations were muted and quiet, and, without his usual gruff demeanour, Witters turned and left the vehicle. Witters recounts, "Eadwards had flown drones through hurricanes without so much as earning a scratch to them. The failure of one flight immediately left me feeling cautious, and I asked her what was wrong, she answered that the drone had simply stopped responding, as if it had flown out of radio range, which should have been impossible. Those drones could fly for hundreds of kilometres without even showing a momentary lapse. By the time I got to her she was already running diagnostics on all of her systems. I felt confident in her ability, so I left in order to recover the drone."

But Lance Cpl Malloy had taken the initiative.

"As soon as she saw the drone fall," Gilmore explained, "Malloy grabbed my shoulder. Since we, including Lance and Molan, were at point, we would be able to get to it first. I heard Malloy over the Tac-Net as she explained what we were doing. Sgt Witters attempted to reply, but his signal was already getting fuzzy to my ears."

They four of them ran towards the drone, each one wary of an ambush, but they made it there without incident.

Gilmore continued. "It had crashed at the edge of a tiny field. As soon as I got to the treeline, I took cover and watched out for an ambush. Malloy did the same. Lance and Molan, covered by us, ran out into the field and grabbed the drone. The damn thing was in one piece, without any damage to it save a few nicks it had earned in the fall."

Malloy embellishes, "The drone was still attempting to transmit and receive. I had tuned my transponder to its signals and could clearly hear the bursts of information as it tried to re-establish communication, but our Tac-Net was silent. I could only hear [the other three] who were with me."

It was a strange sensation for them to be so isolated. Throughout their tour, the entire platoon had always been able to hear everyone through the Tac-Net, an open channel that was like a conference call which involved everyone.

The radios on the Ormarr combat armours were wide reaching, high frequency devices that both beamed horizontally, and vertically, to the many communication satellites that had been seeded orbiting the planet. If that failed suits could talk to each other either via closed contact, where a trooper touching another which would link their suits through a mild electrical field, or by laser communication devices, but they had to be aimed precisely at who one wanted to communicate with, and since the fire-team's line of sight was blocked by the foliage, they could not use that method to reach the rest of the team.

Molan: "It was scary suddenly not being able to hear the rest of the platoon. Grabbing the drone, I lifted it and turned back, practically ready to sprint for the safety of the others." But then Malloy spoke up, and her voice, which was level and serene, brought much needed relief to the team.

"Her controlled voice soothed my nerves." Molan continued. "And brought me back from my state of panic. I could have kicked myself right then and there for almost freaking out."

Back in better shape, the four began to leapfrog backwards.

Gillmore: "We were tense. It was as if we were being jammed. We were ready to be ambushed, but that didn't happen. As we withdrew from the field, the Tac-Net began to become louder with the others' voices."

The familiar sound of Sgt Witters' voice became predominant in their ears. Everyone else in the platoon had been hearing his rather indignant tone climb, and as Trooper Vojin put it, "I had never heard the Sarge use such profanity before. I learned a few new words that day."

Sgt Witter's tirade came to an abrupt end.

Witters: "No sooner did Molan's team return than Eadwards called me back to her APC. Alvar was with her, and I could tell by the new dent in the wall that they had found something that neither liked."

They were alone.

* * *

Back in the air, Specialist Gliffs was worried.

"I'd never seen anything so spontaneous or dense. [It] was so thick that my sensors couldn't penetrate past a few meters into the clouds. After a few attempts, I turned to [Commodore Cyphers], and informed him what was going on."

Cyphers looked intimidating to new recruits. The whole left side of his face was coated in synth-skin, an artificial flesh, thanks to a battle many years before. He scowled at the news, before he ordered a geo-synchronous orbit over the lost platoon.

Determined to reach them, Gliffs busied himself by trying alternatives.

* * *

Eadwards had discovered some strange particles in the air. Whatever it was, it was scattering all of their communications once the signal travelled beyond a range of only a few dozen meters. Silently elated at the revelation, she began collecting samples.

Lt. Ra'id ordered first section awake, as a precaution, before he called the section leaders together for a brief meeting. Cpl Quan remembers it fondly. "It was Sgt Witters, Cpl Bevin, Lance Cpl Molan and I. It wasn't that Ra'id ran a diplomacy, but he did use us for advice. Both Kenward and Casper listened in, but as usual, neither of them got out of their mech's. After a briefing of our situation, we all thought about our options. Ra'id wanted to continue on but was swayed by Cpl Kenward."

Kenward: "There was no point continuing forward. We'd just be wandering blind. Without the capability to see more than a few meters ahead we'd easily have missed our targets if they passed us by. We could have turned back, but we didn't know how long the storm would last for; it could have dissipated in a few short hours."

The team had all the data from the geo-mapping that had already been performed. There was a hill not that far away that was the tallest thing around. Leaving Sgt Witters in charge of forming a perimeter, Ra'id took Alvar, Marksman Armand, thump-gunner Tosh and troopers Kim and Zander to try and re-establish communications with the rest of the forces.

Lance Cpl Norward watched them go. "I felt nervous all of a sudden. As they disappeared into the trees, I imagined I saw ghosts walking with them."

Known to be a strong believer in elastic defence, Sgt Witters was left in an unfavourable position. The little copse of trees that his soldiers were hiding in was barely large enough to hold everyone together. Between them and the rest of the woods was open field, in some places only a few meters away, but behind them, they had almost thirty meters of open terrain. If they were attacked, any enemy would have to cross the open ground, but they had the option of encircling the platoon by moving through the surrounding bush.

In order to solve that, Witters ordered the freshly awakened 1st section into the surrounding tree line, where they began to install flashers, trip-wires, and claymores. The other two sections hurriedly dug in as the APC crews grumbled before entrenching their vehicles.

The worst struggling that had been done by 2nd Lt. Ra'id's team was getting up the hill. It wasn't too steep, just ponderous. After a jog, they had scaled the terrain on hands and knees. Ormarr combat armour functioned well through swamp, water, and relatively flat ground, but scrabbling up the incline had left the team tired.

On the crest, Alvar spent two hours trying to get through to anyone. Even laser communication was unable to raise the rest of second Platoon, although they could clearly see them from where they were.

They could have tried using visual communications, Alvan was well versed in semaphore and Morse code, and he did have a bright multi-light with him, which was more than strong enough to be seen by Eadwards in the growing dusk, but they didn't dare risk it. A thick and dark pillar of smoke could be seen growing in the direction that Second Platoon had been heading.

Accepting the futility of their ability to communicate with anyone, LT. Ra'id's team began a subtle descent, but unfortunately, dense foliage hid them from even the sight of the walkers.

Back at the defensive line, Trooper Gann, one of the mortar operators, was checking the state of her weapon when she heard something she didn't recognise. "I'd often listen to the external pickups because I found ambient noises soothing, but then, in the background, I heard a rumble like nothing that we had heard before on this planet."

Trooper Fremont, Gann's associated partner with the mortars, recalls that moment. "As soon as [Gann] stopped, I knew something was strange. [Gann] has this tendency, when something isn't right to cock her head and listen with her left ear. She froze in a tableau, mortar tube in her hand, kneeling, helmet bent to the side."

Trooper Macen, section 3's marksman and little brother

to Lance Cpl Macen, was lying prone on top of the section's APC. "I had been using my telemental link to scroll through all of my helmet's and scope's visual sensors, and anything beyond twenty meters became snow, except for my optical view. I was bored, and about to grab a nap when I felt something thumping through the ground. I knew it wasn't the APC; it had been off since the stripes and his team had left."

"It was like a collection of heavy drums were being beaten all at once." Gilmore.

Norward: "It felt like my suit was thumping like a speaker."

Sgt Witters reacted almost instantly to the new sensations, and called for Eadwards to bury a sonic spike. A thirteen and a half centimetre tube, filled with microphones, was pneumatically launched into the earth from the APC, and buried itself, using a small drill bit, into rock so hard that its drill bit snapped.

As soon as it was deep enough, Eadwards broadcast the signal over the Tac-Net.

Malloy: "It was like the sound of a football riot. Hundreds of impacts against the ground all at once, growing steadily larger."

Aboard the walkers Kenward was noticing a similar event as the trees around them began to tremble. "My walker was shorter than most of the old-growth trees around me. However, I noticed all of them shaking as if their roots were being forced around by some titanic force."

Lt. Ra'id's team was only a few hundred meters from the hill. They all stopped when the vibrations became too powerful to ignore. With a motion of his hand, the few members of his group spread out in preparation for an ambush.

With a roar, every APC came to life as the drivers started their engines. Each of the crew who weren't in the driver's seats ran to their individual vehicle's targeting computers. Weapons of all calibres came alive under their command, and friendlies immediately became non-targets. Marksmen prepared their rifles, and the walkers sank low into battle formations. The armoured behemoths carefully aligned their heavy metals over their joints and weaker, softer materials.

Worried, Witters gave the order for 1st section to return, but they were spread out, and only Asim, Vojin and Williams, who were laying sensors to the rear, returned. Cpl Bevin, Lance Cpl Norward, and the remaining thump-gunner, Finlay, were still in the woods to the side of the front.

As the thumping in his chest continued, Norward suggested a tactical withdrawal to his companions. "We started back, and we were almost to the tree line when everything went tits up."

A wave of creatures, unlike anything the troops had seen before, exploded from the front and charged directly towards Second Platoon's position.

"What the hell are they?" Gilmore asks. "They don't look at all like any greys we'd ever seen.

"They were short, tall, mixed builds, alternate colours, and armed with a variety of weapons for close in, not long range warfare," Maloy recounts with an uncertain tone. "But there were hundreds of them."

Sgt Witters did not hesitate. "When there's a thousand guys with pointy sticks intent on killing you, even if you're in a tank, their sheer numbers would do you in." Despite still having three troops from First section in an unknown position, Witters made a call that would find him facing a tribunal months later, for having endangered those still in the woods. He ordered his soldiers to open fire.

The opening salvo was all shock and awe, and under such an intense barrage, few things survived, but those that did, stunned the soldiers.

"It was not what we expected." Kenward recalls. "My walker's lasblast hit the front ranks, but where greys withered and vanished, these things, although the first few died, others kept coming, even though they were missing arms, legs, and bits off of their torsos."

Gilmore "I fired a single shot, and my first round hit this lanky, twisted beast. It had a huge mouth and carried a spear that looked like it was made from guts and bone. My round caught it above one of its squinting eyes, and the thing staggered forward, even with half of its head blown off. A second shot dropped it."

The opening barrage was not missed by the three in the woods.

Finlay: "We dropped prone, and the trees above our heads exploded. They were shredded by the sheer firepower. From where we were, we could see the enemy." [Shudders] "It was as if they had been dragged from my worst nightmares. I couldn't look at them without feeling like I was going to go insane."

Norward: "We could see them, just a hoard of them, charging the rest of the platoon. They either hadn't seen us, or didn't care about us, but we watched them get cut to pieces, and still keep fighting.

"And then, that's when I went dark."

The old trees that surrounded them surrendered to the scythe-like action of all the ordnance that had been used. Several of the stout trunks, which had survived centuries of fires, floods, and other acts of God, failed under the stress of mankind. One of the collapsed trees landed directly on top of Norward. The impact literally drove him into the ground and dented his armour, but despite his communication and sensor packages being destroyed, his suit remained intact, and his life support continued to function. Since he was the closest to the platoon, and Finlay and Bevin had their backs to him, no one saw him disappear.

Finlay: "All of a sudden, Norward's medical info went flat-line. I turned around to see what had happened, but he was gone."

The communication team was not having it any easier. Ra'id had decided not to press his luck by firing into the charging ranks, and had instead ordered a retreat back up the hill. Marksman Armand was sent ahead, and she had clambered up the risen earth at a full sprint before she found a position to cover the fire team's retreat. The others had begun a more careful, leapfrog movement, when the enemy finally noticed them.

Kim was the first one to fire. Her slivergun barked, and the many small flechettes flew in a tightly controlled pattern directly into the centre mass of the first thing that had noticed them. The result: Cut off, lightly armed, already tired, Ra'id's team became the primary target. Desperate for some relief, Ra'id ordered Tosh, the grenadier, to fire his Hellbound grenades at minimum fuse. The resulting explosions stunned and killed many of their foe, providing a momentary lapse in the enemy's charge, which was just enough for them to scramble to the foot of the hill where Armand was able to provide better cover as the others climbed towards her.

The bulk of Second Platoon was still doing well. They had changed from the opening savagery, and had begun "talking" their guns, where one would fire against a target of opportunity, before stopping, and letting the trooper beside them take over. It preserved ammo, and let the soldiers collect their thoughts, even though there was not a second of silence. There were too many of their foes.

Witters: "They just kept coming. Nauseating light, pain sonics and agonizing microwaves were thrown from the APCs, but didn't slow the enemy in the slightest."

Gilmore: "I don't know what they were, and not one of them looked like another. I saw a thing that looked like an octopus with legs, so I cut it down. Behind it, came what looked like a Minotaur, so I shot it next, and behind that was a bulbous, pink blob with claws for arms, and I emptied the rest of my magazine into it before it stopped moving."

Knight made the call for more munitions, and Malloy put her boys to work.

Molan: "I ran to our APC. The rear hatch was down, waiting for me. I grabbed the box and returned, passing Lance and Gilmore on the way."

Molan got to Knight just in time and was able to reload his platoon commander while Lafayette covered them.

Then there was silence.

The field was a scene of carnage. Creatures of all types, shapes, and forms lay dead and dying. In some places the bodies were piled ten high. Calling out, Witters ordered a status report. The results were promising, as no one was hurt, yet.

With the absence of gunfire, Bevin and Finlay made the

decision to return to the rest of the platoon. Despite their best efforts, they had been unable to locate Norward under the debris.

Finlay: "We had tried, but those trees were so wide and thick that there was no way we could lift them by ourselves. Even the walkers would have had a hard time dragging the logs away. Bending low, we made a mad dash for our front lines. It was hard going, as the bodies underfoot were slippery."

It went from snafu to fubar in an instant.

Marksman Macen saw the two and yelled happily, but his cheer of victory died in his throat. "I was watching them through my scope, when out of the trees, flies this spear. It hits Bevin in the head, and stuck fast inside her helmet."

Bevin died, but her body did not know it yet. She stumbled on for three more steps before she sank to her knees. Tough as she was, she could not survive having her brain scrambled by the crude weapon that had pierced her skull. Finlay paused, turned back to help her section leader, and then the woods exploded again.

The enemy had regrouped and had caught them in an ambush.

Desperate to save the two soldiers, the walkers stood and advanced side-by-side, while Leigh, Asim and Williams hurried to get the wounded out of harm's way.

Kenward: "Caspar and I moved ahead. Our machines

were more than strong enough to protect us, or so we thought."

The two walkers poured their fire at point-blank range into the tree line. Despite their withering barrage, some of the enemies still advanced. When they got close enough, the walkers began stomping their legs, and crushed even more underfoot.

"We were confident. After all, we were giants." Kenward shakes her head. "We thought we were gods."

Asim and Williams pulled Bevin to her feet, and despite the damage to her brain, they convinced her to walk towards the command APC, where Leigh had returned to, and had begun setting up the medical bed. Finlay began to lay down cover fire with her thump-gun, and at Witters' request, the two walkers began to walk backwards towards the rest of the platoon. Despite their best attempts, however, the two metal behemoths were unable to stop all the enemies from crawling on them.

Kenward: "They were all over us. I asked Caspar to 'swat' me, which is where our walkers rubbed against each other. He started on my side, when I saw this little red bastard crawl onto his primary magazine. It looked right at me, smiled, and then blew itself up."

Walkers had a special design in their magazines. In the event of an explosion, the casing was shaped so that the explosion blew out the back of the walking tank, preserving the pilot and most of the equipment, but it just so happened that, when the creature detonated, it did so in such a way that the casing cracked, and the blast travelled inwards.

Caspar never stood a chance, and his machine sagged into itself, before toppling over to lay still.

Other things were clambering up Kenward's machine. In order to protect herself, she activated her machine's APP's, or anti-personal pods. They were bulbous packages of shrapnel between the "knee" and "foot."

Normally, detonations of APP were considered safe, but Kenward was too close to the front rank. The ensuing blast did knock the offending parties off her suit, but at the same time, peppered the troops she had been trying to defend.

Asim was between the walker and the rest of the rescue party, and he took the brunt of the blast. His armour saved his life, but his suit was pierced multiple times. Unable to stand, he collapsed.

It was just what the enemy had been waiting for. They surged ahead and fell upon the wounded trooper.

Finlay: "I picked myself up, shaken from the blast. They were already on top of Asim, and they tore open his suit, even though we were firing all around him."

His screams were audible for all to hear. It was the first real sounds of agony that any of Second Platoon had made and despite wanting to help, the entire group could not advance, since the enemy had attacked with renewed purpose.

Then it was over.

In guilt, Kenward, who had made it back to the safety of the ranks, where Quan and marksman Macen finished off the few hangers-on, took it upon herself to saturate the area, purifying it in artillery fire.

The explosions were not missed by those above. Desperate to help, and unable to communicate with the beleaguered forces, Cyphers asked the rest of the 437th and those who could be spared from the 44th for help. They were mobilised in minutes, but no sooner did they reach the edge of the storm front, than their dropships failed. Without power, they flew a little better than lead bricks, but although they crashed into the ground, their vessels survived with minimal damage, and no hands were lost. While the crews stayed behind, the entirety of the force began a forced march to relieve their brothers in arms.

By the time night had fallen, it was not looking good. Strange light could be seen from the enemy ranks, and their frequent charges ensured that no one got any rest. Despite the ferocity of the attacks, Second Platoon held on, although twice, enemy ranks had made it close enough so that the fighting dissolved into hand-to-hand combat.

When it came to melee combat, each trooper carried their personal preference. Some carried the SlamDance, which was an armoured fist that discharged upon impact, frying synapses and locking muscles. Others carries P-Sticks, which were batons that heated the air around them into a plasmatic state. Still more carried Heat Blades, which were machete-like knifes with a monofilament tip that burned well above 1,800 Kelvin, but most carried the K-Bar mark XX, which were larger, brutal versions of their old counterparts. The mark XX was especially useful against armoured individuals, as it had been designed to ensnare and shatter military gear.

Yet, even with all of their advantages, Second Platoon was wearing down. Several troopers had been wounded, and the command APC was slowly filling with the injured, while their ammo stores were being vigorously reduced.

If it was bad for those in the patch of woods, it was worse for those on the hill. Ra'id's team was exhausted. The enemy had made many attempts to push the small team off the incline. If it hadn't been for Gunner Tosh's careful conservation of ammo, and Armand's skilled shooting, they would have been overrun many times over.

Alvar was still trying to cut through the distortion to anyone, but had no success. He and Ra'id watched though, as the field below began to grow with light as one torch lit another.

The weird firelight was the first thing that Norward saw. "I came to surrounded by dirt. It was slow going, with my suit damaged, but I managed to pull my head and chest out from beneath the fallen trees. I was halfway to freedom when I saw the enemy. They were less than ten meters ahead of me. One by one they were passing a torch, lighting others. It was surreal. I thought of lying still, staying quiet, but then I saw them preparing weapons. They were getting ready to charge."

Despite having a tree fall on top of him, Norward had managed to maintain his hold on his rifle. The Korat rifle he wielded was the common weapon of the footsoldier, but Norward carried the grenadier's variant, which had a grenade launcher underneath the primary barrel. Having been prepared for battle, Norward had brought almost fifty rounds for the launcher, and he still wore six magazines of 50 bullets per, plus the one in his magazine. The 30 calibre rounds were solid, and made of a safe uranium shell. Tracer rounds were a thing of the past, and instead relied upon the mild radioactive coating to be visible under special viewing lenses that the Ormarr armour came standard.

Sighting in on the closest bunch, he fired. "The blast caught at least a half-dozen of them at once. Since the only indication that I was firing was the sound of my weapon, they did not know where the first shot came from. The sound of the explosion though, brought fire back my way."

The rest of the platoon thought they were in imminent peril, and began firing their weapons again into the trees.

"It was a blessing in disguise. Thanks to [Second Platoon's] fire, I wasn't discovered, so I loaded and fired again and again. I had enough targets to last me all night long, at least until the mortars started to range in on me."

As if that wasn't enough, Gann and Fremont's firepower fell almost on top of the beleaguered corporal, but the same trees that had pinned him behind enemy lines, also protected him from the devastating ordnance falling on his head. Saying a prayer of thanks, he continued choosing his targets.

The mortar blasts only brought worse panic to Ra'id and his small team. Frustration had reached a boiling point, and so he ordered Alvar to launch one of his min-sats. Min-sats were rockets that carried packed communication into orbit as a last resort. Alver had brought three with him.

The moment Gliffs received the request, he informed his CO. "It was a demand for testing fire. It read, fire four corners, we will adjust."

It was a call to bring the rain. Artillery fired one shot, paused, another, paused, another, paused, and finally the last round. Alvar and Ra'id examined each impact, noted where each round fell, and if it was effective, or too close to friendly lines. They busied their calculations, and then launched the second min-sat.

The next time the ten mile snipers fired, they did so with all their guns, and the explosions on the ground were horrifyingly effective. A large swath of the old forest was decimated under the ten minute barrage, and the landscape was forever altered into a pocked and cratered field, and despite the brewing storm that affected sensors and blocked the line of sight, the destruction was visible from orbit.

The support from above also did something to the troops below. It was a well needed shot of esprit de corps. Molan: "We had been too busy to notice the ranging shots, but when the barrage happened, we all took heart. The ground shook and the flashes of explosions lit the night into day. Even though the fire was not close to us, we still felt the wind and the vibrations of the impact. I couldn't help myself, and I cheered. It didn't matter that it wasn't effective against our immediate threats, it mattered that we were not forgotten."

There was another issue: the firing galvanised the enemy forces, and they charged both the hill and the copse of trees with renewed vigour. The massive force finally dislodged those on the high ground, and Tosh, Zander, and Kim gave their lives protecting their comrades. Unable to stem the tide, Ra'id ordered Armand and Alvar to hide. Armand, who had climbed a tree for a better position, simply ceased firing. Her headcam caught Alvar's end. The radio gear was too noticeable, so he disposed of the useless equipment. Ra'id had pointed to a bundle of rocks that would have provided a place to hide, but as Alvar turned to follow his commanding officer, he slipped, and having lost his footing, rolled down the hill, into the swarming masses. Unable to help, Ra'id hurried to the rocks, but not before he threw his last grenade into the swelling melee. The explosion was brutal, and the result was a merciful death for the radioman.

At the front, the troops were involved with the charging enemy. Ammo was reaching a critical low, especially for Lafayette's gun. Alarmed, Lance Cpl Malloy ordered her boys to scavenge every available round that they could, even removing the same ammunition from the APC's forward LMG's. The only one that was spared such salvaging was the command unit, as casualties had mounted. Williams had been delivered with a missing arm which had been bitten clean off, and Nabhan, Section 2's nanite boy, had been impaled in the stomach by a crude sword that looked like it was built out of bone. To add to the chaos, Leigh was still busy attempting to save Cpl Bevin, even though it was a lost cause.

In their haste to bring the much-needed ammo, the three troopers missed something that still haunts them to this day. Gilmore: "We didn't see it, no one did. The APC's were all facing the front. We all were, that's where the enemy was attacking us. I've hated myself ever since. When I checked my head camera the next day, I saw them, clearly and obviously."

None of them noticed that the enemy had begun an approach from their rear. No sooner had Malloy's boys returned to the guns than the growing force charged. Section 2's APC's door was open, as Eadwards was loading supplies of ammo onto the ramp for pickup, and the command APC was unlocked, so that wounded could be quickly ferried inside. The foe were almost at the foot of the ramp when Eadwards noticed, and she hurriedly brought her sliver gun to use, but it was little more effective stemming the enemy tide than she would have had against a tsunami. Her screams of rage alerted the rest of the platoon.

Molan: "I had never heard a human sound so, primal. When she screamed, Gilmore, Lance, and I hurried to assist. Kenward had already turned her walker at the waist and was firing everything she had. We saw Eadwards as she kicked one beast in the chest, shot another in the head, and when her gun ran dry, she swung it as a club. We couldn't get to her. Lance broke rank, charged ahead, and then, one of the bigger ones got him with a club, and his body was flung back at us and it knocked Gilmore and me, over."

Unable to stop them, Eadwards was pushed back into the bowels of the vehicle. Its crew, specialists Drake and Montcalm, grabbed their side arms and joined her in battle. Their screams were muted though, when Leigh's cry of agony joined the chaos of the Tac-Net.

The medic was under attack.

Marksman Macen: "The command APC was done. Enemies were pouring into it. I tried to help, and I fired until my rifle's barrel glowed from the stress. It was useless. The sheer number of invaders caused the APC to rock back and forth, and Leigh's screams, and the two crew, just sounded horrible."

It was then that Witters would make another call that seems brutal to those who practise war from the comfort of their couches and homes, but in the pitch of battle, it was, at the time, an attempt at mercy.

The platoon's remaining nanite boy, Vojin, was dragged to the rear by Witter and Finlay. Raising his weapon, he sprayed the advancing ranks with tiny machines that looked more like a liquid than a cloud of solids. Within the swarm, tiny machines moved about, searching for anything even partially organic to destroy. The rain of death evaporated flesh where it fell, creating a field of serenity where there had been chaos moments before. As Kenward hurried her walker over the dead, Vojin walked to the medical APC's door, and sprayed the inside of the vehicle. If there had been human survivors, brutalised by the enemy, they were no more.

Lance was dead. His armour had done little more than keep his corpse together. Enraged by the death of their comrade, Gilmore and Molan charged into Section 2's APC. Gilmore: "We emptied our guns into the bastards, and when we were done, we finished the last with our K-bars. We weren't nice about it. They hadn't been nice to Eadwards or the crew. The bastards had been torturing them. Eadwards had both her legs ripped off, and the crew were disembowelled, and the monsters were eating their insides while they watched. We slaughtered them, and to this day, I'm not sorry for what we did to them."

Witters arrived as the last of the enemy was being cut in two. His normally gruff tone broke as he leaned down to talk to the engineer. Their suits touched, and what passed between them was silenced from the rest. Whatever Eadwards said to the sergeant, was the last words she would ever say. The damage to her body was too much, and her heart ceased to beat.

Removing her helmet, Witter closed Eadwards' eyes, and then he made his own order.

Gilmore: "Put her in reverse and get the fuck out. That's what he said to me. It was cramped in the cockpit, but I did what I was asked. I jumped out the driver's door and watched as the APC rumbled behind us. Witter and Molan had already left the vehicle. It crushed the enemy who were still coming, and when it was entirely surrounded by them, Witter blew it, and all of the claymores that Bevin had died to put into the trees, up."

The explosion cleared a swath about them. Hundreds of enemy fell like scythed wheat. The exploding APC was still loaded with fuel, which ignited, and transformed their rear into an inferno. Creatures of all types ran screaming towards the remnants of second Platoon, who happily cut them down, or let the flames finish them off.

Marksman Macen: "We let them die. It felt good. We laughed as they burned."

Cpl Quan: "It was satisfying."

Sgt Witter: "Eadwards always wanted a funeral to send her on her way to Valhalla. I hope that she appreciates what we did for her."

The detonations of the perimeter explosives saved Norward's life. A group of enemies had figured out where he was firing from, and had assembled a task force of their own in order to wipe him off the face of the planet. Norward: "I was out of explosives, and down to my second last mag. I saw them, surging towards me. I switched to full-auto, destined to go down without a fight, when a claymore that was stuck to the tree above me, let go. I was directly beneath it, so I was spared from the shrapnel. My opponents, on the other hand, were blown to smithereens."

And so, Second Platoon continued to endure.

Without constant communication, the artillery continued to pound the ground, but their pacing had slowed. Their sporadic shots landed at random throughout the targeted zone, and although they doubted if they were having an impact on the battle, or if their shots were only hurting the taxpayers back home, they, too, refused to give up.

Just like the reinforcements, who doubled their speed, the Commander of the 437th, Captain Jabari, was worried that the troops would arrive too tired from the march to fight, but when he asked his troops if they were prepared, he was greeted with a unanimous reply. "We can sleep when we die." He heard, and more than one trooper requested that they all: "Pick up the pace."

* * *

Time passed slowly for Armand. She had a frighteningly clear vantage of the battleground, and she saw the chaos that surrounded the remains of the platoon. She also had a front row seat to the desecration of Tosh, Zander, and Kim's corpses. Their bodies were stripped of the armour, abused, and then torn asunder and consumed, and it was all recorded on Armand's headcam. Despite her revulsion, she did nothing. There was no point. Any action on her part would have led to a swift death, and she still had one final part to play.

Finally satisfied, her enemies moved off the hill. From her spot, Armand had also seen where the foes were originating from. A fissure, at the far side of the woods, just outside of the artillery zone, had begun to glow with the neon green hue, of Mountain Dew. The monsters' energising substance must have caused local life and fauna to mutate, or maybe it was a by-product when the energy had reached critical mass. As she watched, the numbers grew, swelled, gathered, and then they marched across the field of death. Leading them was something that is still analysed to this day. It was big, horned, red-fleshed, long-necked, with claws for fingers and a mouth filled with crooked and serrated teeth. Whatever it was, it was twice as tall as a walker, and, if it had made it to the remnants of Second Platoon, it would have been the unit's end.

Desperate to prevent her friends' destruction, Armand left her concealment and hurried to Alvar's leftover gear. She had just begun to study the late radioman's equipment when Ra'id appeared. Together, they transferred all of their collected data onto the last min sat, and by the time they were completed laying in the new firing coordinates which also included the fissure, the large beast was beside the hill.

"This is Lt. Ra'id" Were the last words he ever spoke. "Bring the rain. Do not stop until dry. Danger close on our position. Immediate."

They launched the final satellite.

Upon reception, Gliffs read the order out loud to his companions. Everyone was quiet. They knew that their act, if they followed through, would more than likely mean the death of the Ra'id and Armand, but they also knew that time was valuable, and every moment of hesitation, meant another moment the rest of Second Platoon was closer to destruction. Together, the entirety of the 521st Light Artillery Brigade, which had been redeployed at the edge of the storm's front, opened fire with everything that they had.

The destruction was absolute, and those in the copse of trees had no idea what was happening until the first explosions shook the ground.

Gilmore: "It was magnificent. All of a sudden, night became day, and the explosions knocked most of us who were still standing to our knees. I was right behind Knight, and when the shockwave hit us, he was flung into me, bowling us both over. We simply lay there and watched the show. The attack definitely took the wind out of their sails."

If the explosions were so powerful against the armoured troopers at a distance, they were devastating to anything inside the fire zone. Survey crews would later labour over the change in terrain. The hill that Ra'id's fire team died on was flattened then reversed into a crater which widened and grew over the entirety of the barrage. The fire mission continued for upwards of half an hour, during which time, every gun fired continuously, unless they ran out of ammo or jammed.

With an uncharacteristic cheer of his own, Quan ordered his mortars to join the fray. "We turned all of our weapons and opened fire. I don't think anyone held anything back. We levelled the surrounding woods, drained our remaining magazines until we each only had one left, and ran the batteries dry."

As the last shells fell to their targets, the mysterious storm began to dissipate. An hour after Ra'id's last command, Captain Jabari's voice reached Gliffs. They had made visual contact with the beleaguered platoon.

The remaining soldiers were standing at attention. Witters had organised most of them into a position worthy of parade-ground inspection. Despite having fought against an inexhaustible foe, without contact, low on ammo, and having suffered the highest casualty count in the recent campaign, Second Platoon stood proud as they faced the rest of their company. Against protocol in the field, Witters faced his survivors, and ordered a salute to the Captain.

The only ones left who weren't there to raise their arms were Finlay and Vojin, who had ditched his spray for Viljo's rifle, who was too wounded to use it anymore. The two had returned to the bush, desperate to find out what had happened to their section's second in command. Norward was found, unconscious from the shockwaves, which had buffeted his armour. The trees that had pinned him had protected him from the shrapnel that the woods had become. It was not hard to find him. All around him were the remains of dozens of the enemy. When they pulled him from the wreckage, they found his armour covered in dents and scratches, and an inspection of his gear revealed that he had only one round left in his remaining magazine, and one in his rifle's chamber.

With the dropships able to fly again, they hurried to lift out the worst of the wounded, but only Norward and Viljo, who was ordered by Witter, were taken away. The rest of the platoon, now reinforced, rearmed, and refuelled, requested permission to finish the job they had started. Although they were less than half the size they had started out with, Captain Jabari saw no need to force them back against their will, although he, and the rest of the 437th, joined them in the conclusion of their mission.

It wasn't long. When rumour of "Ra'id's Raiders"— which was the name the platoon adopted for themselves— victory against the strange forces reached the ears of the remaining resisting grey's population, and it signalled the end of the local resistance.

To this day, no human truly understands what it was that they fought or how the monsters' energy caused such mutations, but Second platoon would never let themselves forget the night that they had held their own.

Into the Lungs of Hell

By Raven Corinn Carluk

"And I thought the desert was fucking ugly before," Kramer grumbled, hunched down beside me, plasma rifle cradled against this chest. I continued to study the compound through my binoculars, unable to comprehend the changes Area 51 had undergone.

Granted, rampaging aliens had changed a lot of things during the last six years.

Straggly plants had reclaimed the runway, only some of Earthly origin. Smoke stained the sides of several buildings, and rubble scattered from walls that had collapsed. Sand dunes piled up in the lee of all stationary objects, softening the lines humans had attempted to carve in the desert.

Biological structures rose from the sands, casting heavy shadows in the evening light. Burnt-out vehicles were barely recognisable beneath ropey masses. The hulks of dead beasts had mummified over the short years, proving the sun stronger than any life.

Two days we'd skulked through this mutated desert, watching as the signs of the Storming and original infestation grew more obvious. Wrecks were closer together, alien infestation becoming more obvious. Sporadic human skeletons dotted the sands, some not human, most scoured by the relentless desert.

November wasn't unbearably hot, though the nights were biting cold. After all the wet camps we'd endured in the last year, I found it rather refreshing to be merely cold while on guard against alien attack.

We hadn't seen much alien activity while making our way across the Nevada desert. Not much was known about this region since the Storming, with no concrete numbers of Swarm drones or other monsters. There always seemed to be more, so there had to be a considerable amount.

Lucky for us they'd been drawn to the other side of the battlefield.

"Captain Isaacs," Liam said from his sniper position. "I'm seeing a lot of movement by that far building." The young man came from a military family, and even though there was no such thing as the US Marines anymore, he still showed me the respect of my former rank. He would have made a good soldier before the Storming.

I shifted my gaze to the building in question, the binoculars giving me almost as much detail as Liam's scope. Watching the bugs work ceaselessly, moving with the smooth glide of a machine, mouth parts constantly chewing at nothing, I wished I hadn't gotten a closer look. The Swarm were repellent in every stage of life, but this second stage gave me the actual creeps.

"Nought, what's in that building?" I asked the Reaper. I hadn't been pleased when the bio-enhanced soldier had been put on my team, but his knowledge of Area 51 should come in handy.

He lowered his own binoculars, releasing a tiny sigh. It was the first emotion he'd shown since the mission began. "Containment. Deep lockdown of the deadliest species ever encountered. Including a Swarm hive mother."

We'd fought the Swarm for years now. Hive creatures that needed living hosts for their larva, and ate all flesh they encountered during their second stage. Their third form looked like mutated stingrays and laid the eggs in helpless creatures. What could a hive mother possibly look like?

"Well fuck me," Kramer said. The entire team nodded in agreement. This was worse than the hell we'd agreed to march into.

* * *

Former general Barclay made the introductions. "Samuel Isaacs, leader of Isaac's Irregulars. Rafe Drybrough, medic. Ania Machen, tech. Daniel Kramer, soldier. Liam Collins, sniper." He nodded briefly at me before gesturing at the group standing across from us.

"Reaper Hans Nought. Jacob Donaldson, head scientist. Paris and Calais Finch, psychics. And Seandra..." He trailed off while our attention fell upon the Pleiadean at the end of the line.

The alien woman was beautiful. Tall, bright blue skin and large eyes, long black hair, with high cheekbones and bright red lips. Far more beautiful than anything we'd seen in years. The Irregulars worked to rescue civilians from monster attacks, spent most of our time dealing with slaughter and death. Being near Seandra though, washed all that away, made me feel warm and welcome.

For the first time since the Storming, I felt hope.

Donaldson cleared his throat, breaking the moment of reverie. "If everyone would take a seat." He remained standing, his gaze roaming the group, though he never made eye contact with anyone. "Thank you all for coming. I'm sure you have many questions."

"No shit, Sherlock," Kramer spat. He slouched in his chair, not quite so rude as to put his feet on the table.

I didn't reprimand him for his outburst; I'd rather be back in the field than at a meeting in the old Oregon

Museum of Science and Industry. The food and company were good, but there were reports of alien activity a few hundred miles away. Maybe Swarm, maybe one of the nameless monsters that kept coming through spatial tears.

"Yes, um, well," Donaldson stammered. As a team, we stared at him, waiting for the scientist to continue. He adjusted his shirt, cheeks turned red, and seemed to shrink in on himself. My opinion of the super brainy types wasn't improving any. "The situation grows worse by the day. We humans have only survived this long because of the technology released from Areas Forty-two and Thirteen. We are unable to make headway against the alien threat, however, and have begun to lose ground. It seems the spatial anomaly has remained open, allowing—"

"Get to the point," Barclay snapped. Donaldson flinched, embarrassed, and tugged at his collar. I glanced at the former general, one brow raised; we'd been told time was of the essence when called back into Portland.

"For fuck's sake!" Kramer's exasperated tone elicited a giggle from Machen. Liam choked, clearly uncomfortable with the soldier's irreverence. "Who do you need us to fucking kill?" Drybrough laughed, breaking his stoic reserve.

"Isaac's Irregulars are purportedly the best fire team around here."

Seandra's melodious voice silenced my team, drew their attention. She blinked blue topaz eyes, the faintest of smiles on her lips. Warmth washed through me again, releasing the tension I hadn't realised had built up while Donaldson attempted to brief us.

The scientist cleared his throat again, but it was the Pleiadean who continued. "Humans stole many things from other races, and have spent decades attempting to copy and perfect. Some technologies adapted easily, others not so much." No one interrupted her, so she continued.

"My people have always attempted to help yours, using gentle contact to share our knowledge. Sometimes more than knowledge." She glanced at the two women beside her. Were they really psychic?

"While I was captive at Area Fifty-one, those scientists studied my ship, made every effort to copy Pleiadean Rift Drives. They even attempted to extract the knowledge from me, but does one of your drivers know how to make an internal combustion engine?"

"Did they succeed?" Drybrough asked. The man had always been fascinated by obscure technology, even before the Storming. He'd helped adapt fire team vehicles to a design from Nikola Tesla.

Seandra blinked slowly. "Yes. Though nowhere as elegant or small. I know they opened a Rift, but I'm not certain anyone actually used it. Since the one here cannot lock on a destination, I am certain it is still open, and is possibly causing the rifts seen around the world."

I continued to stare at the blue woman, processing what I'd just heard, thoughts already plotting out how we'd get in and shut down some unknown device.

Kramer and Machen whispered to each other, agitated but too low to hear. Liam fidgeted, but Drybrough began to question Donaldson. "How long have you had a Rift Gate? How does it work? Why haven't you gotten everyone out of here?"

The scientist cleared his throat, licked his lips, then began in a low voice. "We've worked on ours for almost as long as Area Fifty-one has, but private funding helped us make more headway. We also used much of the research Montauk broke ground on, which the fools at Fifty-one didn't—" Barclay coughed softly, and Donaldson lowered his eyes. "We want to use our Gate, but are unable to lock onto a destination while the other is open. We need you to return and shut theirs down."

Shock rolled through the team, rendering even Kramer speechless. I had assumed this was what they wanted, why Seandra had praised us, but it still rattled me to hear the actual words.

The Reaper met my gaze when I looked his way. A generic looking but big man, with broad shoulders and thick arms, he had the air of a killer that reminded me of a Marine. Perhaps more psychotic. "So, what's your role in this mission?"

He didn't blink, but his nostrils flared slightly. "I'm not surprised a man with your reputation figured that out." Nought gave me the slightest of nods. "I know the complex. The main routes and the secret. I also have that little extra to help slay aliens."

Machen leaned forward, elbows on the table. "So what are you girls for? Going to tell the monsters their futures?" Kramer snorted a laugh.

Psychics were rare, their powers misunderstood. These two were clearly twins, identical in all aspects, even the way they tipped their heads to glare at my tech. They blinked rather than answer, and the moment drug out.

"My daughters will provide cover," Seandra said, hand over her heart. "They can mask your movements from various races, including the Swarm, providing an extra level of stealth. Not hiding you from them, mind you, simply helping."

"I suppose we're just gonna drive down there and hope they don't see us," Kramer snapped. "Let them hide us, fight everything they can't stop? I mean, fuck that."

Barclay slapped a hand on the table, interrupting Kramer before he could really get going. "Seandra has offered her private transport to bring everyone to the front line. The Utah militia will move in from the eastern flank, with two gunships coming in for a little ground pound. While the enemy is distracted, you make your move."

I frowned at Seandra. "You're coming with us?"

She smiled, teeth startlingly white against her blue skin and ruby lips. "We Pleiadeans do not commit acts of violence. While self-defence is permitted, I could not take an offensive action against an enemy not directly threatening me."

"That's an awfully fine distinction," Drybrough observed.

She turned glittering eyes his direction. "It has served my people well for six millennia." I admired any people that merely didn't destroy themselves, so I couldn't imagine the amount of willpower necessary to live that way.

I glanced at my team, read their body language, judged their moods. Liam would do anything he was told, but he'd shrunk in on himself. Kramer and Machen both fidgeted ceaselessly, shoulders tight; they'd needed a little R and R before hearing about this mission. Drybrough sat straight, quiet, and gave me a nod when our eyes met.

"Who would you send if we said no to your suicide mission?" I asked Barclay.

The former general's jaw tightened, and he lowered his eyes. He sighed when he answered. "Howdeshell. They're bringing in a caravan that made it up from Mexico."

"Fuck that bitch," Kramer blurted out. "She might know how to kill, but she doesn't know her ass from a hole in the ground. And her second is a real piece of shit. If you want that Gate closed, don't send Howdeshell's Howlers."

Barclay looked up, met my eyes with a questioning

look. I simply nodded once, steeling myself for an assault on Area 51.

* * *

I lowered my binoculars and glanced over my shoulder at the sun. "We got at least another hour until the light's gone. Break out some rations and water, rest while we can. Nought, we're going to plan our assault."

The Reaper and I stepped away from the rest of the team to confer. I heard another set of steps and turned to see Paris nearby. The young woman's powers had proven useful so far, helping us avoid a few encounters since we'd touched down. I gestured her closer; maybe she'd have some insight that would help us get in safely.

"All right," I said to Nought, jerking my head toward the base. "Tell me about that, because I'm pretty sure I heard that containment was breached during the Storming."

Nought crossed his arms, glaring across the distance to the remains of the base. At a klick out, we weren't likely to be seen by the Swarm, but he stood near a bush to break up his silhouette anyway. "I was at Area Twenty-one during the Storming, so I only know what was in Nil's report."

He paused and I waited. He wasn't the most forthcoming with information, but he'd proven to be an efficient killer, able to stay on watch longer than any of my team. Two days camped in the desert had been made easy by his presence, though I'd never tell the Reaper he had become a welcome addition to my Irregulars.

"Facility One fell due to internal sabotage. Most of the aliens were kept there, including some dangerous ones. High containment inside there was breached, and those were some of the monsters we first encountered post-Storming.

"But that building is a hardened target, reinforced against the worst threats of the galaxy. The Storming never got through because they were probably running for their lives by then."

I narrowed my eyes at the building in question. Details were impossible in the dusk, but I could see the constant motion of the drones. Always moving, carrying things, going into tunnels and coming back out. My skin crawled, even though I couldn't really see the creatures.

"Where do we have to go for the Rift Gate?" None of the details had mattered during the trek here. There had been a possibility of the Reaper dying in an attack, but Nought was still a secret agent and refused to share critical details unless absolutely necessary.

"Facility One, basement. Right next to the Tesla generator, which is why it still has power. Some security doors are probably still locked, but no one's changed the code in six years, so we'll breeze right through."

"I heard plenty of mixed reports from survivors." I pressed my luck, hoping to get a little more information while he was being forthcoming. "What was in those other buildings?"

Nought sighed, pointing at two of the other large buildings. "That one had the Greys, and over there were artefacts." He cocked his head, looking at me with a vague smirk. "Do you want to know what we had at Area Twenty-one?"

Paris piped up. "I do." The young woman smiled, eyes glowing in the darkening day.

"We had mostly magic. Elves, talking swords, vampires. Rumour was a couple of dragon eggs were in deep containment, but I never saw them." Nought returned his gaze to me. "Now let's talk about our way in."

Planning took most of the hour only because we went over the route multiple times, including what we'd do once we got inside. My blood started to heat as we talked, urging me to action. The last moments before a mission were always the hardest for me, anticipation building to a painful level. Once underway, I was calm and cold.

Just needed to get there first.

The three of us re-joined the team, and I was pleased to see the other five, including Calais, ready to move out. Our reputation as the best seemed to be earned.

"All right, here's the order." The other Irregulars

gathered close and took a knee. Paris took her sister's hand and they closed their eyes. The Reaper sent a message back to home base, letting them know we were about to launch, and warning them of the hive queen's imminent release.

"Nought's on point. Kramer, I want you on his ass. Calais after that, Liam at her side." He'd already packed his sniper rifle back away and carried his plasma rifle. "Machen, Paris, then Drybrough. I've got the rear.

"We're going from truck to truck and that big carcass, right to the south entrance. The drones shouldn't see us, but you two are going to have your work cut out for you." Paris nodded, eyes still closed. "Once we're inside, we head to the basement and shut that Gate down. Check your corners and keep each other covered. There's extensive damage where things have escaped, but that doesn't mean they haven't gone back inside. Ready?" They gave a quiet oorah and rose.

By the time I had my goggles on and armour secured, the last of the light had faded from the sky. I'd never known the sunsets took so long in the Nevada desert, and I briefly wished I'd seen it pre-Storming, without the pressures of life and death, and with enough time to fully appreciate the wonders of nature.

No time to pine for a lost world. I slung my pack under a bush, settled my plasma rifle and joined my team. "Time to save the fucking world," Kramer said. We all chuckled, ignoring the gallows tone of his voice.

The Reaper started toward the first vehicle, crouched, plasma rifle at his shoulder, taking careful steps over rocks and debris. We all did the same, even the twins. They'd proven themselves capable of keeping up with the rest of us, though they'd never soldiered in their lives.

I brought up the end of the line, constantly scanning our surroundings, checking for any threat approaching. Though many had described this as the most stressful position, I enjoyed the responsibility. These were my people to take care of, and I would damn sure do so.

We bunched up against the husk of an M1 Abrams tank. One track had been destroyed, leading to its abandonment so close to the goal. The hull had been scarred by .50 cal rounds and scorched by fire, but otherwise looked driveable. Someone had painted a logo and message on the side. Desert winds had scoured at the paint, leaving the faintest remains of the original words, "E.T. Phone Home". Seeing the faded joke, I wondered how the Stormers had even gotten this far.

Nought pointed to the east. "Looks like the Rainier and Capitan have started their bombardment." Tiny lights flashed above, larger ones below. At least a hundred klicks away, the explosions seemed like mere fireflies twinkling.

"Good. At least most of the creeps are the fuck over there." Kramer spat. If the two big airships thought there were enough aliens to warrant using their bombs, I was glad we didn't have all those aliens here to fight through.

Nought lead the way to the next vehicle, a Humvee flipped on its side. Something had punched through the bottom, shattering drive shaft and axles, and other aliens had excreted ropey strands around the front in an attempt to make a nest. Luckily, nothing seemed to be at home.

Wait a moment, cross to cover, wait another moment. Stop by stop, we got closer to the first buildings. Hunched behind the dried carcass of a massive alien beast, tension clenched my spine. I could hear the Swarm from here, a wet susurration that compared to nothing on Earth. Nothing could sound gooey and crunchy and mechanical all at once.

Drybrough cried out, lunging away from the cover, reaching for something on his neck. Paris hissed, her increased power creating the sensation of a damp blanket smothering us. I lunged for the medic, knowing she couldn't mute everything, especially as his grunt turned to a scream.

"Get it the fuck off me." His voice shook, and he pulled away from me despite the demand for help. Machen arrived, grabbed the man's arm, and held him while I pulled at his collar.

The green tint turned the bloody wounds to shades of darker green, but they couldn't hide the damage that had already been done. Half a dozen worms burrowed into his flesh, feasting and coiling like whips across his skin.

Drybrough cried out as they chewed their way deeper, eating muscle, nerve, bone.

I grabbed one of the things, and it whipped wildly, then slipped out of my glove. It left a viscous slime everywhere, but it pulled out of Drybrough's flesh and lunged for me. I flinched, but there was no dodging two feet of lightning fast creature. It found a gap in the armour at my wrist and immediately bit down.

Pain lashed across my nerves, blinding and hot. Worse than any bullet ripping through flesh. I couldn't feel the teeth themselves, but the sensation of being burrowed into was like having rusty concertina wire scraped across my nerves.

It kept slipping from my grip, refusing to come free now that it had lodged in flesh. The rest of the team moved away from the carcass and any more of the aliens. I managed to keep my voice down, but Drybrough couldn't. He screamed, clawing at his own neck in desperation. Machen tried to pull them free, but they slipped from her hands too.

I drew my sidearm, a compact plasma pistol with a small discharge. I aimed at my own wrist, shallow across the back of the bones, and fired. Flesh was instantly cauterised, and immediately killed both the worm and the pain. I poked at the wound, waiting for signs I still had the worm's head inside me. Nothing.

Drybrough screamed again. I could finally give him my attention again, but there was no sign of any of the creatures gnawing through his flesh. He writhed, pulling against Machen's grip, and begged for help.

But I couldn't do anything for him. Helplessness pinged my mind for a moment before icy resolve took over. I pushed his helmet forward, exposing the base of his skull. "I'm sorry," Machen whispered, then I fired a plasma bolt into his brain. Drybrough fell in a slump, and my heart ached.

"Some of them are coming," Calais whispered, her power amplifying the words so we all heard them.

"Run for the door. Short bursts, check your targets." I holstered the gun, helped Machen to her feet, and moved to Paris's side. The young woman looked at me with tears in her eyes, but didn't hesitate when I touched her arm.

Nought reached the door well before the rest of us, but just as the first of the Swarm drones came around the corner. I sighted down the barrel of my rifle, but Liam and Kramer were faster than I. Two small plasma bursts each, hitting the first two drones in the head and body. Ichor flew, the alien monsters fell, and six others took their place.

Of all the horrors unleashed by the Storming, the Swarm were the only ones that actually caused fear in me. Pearlescent white, the size of ponies, with massive chewing beaks, they moved like solifugae with clawed legs, two massive feeler-like arms looming in front of them. They made no sound but that wet scraping.

I fired, splattered one against the side of the building,

and realised why they creeped me out so badly: they had no eyes, no external facial features to speak of.

"We're in," Nought cried out. There wasn't much point in trying to sneak anymore, but he wasn't any louder than necessary. He held the door open as the rest of us raced forward. Rifle at his shoulder, stance wide, he took out the next four drones with four clean shots.

Kramer and Liam bolted through the door, Calais between them. She screamed, rifles flashed, but I couldn't tell what was happening. I fired at a new drone and kept running, Paris and Machen a step ahead of me. We raced through the door into unknown danger, but it had to be better than what waited outside. Nought slammed the door shut, locking us in.

Rifle at the ready, I studied the interior, looking for the cause of Calais's scream. I saw nothing but a long corridor, at least a dozen doors connected, and a T-junction at the end. "Liam, Kramer, sound off."

"In here, Captain Isaacs." Liam's voice sounded weak, and I heard a muttered curse from Kramer, both of them in a room to the left.

"I'll see if I can restore lights," Nought said. A drone banged against the door at his back. "I don't think we have much need to hide."

"Do that. Machen, watch Paris." I lowered my rifle to check on my men.

Liam was down, Kramer applying pressure to a wound on the young man's abdomen. Calais leaned against the wall, blood splattered across her face, but otherwise appeared unharmed. In the corner was a dead drone and a dozen cocooned humans, too close to death to notice the rest of us.

I pieced together the events: they'd stumbled across this nest, and the guard attacked them. How the Swarm had gotten fresh humans back into Area 51 concerned me far less than the bleeding young man. "How bad is it?" I knelt beside Liam, wanting Nought to get the lights on already. Treating wounds was infinitely harder using nightscopes.

Liam winced. "Not bad, Sir. I can make it." His face looked pale, even through the goggles, lips thin. I glanced at Kramer, and he shook his head slightly. "I can make it!" Liam growled, blood staining his teeth.

Kramer lifted the makeshift bandage, revealing the deep gash in the young man's side, blood flowing free in a steady stream, adding to the black pool already beneath him. I could give him the same mercy I'd shown Drybrough, but I doubted he had much longer to live anyway.

The Reaper leaned through the door. "No lights, the panel's too damaged. They're also going to make their way through that door soon."

Liam groaned, reached for one of the grenades on his belt. "I got your six, Sir."

I gripped his hand, fighting back a surge of emotions. This young man could be my own son, had fought with me for years, had killed without hesitation all to save as many humans as possible. I'd lost many men during my life, too many by far, but never this close together.

"Get him up," I said to Kramer, voice low and tight. "Get him into the hall..." I couldn't say anything else.

Kramer buckled Liam's armour back in place, holding the wad of cloth against the wound. It might give him a few more minutes. Did minutes even matter now? We got him up, drug him into the hall, and Nought pointed to a spot a little farther down. "There's a crack here, should collapse when..." He cut himself off, turned away with a grimace.

We settled Liam against the wall. He motioned at his goggles, and I took them off for him. He'd rather wait in the darkness, and I might have made the same choice. I held one of his hands while the rest of our team passed, touching his shoulder. Calais kissed his cheek, Paris his forehead. I remained with him while everyone else made their way to the junction.

Liam pulled out a grenade, clutched it to his chest. He looked at me, tears streaming down his face, and drew a shuddering breath. "It's been an honour, Sir."

I clutched his hand tighter, as if trying to keep him from of the clutches of death. "The honour was mine, Son. Semper fi." Then I pulled the pin for him, rose, and joined the remainder of my team. Liam deserved better than to be left as a dead man's switch, but there wasn't anything else for it.

Nobody looked at anybody else, stood close but not touching. I'd steeled myself by the time I arrived, compartmentalising like any good Marine. Grief was for after the completed mission, if ever. "All right, Nought, lead the way."

Paris flinched at the cold tone of my voice. With Pleiadean blood, they didn't need goggles to see in the dark, meaning I could see the pain and tears in her expression. The twins had held hope of living through this until right this moment. The forced realization seemed to hurt them as much as the two deaths.

The other six deaths had to wait until we got to the Gate.

Nought gestured down the left hall, ending the moment. "Kramer, on me." The Reaper turned, rifle up, checking each open door before moving on, Kramer close to his back. Last thing any of us needed was to find another surprise nest.

Machen jutted her chin toward Calais. "You're with me. Stay close." She followed Nought's path, double checking the open doors.

Paris stepped closer, wiped away her tears. "You're a hard man."

I took a deep breath, staring down at her, emotions

357

locked back down. "When I have to be. Now, let's hurry." The young woman ducked her head and shuffled in the direction of the stairs.

We passed a hall on the right, and Paris came to a dead halt. She turned and stared, and I went on guard. Nothing moved down there, a pile of rubble blocking it several metres in. "What's wrong?" I asked her.

"There's something down there. Like a Rift Gate, but not. Some kind of tear in space-time." She frowned, rubbed at her forehead.

"Hey, Nought." The Reaper returned to our side, jaw tensed. "What's down there to make her feel like that?"

The Reaper held his rifle at ease, not looking at me, jaw locked tight. Refusing to answer.

I stepped into his space, our faces inches apart. "Why the fuck does she say there's a tear down the hall?"

Nought turned slowly to look at me. I felt his hard gaze even through two pairs of goggles. The eerie green only made him seem stranger, like the inhuman bastard Reapers were. If I didn't need him, I might kill him.

"That's where our translocation Tunnel was." He glanced at Paris. "Your mother thought the Tear Gate was something new to us."

I shoved him back, grabbing a strap on his chest. Paris laid a restraining hand on my forearm. "What happened to it?" she asked. "Why is it broken?"

"Nil and his men set charges on their way out. Didn't need the Stormers or the traitors escaping to any of the other sites. He blew the Tunnel, collapsing that end."

"But?" she prompted, tipping her head.

Nought swallowed hard, tugged on my hand. I gripped tighter, waiting for his answer. "All the Tunnels collapsed. Every single one went dead at the same time. We had to open the sites if any of us wanted out."

"You fucking idiots." Paris stepped away, clutching the side of her head. "You're the reasons for all those random tears."

I released Nought, and the other three joined us. "What do you mean?" Paris passed, muttering to herself, not responding.

Calais touched my arm, drawing my attention. "I shall explain." We turned toward her, letting Paris continue to pace.

"Near as we can tell from his thoughts, the Tunnels are similar to our Rift Gates. They both create openings in space-time, allowing the traveller to pass through to far distances. Ours are not permanent, and they allow space-time to heal afterward. Theirs are permanent, linked to each other, leaving constant holes and trails, like a rabbit warren.

"When this one was destroyed, it caused a backlash, creating rips and instabilities all over your world. Paris is certain that's what caused Bảo Lộc, and the one at Brisbane.

Most likely what triggered Kilimanjaro to go active." Calais narrowed a look at Nought. "Hopefully the Tunnels were confined to Earth, hadn't spread into the rest of the universe."

The Reaper stared down the hall, ignoring the woman's implication. "If the Tunnel is open, does that mean there might be other creepers down here?"

Paris rejoined us, hair frazzled and eyes wide. "Most definitely. It doesn't feel like it's always open, but it has been recently. Many things have used it in both directions. Not all things were good."

"You can tell all that?" Machen asked. Her normal exuberance had faded, but she didn't seem despondent.

The twins shrugged as one. "Simply one of our talents."

"Well, that's a great fucking thing," Kramer spat. "But does that help us get down where we need to be?"

"He's right." I touched Paris's shoulder. "We need to get going. Maybe closing the Gate will close this tear." She didn't look too certain, but she nodded.

A grenade exploded, followed by another.

Dust rained down upon us. Machen turned away, Kramer swore, and I closed my eyes. No more delays. We needed to get to that Gate, render it inoperable. "Move out," I said softly, and we resumed our mission.

We moved quietly again, Nought leading us down the stairs. We didn't have to hide from the Swarm right now, just whatever other creatures might lurk down here. The fewer encounters we had on our way to the Gate, the better.

At the door to the basement, Nought motioned me over. "Thirty metres down this hall, first door on the right. If it's locked, you'll need the code." He rattled off the number, then repeated. No guarantee he'd make it to the door, so we all needed to have access. Grimmer and grimmer by the moment.

Machen shifted, ringing her grip on the rifle. "Donaldson said it would need fifteen minutes to process the shutdown sequence. Until then—"

Echoes of noise rose from the stairwell below us. Too distorted to make out numbers, but definitely Swarm drones. A lot of them.

Nought threw open the door, rushing through, Kramer on his heels. Machen stayed close to the twins; the three women were the only ones capable of shutting down the Gate's computer.

I slammed the door just as the first scuttles reached my ears, and shuffled backwards, watching for any that got through. My feet stuck to the floor, and I dared glance down. Black goo covered everything, even splashed up the walls. Hard chunks created an uneven surface, attempting to rob me of my balance.

The drones began pounding at the door, meaty thunks against the metal, relentless, in rapid succession. Unless the base had been fitted with titanium doors, I didn't imagine it would hold any long against their efforts than the outside one.

The first dents showed on the stairwell door, and the rhythmic pounding grew stronger. They'd be through sooner rather than later.

One of the twins screamed, followed by multiple shots from three plasma rifles. "Contact," Machen yelled, though it was obvious. Something growled, and the young woman continued to scream desperately.

I turned to help, immediately assessing the situation, firing even before I fully registered what I saw.

An impossible creature composed of tentacles and gaping snake heads pulled away from the plasma bolts, screaming and bleeding, clutching Calais in a pulsing coil. It loomed near a door that I presumed lead to the Gate, and seemed to be formed from the sticky mass on the floor. Each plasma strike caused it to ooze backward and pull away.

The creature bit Calais in half with one of its many savage heads.

I fired three more shots as I ran, and all three hit one of the screaming snake heads in the mouth. It flinched and cringed back, giving Nought more room at the security panel. Kramer shouted and followed suit, Machen struggling to restrain Paris.

The pounding behind us grew more aggressive, the sound more hollow. The door must be near collapse. If we could just get in the room, maybe the two species would attack each other. At least be distracted enough to let us close the Tear Gate.

Nought opened the door and Machen rushed inside with Paris. Kramer continued firing on the nightmare hydra, shouting obscenities. Metal slammed against the wall behind me, and I turned to fire a few suppressing shots, back-to-back with my teammate. Drones scuttled toward us, filling the hall with their disgusting movements, beaks chewing on the air.

"Inside, now," I ordered Kramer, shouting between shots. Drones fell, others clambered over the corpses as if they were simple obstacles, not the dead of their own species.

"You first, Sir." The screams of the hydra changed in note, becoming aggressive.

A tentacle lashed out, caught us both in the side, battered us to the wall. The plasma rifle slipped from my grasp to hang by its strap. Stars danced in my eyes, the night vision goggles knocked free.

Someone grabbed me while I was still dazed, yanked me through the doorway. I stumbled, fell to my knees, and immediately tried to get my rifle back in my grip. Not that it mattered; my vision wouldn't clear.

"Don't you fucking dare!" Machen's voice cracked, and she fired her rifle. The hydra screamed in the hall, then the door slammed shut.

I blinked several times, realised the lights were on. The world was still blurry, but I could make out Nought leaning against the door, Machen with her rifle pressed against his chest. Paris must have been behind me, near the Tear Gate.

"There was no other way." The Reaper sounded as cold as ever. He kept his weapon at his side, as if he didn't care that the woman wanted him dead.

"You didn't try, because you don't care. Now move!" She pressed harder with the rifle, but made no effort to push the man aside.

Nought simply shook his head, letting his eyes close.

I made it to my feet. "What happened?" There was only one real reason for the standoff, but I felt compelled to ask. I needed to hear the words to truly believe.

"This cocksucker left Kramer to die." Machen pushed away from him, wiped at the blood on her face.

Nought lifted his eyes to stare directly at me. "That thing grabbed him after it knocked you down, and the drones arrived. There wasn't time to get him back."

Thuds sounded against the wall and door, halting further discussion. The hydra roared, followed by more pounding. Fighting each other meant they weren't trying to get us.

I looked at Paris. She stood at a control board beside a massive metal ring. Tears stained her cheeks, and her eyes were wide. "Samuel, it..." She bit her lip and sobbed.

Could things get much worse? I gritted my teeth. "It won't shut down, will it?"

"No. I think it was damaged by that Tunnel upstairs, and it tore a permanent hole here. As long as it stands, so will the rift." Paris wiped at her eyes trying to calm herself.

"Can't you make it self-destruct or something?" Machen's voice cracked as it rose in pitch.

"Not from here. I can't even get it to lock onto a destination." She sounded hollow, close to despair.

And why shouldn't she? Her twin was dead and it appeared we'd failed. Trapped, we wouldn't be able to fight our way to another control room with diminished numbers. I clenched my fists on my weapon, wracking my brain for a solution. Nothing came forth except frustration and bitterness.

Nought stepped toward the Gate, holding a lump of something grey. "I have enough explosives to destroy the machine." The finality of his words reminded me of the closing of a coffin.

"That doesn't look like very much," Machen snapped. I shifted my gaze between Nought and Paris. He was talking suicide and we all knew it.

"It puts C4 to shame. More than enough to finish the job." The Reaper moved forward, kneading the plastic explosive.

"Will that close the hole?" I asked Paris, holding her gaze. "Will they be able to use the one at OMSI?" My stomach churned with worry. I'd been willing to die when we took this mission, but only if we succeeded. Failure had never had a place in my head.

Paris bit her lip, brows drawn into a delicate frown. "It should. It's the harmonies of the Tear Gate itself that interferes with targeting, not the opening in space-time. An explosion should..." She trailed off, letting her shoulders slump.

Machen followed Nought, hand lifted as if to grab and stop him. "Can't we make it do something? Get out of here?" Her strident tone broadcast all her panic and fear. Dying in the heat of battle was not the same as choosing suicide.

The hybrid looked down at the panel, her frown deepening. "I can put in coordinates, but there's no knowing if it will stay set there. It could let us through safely, or it could deposit us somewhere lethal."

A series of thumps from the hallway punctuated her statement.

Nought and Machen turned to me. I raised one questioning brow, but said nothing. We all wondered the same thing, whether to stay here and certainly die or go through a malfunctioning Gate and possibly die.

They both nodded, and I returned my gaze to Paris. We had no supplies, no reinforcements, no way to communicate our progress or destination. We had only our wits, our skills, our few remaining weapons. The odds were slim, but were better than nothing. "Do it."

Paris nodded tersely, then let her fingers fly across the control board. Machen shuddered and whispered a prayer. Nought closed in on the Gate to place the explosives.

"I'm setting a short timer," the Reaper said, kneeling at the base of the ring. He shaped the explosive, set a detonator in the largest piece. "One-way ticket."

"Always has been," I said, moving toward Paris. She concluded her commands, shuffled my way, and looked up with weary eyes. "Ready?" I whispered to her.

She nodded, then surprised me by taking my hand. "Wherever we end up." Paris stayed close, lead me toward the Tear Gate. Machen joined us, hands shifting nervously on her rifle. Nought pressed a button on the detonator, then rose to wait for us.

I stared at the iridescent wall, colours shifting in a mesmerising display of every colour known and unknown. The void waited beyond it, a vast emptiness between space and time. We could step into the lungs of Hell, or feel the sweet breath of Heaven.

We passed through as one, saying goodbye to Earth and hello to the unknown.

Last Night

By Jennifer Shelby

"Mommy, there's something hitting my window!"

I lay down beside her and pull her close. "It's just June bugs, sweetie. Don't be frightened."

Thwack, thwack, thwack at the window. I close my eyes, my head full of visions of the tiny, ravenous alien swarms from the evening news. It's better if she's asleep. I don't want my little girl to die in terror.

Thwack, thwack. The glass cracks. I hear the swarm chewing through the wall. The silenced emergency alert still blinks on my phone.

Her precious, soft snores return. I focus on them.

It will all be over soon.

Two Hundred and Eighty-Four

By D.M. Burdett

2 HOURS 17 MINUTES UNTIL UNLOCK

Mesmerised, we wait, staring up at the counter; our altar, our Jesus upon his cross.

Two hundred and eighty-four pairs of eyes watch the minutes tick by.

1 HOUR 4 MINUTES UNTIL UNLOCK

We kneel at the door, silent but for our breathing. Even the children stare in wonder.

For ten years we've waited; at first, our thoughts were of rescue—surely *someone* would come for us?—and then of survival, but now we tremble in fear of what is on the other side of the door.

12 MINUTES UNTIL UNLOCK

It will soon be time.

I look back at the Containment Unit standing at the side of this cavernous room that has been our home all these years. The Unit is stacked high with the bodies of those that didn't make it—those we held dear, others that deserved the black sack that now swaddles their rotting corpses. I think of Jack, the father my babies have already forgotten. How he would have celebrated this day! Like dreaming of a lottery win, he always spoke wistfully of the life we would have in the *Outside*.

And now it was almost time. Would the *Outside* be the fairy-tale he wished for?

3 MINUTES UNTIL UNLOCK

Someone starts to sing softly, almost a whisper, and one by one we all join in.

One more step along the world I go, one more step along the world I go; from the old things to the new keep me travelling along with you: And it's from the old I travel to the new; keep me traveling along with you.

0 MINUTES UNTIL UNLOCK

In silence we stare as metal slides over metal and moving parts slam into place.

Dark Earth

By Jo Seysener

From space, Dark Earth looked small, hanging in the vastness of our small galaxy. We'd renamed the planet when the atmosphere clouded over, shortly after the massacres began. Fire, dust...we don't know. In the wake of the alien's release from Area 51, destruction purged our world. Soon the planet was nothing more than a formless dot amongst the stars.

And we glided in our perfect orbit, separate from our home, the terror that reigned. Watching, like tiny gods set above it all.

AREA 0.51

"They'll never last, you know that." I took a swig of the pale liquid, grimacing as sour notes raked my tongue, followed by a sudden cooling sensation. Shivering, I drew back to study the drink. "It's green. What the hell did you put in this, Golem?"

Large grey eyes studied me. I wished he would blink, his stillness so unnatural. But having no eyelids made that quite a challenge.

"Chlorfll." His croak blurred the sounds, his next mumble almost unintelligible, tapping his feet on the floor to some internal beat I couldn't hear.

"Cucumber? And Chlorophyll?"

Golem nodded his too large head, reminding me of those bobble heads people decorated their cars with. Used to. Because there were no cars anymore. Or people. Well, mostly.

He swayed in his seat, humming. He'd once told me his colony sang together in their heads, like a hive mind. There were other Greys on the station, but Golem couldn't hear them. Sometimes he greeted the others politely, but never engaged them in his own language. He was alone.

I leaned back, waiting for the kick. Golem had a way with plants I'd never achieved. Like they spoke to him, told him their secrets. I smiled. New talents revealed themselves regularly. Even after all this time, we were still discovering new things about each other.

Living on a space station with eighteen other species had its advantages. Someone had named the station Area 0.51 as a drunken joke, and it had stuck.

Numbness eked its way up my arms, hairs standing on

end. A groggy smile pulled at my lips.

"Some gooo shii—"

Damn words, not coming out right. A thud rocked me. No, that was the floor. Comfy. The numbness reached my cheeks, muscles not responding. I stared at a puddle of drool on the floor as it inched toward my eyes. Then they closed.

* * *

Strobing lights opened them. Everything was orange. My head wailed and I shook it, relieved feeling had returned. What the hell had the Grey put in my drink last night? I tried to sit and flailed about, hand striking my comm. The sound reduced to a low beeping that was much nicer. Everything took a moment to catch up. Oh, alert. Not head. That was something positive. I flopped on my side, drifting away.

My eyes shot open, watering instantly. It took three minutes to get into uniform, two more for my feet to cooperate with my boots. The trip to the command centre wasn't nice and I nearly trod on one of the Mushies darting by.

I headed into the briefing room to find Golem already seated at the table. Four oddly shaped heads and one human turned in my direction. The blonde frowned.

"Long night," I muttered, sliding into my seat. I aimed a kick at Golem under the table but got Culk instead. Mouthing sorry to the large Orioner, I faced the table.

"Quick recap for the doctor," White started, shooting an irritated glance my way, "We've had contact from Base, but it's not good. They think the aliens are onto them."

I swore softly, but no one else reacted. They'd heard this already. I wondered just how late I was. White glared at me, continuing.

"I don't think the Swarm has caught on that we're up here, or that there's still a working visual network. All we can do is watch There's not much we can do from up here."

His shrug indicated his expectation of their chances. With only eighty humans on board the space station, I tried not to disagree with anyone, but White knew which buttons to push. It was my turn to glare at him but Culk moved between us, blocking my view of the Commander. His rocky face split in a grin he sent in my direction. I snorted at him, listening to the rumble of agreement around the table. As it was the remainder of my culture that faced annihilation, I felt the need to say something.

"It would be so much easier if we could speak to them, help them...something." I mumbled.

The room fell silent and Culk drew back to reveal an ugly grimace contorting White's face.

"What was that, doctor?' His voice was soft, but

something in his tone sent alarm shivering through me.

"I just wish we could hear th—"

I never got to finish.

"We've been over this time and again, Ma'am. Thanks to that bloody Silence Protocol from when they first sent us up, we're less than useless. They can't hear us, we can't hear them."

"But if we could re-establish..."

"We just watch..."

"...a way to communicate, tell them we're..."

"...and there is NO WAY to change that!"

White finished yelling at me and snapped the viewer on, waving to it with his back turned. He glowered at me. I sank back into the chair I hadn't realised I'd left. But it wasn't him that made me sit. It was the viewer.

The clouds that covered the Earth had parted in one area, showing land for the first time in so long. Deep craters rent holes in the earth. Gasps sounded around the table as we all took in the level of destruction the aliens had caused our planet, our people.

The commander finally caught on, lowering his tall frame while he watched, knuckles as white as his name as they clenched the back of his chair. The craters looked large even from here. I knew they must be massive on land.

As I watched, land was obliterated in a rush of billowing red and I knew we had lost them. Our last settlement. The cloud cleared in more areas, until the land masses and part of the sea was visible. All pockmarked with the same deep craters as before.

The darkness began to move again, this time in great sweeping arcs that covered continents.

"What is it?" a female Xewl asked, staring at the screen, her four arms tangling her long, silver hair in a great knot.

I knew the answer but it wouldn't move past my lips.

"The Swarm." White spoke, his voice too loud for the silence of the room. The patterns increased, swirling faster and faster in a chaotic motion. I imagined the millions of bodies it would take to make this visible from orbit.

"What are they doing?"

White swallowed, an audible sound. I looked right at him, as he answered, grateful I wasn't watching the screen.

"Dancing. They're celebrating their win."

The argument on communications had become a moot point. White and I were part of an endangered species.

* * *

"How many are left?"

"There's no way to know."

There was nothing more to say. My tears had dried hours before, though we had known all along this fate was inevitable. Still, we hadn't really planned for this day, as those last survivors had given us hope.

"There may still be some female—"

"Don't. You. Dare."

White fell silent under my glare, shoulders bowed, uniform crumpled. I was certain I looked a wreck but no longer cared. Golem walked into the room, passing a pair of glasses to us. I checked there was nothing green in it amidst White's grumbles of aliens who never knocked, unwilling to repeat last night's performance.

I nodded thanks to the Grey, sipping on the clear fluid. It burned all the way down. I recognised it as the last shots in a bottle of Grey Goose I had been saving. Now it seemed appropriate. I downed it in one, smiling as White spluttered at his end of the table.

"What do we do?" I asked the empty room at large, too numb inside to form a more coherent thought. Something inside me needed action, and genetically altering plants for colonisation wasn't going to cut it right now.

White just sat with his head in his hands, staring at the cantina table. It was like he was suffering shutdown—repeating the same thing over and over. I knew how he felt. I'd witnessed the death of the remaining humans on Earth, after all. The enormity of it all hit me. I swayed in my seat.

A cool hand propped me up, and a small glass was proffered beneath my nose. I shook my head and tried to wave Golem away but he prodded me with the damned thing, insistent.

I sighed, taking the glass, but it was longer than I'd thought. And it was empty. I stared at the thin test tube nestled in my palm. Ideas began to form in my mind, visions of tiny embryos growing. A mission, to resurrect humanity. I smiled up at the little grey alien, fresh tears leaking from the corners of my eyes.

"Thank you."

* * *

Two weeks later we had our first viable specimen ready to go. Nine weeks after that, we had ten. Hitting double figures was cause for celebration. I marvelled at the little beings growing in their units, thinking how blessed we'd been to have the necessary labs and equipment right here with us.

Golem had directed us, reforming the lab into a medical unit suitable to grow the tiny bodies that would be our saviour. Relying on the natural method would have been far less...convenient. With only seven females to fifteen males, demand would be high.

We'd given the embryos every chance possible, the Greys showing us how to select traits in the genes we wanted most. Nothing as cosmetic as redhead or blue eyes, rather those that helped build a stronger body, more resilient, increasing their chances. I had baulked at the thought of playing god initially, but in the end urgency won over. We needed the healthiest babies we could create.

I stared into the tubes, saddened for a moment. Not one of them was mine. Apparently, my eggs didn't like the process...or something. Unviable. Even with all the help Golem had given us. The Grey had a greater grasp on science and genetics than we did, and made our first experiments into growing humans far more successful than I could ever have expected.

All except for mine.

Still, I was pleased we had new life growing aboard the station, even though it wasn't quite what our mission had been when we were first sent up, just after the Area 51 storming. A joke on the internet that had gone so horribly wrong. I wondered if someone in the brass ranks had a premonition to send us up so early in the piece.

I ran my hand over the equipment, kept so clean by our resident Mushies. Essentially a type of polyp with a plethora of gangly eye stalks, they resembled nothing more than a cross between a toadstool that ran about on legs similar to coral found—that used to be found—on a tropical reef. I doubted any were left now. One careened by, and I prayed it wouldn't kill anything overnight. There was some precious cargo in that room.

The Mushies preferred to work in the dark, so I flicked the lights off as I left for the night, and went to get some rest.

I doubted sleep would come easily.

* * *

Dreams of red and black clouds had plagued me since the day we lost the Earth. I knew I wasn't the only one who didn't sleep well. The few remaining humans looked increasingly haggard each morning as we went about our tasks. I made a point to send out regular updates on the embryo's progress and any new techniques we learned from our compatriots. The entire station was on tenterhooks with our pregnancy.

Area 0.51 had always been neutral ground but now we banded together as a nation, the friends we had made over the years supporting us, guiding us in our bid to help humanity continue.

I greeted mates on the way to the coffee machine at the end of the hall, having met half the station out on their morning jog by the time I got there. It was a very long hall.

The aroma of organic beans roasting met my nostrils but before I reached the button that would seal my morning bliss, I was interrupted by a tap on my shoulder. Our only Spider gazed down at me through his many eyes. Even though he'd always been friendly, I backed up. That height was so intimidating. Plus, I was on the "critically endangered" list now. Self-preservation was paramount.

A Mushie skittered around my ankles and took off in the direction of the lab, his eyestalks peering over his hat-shaped noggin as he went. Spider moved off after him. My stomach clenched with foreboding. I left my mug on the machine and took off down the hall.

By the time I reached the lab, a group of residents were rubber-necking at the door. I growled impatiently— apparently a little too loudly, as several turned my way, motioning for others to move. I entered the lab, heading straight for the embryos. A broad chest in a freshly pressed uniform blocked my way. As my nose only came up to the fourth button, I knew immediately who it was.

"White, I thought we agreed you wouldn't come down here without calling me first."

His eyes were narrowed on my face when I finally looked up at him and the unease returned in full force.

"What?"

"Maybe you should go have your coffee."

The fact that he knew my routine didn't even register as alarm triggered me into action. I slammed my open palms into his chest, enough to make him raise his arms in defence. I slipped easily beneath them and froze, breath dying in my lungs.

Every one of our embryos was blackened. Slumped in

their beakers, they looked so harmless. We hadn't been able to do it. This was it. Maybe we could make a few babies—maybe. But humanity would die, here, on the edge of space. Not even on our home planet.

"How did this happen?" It came out as a whimper because that's all I had left.

Salt ran into my mouth but I couldn't brush the tears away. I was numb. Warm hands closed on my shoulders and I cursed, shrugging him off. Cool hands found mine. I stared down at Golem, his wrinkled forehead creased as though in a word, the creature of legend we'd named him for.

"Tryyy gain." He nodded, wobbling on his feet. I wet my lips with my tears, swallowing.

"I can't. I can't try again." I got down on my knees so I looked straight into his oversized eyes, "It's too much. Here." I thumped my heart for emphasis. Too late, I recalled the Grey's hearts were located on the other side but it didn't matter, he got the point.

We'd always had a way of communicating. White frequently muttered about "my pet alien" but he had been quiet about it for many weeks now, ever since... I squeezed my eyes shut, refusing to acknowledge the images hovering at the forefront of my mind. Always there, always blocking.

It was exhausting.

The warm hand returned to my shoulder and I looked

up, not fighting him off this time. Desperate eyes met mine, those of a father silently begging to try again. I bowed my head, my heart aching in my chest. I wondered how much loss it would take for it to grow hard and cold, to stone.

I nodded, knowing that's what he wanted. A relieved sigh hit the back of my neck, the cold breath prickling my skin. Golem pressed my fingers, tugging me up.

"Not theirrrss. Yourrss."

I shook my head.

"No Golem, mine didn't work, remember? They...they didn't take."

"Will make them work." His words came out stunted but as clear as he could make them. I sent him a watery smile, knowing the effort he put into learning our language. I couldn't manage more than a few clicks of his.

"Ok."

* * *

Every day I checked her. Every. Single. Morning. I couldn't bear the thought of what happened to the others happening to her. I wouldn't give her a name—there was too much hope in that—but I knew it was a girl. I could feel her when I was close, as she began to form away from the embryo blob into a tiny, perfect human.

We still didn't know what had caused the first batch to

die. White had accused the Mushies of contaminating the lab, but Golem was adamant it wasn't their fault. I was glad for his intervention, the tiny alien standing up to the tall commander, as I felt a twinge whenever I looked at the Mushies, wondering if he wasn't right about them. Guilt assuaged me until I had convinced myself I had caused the damage. My friend had made me another Golem special, and I had spent the night in blessed oblivion.

Since then, I hadn't used anything to numb the pain, instead focussing on collating the endless notes I collected from the Greys, just in case something happened to her. I'd even taken to sleeping near her on the cold lab floor, unable to settle in my quarters on the other side of the station.

No one knew, and I wasn't about to fess up—White had taken to speaking to me like I was mentally incapacitated which irritated me to no end. Culk and Golem were my rocks—Culk quite literally—cracking jokes and providing me with caffeine. Golem lashed into his work to make sure our baby survived, working harder than any of us. It was as though the death of the embryos had lit a fire inside him. He sat at his table, tapping away with his feet as he worked. I found the familiar sound calming.

I folded my handwritten notes into a bundle. My eyes blurred over the lines. I wouldn't be typing them up tonight. I checked her once more, my fingertips pressing the side of her incubator, humming a soft lullaby my mother used to sing to me.

I slipped beneath the table, popping the thick sheaf beneath my head. Her presence was soothing and sleep came easily here.

It was still dark when I awoke, certain it was some ungodly hour of sparrowfart. I was still too tired for that. Grit clotted my eyelashes as I tried to resettle. It didn't work and I turned on my side, finally opening my eyes. A pair of shoeless grey feet stood right next to my face.

I blinked several times, trying to work out if I was still dreaming. The toes bounced up and down. I recognised the rhythm. Why was Golem in here? I slithered out bonelessly from beneath the table, still sleepy.

"Golem what are you—" I stopped, staring at the table.

Golem had our tiny baby out of the incubator, lying on a heat mat. A long syringe protruded from her skin as he injected her with...something. I tried to speak but ended up looking like a guppy out of water.

"What are you doing." The words came out flat, toneless.

"Hep." He coughed and tried again. "Heelp. You." He pointed a long finger at me, as he continued to inject the baby.

"Please stop that. What's in it?"

My thoughts came out jumbled. Golem nodded, easing the syringe from the baby. I checked her perfect little limbs. Small dots decorated the insides of her arms, where they would be hidden from view during the day.

"What have you put into her?" Feeling returned to me in force. I pushed back a screech that built in my throat and tried to speak normally to my friend. "You said you were helping. How?"

"Make her ssstrong. Ger. From. In here." He tapped his head, but I shook mine, not understanding.

"You are injecting her with your...cells? To make her healthier?"

"Your sssells. Stronger. Better. Like you. Live."

It was one of the longest speeches I'd heard him make.

"You mean, so what happened to the other babies doesn't happen to her?" Was he worried? Should I be worried? When had he taken blood from me? He knew so much about genetics and life, I'd never questioned him. Now I wished I had.

Golem waved his long fingers.

"Babies. Pffftzzz. Not sstrong. Didn't need. You sstrongg. More like you."

He pointed to my abdomen. I looked down, covering it with my hands. He wanted more strong babies like me, from me? He nodded at me, placing my baby back into the incubator. Healthy, glowing with life. I swallowed. The unsettled feeling was back.

"Golem, have you been changing my genetics,

passing them to her?"

He nodded happily, tapping his feet.

"And the other babies, they weren't strong, because they didn't come from me?"

More nodding. I bit my lip, eyes sliding shut.

"One girl, qqueeen, have babies. They girls not w-worth. You." He finished triumphantly, pointing between my baby and I.

Breath caught in my throat. Golem came from a colony—a hive. An in a hive, there was only room for one queen.

"Did you kill the other babies? And stop mine fr-from taking, so you could treasure this life?" I remembered the blackened little bodies, floating in their amniotic solution.

Golem nodded, packing away his equipment. How could we have been so stupid? While he learned our language in an effort to communicate, I had ignored his. Ignored his culture because it was all too hard to learn. Look what it had cost us.

Us. Us here and not down there. Golem had always had an aversion to the other Greys, because they weren't from his colony. We'd had a laugh about how elitist he was.

"The survivors. On Earth. You told them where it was." The night he'd given me that damned green drink. While everyone was asleep and I was passed out, he had contacted the Swarm somehow, and they had destroyed the last of humanity on Earth.

My hands covered my face, scratching my skin as they clenched into claws. I didn't need to look at him to know I was right. He hummed away as I watched, wondering if he would massacre all the females on the ship, so his worthy queen was the only one.

Me.

I leaned back, stretching for my comms. If I could get White up here, maybe we could stop Golem before he did anything else. I couldn't reach the blasted thing, but it didn't matter. When I stood up, a large silhouette filled the doorway. Culk moved into the room, followed by White.

I gaped for a moment, wondering how they had read my mind until White gestured to my comms, then at the floor. I looked down to see the unit just out of my reach, near my notes. I must have rolled on it when I got up, opening the channel. White nodded once, confirmed he'd heard everything.

A rapid clicking startled me. Golem chattered at Culk, pointing at the incubator, and then me. As Culk escorted him to the door, still jabbering, White came to stand beside me. New lines marred his face, aging him. Mine might have held the same look, I wouldn't know. I hadn't looked in a mirror for many weeks.

At the door, Golem turned to face me, his large eyes wide and angry. I felt his betrayal but had no words to describe my own. I turned away from him, returning to the incubator, my hands pressed as close to her as I could be.

That day, White had her moved to my quarters.

* * *

On the morning Nassa was born, nothing went wrong. There were celebrations all round. It was the day after the Swarm left Earth. Fortunately, we were on the other side of the world, tiny ships passing in the dark. Apparently, humanity's complete annihilation was all they had required before they departed.

Our celebrations went on all day and into the evening; we cheered so loudly we nearly missed white noise that hissed through the comms system. White frantically motioned for silence from the console he'd collapsed on at the exodus and we settled, expecting some rousing speech.

Instead, a faint voice filtered through, broken with static.

"Area...five one, are you up...ere...can...hear me? Survivors on...rth...come...us?"

Gasps were quickly hushed. Residents clutched each other, hope and desperation written on their faces. Static continued for a long moment then cleared.

"Area Zero Point Five One...who the hell makes up these bloody names? Humans, are you there? We are survivors on Earth, in the old Area 51 shelters...Area Zero Point..."

White launched into action, diving at the console.

"We're here! Oh, my god, how did you survive? We're here, we can hear you!" White's voice broke as all thought of procedure was tossed out the window.

"We hear you, Point Five One. Coming down for a pint?"

The command room filled with laughter, screams of joy. Tears streamed down White's face.

"This is Commander White. H-how many are you, Area Fifty-One?"

"Two hundred and eighty-four strong, Commander. Can't wait to see you."

* * *

A sigh ran through the station. Earth was vacant of alien life. As I held Nassa in my arms, staring out at the stars, I wondered what it would be like to feel the ground—earth—beneath my feet. I wondered how we would survive in a world with nothing left to provide for us. I wondered if they would ever come back; the Swarm. My baby snored loudly, and tears ran down my cheeks anew at this little miracle. A baby born in space.

The ship shuddered as our small shuttle prepared to

launch. It only held six Earthers for its second run, and now it was our turn. The first meeting with the survivors had gone well. I prepared Nassa for her trip.

We were going home.

2219

396

They Had to Come from Somewhere

By Jacob Baugher

CHAPTER ONE

Turning and turning in the widening gyre
The falcon cannot hear the falconer;
Things fall apart; the centre cannot hold;
Mere anarchy is loosed upon the world,
The blood-dimmed tide is loosed, and everywhere
The ceremony of innocence is drowned;
The best lack all conviction, while the worst
Are full of passionate intensity.
--W.B. Yeats, The Second Coming

September 20, 2219, 200 years since Swarmfall

"Will you stop playing with those fucking dog tags, Ohio-1?" Betsy's voice buzzed in his helmet comm.

"Sorry." Dustin Hammish tucked his father's tags back under his shirt and sat back against the cramped faux-leather seat of his T-26 Dragonfly fighter. The spatial tear above Proxima Centauri-B yawned open in the sky, a black void beyond her twin moons. It seemed to swallow the stars twinkling in the perpetual, bloody twilight on this world they'd found for the last of humanity.

"Where do you think it leads?" he asked Betsy. There were only two of them now, since the last Swarm attack six months ago. Since they'd lost their squad leader. Since he'd lost his wife and daughter.

"Dunno," Betsy said. "Anywhere. Nowhere. Who cares?"

She'd been like this since Captain Tasha died. Indifferent. Irritable. It was grating on his nerves. He pushed the throttle open to do another pass of the landing pad, but the ship sputtered, shook, and dropped a few meters in altitude.

"Fuck, not again." He pulled the throttle back, jiggered the manual fuel injector switch, and the engines came to life with their tell-tale insectoid buzz that gave the Dragonfly fighters their name. He put on speed, carefully testing the craft's yaw and responsiveness. The engines kept up their whine without incident.

"You okay?" Betsy asked.

"Injector's malfunctioning." The ship buzzed along

smoothly beneath him.

He'd missed that sound. It was too quiet in space. That obnoxious buzz meant that, finally, after months of running from the Swarm, they'd finally given them the slip, hopefully for good, and humanity could, once again, settle on solid rock. At least, that was the idea. And not a moment too soon. His ship was badly in need of repair. Betsy's was in worse shape, and even the *Salvation* had whole wings quartered off from where the Swarm had breached the hull and left rooms open to the sucking vacuum.

"Salvation-5 to Ohio squadron, we have visual on you. Well done, Dustin. This one's a beauty isn't she?" Delli's baseball-announcer voice crackled over his comm.

"Copy, Salvation-5. Proceed to the marked landing platform. Airspace clear. No sign of Swarm activity. Confirm when you have visual. Ohio-1, out."

He killed the comm line and observed the planet. He supposed that some would say that Proxima Centauri-B was beautiful. When he and Betsy had scouted it weeks ago, They'd discovered a tidally-locked world full of red rock and arabesque deserts and a perpetual sunset. It had liquid water on the dark side, blue oceans, open plains, and dramatic red-ridged mountains that provided ample cover and protection from the Swarm. Wind currents distributed the heat from the constantly-baked side permanently facing Proxima Centauri, a dying red dwarf, to the rest of the planet, keeping the temps at a cool 76 degrees. As long as they stayed in the twilight zone or on the dark side, the gamma rays wouldn't microwave them like a cheap cut of frozen tilapia.

Sure, it was safe (mostly) and pretty, but it wasn't Earth, and that cold, simple fact made the planet ugly in Dustin's eyes. It wasn't Earth. It wasn't home. Not that he'd ever had a home besides a 10x10 room that he'd shared on Salvation-5 with Carly and Lucy before they died in the last Swarm attack. Photos of them flashed up on the viewscreen he'd rigged to the Dragonfly's dash.

Carly, holding Lucy against her chest just after birth in the medbay. On the little nightstand next to her was an ultrasound photo in a baby blue frame with the words "Baby Lucy, Almost in our Arms!" printed in soft green letters.

The photo switched to one of their wedding. Carly in her white dress in the small hall they'd rented out on the *Salvation* with a window that overlooked the starfield. That was years ago, back before they'd gone through the first Spatial Tear near Io. Saturn filled the viewport when they said "I Do."

He shut the screen off and sat back in the cockpit. Not today, he thought to himself. Not on landfall day. Tomorrow. Tomorrow I'll bury the pictures and start over. But not today.

"What I wouldn't give for a drink," he muttered under his breath.

"What was that?" Betsy again.

"Nothing." The last thing he wanted to do was open up to Betsy.

"We have a visual on you, Ohio squad." Delli's voice crackled, interrupting his thoughts.

"Roger that, Salvation-5. Can you see the landing pad?"

"Affirmative. Dropping landing gear now. Looks like a good spot."

"Welcome home," Dustin said, as the battered old generation ship cut through the sky like a wounded whale (He'd never seen a whale, but he'd read about them in books). "Hopefully this one lasts."

"Copy," Delli said. "Salvation-5 over and out."

The comm crackled and went silent again. Dustin wheeled his Dragonfly around and began circling the descending ship in the traditional defensive formation."

"Boy, I wish Tasha could be here to see this," Betsy said.

He was pretty sure that Betsy and Tasha were lovers.

"Eh, it's not Earth, but I guess it's home." He took one last look up at the spatial tear, that cold, dark void that seemed almost blacker than space itself and wondered again where it led. It was their contingency plan. If the Swarm found them here, they'd plunge through the void and into darkness. Dustin hoped it wouldn't come to that. There was no telling what was on the other side of this particular tear. Most of them ended in the centre of supermassive black holes or spat you out in a raging star furnace. No, that last, ditch effort would most likely end in disaster for Salvation-5, the last generation ship to launch after that group of fucking internet trolls breached the Area-51 base 200 years ago and allowed the Swarm to open the first spatial tear, directly onto Earth.

The whine of his engines faltered again and the Dragonfly started doing its typical *coughcoughsputterjerk* routine.

"Betsy, my engines are going, I'm gonna cut the escort short."

"Roger," she said, "See you down there."

He'd need to take the fighter in for maintenance, but everything needed maintenance these days. Even Salvation-5, which, 200 years ago, had been the pinnacle of human and scientific achievement, seemed like a barely held together bucket of bolts wrapped in duct tape, luck, and a prayer.

But that was to be expected. This contingency of humanity had been on its own for a quarter of a millennium. Things break and can't always be fixed, especially with the Swarm attacks at every turn. Betsy's fighter was in worse shape than his was, and she'd use her ballistics at the last encounter. The one where Lucy and Carly died.

He shivered involuntarily at the memory of those four nukes going off, glassing the settlement on Io and wiping out nearly a quarter of innocent civilians. Dustin had barely made it out alive, and the *Salvation* had sustained massive hull damage. He hoped he never had to see those mushroom clouds again.

Dustin, once again, pushed the thought from his mind and focused on wrestling the Dragonfly through the atmosphere. Delli had already landed the *Salvation*. When he was in space, with no point of reference but pinprick stars, it was easy to forget how big that hulking hunk of metal was. 800m long, sixty stories high, powered by two nuclear high-core reactor engines, supplemented by nearly a dozen solar auxiliary engines. The ship was a skyscraper turned on its side. (Not that he'd ever seen a skyscraper, but he'd read about them on the net). Hundreds of maintenance crews were already inspecting her hull, taking notes, applying patches, Dustin sputtered past them and set the Dragonfly down as gently as he could on one of the secondary pads. Another maintenance crew broke off from the *Salvation* and started toward him.

Yes, humanity was on its last legs. They were crammed on a half-broken ship, protected by half-broken fighters. Their food stores were running thin and they'd been drinking recycled piss for the last 200 years, but, looking around at the red mountains, the stars overhead, glittering in the twilight, feeling the wind soft and sweet against his skin as the cockpit slid open and he stood, stretching his limbs and feeling the heavy weight of gravity press against him, a blissfully secure pressure that no one realised they missed until they lost it, he felt the very first vestiges of home creep into his stomach like butterflies. Yes, it wasn't Earth, but maybe, at last, they could start over here. Maybe this was finally home.

But it never would be. Not without Lucy. Not without Carly. Without his girls, Proxima Centauri B would be nothing but a pretty piece of rock with no one on it who he cared about.

And just like that, the feeling of "home" passed. Dustin grabbed the little viewscreen from the Dragonfly's dash, and went to set up camp. He took one last look up at the stars, at the spatial tear as he clambered down the fighter's ladder. It yawned open like a waiting mouth. Waiting, a voice echoed in the recesses of his mind, for him.

CHAPTER TWO

Surely some revelation is at hand;
Surely the Second Coming is at hand.
The Second Coming! Hardly are those words out
When a vast image out of Spiritus Mundi
Troubles my sight: somewhere in sands of the desert
A shape with lion body and the head of a man,
A gaze blank and pitiless as the sun,
Is moving its slow thighs, while all about it
Reel shadows of the indignant desert birds.
The darkness drops again; but now I know
That twenty centuries of stony sleep
Were vexed to nightmare by a rocking cradle.
And what rough beast, its hour come round at last,
Slouches towards Bethlehem to be born?
--The Second Coming, W.B. Yeats

September 28, 2219, 7 Earth-days since Planetfall, Proxima Centauri-B

Sometimes, when Dustin was drunk, he talked to dead people, or, rather, they came to visit him and talked at him while he tried to ignore them. Sometimes it was Carly or Lucy. Others, it was Captain Tasha, still others, it was Yarvin—the pilot who had first taught him to fly. Today, tonight, though, it was his father.

Dustin sat on the lumpy cot that he'd set up in the corner of the flimsy temp-shelter. The viewscreen that held the photos of his wife and daughter rested on a folding table in its projector mode, casting a 4x3 square of memories onto the wall. He still hadn't buried the photos.

The vision of his father, Tim Hammish appeared much like he always did—in a hospital gown, emaciated, with greying skin. He looked like he did in the days before he died of massive organ failure from the cancer that had riddled his spleen, liver, bowel, and stomach. It was something that, sooner or later, got all Dragonfly pilots. The radioactive ballistic core, kept beneath the cockpit for emergency measures like a Swarm attack, slowly corrupted their cells until the body's repair mechanism gave up. No Dragonfly pilot had ever made it to fifty-five. Dustin tried not to think about it, just like he tried to ignore the vision of his father. It was always the same conversation. The same conversation they'd had on his father's deathbed. He'd hand Dustin the dog tags with the same, strange string of numbers on them.

"My son, my son," he'd said, laying his hands on Dustin's head. The medbay bed creaked on cheap metal springs as his father shifted his weight. "My wish for you is to be the first of our family to make it back to Earth that was. May you live long and well and, when you're dying like me, let you pass with the breeze on your face and the sun on your skin, the scent of lavender and salt in your nose and the warm sea wind in your ears."

Then, his father would lean close, cup Dustin's face and speak urgently, "I don't want to be launched into the void as is our custom. I want to be scattered to the wind at our ancestral home. Promise me, Dustin, promise that if you make it back to Earth that you will do this for me. Promise me, that if you don't make it, you'll give your own son the same instruction. Promise me. Promise!" his father screamed, lunged toward him from the hospital bed and dissolved into sparks.

Dustin sat back against the cot. When they'd first started, the visions disturbed him. Now they were just an annoyance. He popped open another bottle of the homebrewed wine that he'd traded a pack of rations for and glugged down a quarter of it, waiting for the next vision.

Lucy. Her blue eyes burned with tears and she clutched at her stomach, making tiny gasping sounds. She never spoke. She'd been too young to speak when the Swarm got her. Pried open her mouth and choked her airways full of their eggs. His little girl. The little girl that he had been too weak to protect. Dustin closed his eyes. She was the only one that he couldn't look at. He couldn't watch her tiny body writhe and twitch and turn blue until she finally fell still. It always took three minutes and forty-eight seconds. Every time. No more, no less. He started counting. By the time he reached 228, she was gone. Usually, there were only two visitors.

He opened his eyes, numb, sweating, drunk. Lucy, as she was in life, smiling, bubbly; was on the viewscreen, hugging Carly. Tears welled up in Dustin's eyes at the sight, but he didn't cry. He'd stopped crying about their deaths, his girls, his world, months ago and now, whenever he saw their faces or remembered them, or when they visited him in the strange not-dreams that troubled his drunken nights, he didn't really feel anything. Dustin often wondered if that made him a bad person. He wondered if the reason why he obsessively looked through the photos while drinking any liquor he could get his hands on was that, deep down, he was waiting for the tears to come so he could just grieve, move on, and bury the photos or launch them into space in the direction of Earth like he'd done with their Swarm-infested bodies. Instead, he kept the little projector in screen mode, mounted to his cockpit as if he were a soldier, far from home, who needed the reminder about what he was fighting for. Instead, he tortured himself with their faces near-constantly.

He thought about his wife and little girl floating, cold, in the vacuum of space, unable to rot, unable to decay or turn to dust. Unable to be put to rest. He wondered if their ghosts wandered the stars and nebulas like some sort of cosmic haunted wood of black holes and star furnaces. He wondered if, maybe, somewhere, their spirits were still out there and that's why he couldn't seem to let go. That maybe, deep down, his soul still cried out to theirs across the light years: signals that would never reach their destination.

Dustin drained the wine down to its last, sulphurous, yeasty dregs, spat out the grit on the dirt floor and popped open a third bottle. Maybe. He didn't know. Dustin wasn't good at "deep down." So, instead of thinking about it too hard, he took a swig from the bottle and got up to piss. The world spun when he rose from the cot. Red coloured his vision.

"You know," his wife's voice said, "your little girl doesn't blame you."

Carly Hammish stood in the middle of his shelter, naked. She appeared much the same as she did on their wedding day, with that sultry "I know you like what you see," smile curling her lips. She crossed the room, leaned over him. The tips of her breasts brushed over his bare chest as she leaned down, opened her mouth, and kissed him. Dustin melted into the human contact, kissing her back and drawing her hard against him. It was a dream. He knew it was a dream—vision—hallucination—whatever, but he couldn't help himself. Months of cold beds and colder nights had worn on him. Even though he'd stopped crying, one thing Dustin knew: he needed his wife.

"I missed you so much," he tried to say, but he couldn't.

Carly wouldn't let him. She still kissed him. But her soft lips smoothed, turning cold and leathery, like clammy worms. Something slid down his throat, blocked his airway. Golf ball sized globs dripped into his mouth like soft boiled eggs. He choked on them, bit down, salty goo exploded in his mouth. He spat it out; opened his eyes—his wife wasn't kissing him anymore, it was one of the Swarm. Praying mantis eyes peering down at him, four of its eight legs straddling him, its reproductive organs positions over his mouth. Small white sacks, wet with creamy ichor dangled on its underbelly, undulated, and belched forth another soft-boiled egg with a fleshy squelch.

More salty goo slid in his mouth. Dustin bit down hard at the egg, spat it out, and headbutted the alien right in the egg sack. Species aside, he didn't know of any being that particularly enjoyed blunt force trauma to the naughty bits, and the Swarm was no different. It squealed that high-pitched insectoid scream and leapt off him. He rolled off the cot, blankets sticking to him, and retrieved his gun from the bedside table. The Swarm was on its back, all eight legs grasping at its egg sacks. White goo covered the floor.

Dustin stepped around it, still holding the eggs in his mouth, making sure to stay clear of the flailing legs, and executed it. Even aliens aren't immune to double taps to the head. The thing convulsed once, twitched, and went still. In the sudden silence, screams rang out across Proxima B's eternal twilight. Somehow, the Swarm had found them, even here.

The camp alarms blared, that annoying *wermwerpwerp* that signalled an attack. Dustin holstered the gun, checked his clips. He spat the goo out. Small white worms wriggled on the ground. A chill crawled down his spine. One of the egg sacks had ruptured.

He opened the small nightstand drawer next to his cot, pulled out a brown bottle unstoppered it, and drank down clear liquid that smelled like acetone. Hands shaking, he squatted next to the Swarm's corpse, held his breath for as long as he could, then vomited in three heaving gasps that left wine, rations, and more fleshy worms wriggling in it.

"Fuck." He hit the bottle again. More worms. Again. Vomit. Nothing, just pink-tinged fluid. "No," he growled, and drank the last dregs from the bottle. More pink vomit. A single worm, this one with its barbs extended out of its mouth, flopped out onto the floor.

"Christ, no." He picked the worm up, dug out a small metal box from his pocket, and placed it inside.

They were within him now, he wasn't sure how many, but they were there. He needed to get to the medbay. They could use this worm to target the others. It was possible. Others had been saved before. His guts twisted and he heaved over again. More vomit, this time, crimson. He had a day. Maybe two, before the neurotoxins began to take hold. He drew his gun, took a deep breath, and ran out into the twilight, into the screams. He took the viewscreen on his way out.

Chaos reigned. Dustin sprinted across the rocky ground, trying to ignore the convulsions in his stomach. Two of the Swarm tore into the shelter across from his, giant insectoid mandibles thrashing at the flimsy sheet metal, and drug out a screaming man, clutching his son to his chest. The klaxon alarms blared, but he could still hear the screams. He skidded to a stop, took aim with the pistol, and opened fire. The pair dropped the man and skittered towards him, blinding fast for insects the size of small starfighters.

Dustin dived toward the first, rolled, and came up right under the thing's underbelly. He put three staccato shots into its abdomen. The first Swarm crumpled. The second seized him from behind with its forelegs, lifted him up, nearly three meters off the ground, and held him close to its face, so he was looking into those multi-faceted red insectoid eyes.

Host. A crawling, mucous, gargles-with-razor-blades voice slithered through his mind.

Dustin struggled to raise his pistol, but the Swarm pinned his arm at his side.

Foolish human. You are now a progenitor of our race. You are Swarm. Do not resist.

Holy shit, it can talk.

Yes, mortal. We can speak. We learned your tongue

from the research facility. From your scientists.

The Swarm's voice seemed to rebound from everywhere and nowhere all at once. It bounced around his brain. It resonated from the rock, from the air, from the sky. The monster shifted its grip on him. Dimly, below, he could hear the alarms, the shouting, the screams.

Your race is ended, now, the Swarm said, *just as we have ended all races for all time. We were here at the beginning. We were Outside for so long, until your kind let us back in. It is finished. You are ours. Even now, our kind writhe and wriggle through your blood.*

And the Swarm raised him up and turned him around in its claws so he faced the sunset. Trillions of black specks coloured the twilight, blocking out the crimson sun, plunging the camp into near-darkness.

It is over, Dustin Hammish. You have los—

The mental contact broke. The Swarm twitched, dropped him. His stomach dropped out of his body for what seemed like an eternity. He struck the ground, turned his ankle. Pain shot up his leg.

"Come on, Hammish, we're not dead yet." Delli's radio announcer voice snarled in his ear. "Help me!"

"They can speak," Dustin said. "I heard them."

More hands grasped him on his other side. "Get up, Dustin, do it for Tasha."

"Fuck Tasha," he groaned, but allowed Betsy to hoist

him up.

The world spun around him as he allowed them to half-carry him through the chaos of the camp. Soldiers formed up on either side of them, heavy calibre machine guns chattering through the night. Delli stopped at one of the sirens, and keyed into it, pulled down a microphone. The klaxons cut off.

"Citizens of Salvation-5, make your way to the generation ship. Takeoff in three minutes."

He replaced the mic and the klaxons began again. Dustin shook Betsy off and tested his weight on the ankle. It throbbed dully. He wouldn't be doing any sprinting, but he could move. He recovered his pistol. One of the soldiers surrounding them offered him a rifle that he had slung over his shoulder.

"No," Delli said. "Dustin, Betsy, I need you in the air now. If the Swarm gets here before we can take off, we're finished."

"Aye, aye, Cap," Dustin said with false cheer. His voice rasped in his throat. The world was still spinning, though he wasn't sure if it was from the wine, the Swarm's mental link, or from the worms in his guts. "I'll need the medbay soon." He dug the box with the worm in it out of his pocket and handed it to Delli.

"Understood."

The sky darkened further. The Swarm were coming.

CHAPTER THREE

What passing-bells for these who die as cattle?
— Only the monstrous anger of the guns.
Only the stuttering rifles' rapid rattle
Can patter out their hasty orisons.
No mockeries now for them; no prayers nor bells;
Nor any voice of mourning save the choirs,—
The shrill, demented choirs of wailing shells;
And bugles calling for them from sad shires.
--Anthem for Doomed Youth, Wilfred Owen

"Cover our 6, Ohio-1," Delli's voice was strained. "If they breach the hull again, it's over."

Dustin strapped into the Dragonfly, toggled the fuel injector switch, and punched the engines to life. They came online with a roar. His indicators flashed green and that telltale buzz filled the cockpit.

"Copy. Taking off." The ship started the takeoff sequence, but he overrode it, pulled back on the throttle, and rocketed into the sky. The ground dropped away and he snap-rolled to about-face toward the setting sun and the Swarm. They'd grown in numbers, stretching across the horizon line as far as he could see. The sun painted the desert that led up to the mountains sanguine.

"Ohio-1, engaging," he said.

"Ohio-6, engaging," Betsy echoed.

"Taking off," Delli responded.

Dustin peered over the edge of the Dragonfly's cockpit to the ground below. People Swarmed up the *Salvation*'s ramp even as the engines blazed to life.

"Negative, negative!" he shouted into the mic. "There are still people down there."

"Leave it, Ohio-1," Delli's voice was sharp. "It's too late."

"Delli—"

"Survival over everything, Hammish. Now isn't the time to find religion."

Dustin snarled a curse into the mic, but turned back to the approaching Swarm. There were so many. Too many to fight. A great cloud that engulfed the sun. He could hear them calling out to him, silent cries in his brain. Hear half-whispered promises of seeing Carly and Lucy again, of seeing everyone he'd ever lost in the Swarm attacks, if only he would just submit, he could relive the past for eternity, wallowing and lost in his memories, in the collective memories of every species the Swarm had ever exterminated. He couldn't resist. Honestly, he didn't even want to. But, fortunately, Dustin Hammish didn't have to resist, he just needed to drop a bomb.

"Salvation-5," he barked into the mic. "Divert all power to rear deflector shields. Starting ballistic launch sequence."

"Negative, Hammish," Delli said. "We're too close. Engage at point-blank range."

The voices in his head were getting louder now. His guts twisted. He convulsed. Hot, acidic vomit splattered onto his flight suit. More worms.

"Hey, Delli, you insufferable fuckwit," he shouted into the mic. "I got Swarm larvae spilling out of my mouth. I can hear them in my head. I'm launching the goddamn nukes whether you're ready or not. Ohio-1, out."

Angry shouts sounded over the comm, but he shut it off. The *Salvation's* rear deflectors blazed to life in a shower of blue sparks as it cruised by. Dustin opened the Dragonfly's console, pressed the emergency button. The craft shuddered as the nuclear power core separated and dropped into four ballistic missiles at the end of each of the quad wings. Dustin glanced up at the stars, at the cosmic tear, the black void that seemingly engulfed the sky.

Dear God, don't let me die. The viewscreen showed a picture of Carly kissing Lucy on the cheek. Lucy's smile lit up the screen.

The Swarm screamed toward him, bulbous praying mantis eyes black and bloody, reflecting the sunset. Their voices raged in his head. Somehow, they seemed to know what he was doing. They started to climb. A formation of them broke off from the main cloud and sped at him. *They can hear my thoughts too*, he realised. His guts twisted again. He snarled.

"Enjoy the light show, fuckers."

He pulled the trigger. The high-pitched buzzing of the Dragonfly dropped back to that diseased drone that had indicated the injector failing during planetfall. Four streaks of light rocketed from the edges of the Dragonfly's wings, sending the fighter into a tailspin. Dustin pulled back the throttle, pointed the ship's nose at the sky, and punched it forward. The Dragonfly's engines coughed, sputtered, and stalled.

He should have been terrified, but all he could think was, *Goddamn mechanics.*

The ship fell, spiralling toward the ground, toward the Swarm. There was a thunk as he sheared through one of their wings. He ripped the control panel open, jiggered the injector switch, punched the engines. Nothing.

Come on, come on, it can't end like this. He slammed a fist into the console, pulled back the throttle, and punched the ignition.

The engines roared to life. He slammed the throttle forward, and the ship shot toward the sky, climbing out the Swarm, but he wasn't out of the woods yet. If he wasn't at a high enough altitude or behind the *Salvation's* shields before the blast.

There was a muffled *whumpwhumpwhumpwhump.* Light exploded in the cockpit and suddenly, the Dragonfly had lift, baby. He shot past the *Salvation*, into the upper stratosphere, and finally into the black. Only then did he realise that he was screaming.

He whipped the ship around and killed the engine, watching as the debris settled. The *Salvation* sped toward him, the fireball blazed behind it and then faded to nothing. Just a crater in the background filled with a cloud of settling dust composed of bug guts and those too slow to make it onto the *Salvation*.

"Ohio-1, report in." Delli's voice snapped in his ear.

"Ohio-1, reporting in. All's quiet on the Eastern front."

"You'd better fucking hope so after that display. Can you make it through the tear?"

"Yes." Though the Dragonfly shuddered beneath him. "Pretty sure I can," he amended."

"Wonderful. Stay close. No more heroics."

They sped toward the void. That wide slot of blackness that seemed to stretch for kilometres in the sky above them and swallow the very stars.

"Approaching anomaly," Delli's voice was low, but still shook with nerves. "Brace for impact."

Dustin couldn't really brace, so he held his breath. The void grew closer and closer, just cold blackness expanding and seeming to swallow the sky. He powered down the internal cabin lights, the portable viewscreen that rotated photos of his daughter and wife, and watched the darkness grow nearer.

"Do not go gentle into that good night." The words rose unbidden to his mind, spoken in his mother's voice as she read to him from an old, cracked, Norton Anthology of English Literature. But, looking closer, tiny points of light flashed out along the edge of the void. Electric blue and neon green and angry, bloody crimson. Midday yellow and sunset orange. Deep, nebula purple. They seemed to bend in on themselves, swirling and coalescing until three spheres of technicoloured fireflies hung in the void, surrounded by blackness.

"Ohio-1, you seeing this?"

"Copy." The firefly orbs grew closer and closer. The spheres filled the viewport, looming like so many coloured suns, dwarfing even the *Salvation*. But between them, an even deeper blackness that was still-water calm filled the spaces. He remembered a documentary that his mother had once shown him, a series about old-Earth. It had shown the depths of a great salt lake, larger than the generation ship, called an ocean. Under the miles and miles of crushing depths of dark water, something extraordinary would happen—heavier, more concentrated salt water would sink to the ocean floor, forming a salt lake beneath the miles of darkness. This space between the glowing spheres was like that. Concentrated Darkness. Concentrated void. *Concentrated death*, rose the Swarm's voice in his head. But they headed for it.

Dustin followed, passing between the spheres, lights

winked and twinkled like fireflies outside his ship, and, for a moment, he thought he could stay there forever.

Thump. All at once, the lights winked out. The Dragonfly stalled. His instruments went dark. The floodlights flickered out and the red emergency lights in the cockpit popped on. The comm squealed. He cursed and ripped it out of his ear. The viewport fogged with his breath. Then, even the emergency lights shorted out too. Dustin sat there in the darkness, trying not to let panic take hold of him.

He tried the comm. Nothing. He tried to steer the ship. Nothing. He couldn't tell what was up, down, or sideways, if he was going forward of backward or just stalled in space.

Panic rose up again, his guts clenched, he vomited between his legs. He couldn't see anything, but he could taste the blood in his mouth. It just wasn't fair. He didn't want to be stuck here in the blackness. This couldn't be the end. He was supposed to be able to see Earth before he died. That's what his father had said. He promised him he'd spread his ashes. The ashes. The ashes he'd kept in the little metal box in the Dragonfly's storage compartment for the past 10 years. He wasn't supposed to die in a cold void surrounded by dead metal.

'My son, my son, you will pass with the breeze on your face...' the words came back to him, but they held no comfort. His father was just a man. He wasn't God or Fate or whatever cruel power seemed to dictate the rhythm of the universe. He was going to die here, in the void, either from lack of oxygen or from his Swarm-infested guts. Just like Carly. Just like Lucy. Just like they all would, eventually. There was no hope in the darkness.

"I can't, I can't, I can't..." His chest heaved, constricted. More vomit. He couldn't do it. He clutched the viewscreen in one hand, the dog tags in the other, and wept. He'd failed everyone he'd ever cared about. His father, Carly, Lucy, all of them. Their faces exploded in his brain now, and finally, the tears came, gushing forth like a waterfall. They flowed hot and swift over his cheeks, his nose clogged up, and his face took on that congested, buzzing quality so familiar to new widows and orphaned children. He'd failed, and he'd die out here, alone with a belly full of parasites, like a rabid dog. He supposed it was what he deserved.

"I can't, I can't, I—"

The engines roared back to life, the headlights came on, the whining buzz of the Dragonfly filled the cockpit one again. And, thank God, the headlights illuminated Salvation-5 dimly in front of him. The generation ship powered back online and lights blazed out, her engines glowed blue. Dustin punched the thrusters on the Dragonfly and followed. The darkness was fading. Dim, blue light seemed to emit from everywhere and nowhere at once, illuminating a round tunnel of blazing, twinkling stars. They whizzed by on all sides, too fast for his eyes to track until, suddenly, two starkly different scenes emerged on the horizon. One, a starfield filled with strange constellations and dark, shapeless rocks floating in the vacuum.

And in the other? A small blue marble of a planet hung lonely against a black background. Green continents coloured its surface, surrounded by blue oceans. Dustin's breath caught in his throat. It was Earth-that-was. The ancestral home of the human race. The planet his family had fought and bled and died on. He clutched the dog tags around his neck. His home. His father's last wishes. Maybe Carly and Lucy's corpses had found their way here through the lightyears. Maybe, maybe someone down there remembered his family, how his great-great-great-whatever ancestor all those generations ago survived the Area-51 invasion that set off this whole shitshow.

'Ohio-1," Delli's voice crackled in the helmet. He picked it up, wiped sick off of it.

"I copy."

"Stay close," Delli said. "We're heading for Deep Space. The Swarm may still be on Earth. We cannot violate Directive-1."

"Where's Betsy?" Dustin said.

"Her comm went dead in the tear. She's on our blindside watching the sky. Form up."

"Copy." But he didn't form up on the *Salvation*'s wing. Instead, he hung back, behind the engines as Delli steered the hulking ship toward the starfield to nowhere.

"Dustin, form up," he snapped again.

"You go," Dustin said. "Having engine trouble. Ballistics must have knocked something loose. I only have one thruster. I'll rendezvous with you on the other side. Hammish out."

He killed the engines and waited as the *Salvation* hit the event horizon, flickered, and was gone. The comm squealed with the static feedback from the background radiation, but he could still hear Delli in snippets: "Asteroid belt. 2 a.u. past Kepler-22...look for suitable...thrusters...habitat...copy?"

Dustin turned the mic off, coaxed the Dragonfly to life and fought down another wave of nausea, and not just because of the Swarm larvae in his guts. The *Salvation* was all he'd ever known. Everything he was he owed to that ship and to Delli. Suddenly, the Earth didn't seem so welcoming, it seemed to hang, almost sinister in its tranquillity. What if no one was there and it was just another dead world? What if the Swarm were still there? What if he didn't get there in time and died in the fighter, leading the Swarm back to Earth via their hivemind? He could still hear them whispering vaguely in the back of his head. He quashed the thoughts away. It was simple. Either there were humans there and they could help him, or he'd die alone on a field of green grass at his ancestral home while scattering his father's ashes. A win-win, in his opinion. He whipped the Dragonfly around, punched the throttle, and headed towards the little blue marble.

CHAPTER FOUR

If you could hear, at every jolt, the blood
Come gargling from the froth-corrupted lungs,
Obscene as cancer, bitter as the cud
Of vile, incurable sores on innocent tongues,—
My friend, you would not tell with such high zest
To children ardent for some desperate glory,
The old Lie: Dulce et decorum est
Pro patria mori.
--Wilfred Owen

The computer screamed warnings at him. He'd punched in the coordinates on his father's dog tags into the autopilot but the Dragonfly was now losing altitude entirely too fast. Okay, okay, technically, he was falling. The engines had given out somewhere in the upper atmosphere, and he'd tried to use the air currents to glide in for a landing, but without the autopilot, the ship didn't scan the air for turbulence, and he'd gotten caught in a downdraft. The Dragonfly wasn't really meant for air travel, she was primarily a space-faring vessel. For what he hoped would be the last time, one way or another, Dustin ripped open the control panel and jiggered the engine choke. They coughed, sputtered, buzzed, and he regained control of the ship. The autopilot came back online and corrected his course west. He flew over a blue-green ocean, small rounded mountains covered with evergreens and trees with fiery leaves.

Then, seemingly all at once, a vast flat plain opened up beneath the Dragonfly like tranquil sea. But instead of blue, it was green, amber, and golden. The colours of vegetation that he'd only heard about in books and on the net. Long, dappled grass swayed in the noon-day sunlight. Still the plains continued on. The Dragonfly swooped lower, dropping below the cotton-candy cumulus clouds that raced hazy shadows across the flat ground. And somehow, despite the writhing in his guts and the unexpected melancholy of abandoning Delli, Betsy, and the *Salvation*, he felt, oddly, a feeling of warmth wash over him like the golden sun. A feeling that spoke to him on a primal level. The same feeling he felt when he held Lucy for the first time or his first kiss with Carly: a deep, warm, harmonious peace that seemed to radiate out from his core and spread to his fingertips: a feeling of home.

The Swarm larvae sort of ruined it for him. His guts twisted and, for the fourth time in the last two hours, he spewed red vomit onto the floor. The entire cockpit smelled of it. He scanned the plains for something, anything. A hospital, a settlement, a farmhouse, but what few houses he could see were clearly abandoned, falling down or completely in ruins. So, he sat back and let the ship fly itself and tried not to think about the parasites. Surely, someone would be here. The entire planet couldn't be vacant.

He came upon the farmhouse suddenly. It was a big, three-story white-sided building with a faded red roof and what looked like the remains of wrap-around front porch. He'd been flying for the better part of four hours. The Dragonfly's engines had failed twice, he'd vomited six more times, the fluid turning progressively bloodier. His legs had started cramping. He needed fluids. He supposed he could have made the trip faster. The Dragonfly was a fighter, but he hadn't wanted to push the engines. The vast plains had continued on for the better part of the trip until the last 20 minutes where lofty mountain peaks had materialised out of the horizon. White snow caps were atop some. Others were barren brown. Dustin didn't like them. They reminded him too much of the mountains on Proxima B.

The farmhouse faced the plains, dilapidated, rotted, but still standing, somehow, after all these years. The Dragonfly circled it once and started the landing sequence. The ship set down surprisingly gentle for all the damage it had sustained. Dustin wasted no time in popping the cockpit open. The internal pressure released with a hiss. His ears popped and, finally, he took his first breath of Earth air.

Instead of the scents of the sea, lavender, and wildflower, the smells of smoke, rot, and dead animals filled his nose. Dustin tried to fight down another episode of vomiting. He heaved twice, and a single, bloody string of mucous dripped onto the Dragonfly's floor. He spat it out, took another deep breath, regretted it, and climbed out of the cockpit. The grass was almost head high on him, but he pushed through it and toward the farmhouse's front door.

He had to clamber up onto the porch (the stairs had rotted out long ago). The boards creaked under his weight but still he continued on and entered the house. The letters HAMMISH were blazed golden on the front door, though they were cracked, faded and peeling. The door was slightly ajar.

It opened on a dead house. The smell of mildew and rot had seeped into everything. The room was wide, high ceilinged, with textured walls covered in flaking paint that had long ago been...a pale green? He couldn't tell. Dust covered the hardwood floor like snow flurries. On the far wall, a fireplace with a wooden mantle stood, dark as a void. Pictures cluttered the mantle's surface. Photos of dead ancestors?

"Hello?" Dustin said. "Is anyone there? The house creaked around him in answer.

"Hello?" His voice fell flat against the dust and decay, like he was shouting outside after that snowstorm on Illien, that small exoplanet they'd stumbled upon years ago. Lucy had only been three or four, but he remembered her tottling around unsteadily outside their shelter in a puffy pink snowsuit.

She fell, cut her hands on a piece of metal hidden in the snow. She screamed. Drops of crimson blood dripped out onto the blanket of pure white. Dustin ran to her, cradled her in his arms, and as hot, fat tears rolled down her cheeks, red from the cold, she buried her face in his shoulder and sobbed while he held her.

"Carly!" He'd yelled for his wife and that same, flat quality overcame his voice. He stymied the blood that was melting the fallen snow. His daughter's blood.

Something inside Dustin finally broke. He'd been there for his daughter in that moment. He'd been able to hold her, to comfort her, to help her. Tears blurred his vision. He sank down to the floor, pulled his knees up to his chest, buried his face in them, and wept for his daughter, his wife, himself. Alone. The only voice on the planet.

He stayed there for a long time, but eventually the tears had turned to sobs, and the sobs to vomiting. He wiped his mouth and pushed himself to his feet, took a deep breath of the dead air. He needed to get out of here. This wasn't the Earth that was promised. This was a tomb. The Swarm had taken everything from him, and here he was, ready to succumb to their infection. Was he really that much of a coward?

He turned to leave, but stopped, footprints in the dust by the fireplace catching his eye. Could there be someone else here? He crossed the room, crouched, and studied them. No, they were faded, maybe weeks old.

Weeks? Could there be other humans on Earth? Then he dismissed the thought. The footprints didn't matter. They were too old to be someone who was still living in the house and, if they were still nearby, they certainly didn't have the medical capacity to help him recover from the Swarm's infection. He was alone, but he had a promise to keep.

Slowly, shakily, he made his way back to his Dragonfly, popped the storage compartment and retrieved the small metal box that housed his father's ashes as well as the vidscreen that held the photos of Carly and Lucy. Dustin clambered back onto the dilapidated porch, opened the urn, waited for a strong wind, and flung the ashes into it. They carried on the breeze up and away, out of sight. He cupped the vidscreen in his hand, walked into the house, and set it on the mantle, among the countless other yellowing, disintegrating photos of the relatives that he'd never met and would never meet. He made to leave, but turned back, grabbed the small screen and kissed it once. It displayed a photo of Carly and Lucy laughing together, both with their blue eyes warm with love, looking at him, behind the camera.

"I love you," he said for the last time.

He left. He headed back to the Dragonfly, powered it up, and sent a distress signal to Becky. The Dragonfly's console showed she'd received it. A message came crawling back:

Glad you're not dead. On my way.

There was nothing for him on the Earth anymore, just memories and ghosts and old bones. No, he belonged among the stars.

EPILOGUE

Like the generations of leaves, the lives of mortal men. Now the wind scatters the old leaves across the earth, now the living timber bursts with the new buds and spring comes round again. And so with men: as one generation comes to life, another dies away.

--Homer, Iliad

The planet was perfect. Captain Dellitino Moss surveyed its pockmarked, baked clay surface from the bridge of the *Salvation*. Carbon based. 1.12 times the size of Earth. Fresh water in deep ice cores, everything you'd want in a planet. It wasn't as pretty as Proxima-Centauri B, but it would do. Also, if his compositional readouts were correct, it contained high levels of lead and gold; good natural cloaking mechanisms. Not to mention the gold could be the basis of a future currency. "Currency is the basis of society," his father always said.

He tried to get used to the idea of living on yet another planet on the long list of planets they'd tried to colonise in his fifty years as captain, instead of on the *Salvation*. He wasn't sure he liked it, but it was necessary. He wasn't part of a 200-year dynasty of pilots to let a little thing like personal desire get in his way. He had a responsibility to these people, likely the last of humanity, to keep them safe.

Sure, he'd seen the Earth through that distant wormhole, and he knew the fact that Hammish hadn't joined them yet meant he'd deserted for it. If Delli had been a scrub pilot he'd probably have done the same thing. But the Earth wasn't safe for anyone anymore. Not for him, not for humanity. It was more than likely still Swarm-occupied, and, as much as Delli wanted to breathe free air again, he'd settle for filtered and recycled air instead. Safety over beauty. That was Delli's motto, and this planet fit it. It was in close proximity to the spatial tear, and the randomness of the nearby asteroid belt would help to throw off any searching Swarm, especially if they made it underground in the next few months. Sure, they'd have to strip the *Salvation*, dismantle the shield generators and reinstall them over the settlement to protect them from the asteroid belt. They'd have to wreck his ship, but safety over beauty. Safety over convenience. The shield would keep them safe from impact. The *Salvation's* cloaking device, along with the heavy metals beneath the planet's surface and the cloaking background radiation and sheer randomness of the belt would keep the Swarm off their tail.

It was worth it. Delli had finally achieved his purpose—his whole family's purpose. No one else, no other generation ship pilot, so far as he knew, had done that. There had been four others: Genesis-1, Exodus-2, Journeyman-3, Interstellar-4. He'd lost contact with all of them.

A warning alert cut through the bridge. Three quick beeps and a long drone. A ship had taken off from the planet's surface.

"Status report?" Delli snapped.

"Ohio-6 has taken off, Captain," the sensor relay's technician said.

He turned back to the viewport. A single Dragonfly fighter streaked through the sky and headed for the tear that hung ominous in the sky above them.

"Let her go," Delli said, "Ready the medbay for emergency Swarm detox." Then, under his breath, "Welcome back, Hammish. Hope you're not too late." He watched Becky's ship until it disappeared into the special tear.

"Sir?" Ketra, his co-pilot, asked. "Your orders?" No time to think about Hammish. Security over comfort.

"Dismantle the *Salvation*. Deflectors first. Shield the settlement. This is our new home."

"What should we call it, sir," asked Ketra.

He thought it over for a long moment, then he thought of the *Salvation*; the ship that'd served humanity so well for twenty generations.

"Safe Harbour," he said. "Safe Harbour. We're finally home."

2519

Delaying Action

By Peter J. Foote

The bridge speaker pops and hisses as it's powered up, and then; "...are a peaceful people of over 270,000 souls. We don't have the resources to stop the asteroid or flee Earth. I have ordered the whole population to make their way to the capital cities and assist with the construction of underground bunkers, though we have little hope they will protect the population. Please, is there anybody out there?"

"The message is still on repeat, Captain," Com-tech Morzycki says as he turns a dial on his bridge console and the scratchy transmission fades into nothingness.

"Thank you, Morzycki," Captain Hammish says. He continues his path around the bridge, his shoes scuffing the carpet as he goes.

Poor Morzycki, the youngest of us and seen by many as a little brother, now all the transmissions of a doomed people are being filtered through his ears. I know this isn't what he thought he would do when he signed up to serve his planet.

Cradling his coffee cup, the steam bathing his face, Captain Ira Hammish meanders around his bridge, adding to the wear marks in the ship's carpet like an established animal trail through old forest growth. Passing bridge consoles with chairs repaired with tape and keypads with hand-painted icons to replace those worn off by countless keystrokes, he finishes his loop and returns to his command chair at the back of the bridge.

Peering over the curve of his cup as he takes a sip of the cooled coffee, Captain Hammish scans his officers as they go about their assigned tasks, and smiles.

I couldn't have asked for a better bunch. I hope they can forgive themselves for what we must do today, they're trained to accept that they might lose their lives in the call of duty, taking the lives of others, especially innocents, is a different matter altogether. Doing the right thing can be a bitch sometimes.

Swallowing the last of the coffee, straining the grounds between his teeth, their bitterness makes his left eye twitch as he chews them. The ritual forced upon them by the failing coffee machine complete, Captain Hammish clips the stained cup to the carabiner on his belt.

"Morzycki, what's the ETA of The Swarm?"

At the mention of the alien menace that is heading their way, the mood of the bridge becomes further subdued; voices shift to whispers and several crew members lean closer to hear the reply.

"Unchanged, Captain. Just under seventy-two hours until they reach the planet," Morzycki replies.

"Well good. Open a channel to Earth."

"Right away, Captain," Morzycki says, his eyes never meeting the Captain's, and his shoulders stiff as he taps away at his console.

With a sad smile at the back of the young officer, Captain Hammish shakes his head. Get your mind in the here and now, the crew will be fine, he thinks as he turns to the pickup monitor and stares at the face reflected back at him. A thin man, his youth going the same way as his receding hairline. A man no one ever called handsome, but the laughter lines around his eyes suggest that looks aren't everything. Buttoning up the collar of his faded grey coveralls, Hammish brushes an imagined piece of lint from the ship's badge, hand-sewn to the breast of his coveralls—an embossed white orchid with the words *Long Night* beneath the flower as if cradling it. Tattered and threadbare after three years in deep space the ship might be, nevertheless, it's a point of pride of those who sail on her that their ship's badge looks as crisp and clean as the day they set sail.

The monitor flickers to life, and a red dot in the bottom right of the screen blinks. "Recording now, Captain," Morzycki calls from his console without turning.

With a sigh and a small nod at the back of the Com-tech's head, Hammish lifts his chin and speaks. "Greetings, citizens of Earth. My name is Captain Ira Hammish of the *Long Night*, a Sol System deep space patrol ship from the planet Safe Harbour. We have received your pleas for aid and are responding to the crisis with teams on the surface of the asteroid which we have dubbed Solar Body One. These teams are outfitting SB-One with reaction thrusters stripped from our survey probes in the hope that SB-One will change its course. At its current heading, SB-One will brush your atmosphere in seventy hours, causing major widespread devastation. I recommend that you continue your efforts in building your underground bunkers at the capitals." Looking away at another display, Captain Hammish continues, "I will contact you again in twelve hours with a status report. *Long Night* signing off."

Tension leaves Hammish's shoulders as he turns away from the monitor. "Morzycki, send that off to Earth every twenty minutes and keep broadcasting until we get a reply." Com-Tech Morzycki gives the captain a slight nod and bends over his workstation. Captain Hammish sighs and turns to the bridge crew. "I'll be in my quarters," he says as he leaves the room.

* * *

With a glass of amber liquor balanced on his knee, Captain Hammish stares at his cabin's ceiling, ignoring the concerned glances he is receiving from his first officer.

Perched on the edge of her chair, First Officer Althea Foglund glares at her captain and, for the thousandth time, tries to guess his thoughts. As the amount of liquor in the captain's glass lowers by several centimetres, Althea frowns, clears her throat, and gives voice to her concerns.

"Maybe it would have been better if we'd stayed silent, Captain. They've been lost to the rest of humanity for so long, aren't we getting their hopes up?"

What you mean, Althea, is that I'm a cold, heartless bastard and that by giving them false hope I'm displaying the worst aspect of humanity. Maybe you're right, but if the citizens of Earth know what's coming, they could scatter and hide. To save the rest of humanity, I need them contained. I hope you never have to make a similar decision when you make captain.

Swirling his drink, watching the liquor creep higher and higher up the sides of the glass, Hammish says quietly, "It may be easier for us, Althea, but those people on Earth have a right to know that the rest of humanity is out here and will remember them. When humanity threw itself out into the void of space, every soul took the risk of starting over, but that same drive that pushed us outward still connects us to our common heritage."

Making eye contact with the first officer, Hammish concludes, "If there isn't anything further, I need a couple hours shut-eye, and you're supposed to be on bridge duty."

With a blush blistering her young freckled cheeks, Althea nods and hurries from the room, missing the world-weary smile aimed at her back.

When his cabin door closes, Hammish sees his wet hand, the swirling of his drink had become too violent and he didn't even notice. Putting the glass down, he sucks the liquor off his fingers and turns off the light.

* * *

"I'm sorry to wake you, Captain, but we have a problem on SB-One." First Officer Foglund's voice crackles through the dented communication grill in the cabin's wall beside Hammish's head. Flailing, Hammish knocks his glass off the table, watches the liquor soak into the carpet before stabbing the comms button. He gives a curt "Acknowledged", and lurches to his refresher.

Hammish, his face scrubbed and a stim patch behind his ear, walks past the glass on the floor and out of his quarters.

Rising from the command chair to stand beside it, First Officer Althea Foglund waits for him to unclasp his coffee cup from the carabiner on his belt and fill it from the wall dispenser before speaking.

"Captain, Team Three has their last set of thrusters mounted to the asteroid's surface, but they are refusing to connect the drive controls to the ship. Without that link, we can't program the firing sequence."

"I well know that FIRST!" snaps Captain Hammish.

As if struck, First Officer Foglund jerks upright and stares straight ahead.

"I'm sorry, Althea. It's a bad captain who takes out his frustrations on his crew. Team Three? That's Medic Dummell's team, isn't it?"

With a tight nod, First Officer Foglund strides away and sits at her workstation.

You're a fool Ira, an old broken down fool, Hammish thinks as he rubs the stim patch behind his ear, willing it to work faster.

Captain Hammish breaks the silence that has engulfed the bridge and says, "Morzycki, please open a channel to Dummell for me."

"Channel open, Captain," his tart reply.

Captain Hammish squeezes out his words, his levity forced from between locked jaws. "Hey Russ, it's Ira, what's going on down there?"

Heavy breathing flows out of the bridge's speakers, like wind through a graveyard. A hollow voice speaks. "We can't do this, Captain. You know this isn't right. We can't kill these people, we should save them."

Putting his coffee cup aside, Captain Hammish leans forward in his chair, lacing his fingers together. "Russ, you know what's at stake here. This isn't just about the people down on the planet. This is about the safety of everyone back home. If The Swarm find a way to Safe Harbour, humanity will die."

Muffled weeping drifts through the speakers until Medic Dummell can speak again. "Captain, you know my team and I would follow you to the end of the universe. But this time you're wrong! Please don't force us, we don't want to fight shipmates...friends. It's pointless anyway, we trashed our thrusters."

A gasp from First Officer Foglund causes Hammish to glance her way, and he sees her punching keys on her workstation. Shifting his focus back to the team on the asteroid, Captain Hammish closes his eyes. The veins in his forehead become pronounced and throb in time with his anger. After a deep breath, his face relaxes and he speaks again. "Ok, Russ. You win. Gather your team and make for the umbilical back to the ship. You have my word that nobody will move against you."

"Morzycki," Captain Hammish says, "close that communication channel and connect me to the marine deck. Get me Lt. Knowsiacki."

"Aye... What? Yes, Captain!" Morzycki says, his eyes

wide. He turns away from the captain and back to his duty station.

The captain's monitor flickers to life, the image wavers as if afraid, but then resolves to show a pale female face. Her steel-grey eyes come to attention, and she salutes. "Lt. Knowsiacki here, Captain."

"Lieutenant. I assume you heard what's happening down there?" She knows, maybe even before I did, nothing gets by those eyes.

"Sir!" she replies.

"Medic Dummell and his team will come up from SB-One in a few minutes. I want you to meet me at the umbilical with your sidearm only, no need to go into full-blown soldier mode."

"Captain, there's no need for you to come down here, I can escort them to the brig with no—"

"Belay that, Knowsiacki, follow your orders, you will wait for me," Hammish barks, and the lieutenant goes rigid.

"Aye, Sir. Sorry, Sir." Knowsiacki salutes and the monitor goes blank.

Captain Hammish shakes his head and turns his attention back to the bridge crew, noticing that only his first officer will make eye contact with him. *It's a poor Captain who yells at his crew,* Hammish thinks as he scans the bridge, noting stiff shoulders, furtive glances, and lowered voices. *Dear lord, I hope their spirit is strong enough for this dirty work ahead of us.*

"I'm going to go talk with Dummell, Althea. While I'm gone, I want the math run on whether we can still steer SB-One to target in the time available, and if not, I want options on how we can destroy that colony," he says, and after receiving her nod, he turns on his heel and marches off the bridge, a weighty silence following him out.

* * *

Entering the cargo bay, Captain Hammish finds his nostrils assaulted by the sharp smell of metallic dust from the asteroid. No matter how hard the air scrubbers work, they never get it all, they have tracked the powder fine dust from one end of the ship to the other.

I wonder if this is what brimstone smells like? Hammish thinks. *How very apt that we are turning our home into a living hell; all we need are some devils with pitchforks and the scene will be complete.*

Thought turns into reality as the airlock doors retracts—the fine dust in the track causing a painful high-pitched squeal—and Medic Dummell and his four-person crew stomp out of the airlock, their EVA suits stained with the black dust of the asteroid and drilling lances in their hands.

I keep telling myself that we're on the side of the angels, making the hard choice to sacrifice a few to save many, but could Dummell be right? Is it our place to make these decisions? Are we playing God?

Knowsiacki and eight marines burst into the cargo bay cutting off Hammish's thoughts. Tasers at the ready, they hurry to put themselves between their captain and the suited drillers. The sounds of humming tasers and spinning drilling lances fill the cargo bay as the two groups stand off. Crisp and clean-looking marines all standing in a perfect line in front of their captain against the five crew members just up from the asteroid, coated in black dust, their face shields polarised, they looked like the stuff of nightmares made flesh.

It would be so easy to see them cast in the role of evil, and the marines as agents of the light, but life isn't that clean.

Hammish puts his hand on Lt. Knowsiacki's shoulder pushes past her to stand between the two groups and says, "Stand down all of you, that's an order."

The eyes of the eight marines shift from the captain to Lieutenant Knowsiacki who gives a slight nod. They holster their tasers but stand poised to leap into action.

Turning his back to the marines, Captain Hammish steps forward until the sharp scent of metal grindings fills his nostrils, the hum of the drilling lancers fills his ears, and he sees five versions of himself reflected at him from the visors of his crew. "Russ, let's end this now." Nodding at the marines behind him, Hammish continues, "I didn't want it to go like this, and for that I'm sorry. You've served under me for almost ten years, you know that isn't my style. Can't we just talk?"

For a dozen heartbeats the only sound in the cargo bay is the hum of the drilling lances mixed with the controlled breathing of the marines, until one lance shuts down, falls to the deck, and the tear-stained face of Medic Russ Dummell removes his helmet.

You forgot about those doing your dirty work, didn't you, fool? You were safe and insulated from getting your hands dirty on the bridge and forgot that others weren't.

"Russ, I can understand your reluctance..." Captain Hammish begins, but Medic Dummell raises his dust coated glove and cuts him off.

"You're wrong, Captain! Those are humans down on that planet, family we didn't even know we had. We're slaughtering our own kind. We should be doing everything in our power to save them, not kill them. We don't have the right!" Dummell yells, his face red, his cheeks wet.

The right? Maybe, maybe not. Humans have been killing each other since time began, I doubt we'll ever grow out of it; it's bred into our bones.

"I hear what you're saying, Russ...God, I really do...but it's my responsibility to see that The Swarm doesn't find a path to Safe Harbour, and right now Earth is letting them know they're on our doorstep," Hammish says to the ship's medic. "If I thought we stood a snowball's chance in hell of leading The Swarm away, we would do it, and I know you and the rest of the crew would be happy to sacrifice yourselves to save those people down there, but the risk is just too great. I need to think of the billions back home, too."

Shaking his head, his tears landing on the stained deck of the cargo bay, Dummell says, "You're wrong, Captain. Might doesn't make right, and when you put some lives ahead of others, you become a monster...worse than The Swarm." Waving a hand to the crew members behind him to drop their drilling lancers, Dummell finishes, "But we will not fight crew. With our thrusters trashed you won't be able to steer the asteroid, so you must save the planet now, Captain." The medic's eyes, puffy with tears, are nevertheless steady as they lock with those of the captain.

"OK, Russ, I understand. Lieutenant Knowsiacki, escort these crew members to their quarters and confine them there until further notice."

With a shuffling of bodies, the detachment of marines escort the suited crew members from the cargo bay. Lieutenant Knowsiacki pauses at the hatch and looks back at her captain for a moment before following her men out the door.

Alone, Captain Hammish stands in the dust-stained cargo bay holding Medic Dummell's helmet in his hands, staring into the mirrored visor.

* * *

Captain Hammish enters his bridge and the crew's voices stop instantly, the void of their silence louder than any words. Standing in the hatchway for a moment, Hammish meets the eyes of the bridge crew who stare at him like kids caught while the teacher was out of the room.

Likely they watched the whole scene in the cargo bay from here. How many of them would side with Dummell if given the chance?

Shaking his head, he steps into the bridge and walks to the refreshment unit on the wall, unclips his coffee mug from his belt and hits the faded dark roast button before turning his attention to the first officer. "Can we still do it, Althea?"

First Officer Foglund walks up to him, pauses, takes a handkerchief from her pocket and whispers, "Smudge on your cheek, Captain."

Taking the handkerchief from her, Hammish wipes the asteroid dust from his face and gives her the ghost of a smile of thanks.

Clearing her throat, Foglund says, "If we run the remaining four thrusters at 128% of their rated capacity, and start the burn..." She glances back at her work pad, "twenty-four minutes earlier, we can still do it, Captain."

Walking to his command chair, Hammish hides his weary smile as he takes a sip of coffee.

She probably ran the math three times to give herself and the rest of the crew something to do other than just sit and wait, dwelling on the reality of the situation. She will make a great captain someday.

"It's OK to run them into the red, Althea. It's not as if we have to pay for them."

An attempt at a weak smile from his first officer is the only response to the captain's humour.

"Continue with the efforts on SB-One," Hammish says. "Let me know when we're ready, I have paperwork to catch up on."

* * *

Buried in a lap filled with duty logs, inventory listings, and department reports, it startles Captain Hammish when the first officer speaks from his elbow.

"It's time, Captain."

"Thank you, First Officer."

I wonder if anybody else has noticed how formal we've all become, as if it's a way to protect ourselves from our feelings. I miss the days when the bridge rang with jokes and laughter, and the constant complaints about the three-year-old freeze-dried coffee. We won't see those days again, at least not on my watch.

Putting his paperwork aside, Captain Hammish looks around at the bridge crew. The room is under a cloud, subdued voices speak into headsets. Several sets of eyes gleam with moisture, the Captain sees all the faces focusing on him.

"Report," Hammish says, his tone commanding, breaking the heavy quiet weighing down on them.

"The crew have installed the last four thrusters at their designated coordinates, and I've locked their controls into the helm. Surface teams are back on board and the umbilical to the asteroid is retracted. All stations report ready, Sir." First Officer Foglund says, her voice steady.

"Great. Good job, everyone." With that, Captain Hammish stands, his back ramrod straight. He walks over to the helm station without hesitation. He stabs a button, his fingernail scratching the painted key, starting the firing program of the thrusters mounted to the surface of SB-One, that will affect the lives of over 270,000 people on the planet below, and the three hundred thirty-six above.

"Program started and controls locked. All thrusters responding," says First Officer Foglund.

Nodding, Captain Hammish walks back to stand beside his own command chair. Buttoning up his collar, he pulls himself to attention. "Morzycki. Open a channel to Earth."

"Contact established, Sir."

* * *

Hammish stares at the screen as the asteroid shifts its course and drifts towards Earth, then speaks;

"Citizens of planet Earth. This is Captain Ira Hammish of the Sol System Patrol Ship *Long Night*. Just moments ago, I started a program that is directing the thrusters I ordered to be installed on asteroid SB-One several days ago. What you don't know is that the asteroid wasn't a hazard to Earth until that order. SB-One will collide with your planet in less than three hours. I repeat, the asteroid will collide with Earth in less than three hours. Computer models show that the force of the impact will be like that of the strike that caused the extinction of the dinosaurs."

His fists clench the fabric of his coveralls, and the veins on his forehead pound.

"The Universe isn't the empty place we thought it was three hundred years ago when our colony ships left for Safe Harbour. Humanity is nothing but a minor player in a deadly game. One false move will sweep Safe Harbour and all its colonies away...it will be like humanity never existed."

"By far one of the most dangerous species in our galaxy is a race called The Swarm. We're not even sure they are sentient by our understanding. All we know is that The Swarm obliterates any race that it comes into contact with. We are now transmitting our images of what The Swarm has done on other worlds."

Captain Hammish gives a nod to Morzycki and he taps

his workstation. All the monitor in the bridge show the same footage now being sent to the planet below. One member of the bridge crew cries out.

"As you can see, the individual insect-like members of The Swarm spend most of their time naked to the void of space, only entering a gravity well to breed. Their reproductive cycle isn't anything like ours. Two or more members inject their seed into any large warm-blooded body, like a human, where they grow and feed upon the living person until their violent birth. No race is safe, no race has survived contact with The Swarm."

Captain Hammish's face ages in mere moments. His skin has gone pale and a tick flickers in his left eye. With a force of will, he continues.

"Two months ago, the *Long Night,* while on a deep space deployment, stumbled across the leading waves of a branch of The Swarm. The *Long Night* investigated and scouted ahead of their projected course and were dismayed to find you—our long lost and forgotten cousins—and the Spacial Tear our people used long ago to flee Earth."

"We can't save you, people of Earth. Our ship can't enter your atmosphere, and we have no shuttles. If The Swarm even gets a hint that Safe Harbour and her billions are close through the Spacial Tear you found, we would lose humanity. By my actions today, your deaths may save our species."

"This channel will remain open until the strike. We will record all transmissions you send us. It is a cruel fate that has brought us together, people of Earth, but I encourage you to send us your stories, your history, that some part of you will live on."

"We will remember you. I'm... sorry."

Captain Hammish collapses into his chair and rubs his temples but waves away his first officer when she starts towards him. Hammish controls his breathing and before speaking to the communications officer.

"Morzycki, record all transmissions from the planet. Direct all communications to my station. Althea, please convey my thanks to the crew...I know the strain they have been under."

"And Dummell and the others?"

"Best leave them confined to quarters until we're out of this system. Also keep an eye open for anyone else who might be struggling," he says before returning his focus to the view screen.

* * *

The countdown ends. The fiery streak that was SB-One also ends as it hits Earth Shockwaves ripple across the landscape, mountains collapse like a house of cards, oceans empty leaving seabeds exposed for the first time in millions of years, and a city-sized crown of ejecta plumes into the atmosphere to mark the resting place of the last human colony of Earth.

"Have we recorded all communications from the planet?" Captain Hammish asks, and a pale-faced Morzycki gives a shaky nod.

"We have retrieved their satellite, correct First Officer?" Hammish asks, and he turns to Althea, her eyes wet with moisture but her voice is firm.

"Yes, Captain. Safety stowed in the cargo bay. Also, our long range scans show The Swarm are still heading this way, course and speed unchanged."

She's handled this better than I have. Dealing with grieving crew coming to her for support, and a captain who demands that she perform her duty as if this were a routine mission. I'm proud of her...proud of them all.

"Back us away from Earth, First Officer, just to the edge of the sensors, and go to silent mode. I want no emissions to escape this ship until The Swarm has passed. If for any reason The Swarm gets an idea we're out here, I want the *Long Night* to make best speed in the opposite direction of the Spacial Tear. They can't know it's here," Captain Hammish says as he settles in for a long wait.

* * *

"Report," Hammish whispers, the oppressive silence of the bridge affecting them all.

"Passive scans show The Swarm has circled Earth twice without entering the atmosphere and are moving away. No sign they detected us or the Spacial Tear," First Officer Foglund replies.

"Althea, power up the ship slowly and head towards the Spacial Tear. Keep sensors on the retreating Swarm. If they shift course even a millimeter, I want to hear it."

"Aye, Captain." First Officer Foglund gives whispered instructions to the crew.

Hours later, the air on the bridge heavy with stale sweat and coffee, the *Long Night* slips through the Spacial Tear and finds herself years closer to Safe Harbour than normal travel would allow.

"Morzycki, drop a communication beacon outside the influence of the Tear so Safe Harbour can find it again. I'm sure our people back home will be very interested in exploring the other side," says Captain Hammish.

"Yes, Captain."

"And when you're done, report to First Officer Foglund, she's in command now. That goes for the rest of the bridge crew. I'm stepping down as captain and will present myself for court martial when we get home."

Ignoring the gasps and frantic whispering as the bridge crew absorbs this information, Captain Hammish walks over to the stunned first officer.

Giving her arm a gentle squeeze, Hammish says, "Althea, my last orders are that you make best speed for Safe Harbour and report *everything* that has happened. Keep an eye on the crew; shock hits different people at different times and in strange ways. Watch the quiet ones they will need the most support."

With that, Captain Ira Hammish picks up his empty coffee cup and walks to the dispenser. He stares at the years of staining inside, the rings of dried coffee akin to tree rings that remind him of the years spent on this bridge with this crew.

He drops the cup into the trash and walks off the bridge without looking back.

461

AUTHORS

Angela Zimmerman

Author of *Claire and Gabe Hammond*

Angela Zimmerman is a writer living in the Southern United States. She has been published in Unnerving Magazine and Coffin Bell. You can find her personal writings at Conjure and Coffee.
Website: conjureandcoffee.com

Bob Adder

Author of *Brittany Jenkins*

Bob Adder is an aspiring author and superhero geek from Melbourne, Australia.
Instagram: @bob_adder_

Brandi Hicks

Author of *Karen Thomas*

Growing up in West Virginia, Brandi Hicks loved to have her nose in a book, her eyes toward the night sky and putting a pen to paper. Her imagination was always sparked by her grandfather and her mom taking her to new places and teaching her about the unusual. She loves fantasy, sci-fi, and learning about science and history. She has two beautiful children, and hopes to instil creativity and a love of reading in them. Finding new crafts to try keeps her busy when not playing with her kids or working.

BLACK HARE PRESS

C.L. Williams

Author of *Allen Parker*

C.L. Williams is an international best-selling author currently living in central Virginia. He has written eight poetry books, four novellas, one novel, and a contributor to a multitude of anthologies and magazines. His most recent anthology appearance *ANGELS: Dark Drabbles #2* from Black Hare Press became a number one in hot new releases. C.L. Williams is currently working on his second novel and a new poetry book.

Cecelia Hopkins-Drewer

Author of *Angela Lazza*

Cecelia Hopkins-Drewer lives in Adelaide, South Australia. She has written a Masters paper on H.P. Lovecraft, and her weird poetry has been published in THE MENTOR (edited by Ron Clarke), and SPECTRAL REALMS (edited by S.T. Joshi). Her novels include a teenage vampire series comprised of three volumes, MYSTIC EVERMORE, SAINTS AND SINNERS & AUTUMN SECRETS. Short stories have been published in WORLDS, ANGELS & MONSTERS (Dark Drabbles anthologies edited by D. Kershaw).
Amazon: amazon.com/Cecelia-Hopkins-Drewer/e/B071G968NM
Website: chopkin39.wixsite.com/website

Charlotte O'Farrell

Author of *Jasmine Smith*

Charlotte O'Farrell is a lifelong horror fan who writes about all manner of the weird and wonderful. Her work can be found at the Drabble, the Rock N Roll Horror Zine and Horror Tree, among other places.
Twitter: @ChaOFarrell

Cindar Harrell

Author of *Rachel Montgomery* and *Belladonna Pryor*

Cindar Harrell loves fairy tales, especially ones with a dark twist. Her stories are often fairy tale inspired, but she is also working on a mystery series. Her stories can be found on Amazon and in various anthologies. You can follow her on Facebook and visit her blog, which she promises to try and update more often,
Website: cindarharrell.wordpress.com
Facebook: CindarHarrell

D.M. Burdett

Author of *Jessie Gilton* and *Two Hundred and Eighty-Four*

D.M. Burdett initially roamed as an army brat, but now lives in Australia where she spends her days avoiding drop bears and killer spiders. She has published a Sci-Fi series, has short stories in various anthologies, and has published two children's series. She is currently working on the first book in a dystopian series.
Website: www.dmburdett.com
Facebook: DMBurdett

David Bowmore

Author of *Soldier* and *Daniel MacBride*

David Bowmore has lived here, there and everywhere, but now lives in Yorkshire with his wonderful wife and a small white poodle. He has worn many hats in his time; head chef, teacher and landscape gardener. His first collection of short stories 'The Magic of Deben Market' is available from Clarendon House.
Website: davidbowmore.co.uk
Facebook: davidbowmoreauthor

BLACK HARE PRESS

Dawn DeBraal

Author of *Emmett Trowbridge*

Dawn DeBraal lives in rural Wisconsin with her husband, two rat terriers, and a cat. She successfully raised two children (meaning they didn't return to the nest!) After many years serving the government at the Federal and County level, she recently retired. Having extra time on her hands she started to write after a paralyzed vocal cord took her ability to speak for two months. Not finding her voice, she discovered that her love of telling a good story could be written. Her works have been published in Palm-Sized Press, Spillwords, Mercurial Stories, Potato Soup Journal, and Blood Song Books.

Eddie D. Moore

Author of *Jane* and *Josh Tillman,* and co-author of *Al Woods*

Eddie D. Moore travels hundreds of hours a year, and he fills that time by listening to audiobooks. When he isn't playing with his grandchildren, he writes his own stories. You can find a list of his publications on his blog or by visiting his Amazon Author Page. While you're there, be sure to pick up a copy of his mini-anthology Misfits & Oddities.
Website: eddiedmoore.wordpress.com
Amazon: amazon.com/author/eddiedmoore

Gabriella Balcom

Author of *Stewie*

Gabriella Balcom lives in Texas with her family, loves reading and writing, and thinks she was born with a book in her hands. She works in a mental health field, and writes fantasy, horror/thriller, romance, children's stories, and sci-fi. She likes travelling, music, good shows, photography, history, interesting tales, and animals. Gabriella says she's a sucker for a great story and loves forests, mountains, and back roads which might lead who knows where. She has a weakness for lasagne, garlic bread, tacos, cheese, and chocolate, but not necessarily in that order.
Facebook: GabriellaBalcom.lonestarauthor

Gregg Cunningham

Author of *Cody and the Agent* and *Zac "Boomer" Butcher*

Gregg Cunningham 48, short story writer who has had to pick up his game since stumbling into Facebook writer's groups. He has stories published by 559 Publishing in in 13 Bites volume 3,4,5, Plan 9 from Outer space, Other Realms, Heard It on The Radio, 559 Ways to Die, short stories publishing by Zombie Pirate Publishing in Relationship odd Vice, Full Metal Horror, Phuket Tattoo, World War four and Flash Fiction Addiction (flash) with Zombie Pirate Publishing, and also in Dastaan Magazine Chapter 11 and Brian, Rich and the Wardrobe.
Amazon: www.amazon.com/-/e/B016OTHX0K

J.B. Wocoski

Author of *The Knowsiacki Family*

J.B. Wocoski is the author and narrator of the shortstorypodcast.com with three flash fiction short story books published in the last three years. He is currently working on book 4 "Short Story Podcast 2019." He writes mostly science fiction, fantasy, and horror stories. He won the 2016 Little Tokyo Short Story Writing Contest with his short story "The Last Master of Go"
Website: shortstorypodcast.com

J.W. Garrett

Author of *Cal Davis, Emily Sparrow,* and *Josh McKennan*

J.W. Garrett has been writing in one form or another since she was a teenager. She currently lives in Florida with her family but loves the mountains of Virginia where she was born. Her writings include YA fantasy as well as short stories. Since completing Remeon's Quest-Earth Year 1930, the prequel in her YA fantasy series, Realms of Chaos, she has been hard at work on the next in the series, scheduled to release June 2020. When she's not hanging out with her characters, her favourite activities are reading, running and spending time with family.
Website: www.jwgarrett.com
BHC Press: www.bhcpress.com/Author_JW_Garrett.html

Jacob Baugher

Author of *They Had to Come from Somewhere, Kelly,* and *Kyle Koch*

Jacob Baugher teaches Creative Writing at a small university near Pittsburgh, PA. When he's not teaching or coaching the track team, he can be found in the Cuyahoga Valley hiking with his wife and son or brewing beer on his front porch. He's received honourable mentions for his work in the Writers of the Future contest and he co-edits a series of Fantasy and Science Fiction anthologies titled Continuum. His work also appears in Black Hare's Deep Space and Area-51 anthologies, as well as in the Dark Drabble Anthologies Worlds, Angels, Monsters, Beyond, and Unravel. He also hates pineapple on pizza.

Jennifer Shelby

Author of *Last Night*

Jennifer Shelby hunts for stories in the beetled undergrowth of fairy-infested forests. She fishes for them in the darkness between the stars. As part of her ongoing catch-and-release program, her stories have appeared in Cricket, Unlocking the Magic, Andromeda Spaceways, and other places.
Twitter: @jenniferdshelby
Website: jennifershelby.blog

Jenson Reed

Author of *Janitor Jared*

Jensen Reed is a multi-published short story author, lead admin for Writing Bad, and mama to two boys. She dabbles in reading and writing genres but particularly enjoys feeding characters to zombies and making readers cry. Find her book links, flash fiction, and connect with her on her website.
Website: authorjensenreed.wordpress.com

Jo Seysener

Author of *Bettina White* and *Dark Earth*

Jo Seysener is a mum of three crazies, a scatter of chickens, a decrepit kelpie and a rambunctious GSD. She lives with her husband near Brisbane, Australia. When she is not exposing her kids to cult story books from her childhood, she can be found in the kitchen experimenting with new flavours and pairings. She adores alpacas.
Facebook: joseysener
Website: www.joseysener.com

Marcus Cook

Author of *Cherish Salazar*

Marcus Cook, lives in Cleveland, Ohio native with his wife and cat. He loves Sci-Fi and thrillers. His short story, Ava Edison and the Burning Man was recently published in Burning: An Anthology of Short Thrillers by Burning Chair Publishing which can be purchased on Amazon.
Facebook: ReadMarcusCook

Mason Harold Hilden

Author of *Alastair Harp*

Mason H. Hilden is a Bluenoser, who currently resides in Saint John, New Brunswick, with his family. Over the last twenty years, he has written comic-books, including one professional work. He has also dabbled in mini-biographies, interviews, baseball articles, and animation scripting. Mason recently began writing fiction, and believes that BHP may have created a monster by accepting his submissions.

BLACK HARE PRESS

N.M. Brown

Author of *Aidan Charles* and *Evan Dean*

Since N.M. Brown made her first post to a popular Internet forum, she's taken the horror community by storm. Her ability to create, terrify, and drive home her stories is insurmountable. N>M> Brown's published works can be found in multiple anthologies for all to read, but be forewarned, if you do... you may want to call your therapist after, her stories are terrifying, disturbing and devilishly unsettling. She is not only a fright visually, but also has a creepy tentacle in horror podcasting as well. Sinister Sweetheart writes, voice acts and is the media director of the Scarecrow Tales podcast.
Website: Sinistersweetheart.wixsite.com/sinistersweetheart
Facebook: NMBrownStories

Peter J. Foote

Author of *Delaying Action*

Peter J. Foote is a bestselling speculative fiction writer from Nova Scotia. Outside of writing, he runs a used bookstore specialising in fantasy & sci-fi, cosplays, and alternates between red wine and coffee as the mood demands. His short stories can be found in both print and in ebook form, with his story "Sea Monkeys" winning the inaugural "Engen Books/Kit Sora, Flash Fiction/Flash Photography" contest in March of 2018. As the founder of the group "Genre Writers of Atlantic Canada", Peter believes that the writing community is stronger when it works together.
Twitter: @PeterJFoote1
Website: peterjfooteauthor.wordpress.com

Raven Corinn Carluk

Author of *Reaper John Nil* and Into the *Lungs of Hell*

Raven Corinn Carluk writes dark fantasy, paranormal romance, and anything else that catches her interest. She's authored five novels, where she explores themes of love and acceptance. Her shorter pieces, usually from her darker side, can be found in Black Hare Press anthologies, at Detritus Online, and through Alban Lake Publishers.
Twitter: @ravencorinn
Website: RavenCorinnCarluk.Blogspot.Com

Rhiannon Bird

Author of *Running* and *Newsfeed*

Rhiannon Bird is a young aspiring author. She has a passion for words and storytelling. Rhiannon has her own quotes blog; Thoughts of a Writer. She has had 4 works published. This includes 3 short stories and 2 poems. These are published on Eskimo pie, Literary yard, Down in the Dirt Magazine and Short break fiction. She can be found on Facebook, Instagram, and Pinterest.

Rich Rurshell

Author of *Cody Redman*

Rich Rurshell is a short story writer from Suffolk, England. Rich writes Horror, Sci-Fi, and Fantasy, and his stories can be found in various short story anthologies and magazines. Most recently, his story "Subject: Galilee" was published in World War Four from Zombie Pirate Publishing, and "Life Choices" was published in Salty Tales from Stormy Island Publishing. When Rich is not writing stories, he likes to write and perform music.
Facebook: richrurshellauthor

BLACK HARE PRESS

Shelly Jarvis

Author of *Earl Justice*

Shelly Jarvis is a speculative fiction author from West Virginia, US. She found a life-long love of sci-fi and fantasy in the 3rd grade when she found Madeleine L'Engle's "A Wrinkle in Time." Shelly is an avid reader, a Whovian, the ideal viewer of dog rescue videos, and undoubtedly Ravenclaw. She currently has three YA sci-fi books available for purchase on Amazon.
Website: www.ShellyJarvis.com

Stephen Coghlan

Author of *Sexy_Kikashi_69, Monster Energy* and *They Held Their Own*

Stephen Coghlan is an ever-expanding, multi-genre author who writes out of Canada's National Capital. His works include The Genmos series, The Nobilis series, and the Dreampunk novella, URBAN GOTHIC.
Website: scoghlan.com
Twitter: @WordsBySC

Stephen Herczeg

Author of *Bradley Lutkins*

Stephen Herczeg is an IT Geek based in Canberra Australia. He has been writing for over twenty years and has completed a couple of dodgy novels, sixteen feature length screenplays and numerous short stories and scripts. His horror work has featured in Sproutlings, Hells Bells, Below the Stairs, Trickster's Treats #1 and #2, Shades of Santa, Behind the Mask, Beyond the Infinite; The Body Horror Book, Anemone Enemy, Petrified Punks and Beginnings. He has also had numerous Sherlock Holmes stories published through the Belanger Books - Sherlock Holmes anthologies.
Amazon: amazon.com/-/e/B07916SQQS
Facebook: stephenherczegauthor

Sue Marie St. Lee

Co-author of *Al Woods*

Sue Marie St. Lee is a retired Finance Manager who has been freelancing, researching, writing content, designing corporate websites and brochures over the past fifteen years. She also started a small business specializing in digital photo restoration. Born and raised in Chicago, she moved to Canada where she and her husband raised their sons until her husband's untimely death. As a young widow, Sue Marie employed her skills, tenacity, strengths and wisdom to support her young family. Currently, Sue Marie contributes to several blogs, is a ghostwriter for numerous online publishers and corporate websites. Her sons are grown, productive adults.

Terry Miller

Author of *Eric Dyer*

Terry Miller is an author and 2017 Rhysling Award-nominated poet residing in Portsmouth, OH, USA. He has self-published a dark poetry collection on Amazon and one short story to date. His work has also appeared in Sanitarium, Devolution Z, Jitter Press, Poetry Quarterly, O Unholy Night in Deathlehem, and the 2017 Rhysling Anthology from the Science Fiction and Fantasy Poetry Association.
Facebook: tmiller2015

Vonnie Winslow Crist

Author of *Ivan Hawks*

Vonnie Winslow Crist is author of The Enchanted Dagger, Owl Light, The Greener Forest, Murder on Marawa Prime, and other award-winning books. Her fiction is included in "Amazing Stories," "Cast of Wonders," "Outposts of Beyond," Killing It Softly 2, Defending the Future - Dogs of War, Midnight Masquerade, Chaos of Hard Clay, and elsewhere. A cloverhand who has found so many four-leafed clovers she keeps them in jars, Vonnie strives to celebrate the power of myth in her writing.
Website: www.vonniewinslowcrist.com

BLACK HARE PRESS

Wondra Vanian

Author of *Jordan Matthison*

Wondra Vanian is an American living in the United Kingdom with her Welsh husband and their army of fur babies. A writer first, Wondra is also an avid gamer, photographer, cinephile, and blogger. She has music in her blood, sleeps with the lights on, and has been known to dance naked in the moonlight. Wondra was a multiple Top-Ten finisher in the 2017 and 2018 Preditors and Editors Reader's Poll, including the Best Author category. Her story, "Halloween Night," was named a Notable Contender for the Bristol Short Story Prize in 2015.
Website: www.wondravanian.com

Zoey Xolton

Author of *Caroline Walters* and *Elayna*

Zoey Xolton is an Australian Speculative Fiction writer, primarily of Dark Fantasy, Paranormal Romance and Horror. She is also a proud mother of two and is married to her soul mate. Outside of her family, writing is her greatest passion. She is especially fond of short fiction and is working on releasing her own themed collections in future.
Website: www.zoeyxolton.com

475